PRETTY LITTLE DEAD THINGS

"Gary McMahon's vision is as ple~~~ ~~~ ~~~ ~~~ ~~~
but it glows with a wintry light that illuminates the dark
we live in. His prose and his sense of place are precise
and evocative, and his characters are as real as you and
me. He's one of the darkest – which is to say brightest –
new stars in the firmament of horror fiction."

RAMSEY CAMPBELL

"Thomas Usher is a great character treading a twilight
world between Manhunter and Most Haunted; conflicted
by grief, haunted by blame, a 'magnet for ghosts' who
sees the skull beneath the skin. In *Pretty Little Dead
Things*, Gary McMahon nails genuine horror as few
British writers can – or dare. He gets under your skin,
then burrows even deeper. Terrifyingly, dangerously,
hauntingly so."

STEPHEN VOLK, CREATOR OF TV'S *AFTERLIFE*

"*Pretty Little Dead Things* is a very disturbing read. Gary
McMahon seems intent on taking readers through the
looking glass and tearing down the walls between the
living and the dead. He creates dark, hallucinatory
images that burn in your brain forever."

CHRISTOPHER FOWLER

"Gary McMahon's horror is heartfelt, his characters
flawed and desperate, and this book is a rich feast of
loss, guilt, and redemption. His vivid ideas are given life
in beautiful prose, and the book leaves you staring into
shadows that weren't there before. His talent shines,
and is set to burn brighter still." TIM LEBBON

ALSO BY GARY McMAHON

GARY McMAHON

PRETTY LITTLE DEAD THINGS

A THOMAS USHER NOVEL

ANGRY
ROBOT

ANGRY ROBOT

A member of the Osprey Group
Midland House, West Way
Botley, Oxford
OX2 0HP
UK

www.angryrobotbooks.com
All in a row

An Angry Robot paperback original 2010
1

A catalogue record for this book is available
from the British Library.

ISBN: 978-0-85766-069-5
Ebook ISBN: 978-0-85766-071-8

Set in Meridien by THL Design.

Printed in the UK by CPI Mackays, Chatham, ME5 8TD.

For Emily

AUTHOR'S NOTE

I have taken certain liberties with the geography of Leeds. Let's just call it artistic licence. The city in this novel is the Leeds of my imagination – part fact, part fiction, wholly extraordinary. I hope keen-eyed readers will forgive me for transforming the place in these subtle ways, and that they enjoy the haunted landscape I've created.

PART ONE
A KNOT, TIGHTENING

*"Nothing exists which is not subject
to the conditioning of death."*

The Tibetan Book of the Dead

I have never visited their graves. The grief I carry always inside me would be too much to bear, so I choose to remember them in my own way, in my own time. Not a day goes by when they are not in my thoughts. They haunt my every movement, but still I have not seen them: they have not come to me in the way that others have, asking that I bear witness to the memory of their passing or simply requesting that I help guide them towards the next part of their journey. But someday, somehow, I hope that they will find their way back to my side.

ONE

Fifteen Years Ago

The Mersey is a broad, black ribbon, the shimmering lights of Birkenhead promising a world of untold stories on the opposite bank – dark stories, probably told by old men in their cups and women whose skin has been bruised by careless husbands too many times to count. I stare through the passenger window, lost in thoughts of nothing in particular – just thinking, as I tend to do, about life in general: my dull job, paying the bills, the things I think I might be missing out on because I married so young and the things I gained by doing so.

The broad shape of a ferry trawls slowly across the darkened waters, seeming to heave upwards on waves that are not quite visible, as if a giant submerged hand is struggling to lift it above the busy surface of the river. Darkness then presses down on the vessel, giving the illusion that it is now sinking gradually beneath the waves. The motion is so lazy and incremental that it looks like a cartoon animation. I wonder why a ferry is crossing so late at night, and what haulage it might be carrying.

The car swerves to avoid an animal that has run into the road – a dog or a cat or perhaps even a roaming river rat – and

Rebecca turns to smile at me, the delicate yellowish hue of the streetlamps at the side of the road catching her face and holding it for a moment in a wash of amber. In that instant I know that I have missed out on nothing in life, because all that I will ever need is inside the car with me. Past mistakes and misdemeanours no longer matter; what is important is how I feel right now, sitting in the dark with my wife and daughter.

"Sorry," she says. "Did I disturb you?"

I shake my head, smiling. "No. It's okay. I was just woolgathering." I have never known exactly what that phrase means, but have always enjoyed the way it sounds. Like a snatch of crude poetry lodged in the back of my mind, or part of the verse from a folk song I might have heard as a child.

Allyson sleeps soundly in the back seat; the sudden deviation of the vehicle's path has not broken her slumber. Her breathing is even and her hands are clasped tightly in her lap. I turn around in the passenger seat and watch her, my heart breaking just a little, as it always does whenever I take a moment to realise how much my infant daughter means to me. Her small white face is the face of the world. Her loosely closed eyes are windows through which I might glimpse the truth of my own existence.

"We should be home before midnight. Traffic's light." Rebecca's face is stern; she watches the road intently, on edge because of what has just happened with the animal running out in front of her. She is a skilled driver – better than me – and she resents the thought of anyone thinking otherwise. Her angry pride is one of the things I love about her.

One of the *many* things I love about her. There are about a million other reasons to go along with it, but that one will do for now.

The strong German beer I have consumed earlier that evening sloshes around inside the pit of my belly, making me feel bloated and uncomfortable. I need to urinate, but I do not want to ask Rebecca to stop the car and interrupt our journey home. I should have gone to the lavatory back at John and Emma's place, before we left. When I think about it, I realise that we should have stayed the night with our friends. The offer of a bed was there but I'd wanted to get home to make an early start in the morning. I am booked in to referee a football match for Ally's school team at 9am and hate the thought of breaking a promise even as small as this one. The scars of adulthood are sometimes caused by such tiny blades.

There was also the fact that things had grown tense as the evening wound down. John's usual gently mocking demeanour had caved in and given way to something darker and slightly more vicious as he had gone well beyond his usual lager quota. He and Emma are on the verge of splitting up; she has even asked him for a divorce. I suspect that a third party is involved somewhere along the line, but am not quite sure on whose side the weight of infidelity falls. As usual in these situations, there is no one person to blame. Something has come between them, blocking the way they used to feel about each other, and it looks like whatever it is will not budge as much as an inch.

"How much did you drink earlier?" Rebecca speaks without taking her eyes off the road.

I wonder, briefly, if she has ever been tempted to sleep with someone else. God knows, I have been attracted to other women during our marriage, but have only once acted upon it. Despite my flaws I consider myself a good man, a loyal husband, and I would rather damage my own body than harm my family. That one time was a terrible mistake I know I will never stop regretting and will spend the rest of my life trying to make up for – a shame I will always carry with me, like a leaden weight around my neck.

"Just a couple." It is not exactly a lie, and even years later I will still ask myself why, in that near-perfect moment of potential connection, I failed to tell the complete truth. If I'd admitted that I was slightly woozy, that the relatively small amount of beer I had consumed was stronger than I'd expected, then things might have turned out differently. My life might have been better. Then again, this might all be wishful thinking. Some events, I have learned, are just meant to happen. Some things are meant to be taken from us, no matter how hard we try to hold on to them.

Ifs, buts and maybes: the eternal stumbling blocks to happiness.

"I'm tired." Her eyelids are drooping and her mouth twists into a yawn. "Really tired." She is blinking rapidly, which is always a sure sign that she needs a rest.

"Pull over. I'll take it from here." A sense of déjà vu hits me then, a strange feeling that I have lived through all of this before – perhaps many times – and the last time it had turned out badly, maybe even fatal. I feel a great desire to take back what I have just said, but the sight of Rebecca's suddenly dough-white face and her eyes that are now open too wide to try and combat sleep cause me to hold my tongue instead.

The moment passes. I actually feel it leave, like a physical presence passing over us within the confines of the car and moving on elsewhere, towards other unwitting travellers. Is fate a sentient entity? Did it touch me that night, making itself known to me? I suppose I will never know.

"It's okay. I can make it."

"No. You should rest. It's my fault we left, so it's only fair that I should drive. The beer's out of my system now. I feel wide awake. Honest."

"You sure? I don't like the idea of not knowing how much you drank. Remember, we have a daughter asleep in the back."

Lights blur past the window, but no sounds penetrate the car. I feel like we are in another world, or perhaps hurtling through a cosmic void. I have not really lied about my current level of intoxication, yet I feel odd. Detached. It is not a feeling of drunkenness, but a sense of the world spinning on its axis, of things moving too fast for anyone to stop and think. Particularly me.

"Here," I say. "Pull over here." I point at the bright service station lights, and before she has the chance to change her mind, Rebecca is pulling into the entrance and stopping the car on the clean concrete forecourt, next to one of the stubby petrol pumps.

"We need fuel, anyway," she says, undoing her seatbelt.

Lights flicker outside; darkness seems to fall in layers, coating the footpaths and the verges and the squat service station buildings.

Ally sleeps on in the back of the car, her state of near exhaustion after that evening's excitement and the hypnotic lull of the motorway conspiring to keep her under. Cold light bathes her face, making her look older than she actually is. Instead of a seven year-old girl, for a brief moment I feel that I am looking at a little old lady snoring on the back seat, her small, claw-like hands making fists in her lap. The bones of her knuckles shine white for a moment as she grasps something in her dreams. I wonder briefly where my daughter has gone, and who has replaced her with this wizened little doppelganger...

The car door opens and Rebecca steps outside into the chill night air, which rushes suddenly into the car, filling it up. My ears pop from the change in pressure, as if we are travelling at high altitude instead of sitting parked by a petrol pump on a lonely motorway refuge.

"This should wake me up, actually. I can drive the rest of the way." She slams the door and walks to the back of the car, twisting off the petrol cap and slotting the nozzle of the pump into the tank. She leans on the side of the car, her attention focused somewhere else, and I watch her without her knowing. I love to catch her unawares like this, when her guard is down and she looks lovelier than ever. Rebecca's beauty is purely an unconscious one: she never realises how attractive she is, and is always amazed whenever anyone chooses to compliment her appearance.

She smiles, still staring into space, and I wonder exactly what crosses her mind at that particular moment. Is it something to do with me, or Ally? Or is it the memory of a joke we shared earlier in the day? Perhaps it is nothing more than the mental equivalent of breaking wind.

Just another mystery: one that I will never solve. Some secrets are best left alone.

Before long Rebecca replaces the nozzle in its clamp at the side of the pump and walks across the forecourt to the single-storey building, fishing her purse out of her jeans' back pocket. There are no other cars on the lot; no other customers stop by while we are there. The place is almost silent, and the emptiness seems eerie in a way I cannot pin down.

I get out of the car, walk around the front, past the bonnet, and climb into the driver seat. I watch through the windscreen as Rebecca pays for the petrol, enjoying her sleek profile, and smiling as she walks back towards the car, doing a silly little dance for my entertainment. Then I glance over my shoulder at Ally.

"Come on," says Rebecca, grinning as she opens the driver door and leans in, her perfume and her breath filling the space. "Get the hell out of there and let me take the wheel."

"Don't be daft," I say, grasping the steering wheel. "You take a break. I'll do the rest of the journey. Honestly, I'm completely clear-headed."

Rebecca tenses, as if she is about to say something more, then simply shrugs, slams the door, and strolls around to the passenger side. She climbs in and hands me the keys. As I take them from her, I feel her cold hand against mine, her thin fingers resting in my palm, and for some reason I cannot quite understand but which seems somehow inevitable, the sensation makes me faintly and absurdly nauseous. I can feel the bones beneath her skin.

It is only much later that I will identify that passing emotion as fear.

I head for the motorway slip road, the night sky almost as clear as day but clusters of dark clouds closing in to obscure the view. Rebecca fiddles with the stereo as we descend the slope to join the motorway, and the sound of easy-listening music fills the car. "Whoo!" says Rebecca, pressing back into her seat. "Groovy!"

Laughing, I stifle a sudden yawn. Perhaps I should have let her continue driving after all. I shake my head and work the muscles of my jaw, trying to overcome the sensation of falling.

When Billy Joel begins to sing about an *Innocent Man*, Rebecca closes her eyes and starts to sway her head to the music. Joel is one of her favourites; she has all his albums at home, and never sickens of playing them. I will burn them all exactly a year to the day after that night. Even now, the sound of the singer's voice as he hits a high note is enough to make me weep with loss.

I fight to remain focused on the road ahead, but the unusual lack of traffic and my overactive brain make it difficult to focus. I think now that if there had been more cars on the road it might have been easier to keep my act together. I would have been forced to concentrate.

The music lulls me; my eyes begin to feel heavy and the road ahead blurs and blends to form an endless swirling ocean of grey. The lights far ahead and on either side of the car turn to watery streaks of illumination, and what few other vehicles there are present on the road recede, swallowed up by distance and the burgeoning weight of something soft and heavy that is pulling me down, down, down...

We enter a narrow aisle formed by traffic cones, where the two lanes are forced into a single passage because of some mysterious, unseen roadworks. The cones flash past. My vision flares.

In that moment I fail completely to see the other car speeding towards us along the left-hand lane, its extinguished headlights and radiator grille looming like the eyes and jaws of some giant mythical beast, like a dragon. Perhaps if I'd seen it earlier I could have turned the wheel to avoid the collision but the dull red Ford Sierra just ploughs on, its dusty (how on earth can I pick out such a minor detail while so much else remains out of reach?) front bumper and number plate growing larger and more terrifying in the windscreen.

Terror bears down on me, coming towards me faster than I could ever have expected.

When at last I truly notice that something is amiss about the way the car is racing towards us on the wrong side of the road, the opportunity for action has long passed and I simply brace myself for impact, throwing one arm out instinctively to protect my wife.

Rebecca has her eyes closed, lost in the simple pleasure of a good song; Billy Joel's bruised voice is fading to make way for the next tune. Ally – thank God – still sleeps in silence in the back, so she is completely unaware of what happens next.

But I am aware of it. All of it: every hellish second.

TWO

It was raining again. Why does it always rain in situations like this, when you're stuck out on a street that you aren't too familiar with, on a dark night in a rowdy part of town? It's like some kind of immutable law, perhaps akin to the strange household hoodoo that ensures you lose one sock from every pair you put in the washing machine, or whenever you put something down it's no longer there, in the same place, when you go to pick it back up.

Some call it Sod's Law, but I just call it life.

A grey blanket of sky hung over the maze of flat grey streets, the horizon line nothing more than a vague, slightly greyer demarcation located somewhere beyond the edge of the city. Clouds and sky were indistinguishable, a vast metal-grey sheet hanging above me, waiting to drop onto my unsuspecting head.

Leeds is a pretty hostile city at the best of times, but on the night in question I felt that hostility rushing at me in waves, pulsing through the heavy air and into my mind like a small mental battering ram. The pubs had chucked out some time ago, but the late bars and nightclubs were still jumping. Bass-heavy music spilled out onto the slick streets, mixing with the vomit and kebab meat that lay in unappealing fleshy patches on the glistening footpaths. Raised voices combined to create a rumbling undercurrent of chatter, but no actual words were audible within the shuddering din.

Cars passed by at a slow pace, their drivers and passengers watching the roadside carnival from behind a protective layer of glass. Most northern cities after nightfall are like zoos, but by that late hour the animals had already been let out of their cages and allowed to roam free for a while. Giggling young women in short skirts and high heels stumbled off kerbs, sweaty men in thin cotton shirts sank to their knees and prayed to some drunken deity, large figures in dark suits watched from neon doorways – uneasy sentinels trained to spot the flame of violence before it even flared beyond a tiny spark.

The girl I was waiting for was standing in the doorway of a pub opposite the Metropole Hotel. She was just twenty-one, wearing a fake fur coat over an expensive Japanese designer dress, and her feet were clad in the latest pair of Jimmy Choos – bought with her father's money, of course. Despite the suggestion of glamour, the girl was more "sauce in the suburbs" than *Sex and the City*. She stood in the recess, leaning against the wall, one knee bent and the corresponding foot resting flat against the dirty brickwork. She was smoking a short hand-rolled cigarette and warbling along to whatever tune was playing inside the pub, her eyes bright from the ingestion of cheap narcotics and expensive alcohol.

I stepped back into my own dark doorway, wary that she might see me. I'd been following her for a couple of days, ever since her father agreed to my slightly inflated fee proposal.

Baz Singh was a well-known Bradford businessman. He owned three curry restaurants, an off licence, and a small strip club in the centre of Bradford which – if the rumours were true – also doubled-up as a brothel. The girl was his daughter, Kareena, and in my considered opinion she was certainly worth watching.

Let me get something straight right from the start. I am not a private eye or some glorified down-at-heel shamus; I do not have an official licence to run around investigating things the police are paid good tax money to look into. My days are not dedicated to Chandleresque sleuthing and I certainly don't spout sudden bursts of clipped dialogue while I hunt down Maltese Falcons or tarnished McGuffins. No, I just try to help people out, people who ask and who are willing to pay me for my trouble. Sometimes this works, other times it doesn't. Often it all goes horribly wrong. But it's a damn sight better – and safer – than what I used to do for a living: better by far than mingling with the dead.

My name is Thomas Usher and I am – well – that's part of the problem. I don't really know who or what I am, not any more. Not since I began to feel the maggot of self-doubt gnawing away at my guts, not since the potentially true nature of my peculiar abilities were revealed to me in a glimpse too brief even to be considered fleeting. Since then I have tried to stick to the right path and avoid all things... *unearthly*, for want of a better word. These days I was more likely to be looking for someone's missing teenage daughter or absent spouse than gazing into the heart of the abyss.

But it wasn't always that way.

I used to be gifted but now I feel cursed. At one time I thought my purpose in life was to help the dead find their way through the dark, but these days it seems that I might have been mistaken.

These days I can't even help the living.

Kareena Singh stubbed out her cigarette against the wall and pushed away towards the middle of the footpath, like someone kicking off from the side of a swimming pool. A small burst of sparks remained in her wake, held in the air for a moment like a tiny swarm of fireflies before being washed away by the rain. The intensity of the rainfall had diminished, leaving behind that fine, wispy rain that seems to get you even wetter than its heavier counterpart. My scalp was soaking and my coat was stuck to my back.

"Come on, Byron." Her voice was pure Bradford: dull, dour, an ugly sound from a pretty mouth.

"Yeah, yeah." The large shaven-headed Caucasian man she was shouting at shook the hand of the even larger bouncer he'd been locked in conversation with and approached Kareena as she opened her arms to take him in a loose embrace. He ignored the gesture and grabbed her slim forearm, guiding her instead out into the centre of the road, where he stood trying to flag down a passing taxi. His hands, as he waved them in front of his face, looked as big as shovels, and just as lethal.

I watched the couple without leaving my hiding place, studying the way they moved, the subtleties of their body language. One of the downsides of my particular type of insight is that I am often unable to read people. The dead are easy to understand if you know the rules – they follow straight lines of logic – but the living rarely think or act in a linear manner, and I am sometimes left feeling confused. I manage to fumble through, but whatever insights I have come from darker regions than those inhabited by the sunlit folk I meet on a daily basis.

The truth is, only death could help me read the living.

The muscle-man's name was Byron Spinks. I'd gathered enough information on him to know that he was a low-level criminal involved in everything from house burglary through car crime to prostitution. Kareena was seeing him simply because her father disapproved – that fact was obvious to anyone who took the time to look, even to me. Baz Singh had already arranged his daughter's marriage to a wealthy Indian business partner, but Kareena wasn't playing ball. She liked the freedom Western culture offered her, the right to make her own decisions and see any man she liked. The right to try before you buy.

And this was where I came in.

Baz Singh had retained my services and asked me to watch his daughter and report on her movements. He was terrified that she was planning to run away with this yobbo Spinks, and that any business capital to be gained from the proposed arranged marriage would go down the drain like so much discarded confetti during a storm.

The couple crouched and climbed into a taxi, so I ran for my car, which was parked at the kerb a few yards away in a No Parking zone where I knew I'd get away with it. I dodged a group of weaving late night revellers and climbed inside, following the taxi as it passed through a series of amber lights and headed out of the city towards the inner ring road. I'd seen enough cop shows on television to know that I should keep at least one vehicle between myself and the car I was trailing, but I was also worried that my lack of real experience in covert pursuit would ensure that I lost them in the heavy night time traffic. The fact that I hated cars and driving was yet another obstacle to overcome.

I didn't like this kind of work. It wasn't what I was made for. Then again, I wasn't really made for anything – that was the other part of the problem.

During my years as what can only be described as a psychic sleuth I'd honed and utilised many specialised methods. Seeing the dead, being called upon by spirits to help guide them to the next level, is a very esoteric field – I had no business rivals and I paid no income tax on my earnings. It was hard work, thankless for the most part. But after the death of my wife and daughter it was the only thing in my life that meant anything. My talent – my ability to see ghosts – was like an anchor, ironically tethering me to the physical world. Without it, I would've taken a hot bath with a cold razor, or dived off the nearest bridge with rocks in my pockets.

But that's another story.

After a few miles the taxi left the ring road at an exit marked for Bestwick, and I cringed at the thought of pursuing these people into what I knew was a rough area. But the taxi continued, passing through the outskirts of the mean-looking estate, and carrying on towards a disused industrial complex called Clara Heights. The place consisted of a wide concrete access road leading to several warehouse units, most of which had been gutted in a serious fire a couple of years ago, and some vacant office space which had miraculously survived the blaze. Prefab huts and squat redbrick buildings were scattered among the blackened shells of the warehouses. I knew the place was dangerous. If red-top news reports were to be believed, the area was used regularly by junkies and sex pests.

"Welcome to the Terror Dome," I muttered, reciting the line from a film, or a book or a song – I'm still not sure which.

The taxi stopped at the kerb and the couple climbed out. By this point Kareena looked slightly worse for the evening's drugs-and-alcohol intake: she was stumbling and her clothes were dishevelled. It looked to me as if she and Spinks had been getting more than cosy on the back seat.

Kareena's black stockings were rolled down to her knees.

According to Singh, his daughter had been seeing Spinks for six weeks – long enough for her to trust him but not long enough to really know him. I had the suspicion that the promise of danger associated with this thug was half the attraction, and that Kareena knew exactly what she was doing and why she was doing it. Pure bloody-mindedness and the desire to hurt her father were the motivating factors in this particular soap opera.

My heart sank. Over the years, I'd seen the bloodied remains of too many women who'd made similar mistakes, the sorry victims of abuse and murder and sexual mutilation, the torn, shredded bodies of those whose only crime had been to make a bad choice on a lonely night. I'd watched them, these murdered women, as they tried and failed to speak to me from somewhere else. They often wept as they failed to communicate the depth of their pain through the barrier of death.

I closed my eyes and held my breath, summoning the courage to go on, to follow these two people towards the edge of their personal darkness. I think even then I knew what was coming, but I kept on going anyway, stupidly hoping that this would not turn into exactly the kind of situation I'd been running from.

When I opened my eyes the taxi had already pulled away; I could see the twin sparks of its taillights as they diminished to tiny pinpricks in the dark.

I glanced over to where the two passengers were now stumbling over a stretch of rough ground towards the shabby heart of the small industrial estate, holding on tightly to each other in case they fell. Hesitating for only a moment, I left the car and followed them over the rubble-strewn ground. I trod softly, as if I were engaged in some kind of guerrilla warfare. I had no idea who else was around, or who they might be meeting here, and the last thing I wanted was to draw attention to my presence on the scene.

I recalled Baz Singh's words to me earlier that day: "Just follow her, and if she gets into trouble, intervene as best you can. If she gets hurt, it's her own decision, but I don't want her dead." The man was as heartless as one of the many stone statues that littered his home – artful representations of the Hindu gods he no longer believed in yet paid lip service to in the name of commerce. It seemed to me that he probably wanted his daughter to be hurt so that she might be punished for her transgressions, but even he drew the line at allowing her to come to serious harm. My role here was as a glorified babysitter, but the money was good so it was a situation worth sticking with.

Or so I hoped.

Not for the first time, I questioned my own involvement in such matters, and with such unappealing people. In the past I'd always sought out the good, or at least the semi good. Now I worked for anyone who would pay me. Not for the first time, I wished that things could be different. That I hadn't once felt the pull of something dark and hungry and powerful as it moved towards me through the spaces between stars.

I regretted the people who had died over the years because I might have unknowingly drawn dark forces towards me. And when I saw their faces in my mind, screaming silent accusations at me, demanding their right to speak, I felt utterly lost.

The truth was I no longer felt able to connect with the departed. Their demands were too intense, and so much more than I was currently willing to handle. I was stuck in some weird middle ground, hating the living and tired of the dead.

Spinks allowed Kareena to go first and followed her towards the blackened entrance of one of the burned-out warehouses. The timber boards barring the entrance had at some point been stripped away from the door, and the door itself had been kicked in. Darkness swallowed Kareena's small, agile figure. Glancing once over his shoulder, his large pale face leering like a clown's mask in the gloom, Spinks entered the building behind her.

That should have been the moment that I walked away. Should have been. But wasn't.

I paused at the doorway when I reached it, sensing something stirring lazily within. Not the couple I'd followed, nor any associate of theirs. No, this presence was something entirely different; it was a thing I'd been fighting not to acknowledge since I'd arrived here at the industrial estate. My failure to see the dead was not an actual breakdown of my ability, it was a deliberate act. For thirteen months now I'd fought against the insight that raged within me, blocking them out, ignoring their voiceless pleas, pretending that they did not still come to me in droves, seeking my aid.

But the dead were never restful. They were always there, peering over my shoulder, stepping into my path, and it was difficult to ignore them for long.

The struggle was taking its toll on my physical appearance – I looked thin and haggard and older than my years – and my head hurt constantly. I devoured painkillers by the packet, their effect diminishing with each passing day. A doctor friend who knew almost everything about me, and had done for many years, often suggested I take harder drugs – morphine, even heroin – but that was a route I didn't want to take, despite his promises to carefully administer just enough to fight my demons. No, I had to do this alone – until I was ready to once again allow the dead access to my battered psyche.

I took a breath and ducked into the warehouse. Every inch of skin on my body was cold, as if I'd sunk suddenly into icy waters.

I could hear footsteps up ahead. Kareena giggled and whispered something I couldn't quite make out. Her voice sounded slurred, unsteady, and I began to fear for her. I never carried a weapon when I was working, but right then I wished that I had a gun. Baz Singh had shown me a small pistol that he'd acquired for my use, but I'd told him to lock it back inside his desk drawer and hide the key. The taking of a human life was an alien concept to me. I had communed with the dead for so long and so often that I had no desire to add to their numbers.

The darkness pulsed around me like a sea of organic black matter, clinging to my clothes, entwining with my hair, sticking to my skin. I kept raising a hand to push it away or wipe it off, but could feel nothing of any substance beneath my fingers. It was an illusion, like so many others I'd encountered over the years. The dark was not alive, nor was it sentient – but there was no doubt in my mind that it did contain *something* which thought and probed and hungered. It was looking for the gaps in my armour, the chinks and damaged areas caused by fear.

Fear was something I could ill afford to show, so I kept it down, kept it at bay.

The sound of a woman giggling came to me again, this time from farther away. Its source could've been miles ahead of me, but that would have been impossible because the industrial building I was moving around inside took up not more than a few hundred square yards. I lost all sense of walls and floor and ceiling. The air opened up, as if sucking me into a vast and airless space. It was a struggle to hang on to my sense of reality; things wanted to move and shift, and transform into other less solid objects.

It was a sensation I was more than familiar with.

Footsteps echoed on the concrete floor and I concentrated on their hollow music, focusing on the sound as if it were a lifeline to what I knew to be real and solid and earthly. Phantoms swam in and out of vision, reaching out to me, clutching at the tattered remnants of my resolve, picking away the stitches of my refusal to accept them.

"Leave me. Let me be." But they wouldn't listen. Instead, they intensified their attempts to snag me in the dark, groping for my weak points.

"This way," said a man's voice – one which I assumed must belong to Spinks. Kareena laughed again, and then fell abruptly silent. I stood there for what seemed like hours, trying to navigate the at once familiar country I found myself in. The landscape was soft, blurred at the edges, but the topography was similar to those places I'd traversed before, many times. This was the realm of the dead, a land where the common laws of physics did not hold sway. What disturbed me more than the ease with which I'd crossed over was the fact that I'd accepted such an extreme transition so readily. Fear gnawed at my insides, a rat in a soft cage, and again I tried to block it out, ignore it, and carry on into the dark.

After thirteen months of denial, I had finally found my way back home – as good a home as any, the only one I really knew.

It was as if a map appeared before me in the darkness, with a route etched in threads and filaments of light. I knew exactly where to go, and accepted that I was being led – by my weird instincts, and by the dead who walked before me, clearing a path like native guides on an expedition deep into their home-land. I can't be sure how long I was in there, delving into a night like no other, but it felt like ages had passed, the world withering outside, people dying and being born. All clocks had stopped; time meant nothing to me.

I followed a narrow passage and stood at the top of a flight of concrete stairs. Each of the steps was blackened by an old fire, their edges chipped and cracked. The banister had fallen away at some point, so I clutched the bare wall as I descended, unsure of what I would find at their base.

The cramped space at the bottom of the stairs was flooded. My feet rested in several inches of standing water. The dark-ness receded, and then rushed back in increments, but this time it was a normal darkness. My guides had abandoned me, deciding that from here on in I would either know the way or could find it without their help. Water sloshed loudly in the hollow chamber. I reached out in front of me to find some kind of purchase. When my fingers fell upon a ragged door handle, I slowly turned it and pushed. The door opened awkwardly, held back by the standing water, but I leaned my weight against it and stepped into the cold room beyond...

At first I was unable to see anything beyond the rubble and the dark reflections in the restless puddles, but gradually my eyesight grew accustomed to the poor conditions. I'd come at them from behind, somehow managing to take a route that would allow me to remain unseen. There were two of them inside the damp chamber, yet I had the sense that someone else had recently departed the scene. Ghost footsteps rippled the surface of the shallow pools of water nearby, and the tableaux on the raised concrete platform up ahead seemed incomplete, unfinished, as if a vital element was missing from the whole.

Darkness shivered in the corners and in the doorways, receding, moving away from me.

Spinks was down on his knees, his large hands clasped in front of his face; he was hiding behind them, afraid of whatever it was he refused to look at. His head was bowed, his thick neck was red and damp, and his broad back was curved in an attitude of defeat. A high-pitched moaning sound came from him, but for some reason it seemed too feminine to associate with such a big man. It was more like the wailing of a little girl.

I wanted to close my eyes, to erase the sight, but I couldn't. I had to see, had to face it. All of it: every single piece of the picture.

Kareena Singh swayed before Spinks, suspended from a thick rope which hung around her throat and upper chest like a trailing brown snake. The rope was wrapped once around her neck and its end terminated somewhere up in the rafters, most of which were lost in shadow. Her smooth skin had paled a shade and her eyes bulged from their sockets, fixing me in their bloated gaze. Her tongue was hideous, like a fat grey graveworm, and it protruded between lips as thick and rubbery as uncooked steaks.

There was some kind of metal stand set up before the body, maybe a tripod for a camera, but my attention refused to focus on the contraption. As usual, I had eyes only for the dead. Her body drew my attention, not letting me go. I stared and I stared and I felt her sorrow like the vibration left in the air by a shriek. I was being pulled back towards death – always, always drawn to it, with any choice in the matter I might once have had now snatched away.

Kareena's feet dangled slack and lifeless. One shoe was missing and the other hung treacherously from her dainty toes.

I could not take my eyes from those feet. Their gentle motion was hypnotic, and it drew me like nothing I have witnessed before or since. They danced in the air with a grace she surely would have lacked in life – the rhythm was that of the grave, the dance of the dead, but she kept the beat well.

I would be standing there still, entranced by that elegant footwork, if Spinks had not abruptly fallen over onto his side and begun to scream.

THREE

"Jesus, Usher, I thought you were dead." Detective Inspector Donald Tebbit stalked the length of the tiny room like an expectant father. All that was missing was the worry frown and a pocket full of cigars. He paused, ran a hand through his sweaty hair, and then resumed his repetitive exertions. "I mean, you just slipped off the edge of the world for a while."

I smiled, but my mouth wasn't too keen on the expression so I ditched it in favour of a grimace. "I was lying low, taking it easy. I've been advising a few people on certain situations, making some easy money. This is the first big thing I've been involved in for months."

Tebbit stopped moving again. This time I thought it might stick. "I was worried about you." He looked coy. It didn't suit him. "We had a few things we wanted to talk to you about, ourselves. You could've returned my calls, you know… or even answered my emails." He stared at me as if expecting miracles – it was a look I'd grown accustomed to over the years I'd known him, and it always gave me a bad feeling. A very bad feeling.

"I don't do that anymore. These days I'm working for the living, not the dead. Strictly for the living." I didn't even believe it myself, so wasn't surprised when Tebbit shook his head before sitting down opposite me at the scarred table. He spread out his broad fighter's hands on the faded wood and flexed his chunky fingers. The wedding ring glinted once, catching the light, and my stomach lurched.

I stared at him. "I'm not under arrest, am I?"

"Don't be silly, Usher. You are a witness – our only one, in fact – but that doesn't mean we can hold you. You're free to go whenever you like."

"I have no plans for this evening," I countered, finally finding that smile.

Tebbit shook his head again, but this time I knew he was softening, his habitual defences coming down. I'd known the man for over a decade, and helped him on several so-called unsolvable cases, so felt that he at least owed me a few favours. "So you found them like that? The girl already dead and her bloke praying to the gods of muscle mania."

"Yes. She was hanging from a rope and he was in no fit state to tell me anything about how it happened. How is he now?"

Tebbit sighed, ran a hand across his lined, damp forehead. "Inconsolable." He rubbed at his right temple, grimacing.

"Do you think he did it? Do you think he murdered her?" I knew by his face that he'd already decided what he believed.

Tebbit nodded once, and then shook his head, slowly. Finally he just shrugged his broad shoulders. "I don't know. Probably. Do you?"

Perhaps I should have spoken up and voiced my doubts, but at that point I was operating without any additional information. The facts were that I'd followed them both to a deserted location, where I'd discovered the girl hanging from her neck and her boyfriend kneeling at her feet, not even trying to cut her down. On the surface of it, this one looked obvious – but I rarely dealt with the surface of things. All my breakthroughs came from somewhere underneath, guided by instincts located far below everything that other people – normal people – try their best to believe in.

"We have him locked up and awaiting trial. This should happen fast – it seems like a simple case of boy-meets-girl-and-kills-her. Sorry if I sound cynical, but I am." He glanced away, trying to hide from me the doubt in his eyes, and the reflection of something I could not help but see and be afraid of.

"She's not the first, is she?"

"I always said you were good. You should be on TV – some sort of psychic hotline, or maybe a chat show." He was trying to rattle me, to cause me to react.

"I am *not* a psychic." I regretted taking the bait, but it had been a long day – and an even longer night. Not matter how many times I saw stuff like this, or how often I was forced to swallow my fear, I could never quite get used to the emotional impact.

Tebbit stared back down at the tabletop, his blunt fingers tracing the innumerable names which had been carved or etched into the wood over many years of intense interrogations: the signs and sigils of so many guilty men and women – and even of some who were innocent. His face was pale, the flesh hung loose on his bones. He looked worse than I'd ever seen him, and certainly worse than our last meeting.

I wondered if the tumour was beginning to take hold, to stamp its mark on his internal organs, on his bones and blood and tissue. He was completely unaware of the cancer, of course; I'd never had the opportunity to tell him, and had promised not to anyway. If there was a chance that it could be treated, I would have sent him to a doctor, but when the ghost of his wife, Tabitha, had informed me several months ago of his impending illness she made it very clear that it was inoperable and that he was going to die.

And that she would make sure he did not get lost along the way.

She was another that I had tried and failed to ignore. The list of names was longer than a trail of tears, and it all led back to the same place: my wretched, broken heart.

"Come on, man. Don't toy with me. Just tell me."

When he finally looked up I saw the skull grinning through the skin of his face, and I knew that his time was drawing near. Tabitha would be pleased: she was waiting for him, and had been for quite some time. He would not need me to help him on his way. He had his wife to hold his hand in the long darkness which was even now reaching out to claim him.

"She's the third in six months. All of them young. All of them beautiful. Each of them hung by the neck to die in agony."

"Is this one of the things you wanted to speak to me about? Did you want my help on the case?" My hands clenched on the table, the knuckles whitening. I looked deep inside myself for rage but found only despair.

"Yes." He held my gaze, God love him: at least he was man enough to give me that. The fact that Kareena Singh's death might have been avoided had he been able to contact me remained unspoken, but it hung in the air like a fog – or like the vague shape of a girl strung up by a length of rough hemp, the flesh of her lovely young throat knotted and twisted, her sad eyes bulging, singling me out and blaming me for it all.

Blaming me. All of them blaming me. All the fucking time.

There wasn't much more to be said so I left Tebbit with his own ghosts – the main one being the ghost of himself – and took a walk over to where my car was parked. The rain had let up but the sky remained grey, as if taunting the city with the promise of even more downpours. My mood felt equally dour, and the prospect of driving again made it even worse.

I sat in the car without starting the engine, waiting for the heavy sense of guilt to lift and disperse. Had Byron Spinks been directly responsible for the deaths of these three girls? I doubted it. Something told me that he had probably not killed Kareena, so it made sense that he'd not done for the others.

At the scene of Kareena's murder the attending officers had found a stash of professional standard filmmaking equipment. Although the victim was still clothed, it was suspected that she and Spinks had gone there with the intention of shooting some kind of pornographic footage. The mystery third party – the one whose departure I'd felt more than witnessed – was thought to be the man behind the camera, an accomplice. No actual film (digital or otherwise) had been found at the scene, so he must have taken with him whatever they'd shot – if indeed they had even got that far before she was killed.

The engine started first time, which was always a bonus, and I eased the big battered Volvo out of the parking space and into the road. It was early by now – 5am – so traffic was virtually non-existent, just a few sombre nightshift workers pacing the streets and whatever party people were still intact enough to take early morning taxis home. I felt like listening to some music but the radio was broken, so instead I tried to clear my mind and think of nothing.

Nothing.

Darkness.

The dancing feet: one shoe off; one shoe half-on. Lithe legs in a tawdry ballet. Swinging. Swinging. Never coming to rest, not now not ever, just swinging all the time, never losing time, always catching the rhythm that waits for us all, singing us toward the other side.

I blinked back tears and concentrated on the road.

The city skulked behind me like an overgrown naughty child – one with learning difficulties and a penchant for hurting people. The road ahead narrowed, becoming my only route through the shuddering darkness. The horizon line shimmered, weak light bleeding up from the slowly opening wound of day. I wasn't sure why I was crying, but it felt like my tears were for more than the immediate dead. I wiped my face with the back of my hand, and for the first time in such a long time my tattoos twitched: the ink on my back started to crawl, the markings across my chest stretched like waking animals, and the designs on my upper arms jigged and jolted like live electricity cables.

Whatever power crouched within me was waking from the self-induced sleep. I had managed to keep it down, to push it under, for a little over a year but now circumstances were calling it back, summoning it from that uneasy slumber. That power was like an animal, a hunter, and right now it had been released back into the world.

This description makes it sound like it isn't part of me, but it is. Without it, I am nothing; without me it is simply unfocused energy swirling around the universe, looking for a home. The car crash that killed my family so long ago (long enough that I was at least able to think about it without breaking down) gave me something more than an immovable rock of grief in my chest. It also opened up doorways within me, forced open fissures, dredged up things from the primordial mind that could never be put back in place. I was granted a gift; a curse, an ability that I could use to help people while at the same time it used me. All I was missing was the knowledge of where it came from and what it was really for.

What *I* was really for.

The countryside usually soothed me, but tonight it just made me feel more alone. The empty fields and broken-down dry stone walls spoke to me of damage done and promises not kept. The slow-rising sun over Otley did nothing to obliterate the darkness; the shadows simply went into hiding, marshalling their power before returning to engulf the land.

My house lay twenty miles from the city, near Bramhope. It used to be a home, when my family and I first bought it, but now it was merely somewhere to store my things and a place to sleep. I remembered first viewing the property with Rebecca and Ally, moving slowly from room to room, each of us smiling, feeling that the building had been waiting for us to find it. The house was everything we had ever wanted: big, located far away from the city, surrounded by open countryside, isolated enough to be private but not so much that we would feel like a family of hermits.

Rebecca had loved the place, and seeing her face I'd fallen in love with it too. Ally – a mere baby at that time, not even ready to toddle – had crawled around on the floor and gurgled at the dust and the cobwebs. We'd mortgaged ourselves to the hilt to buy it, and struggled for a while to make the repayments, but the glow in Rebecca's eyes was enough to convince me that we'd made the right choice. It sustained me, that glow, through the tough times we experienced at the beginning of our marriage.

Now the rooms still echoed with their laughter, the floors reverberated with their long-ago footsteps, and I was never at peace. But I could not leave the house. Selling up was not an option. Some day, I thought, the ghosts may come – my family might return. So I stayed there, counting away the years, hoping that this night, any night, might be the one when it happened and my loved ones would come calling to find me waiting there, right where they'd left me.

Blaming me. Always blaming me. Always blaming myself.

I parked on the drive and walked up the gravel path to the front door. I felt a vibration when I placed my palm against the old wood, as if machinery were operating somewhere deep inside. My tattoos swarmed, responding to the energy. I unlocked the door and stepped inside.

The house was too big for me so I kept mostly to the downstairs rooms. I even had a bed set up in the main reception room, facing the rear patio doors where I could look out onto the overgrown garden to watch the sunrise. Upstairs was all dust and shadow; mourning and memory. I had not been inside the master bedroom for such a very long time.

I took off my coat and hung it in the cupboard under the stairs. The boards creaked; something vague as a memory scuttled away out of sight. I trod softly towards the room I used as a study, switched on the desk lamp, and powered up my laptop. It was an old model but it had served me well. I have never believed in replacing something just for the sake of it, only when it is broken and can no longer function. Even then, when a replacement is entirely necessary, it pains me to throw things away.

I poured myself a large whisky and felt the radiator under the window with the palm of my hand. The hand was shaking only slightly, but I knew the whisky would settle that. The radiator was warm but not hot; the system must have just come on. I'd probably forgotten to reset the timer after the clocks were last turned back. I was always doing that, forgetting everyday things. Time was like an enemy, mocking me from afar, tearing away parts of me that would never grow back and leaving me twitching at its mercy.

I sat at my desk and logged on to my email account. Twenty messages: less than usual. Maybe people were taking the hint and realising that I'd given up the ghost on dealing with ghosts.

Ha fucking ha.

The joke was so weak that I couldn't even raise a smile.

My usual routine was to delete all emails without even reading them, unless it was from someone I could guarantee wasn't looking to recruit my services or the message in the title header moved me in some way. I didn't advertise in newspapers or magazines, nor did I peddle my services from door to door like a window salesman. People heard about me through others I'd helped, and they always found a way to contact me. If they failed to find me, their desire for what I had to offer was obviously not great enough.

DI Tebbit had sent me something. The cursor hovered over his name as I gripped the mouse, but I couldn't yet find the strength to press the button and open his message. The shakes had passed, but other tremors – the deeper ones which had nested within my bones – would never go away.

The email attachment – symbolised in the software program by a small paperclip – taunted me, and finally I could put it off no longer. I opened the email and leaned back in my chair, ready for anything. Ready for nothing. Not ready at all.

The email read as follows:

Usher,

I thought you might like to see the attached. No pressure. Just take a look and get back to me if you feel like it.

Tebbit

His manner was always brusque yet it hid a heart the size of a continent. Tebbit was one of those men who let no one inside; their armour is always up, protecting the soft tissue beneath, preventing any potential harm. Like most people, he hid behind whatever armour he possessed, and also like most people he was utterly transparent in his motives.

I clicked on the attachments and waited for a software programme to respond.

There were three photographs attached to the email, unoriginally titled #1, #2 and #3.

The first showed a young, slim white girl dressed in a smart business suit. She was hanging from what looked like a thin length of plastic-insulated electrical wire. Her throat was cut by the wire down to the vertebrae. A wash of blood decorated the front of her white blouse.

The second shot was of a young black girl. She was wearing gold lamé hot pants and clear plastic stilettos – stripper shoes.

Her hair was styled in a theatrical manner, like a big Seventies afro. Her make-up was equally elaborate, as if it had been applied for a part in a film. There was a long woollen scarf looped around her neck. Her head was tilted at an angle that was all wrong.

I did not need to look at photograph #3. I knew it was Kareena Singh and I knew I'd already seen the image, but in the flesh. I shut down the laptop, closing the lid on the horror, and finished my drink. It was only then that I registered the sound.

I held my breath without really being aware of it and glanced around the room. The old leather armchair sat in the same spot it had occupied for years, the coffee table squatted beside it. My bookshelves reached up the walls to caress the ceiling. The sound continued. It was like a gentle thumping noise, as if someone were knocking on a door somewhere far away yet close enough for me to hear. But the rhythm was off, as if they were not concentrating too hard as they knocked. The thuds seemed random, yet still held some kind of elusive beat. Then I realised what it was that was so weird about the sound: the knocks were too far apart, as if the knocker was doing so slowly, leaving a long time between each individual sound.

I stood and walked softly across the room towards the door, my head cocked, ears pricked and listening to the sound. It did not increase or decrease in volume, nor did the beat change. The gaps between thuds remained regular.

I opened the door and went out into the hall, where the sound grew slightly louder. I glanced at the stairs, my gaze climbing them but my feet remaining immobile. The sound, I realised, was coming from somewhere on the first floor. It could not be an intruder – who would be foolish enough to break into a house and start rapping on the walls? No matter how hard I tried to tell myself otherwise, I knew that I was hearing sounds made by the dead. Somebody somewhere was trying to contact me, to draw my attention, and the only way they could manage it was through this dull, percussive method.

I began to climb the stairs.

The carpet wrinkled against the varnished boards. Grey cobwebs shivered against the walls where they'd gathered at the edge of each riser – I never had been one for housework, and the place was a mess. The sound continued, pulling me towards it, hooking me like a fish on a line. I stared straight ahead, waiting to see something, but the way was clear. No misshapen figures darted across the landing, no pale hands clutched at the edge of the wall.

The air was musty, unlived in. I rarely came upstairs. My life was focused on the ground floor, where the kitchen, study and two receptions rooms were located. I even used the downstairs bathroom.

Upstairs there were too many memories: the room baby Ally had claimed as her own, the master bedroom where Rebecca and I had slept and made love. Still, after all these years, I hated going up there.

Hated it with a passion.

The volume of the thudding sound increased as I made my way along the landing, passing doors I'd not opened for years. I knew immediately which room the sounds were coming from – it was obvious. The dead, although often vague and gossamer in their manifestations, are rarely subtle in their approach.

I stood outside the master bedroom and took a breath, feeling dizzy and nauseous. The fear was upon me, but I sucked it all up, crammed it all inside.

Why do they always have to go for your weak spots, hit you in the places that hurt most? A lot of ghosts are like that – they sniff out your soft, vulnerable parts and close in on them, prodding and poking until something breaks and they can reach deep inside…

Slowly I reached out and grasped the door handle but couldn't quite bring myself to open the door. The handle was cold in my fist; cold as ice, as if the room beyond contained an expanse of arctic waste. The wood began to groan, warping and flexing, and I knew that I had to push on and enter the room.

The door opened easily. I was sure that I'd locked it years ago, but it opened without a key. They do that, too, the ghosts. They fuck with your mind, making you doubt your sanity until the world becomes malleable, open to interpretation. They enjoy throwing you off balance.

I expected the sound to cease as soon as I set foot in the room, but it didn't; it kept on, slightly louder, more intense.

More immediate.

Demanding.

She was hanging from a dark spot on the ceiling, near the window. Her long smooth legs swung like pendulums, one foot repeatedly hitting the timber panelling – the obvious source of that maddening sound. Her image was at least strong enough to interact with her surroundings, yet still obviously not fully anchored in our world. There was a tragic beauty to it, and its raw, untapped power made me shake all over again, as if an electric current had sent a jolt through my bones.

It was Kareena Singh, of course. I knew it would be. She'd come to me to ask for my help, to force me to remember her and to beg me to keep sifting through the detritus of her life. Her eyes were open, bulging as wide as they had been when I'd found her, and the fat blue tongue was plastered across her chin. She did not speak or even acknowledge me. It was enough that she was here, in my house, making herself known to me.

"Why can't you all just leave me alone?" My voice cracked as I spoke, the words coming apart in my mouth, like shattered teeth.

Kareena Singh did not reply. They never do. Not once have I been spoken to directly; all communication with the dead is elusive, peripheral.

She just swayed on the rope, with that one bare foot bumping against the wall, arms held stiffly at her sides. Her body looked solid, yet it was slightly less than substantial: in the light from the external lamps that bled through the window, I could glimpse her diaphanous quality. As she swayed, her body turning slightly to the side, I saw the outline of the window through her torso, the angle of the wall through her arm. She was there but not there – a representation, a message. A pointer.

I turned and left the room, closing the door gently behind me, so as not to disturb the girl. The thumping sounds finally stopped. My heart almost did the same.

The other two girls were out on the landing, suspended from the ceiling. The black girl in the stripper outfit turned in slow circles, and the other girl was immobile, hanging straight down like a suspended statue, her toes pointing downward, as if straining to touch the floor.

I went downstairs and looked again at the three crime scene photographs Tebbit had so thoughtfully sent me. Then I picked up the phone, my hands gripping it so tightly that I wondered what would break first, plastic or bone.

FOUR

"What are their names?" My voice sounded strange, I didn't even recognise it. There was an anger held between the words that I had not been aware of for months. I felt like spitting – spitting right into that bastard's face.

"Usher. I was hoping you'd call." Tebbit's tone was low and even, betraying nothing of his own emotional state.

"The names, man. Just tell me the names."

"Sarah Dowdy and Candice Wallace. Dowdy was an art student at Leeds University, did well with her coursework, and was by all accounts a popular lass. Wallace was a stripper. She worked at the Blue Viper. Kareena Singh's father owns the Blue Viper – but I'm sure you already know that, considering he's currently paying your bills."

I refused to take the bait. "I'll keep my eyes and ears open, Tebbit – that's all I can promise. Nothing more."

"And your *other* senses? What about those?"

I smiled, despite the grim situation. My anger receded. "Yes, those too. I'll be as receptive as I possibly can and let you know if anything occurs to me." I did not tell him about the ghosts. He didn't need to know about them, not just yet. Whatever message they had come to deliver, it was directed at me. Always at me.

"Thanks, Usher. I was hoping you'd say that."

I hung up the phone, pressed it down hard against the desk. I felt like leaning all my weight down on it until the case shattered, but pulled away at the last minute, regaining control of my emotions. I opened my laptop and hit the start button, then waited for the machine to come out of sleep mode. I accessed a search engine and typed in the name Sarah Dowdy. The results from several news sites told me what I already knew, along with some additional personal information that I didn't. Art student. Quiet, popular girl; she kept herself to herself. Struggling to pay the bills, she'd become involved with a few shady characters and been drawn into selling pornography on the University campus. She didn't appear in any of the movies, but pushed copies of them to all her male friends.

Candice Wallace, as Tebbit had already informed me, had worked as a stripper and waitress at the Blue Viper. She was twenty years old, unqualified, and had a sick mother in a nursing home up in Newcastle upon Tyne. Nothing was mentioned about porn films, but she was linked to the others because she did casual work in a strand of the same industry.

All roads led to the Blue Viper, and indirectly to Baz Singh.

On the surface, it all made sense, but I'd learned enough not to trust what immediately presents itself and wait for the other options to appear. Dig deep enough and you always find those other options – usually too many of them, and the one you least expect to be the truth usually turns out to be exactly what you are looking for.

My head was aching and my eyes felt gritty, so I closed the laptop lid and poured myself another whisky. The drink felt fine in my throat; a purgative. I closed my eyes and enjoyed the burn, trying to clear my mind and concentrate on kick-starting my buried instincts. I was all too aware of the visitors upstairs, but hiding behind them was something else – a vague and shadowy presence that refused to reveal itself for now. I knew it would step out into the open when it was ready, so chose to let it be for the time being, trusting in my experience.

The dead do not like to be rushed. They have their own timetables and dance to their own beat.

I went through into the lounge and turned on the television, simply to distract myself from the problem at hand. Things rarely resolve themselves if you're too focused on them: the answers to life's conundrums usually arrive when you are looking the other way. Wasn't it John Lennon who said that life is what happens when you are making other plans?

I should have asked him about that when I met him, nineteen years after he was killed.

I found a twenty-four hour news channel and settled down on the sofa, kicking off my shoes and rubbing the soles of my feet against the thick carpet. I rolled off my socks with my toes, impressed at my own dexterity, and then splayed out the toes, stretching them as far apart as they would go.

A news report was playing about a missing nine year-old girl on an infamous Leeds council estate called Bestwick (the same estate through which I'd trailed Kareena Singh and Byron Spinks the night before). It was feared by the authorities that the youngster had been snatched by a disgruntled neighbour, a gang of feral kids, or – everyone's favourite bogeyman – a predatory paedophile. The usual suspects, then: media monsters of the month.

Images of a weeping mother, a blank-faced father and countless hard-featured friends and family flashed up onto the screen. They were an ugly lot, dour and pale and apparently clueless, but I felt for them. Losing a child is the worst horror of all. Nothing else even comes close. Not even the loss of a spouse. I could testify to that better than most; my own history was stained by loss.

Feeling depressed, I turned off the television and walked over to the stereo. I put on some Mahler, just for the hell of it, and lost myself in the music for a while. I crossed the room in a trance, almost asleep on my feet, the exploited ghosts of hanged girls dancing provocatively above me, my own ghosts skulking in the background, as they always did. Watching and waiting, but never stepping forward to ease the pain in my heart.

I went through into the other room, where I lay on the bed and dreamed that I was

...lying in the master bedroom, stretched out on the bed I'd once shared with Rebecca. The room is clean and tidy, the furniture scrubbed, the carpet unstained. The walls look freshly painted but I cannot smell a thing – that's how I know I am dreaming: because my senses are all messed up.

It is dark outside; the window looks bigger than it should, the separate panes now forming one single glass sheet. There are no curtains. No stars in the sky beyond.

I look down at myself, examining the length of my body, and see that I am naked. My body is thin and my skin looks strangely colourless, lacking in vitality. My ribs show through the flesh of my sides and my kneecaps jut out like tennis balls.

I climb from the bed, expecting every movement to set off a series of aches and pains. But I feel nothing, not the motion of my limbs, the kiss of the cotton sheets against my skin, or even the gentle impact of my feet upon the floor.

The bodies of vermin lie along the skirting boards, lined up like little victims. Each of them has been killed by the twisting of the neck: the fur at their throat is knotted and torn, their heads facing the wrong way. Their tiny limbs are hairless, claws clenched. I suppose that they must be rats, but they resemble no rodent I have ever seen. Their backward-facing features are monstrous, with huge gaping mouths, elongated teeth, eyes dull and glassy as a child's toy marbles.

For some reason I am drawn to the window, so I step across the room and approach the pane. The sky outside has turned black, like ink spilled across the heavens: I can see its cloudy progress as it stains the view. The geography outside is all wrong. Where there should be

a low wooden fence bordering my property, with a road and scrubby fields beyond and a small area of woodland in the distance, there is instead a vast expanse of blackened ground – earth which has been razed by fire. This scorched topography rises gradually towards a hill, and at the top of the hill sits the charred remains of a single tree. I guess that it is an oak; it must have been a wonderful sight in its prime, but now it is merely a spelk, a sooty splinter.

The branches of the tree are bare and black; thin appendages clutch blindly at the darkening sky. As the darkness spreads, threatening to steal my vision, I see that there is something held suspended within the spindly branches – or rather, something dangling from them.

A dark, squat bundle, something which resembles rags but I know is something more, hangs limply from the burned limbs of the tree. At one time it must surely have looked more like a human being, but now it is like sticks wrapped in untreated leather. I can make out no features; can barely even locate the skull, so when it begins to twitch I initially blame a breeze that is not actually present.

The bundle slumps downward, falling clumsily through the thickest of the denuded branches. Then it gets caught on a stubby limb and halts its agonising descent. What looks like a ragged arm falls from the main body and dangles freely, its motion sickening and somehow unnatural as the darkness turns the sky to onyx.

The last thing I see before I can see no more is the suggestion of a raised head – at least I assume it must be a head, for surely no other part of the human anatomy, however mutilated, could swivel at such a hideous angle…

Then the tree ignites in a flash of yellow-white flame, and the vision is gone.

FIVE

I woke with a scream stuck in my throat but thankfully it did not budge. My lips were sealed with congealed spit and the lower part of my face was numb, as if a cold breeze had been blowing all the time I slept. I sat up and blinked back tears, wondering where they'd come from and why I was so ashamed of them. The dream was thick in my mind, like a mental mud, and I could not rid myself of the terrible image of something dark stirring in that skeletal tree, turning its blaze-blasted face towards me.

I sat up on the bed and rubbed my eyes. They were gritty, aching. Blinking back the sudden moisture, I wondered where the imagery in the dream had come from. Was it an attempt by some restless spirit to contact me or simply the result of my own stressed-out mind approaching a breaking point? There were no answers forthcoming, so I stood and walked to the kitchen, craving strong coffee and something to eat.

It was still dark outside. I'd fallen asleep early, slept all night, and woken an hour or so before dawn. I liked this time of day best of all, when everyone else was still in their beds, the spirits were mostly restful, and the planet seemed to move slower than at any other time. It was almost as if I could see the workings of the world.

I filled the kettle with water from the tap and set it to boil. My hands looked old, worn; the knuckles were swollen and the skin on the backs of them was dry. I held up my hands and examined them, feeling ancient, like a man well past his best. But I had been that way for a long time now – indeed, because of the loss of my family I had never been allowed to enjoy any kind of so-called prime. The best of me had been sliced away like meat from the bone, taking with it any promise of future good times. A loss of such great magnitude destroys people in ways they don't even recognise until much later, and by that time the damage is too old to repair.

The kettle boiled. I poured hot water over instant coffee grounds. It tasted bitter, like my life, my experiences. I drank more, burning the roof of my mouth but barely even feeling the thin layer of skin as it peeled away in tiny patches from the muscle and bone.

I walked through into my bedroom and opened the patio doors, then sat down on the old patio chair, resting my feet on the low table I kept there for use during rare moments of relaxation. The sun was rising in the east, a vague ball of light struggling to illuminate the dark corners of the world. I watched it as it crested the rim of the horizon, weary and unimpressed by nature's wonders. Too many times I had seen beneath the façade and confronted what lay there, concealed by natural mysteries. The underside was not so different from what everyone else saw: it was just as grubby, and just as open to interpretation.

There are no easy answers to be had – the major religions have it all wrong, each in their own way, and at best they simply brush up against a possible truth without even acknowledging it in their simplistic doctrines. Nietzsche was wrong, God isn't dead; he was never actually alive in the first place. Original Sin. Karma. Reincarnation. Heaven. Elysium. It all amounts to so much bullshit.

The truth is that there *is* no truth: everything is negotiable.

My head ached. I drank more coffee. The sun shuddered, threatening to go back into hiding. For a moment I fancied that I could hear the sound of the world turning: the dull hum of complex machines, the flat screams of the lost and the lonely, the endless wailing of children never fed, never clothed, never loved... My own impotency surged within my throat like bile, reminding me of the sheer lunacy of existence, the nonsense of simply being.

Gradually, I began to hear the shrill sound of the telephone ringing inside. I got up and walked through the house into my study, hoping that the ringing would cease. The thing kept on, uncaring, insistent. Wondering why I always found it so difficult to ignore a ringing telephone, I answered the call.

"Yes?"

"Hello, Thomas."

My throat tightened. I recognised the voice immediately, but did not want to acknowledge that it was her. I waited for her to speak again, but she was also waiting – waiting for me to break the silence that stretched between us like a canyon with no apparent bottom.

"Ellen."

More silence, as if she'd suddenly changed her mind. I imagined her lips resting inches from the telephone receiver, and my hand went cold. I stared at the veins in my forearms; my blood pumped slowly, reluctantly, as if it was afraid to circulate around my body and animate my limbs.

"How are you?" Her voice was low, as if she were afraid to raise it and draw attention to the inherent redundancy of her question. "You okay?"

"I... yes. Yes, I'm fine. It's been a long time, Ellen."

The sound of her voice took me right back, to a time several months after my body had recovered from the injuries I'd sustained during the accident. Ellen Lang had been a GP back then, and it was mostly because of her that I managed to find the will to carry on. She believed me when I told her about seeing dead people, and her advice was simple and direct: *just keep going, don't look back and never look down.*

But even before that Ellen and I had a shared history. I'd known her since I was seventeen years old, and in the early months of my marriage to Rebecca, when I was too young and far too stupid to realise the damage I was doing, Ellen and I had slept together. We both regretted the transgression, and it had never happened again, but the bond between us, instead of weakening, had grown stronger, culminating in her becoming my saviour when I needed one.

"I didn't even know you were back in the country. Isn't NASA missing you?"

She laughed then, and everything seemed fine for an exquisite moment, as if nothing else in the world mattered more than the sound of this woman's laughter. I recalled as if it were yesterday the image of her bare legs, the shape of her naked thighs, the way she'd whispered nonsensically in my ear as she came.

"I'm on extended leave. Family business."

Fearing that I might fall, I lowered myself into an armchair and just about managed to focus on what she was saying. "Nothing serious, I hope."

Another pause, but this one was pregnant with possibilities. I knew that this wasn't a social call – she'd had plenty of opportunities for that since moving to America. No, she wanted my help. She wanted my help and I was more than willing to give it.

"Whatever it is, Ellen, the answer is yes. I owe you far more than anything you could ever ask."

She coughed softly and I realised that she was probably trying not to cry. "Have you seen the news?"

"Some. I've been busy. A lot has changed since I last saw you. As I'm sure things have changed for you." I paused, allowing her to move the conversation forward at her own pace.

"Could we meet? Have dinner, perhaps? I know it's been a long time, and I realise that I'm asking a lot here, but I really need to see you. A lot of it is to do with this family business I mentioned, but also I want to *see* you. I haven't thought of you for ages, but as soon as the plane landed at Heathrow I pictured your face, even started scanning the crowd in case you'd caught wind of my arrival. I was disappointed when you didn't turn up to meet me. Stupid of me, eh?"

Rebecca was the love of my life, but like most men I'd also loved others. I would have died for my wife, but I would kill for Ellen Lang. The depth and nature of my feelings had always confused me; she had always been second best, and she knew it, but I had never been able to shake off the effects of her presence – or the wonderful, deeply torturous memory of that one night, long ago, that we had spent together.

I felt guilty even speaking to Ellen. My entire life was constructed around the vague hope – the yearning – that one day I might see the ghosts of my wife and daughter, yet here I was having dirty thoughts about a woman from my past. It didn't make sense. Nothing added up. But then I reminded myself that I was still human, despite my unique ability, and human beings are flawed and self-destructive. No matter how tense or tricky the situation we find ourselves in, we can always manufacture a way to make things worse.

"If I'd known that you were coming I might have done just that. You're my oldest friend, and we haven't spoken in such a long time. I think that probably warrants some kind of ostentatious gesture."

"I'm sorry that I cut you off." Her voice was almost a whisper. "I thought it was for the best. I never intended it to go on for this long – just a break in communications. But I got busy and my life got messy, and before I'd even paused for breath a year had passed. Then another. Then it was too late. I know it's a lame excuse, but it's the only one I have. I really am sorry. It should have been easy to pick up the phone."

The distance between us narrowed, and I felt that I could almost reach out and touch her, just to reassure her that everything was fine between us. "I could say the same. I didn't even send you an email." The truth was that I'd written several, and then deleted each one without sending them. Some relationships are not meant to change; certain kinds of love are too fragile to ruin with romance.

"Listen," I said, taking control of the conversation. "Let's not do this to ourselves, and to each other. We've both been a bit shoddy. We can leave it at that, or talk about it later, over dinner."

I could sense her slow smile. "Okay, Thomas. I agree. There's no point in…"

"Waking the dead?"

She laughed, and the tension was gone.

"Where are you staying?"

"The Crowne Plaza Hotel, in Leeds city centre. Do you know it?"

"Yes, I know it. I performed an exorcism there five years ago, left a double room in one hell of a state. There was spit and ectoplasm everywhere."

"No matter how well I know you, I can never get used to this stuff." Her voice sounded hollow; the tension was returning.

"I was joking, Ellen. I stayed there once, but not on business. I attended a psychology conference in the dining suite."

Thankfully, she laughed again, but this time it was more guarded. My stupid quip had reminded her all over again of the crazy parts of my life, the things I'd seen and done, the dangerous situations I often found myself in. A lot of it was what she had run away from: she simply couldn't handle the knowledge I possessed. Nor was she prepared to let our relationship play second fiddle to Rebecca's lengthy absence – and I couldn't bring myself to blame her for that.

"Dinner? Tonight?" Her voice pulled me back from the brink of too many painful memories, and I clung to it as if her words were a series of narrow ledges over a vast pit.

"Yes. That would be nice. How about I meet you at your hotel? Eight o'clock? I'll book a table at a nice little Italian place I know around the corner – you do still enjoy good tiramisu, don't you?"

"If I could, I'd eat nothing else."

When I replaced the telephone in its cradle, I experienced an odd sensation that felt like I was rushing backwards to meet something terrible. Ellen's call and the events of the past twenty-four hours had forced me to think about things I had not dwelled on in years. I moved across the room as if in a daze, groped for the drinks shelf, and poured myself two fingers of Bushmills single malt. Then I poured some more.

This was at least a three-finger memory.

When I left hospital after the accident my body was almost fully healed. I had a few scars here and there, and my neck ached if I didn't exercise it every few hours, but overall my frame had held up well to the impact.

The psychological scars, however, proved a lot more difficult to treat. I'd spent hours with surgeons to mend my body, but would have nothing to do with the useless counsellors and therapists recommended to me. They did not know me; they had no knowledge of my life before the accident, of who I really was.

And, of course, there were the ghosts.

I see the first one three weeks after the accident, and even then I am aware that never again will I experience it so vividly, so... simply. It is long after midnight, possibly somewhere close to 3am. I am sitting up in my hospital bed, staring at the blank wall opposite, when a young man calmly enters the room. I have been transferred to a private room because my depressive moods and late night rages were affecting the other patients, and to be honest I am glad of the time alone. The young man has no business coming in here, and I turn my head to tell him so.

But the young man is no longer there.

Not there; not visible, yet still present.

I feel the first pangs of terror as a faint gnawing sensation at the base of my spine, then, gradually, it begins to spread, like a virus.

Initially I think I am experiencing a hallucination, having seen him only at the periphery of my vision. But, no, that is impossible. The details are too clear. I know, for instance, that he is wearing faded jeans and no shoes. His hair is long, the ends resting on his collar, and he has a short dark beard reaching across his cheeks and under his chin.

Fear gnawing. Spreading. Flowering towards my heart.

If the young man had been some kind of vision, a waking dream bleeding over from my subconscious, then surely I would not be able to process such tiny details. Yet still disbelief hangs over me – I am not a superstitious man, not once in my life have I experienced anything that could be described as otherworldly.

I close my eyes. Open them. I expect to see a dark veil, my fear manifest, terror stretched across my vision like a drawn curtain. My heart swells, pressing against my ribs.

The young man is now squatting in the corner, his big bare feet splayed wide apart and one hand resting palm down on the floor between them. His face is raised, and his pale blue eyes are staring right at me.

"Hello," I say, too grief-stricken and depressed to fully understand. Too frightened to know how I should act. "What do you want?"

What I really mean is: *What is happening to me? Why have you come? What have I done to deserve this unwanted attention? Are you even real?*

The young man smiles. His front teeth are crooked, the incisors yellow. His mouth begins to move, the thin lips forming words, but I cannot hear his voice. It is as if he is speaking to me through a layer of glass – a barrier which cuts out the sound. He continues to speak, smiling, nodding, punctuating certain passages with a knowing smile, and after making an odd circular motion with his hand – the one that is not resting on the floor – he suddenly stops.

I realise that I am holding my breath. Since being admitted to the hospital, this strange unannounced visit is the only thing that has provoked any kind of reaction other than anger. I am curious, but I am afraid. So very afraid. Of him, and what he might represent.

Unless I have lost my mind, the young man is clearly some kind of phantom – what else could he be? He can not possibly be anything else: his edges are ill-defined, almost ragged, and whenever he moves I catch glimpses of the dull grey plaster behind him. The light from the hallway outside the room, when it catches him, pierces his body and opens up bloodless wounds through which I can see the clumsy brush strokes on the painted skirting boards his crouched body would otherwise have obscured.

"Are you dead?" At any other time, and in any other company, it would have been considered a stupid question. Right here, right now, in this squalid little hospital room, it seems the most sensible question in the world.

Too many questions, with no answers forthcoming... The only reply I receive is more fear, more doubt, more screaming inside my head. I wish that I could pull the covers over my head, like I did in childhood; that single action always kept the monsters at bay.

The young man grins and shuffles around on his haunches like a monkey, turning his back on me. At last I see what he has been trying to tell me. The back of his skull is matted with blood, with white splinters of bone showing through the clumped hair. What can only be brain matter oozes through the cracks, bulging like porridge from a shattered bowl. His narrow back is bare; the light green T-shirt he is wearing has torn right down the middle, the split in the material following the line of his spine.

Damaged vertebrae show through his pale skin like the plastic components of a child's toy.

I press my lips together, holding back a scream. I can feel my eyes growing bigger and wider and coming loose in their sockets.

Those bones. So clean and white. Poking through his back.

Then, slowly, the young man stands, and once again he turns to face me. Tears shine on his cheeks like slivers of broken glass; his eyes are becoming dull, glazing over.

"I'm sorry," I whisper, unable to think of anything else to say. "So sorry." Sadness replaces the fear, acceptance pushes aside the doubt. I am not insane. This is all too matter-of-fact to be anything other than reality.

The young man waves at me, still smiling, but the smile is fading like the final rays of a weak winter sun. He leaves the room by the door: no walking through walls, no magical vanishing acts. He even closes the door behind him.

The bloodstains he leaves behind soon recede to dusty marks on the wall and floor, and after a short time they fade completely. I sit and stare at the spot on the wall, and at the floor around the place he had been. There is nothing there, not even the shape of my fear.

Nothing there: everything there. *This*, I think, *is where it begins*. And then I wonder where the thought came from, and what it could possibly mean.

I know that I will never forget that young man.

The following day I ask a nurse if anyone with head injuries has been admitted overnight. She looks at me strangely, backing away a couple of steps without even realising it, and nods. "A nineteen year old boy. Billy Adams. He and his girlfriend were involved in a motorcycle accident. She was driving his bike. He died five minutes after we got him in the emergency room. Why do you ask? Did you know him?"

"No. No, I didn't. Not really." I thank her for the information and stare at the wall whose subtle imperfections I am growing to know and love. The fact that the boy met his end in a similar type of accident to the one I have survived is not lost on me. Is it simple irony, or a small component of some kind of grand design?

After staring at the breakfast I cannot even think about eating I leave my bed for the first time in over a week (apart from reluctant trips to the toilet) and go looking for the young girl who was in the crash with Billy Adams.

I find her on the women's ward – she is lying on her back with her face turned to the wall. The nurses are busy so no one sees me approach her bed. I sit down at her side, clasp her hand, and wait for her to see me. Finally, after long minutes of pretending that I am not there, she reluctantly turns to face me.

Looking at her battered face, into her eyes, the fear returns. Am I doing the right thing, here? Is that what is expected of me? Was that a dream last night, a fragment of nightmare wedging itself into my broken little corner of reality? I have no way of knowing; all I have is a memory, and the hope that I am not losing my mind.

All I have is belief.

"Billy sends his love," I tell her, tightening my grip on her hand. I am still not sure if I am clinging on to her because I feel like I might faint or if I am just holding her there in case she tries to bolt. "He came to me last night." I picture his thin lips, the words they had formed: the interesting shapes they made.

"Your name is Sally." It was not a question.

Her eyes widen. Silence smothers us, cutting us off from the rest of the ward. At last I hear Billy Adams's words: they come into my mind like a song that has been stuck in your head all day because it was the last thing you heard before leaving the house. I can barely believe that I did not hear the words last night, when my young visitor bequeathed them to me.

I take a deep breath, close my eyes. Open my mouth...

"He said, 'it wasn't your fault. The brakes have been faulty for weeks, but I couldn't afford to get them done. First it was mum's birthday and then I bought you those flowers. I could've still got the brakes fixed, but our Dave borrowed the money to pay off a gambling debt. Let it go, Sal. Let all the blame go and fall in love again. Just remember me as I was and not as I am now.'"

Then I hear nothing more. Billy is once again silent, but his face hovers in my mind, that wide grin still locked firmly in place.

The girl's mouth gapes; her eyes are moist, but they are shining. *Shining.*

My job is done; the task I was given has been carried out to the best of my abilities.

(If only every one was that simple, maybe then I could find a sense of peace.)

I leave Sally to heal. Hopefully she will do so, and perhaps my intervention has even helped in some small way. At the very least she will be sure to forgive herself for the accident. At some point in the future she might even climb onto a motorcycle again. She is young enough that anything is possible.

Shining.

Suddenly, as if it has been waiting patiently for me to realise, my purpose in life becomes clear. Walking back to my private room, I know what it is I must do, and I realise that I need to get started as quickly as possible.

And her eyes – her eyes were *shining*.

But was any of it real?

SIX

I knew I had to visit Baz Singh, but had been putting it off for reasons I couldn't even begin to think about. More than the fact that I'd seen his daughter's body hanging from the ceiling – and still saw her now, on my upstairs landing – was the conviction that Singh was an unhealthy presence to be around. I'm not a fool. I'd known all along that Singh was at best a man of dubious business interests, yet I had accepted his offer and followed his daughter to her death.

I never claimed to be a good decision maker.

I was pondering these thoughts when I heard a knock at the front door.

It was just after noon. Time had run away from me. Ellen had always had that effect on me: in her company, time became irrelevant, simply a measure of how long I was with her.

I got up and went to the door, glancing out the window on my way. A huge light-skinned Indian man was standing on my doorstep, his face calm and dark and intelligent. I knew immediately that all the time I'd been thinking about avoiding Baz Singh, he must have been biding his time before making steps to summon me.

I opened the door.

"Good afternoon," said the man. He was wearing a dark grey suit and a white shirt with no tie. There was nothing threatening about him apart from his build, and the fact that he was standing there outside my door. Otherwise, he seemed very pleasant.

"Hello. How can I help you?"

The man smiled. It was an expression he used often; I could tell because he slipped it on so easily, and it suited his big, kind features. "I'm sorry to disturb you, Mr Usher, but Mr Singh sent me to request your presence. He would like to see you, and he asked me to say that he's rather surprised you haven't called by."

I nodded. "I've been expecting you, or someone like you. Give me a minute and I'll join you."

"No rush, Mr Usher. I haven't been sent to threaten or intimidate you in any way, merely to invite you to come and see my employer. If you don't wish to come, I can pass on a message." He smiled again. And again it wasn't threatening, just… nice. Friendly.

"No, no. I do owe him a visit. It was rude of me not to call by or even telephone, particularly after what's happened. I'll be right with you." Our genteel exchange seemed so out of place that it had begun to take on a surreal air, like a mannered discussion between two psychopaths.

I returned inside and put on my coat, then followed the large Indian man out to the street, where a shiny brown Jaguar was parked at the kerb. The man opened the back door and I climbed in, catching a whiff of leather and the vague traces of cigar smoke.

The man drove off without further conversation. He kept his speed down, watched the road carefully, and handled the vehicle with skill and precision. He probably learned to drive in the armed forces, or perhaps MI5. The man certainly had the bearing of an ex-soldier, someone high up the ladder. I knew that Singh had a lot of shady family connections, and it was rumoured that some of the men working for him were experienced mercenaries.

Again, I questioned my own judgement in associating with such a man.

I'd known Baz Singh for about seven years, since the days when he ran an Indian restaurant in Pudsey and a takeaway in Horsforth. He'd come a long way in a short amount of time, buying up several businesses with money from big-time investors, and finally renovating the one-time massage parlour and clip joint, the Blue Viper.

I'd first heard of Singh when I assisted a close friend of his in a suspected case of demonic possession that turned out to be part of a complicated (and rather desperate) blackmail plan concocted by the man's money-grabbing cousins. After unveiling the scam, my reputation had risen in the Indian community and I came to be known as a man who could be trusted. Baz Singh retained my services when he thought one of his restaurants was haunted. It turned out that he was right, and I was able to help the spirit vacate the building. Ever since then Singh and I had kept in touch, and he maintained an interest in my professional affairs, sending other clients my way if he thought that I might be able to help them.

And now he was putting pressure on me to return those favours.

Instead of heading out into the country towards Harrogate, where I knew Singh maintained his family residence, the Jaguar cruised towards central Bradford. Traffic was no heavier than usual, but it was slow going. Weak sunlight glinted off the car's bonnet, slicing pale arcs in the air. The sky seemed to lift as the day progressed, making room for something beyond even my vision. We passed terraced houses that became second-hand shops, pound shops, betting shops and chip shops. All purveyors of poverty, these stores provided poor diets, cheap products and empty promises of a sense of wellbeing that would never last.

Soon enough we approached the Blue Viper. I should have realised that he'd see me here rather than at home, where his wife and other family members would still be in mourning. It was a tall, thin building flanked by derelict properties and take-away outlets. The neighbourhood was in terminal decline, yet the club was booming. Sleaze, it seemed, was a recession-proof industry.

"We're here," said the driver, unnecessarily.

"Thank you," I said as I stepped out of the car and headed towards the low-key entrance to the notorious strip club. The driver remained at the vehicle, standing with the door open, his hand clenching the panel. He was smiling again, and it was such a nice open, honest smile that I felt compelled to return the expression. I wondered if it was the same smile he wore when he kicked in people's faces.

The door to the Blue Viper was a plain hardwood barrier with a small, square window set slightly above the eye level of an average person. The glass in the window was strengthened, probably bulletproof, and opaque.

Two men – these even larger than the driver – stood on the concrete steps leading up to the door. One was a black man with a bald head and startlingly blue eyes (so startling in fact that I assumed they must be contact lenses) and the other was Caucasian. The two men tensed slightly as I approached, but I held out my hands to reassure them that I meant no harm.

"I'm here to see Baz Singh. I have an appointment."

"What's yer name?" said the white man, coming down a step to meet me.

"Thomas Usher. I have a working relationship with Mr Singh."

The man nodded, smiled. His smile, however, was not a patch on the driver's: it was cold and hard and empty, the smile of a reptile as it eyed up dinner. "You're expected. Go on up. Climb the stairs and take the third door on your left when you reach the landing." His dull Yorkshire tones fell like small blows against my ears.

The men stepped aside in unison, allowing me access to the door. I pushed open the door and stepped inside, feeling them close in like twin shadows at my back. It crossed my mind that I would hate to make an enemy of Baz Singh. On the surface, he and his little empire were above board and welcoming, yet there was a terrible darkness beneath the charade which held the constant threat of violence. The man wasn't a gangster, not really; he was a businessman. But these days, in these times, the concept of business had changed dramatically.

To my left a corridor led along to the main body of the club. Ahead of me lay the stairs. I climbed them reluctantly yet knowing that I'd got myself into this and had nobody else to blame. Grief is something I can deal with, an emotion that fills me to the point that I can easily empathise with it in others. But someone like Baz Singh had his own coping mechanisms, and the emotions he generated were unlike the ones experienced by so-called normal people. Men like Baz Singh work in a different way to the rest of us.

I had to go up there and expect anything: rage, tears, venom, or even a strange deathly calm.

The main door closed behind me, shutting me up in a dark, quiet space that held within it a strong sense of despair. Ghosts walked here, unseen by me but definitely present: they moved behind the scenes, huddled in black corners, watching me with something approaching fear as I passed through their domain. I wondered what had gone on inside this building, either during Singh's tenancy or before he had taken possession of the building. Places like this, hidey-holes for the lost and the lonely, almost always had a history of human misery.

The stairs creaked as I climbed them. I put out my hand and grabbed the wooden banister to steady myself. From somewhere upstairs, I heard the sound of wild laughter, followed by low, mumbling voices. A door slammed; something heavy was thrown against a wall or onto the floor.

With each step I took the dead drew near, ready to expose themselves. I'd managed to ignore them for quite some time, but now my defences were crumbling. I hoped that I was strong enough to resist whatever lay beyond the spirits and the landscape they inhabited. I had glimpsed it once, for a moment, thirteen months earlier, during a supposedly routine job as a consultant, and that was enough to make me fearful of the special sight I possessed.

I made it to the top of the stairs and paused for breath. I felt as if I'd surmounted a great barrier, and my body ached. My limbs throbbed as if from exercise and my joints felt swollen and rigid. Occasionally I experienced physical reactions to the dead, but this was the worst I'd known. It was as if my entire body suffered flu symptoms: aching joints, a pounding headache, severe perspiration of the brow and back.

My tattoos were going crazy. The names on my back jitter-bugged across my skin and the various symbols on my arms and shoulders seemed to roll and shift as if the ink were solid-ifying and trying to break free. I half expected a geyser of blackness to jet from my body, stigmatic wounds opening to bleed pure ink. The proof of my failures along with whatever protection the tattooed glyphs offered me bleeding out onto the dusty floor of this squalid building.

I moved left along the narrow landing, trying to remember which door the bouncer had told me to aim for. Then I heard Singh's voice, its muffled timbre coming from behind the next door along.

I stopped outside the door and knocked. Knocked again.

"Come in."

Coughing into my fist, I pushed the door open and stepped into a small, neat room with a desk pushed back against the window. Framed art prints and photographs of smiling figures decorated the painted walls, the floor was covered with an expensive carpet, and the furniture was modern, functional, and obviously designer.

Baz Singh sat behind the desk with his back to the window. He was replacing a telephone receiver into its cradle and smiling. "Thomas. Thank you for coming. I hope my man wasn't too crude with my invitation." He stood and came around to my side of the desk, his face solemn yet still with the hint of a sly smile at the corners of his mouth.

"No, not at all. I'm sorry I didn't come earlier. I really should have." I stuck out my hand and shook Baz Singh's broad mitt, his thick brown fingers swallowing mine. His grip was solid, immovable. For a small man, he possessed the capacity for great physical strength.

"If I didn't know you better, I'd say you were avoiding me, Thomas."

I smiled, shook my head, and sat down in the chair he indicated. "No, of course not. I've just been busy. Mostly with the police." I sank into the chair, unable to stop the leather upholstery from swallowing me. It was some chair: incredibly comfortable, the kind of chair meant to put people at ease.

Singh lowered himself back into his own chair, letting out a long, loud breath.

"I'm sorry about your daughter. About Kareena."

At the mention of her name he winced, as if from a blow. His eyes narrowed, his dark skin paled and his hands splayed out flat on the desk top, the fingers stretching and flattening like blades. His fingernails were exquisitely manicured. I don't know why I noticed that; I just did, and it disturbed me.

"Listen, Thomas. Just to put you at ease, I haven't called you here to blame you or accuse you of inattention. I know you were following her and that you did your best when you found her there – found her dead." Silent beats; the ticking of an unseen clock; music drifting up from the street; a dog barking in the distance. "Perhaps if the girl had listened to me, she might still be alive today. Perhaps not. We'll never know for sure."

I waited. Listened. There was no way I was going to interrupt the man's train of thought. I wanted to hear what he was about to say.

"I'll get straight to the point. What I wanted to ask you – the reason I asked you here – is, well, I want to know if you think Byron Spinks killed my daughter. Did that animal… did he do it, or was he simply a witness to her murder? Because that's what it was: murder. I need no inquest to tell me that. Even if she hoisted herself up there and put the noose around her own neck, someone made her do it."

I listened to the ticking clock, trying to figure out where it was. There was a bookcase against the far wall, stacked with nameless leather-bound hardbacks, and I guessed that the clock must be located somewhere on the top shelf.

"Well, Thomas? What do you think?"

I stared at him, wondering what he wanted to hear. Then, sadly, I opted for the truth. "I'm not sure, Mr Singh. I really don't know. All the evidence points to Spinks being the killer, and the police think he did it."

"But?" He leaned forward, his face avid. Eyes huge. Lips pursed. Avid.

"But I'm not so sure. When I found him there, he was hysterical. It wasn't an act; he was mortified. Petrified. Whatever he saw, it sent him somewhere he still hasn't returned from."

"Thomas." His chair creaked. "Thomas, I realise that we've known each other for a number of years, and that I'm probably taking advantage of our friendship here, but I need to ask you to please keep your suspicions to yourself. I am a businessman as well as a grieving father, and my business interests cannot be allowed to suffer because of my silly, wayward, murdered little girl. I am well aware of a lot of her naughty little habits and sidelines, and would like to ensure that no one else learns of them."

I'm still not sure if I was shocked or simply nervous, but once again I chose to say nothing. What was Singh implying about his daughter's activities, and what was the exact nature of those activities? Clearly, he knew a lot more than the authorities thought he did.

"I want the police to go about their business and investigate this, to find out who else was there, but at the same time I'd like to retain your services on an advisory level. You have contacts, and your highly specialised talents make you open to other forms of information, information no one else could ever gain access to. I'd like you to pass on any of this information that might come your way – to tell me whatever you see or hear... or sense."

I nodded. What else could I do?

"Whatever I'm paying you, I'll double it of course. This is a special arrangement, just between the two of us, and I'd hate for you to be out of pocket."

In that moment, sitting in a small office with a man I thought I knew but really, truly didn't, I realised that Baz Singh was far from the usual grieving parent. More than his daughter's loss, even more than the absence caused by her no longer being in his life, he possessed an almost manic desire to ensure that her death did not tarnish his business. But there was also anger somewhere behind his mask. A dark and terrible rage that was so intense it had become a facsimile of calm. Like a deep ocean, this anger simply swelled and rolled and waited, passing itself off as a form of serenity yet hiding within its depths the capacity for great harm.

"I'll do what I can, Mr Singh. I can't promise anything – never can I promise. It doesn't work that way. I have no control over what I learn, what I experience. I will, however, pass on any knowledge that comes my way. Despite what you say, I believe I owe you that for failing to protect your daughter."

I stood and walked slowly towards the door, sensing that our meeting was over. There was a tension in the air that I couldn't define, something barely tangible yet still strong enough to fill the room.

"One minute, Thomas?"

I stopped and turned to face Baz Singh, wondering what else he wanted from me. Wasn't the damage limitation he'd already requested enough?

"Just tell me she was already dead when you found her. That she didn't suffer for long. The way I see it, the whole thing happened fast, so if she was dead when you arrived on the scene that means she went quickly." His eyes were wide, eager. He needed me to make him feel better about something, but at that point I didn't understand enough about the situation to even consider lying.

I swallowed hard, moistening my throat. "Yes, she was dead when I found her. But I think that she suffered. I'm not sure how I know this, but I know that she died in great pain. Spiritual pain, if not physical."

Singh lowered his head; light glinted from his balding pate, exposing the light scars there. I'd never seen them before, and wondered briefly how he had come by them. "Thank you," he muttered, barely loud enough for me to hear. "Thank you for being honest. I can't trust many people to tell me the truth, yet you never seem to do anything else. It is both a strength and a weakness."

I nodded without speaking, and left the room.

Outside on the landing I headed back towards the stairs, but when I got there I continued on past the closed doors, the carpet becoming more threadbare beneath my feet. The part of the landing where Singh's office was situated – the area immediately above the club – was truncated, but this side of the building seemed to go on forever. I tried to remember what was next door to the Blue Viper and thought that it was perhaps one of the many fast food joints that proliferated in the area. Kebabs and curries and greasy burgers for the greasy punters who spilled out of the place in the early hours of the morning every weekend, hungry for sustenance after satisfying their other, less specific cravings.

Each of the doors I passed was closed tight to the frame, but the one at the end of the hall, adjacent a stained window that looked out onto what seemed to be a narrow alleyway was open: I could see a chink of light through the gap, shadows passing back and forth like pacing cats.

The touch of the dead was everywhere at this end of the landing. I could sense violence, assault, rapes, and even several old murders. Human life had certainly been taken here at some point in history, savagely and without remorse, but it was too far in the past for me to pinpoint. My mouth went dry; my teeth tasted of copper. My tattoos were going berserk, twitching like frenzied animals stapled to my flesh.

I'd lived with my ability for almost fifteen years, but still I had not learned to control the fear. The two went hand-in-hand: fear and insight. But isn't that always the way?

"I don't want to do it." The voice was small – that's the only way I can describe it. Small and scared and uncertain. The voice of a victim. It belonged to a woman, and it was clear to me that she was under some kind of duress.

"No. I won't. You can't make me."

Then: laughter, vile, horrible, cruel laughter. Underwater laughter, all wet and bubbling and unnatural. The man inside the room sounded like someone I did not want to know, or even see. He sounded like a bad man, a marauder, a taker of innocence. The unseen spirits in the air around me gathered in close, but still kept out of sight. They drew in on me, agreeing with my suspicions, adding fuel to the fire of my vision. I felt their hands upon me, sensed their puzzled fear; even they were afraid of him.

Afraid of whoever was behind that door.

"Not now, perhaps," said the man behind the door. "But you will. Oh yes, you will." Then he laughed again.

I experienced a slight tugging in the air, as if invisible coils of rope were being wound onto a spindle and dragged away from me, and the door, the door that was always ajar, always inviting a stray gaze, suddenly swung open and a small, stocky man in a simple, dark suit stalked out onto the landing, his oversized hands bunched into fists at his sides.

I took a step back, stunned by the sudden, unannounced presence of this stranger, and he liked that: oh, how he liked it. His smile was a knife-cut across his face; his eyes were holes in the world. His bald head glistened, glistened, catching the meagre light and drawing it towards him, nullifying it, and as he glanced towards me I felt cold, so very cold. Despite his lack of stature, he took up so much space that I felt hemmed in, trapped by the sheer force of his personality – a personality that was, ironically, utterly devoid of anything I could latch on to. He was an empty vessel, but one of such magnitude that I felt nothing on earth could fill it.

Then he was past me, heading down the stairs. I heard his heavy footsteps on the wooden boards, the sound of the main door opening, and voices out on the street as he exchanged quiet words with the bouncers.

Shaking, I approached the door. It was still open, and through it I could see a threadbare room, the wallpaper peeling, posters covering the worst of it. The floor was covered in dirty rugs, cords and cables trailing across them like boneless spider legs. A small television stood on a high cabinet. A blurred CCTV image was still playing across the dusty screen: the picture consisted of several hunched figures standing before what looked like a hanging basket – at least something small and compressed attached to a rope. But before I could fully understand the image, the screen went dark.

A woman's bare leg appeared briefly from behind one edge of the door, drawing my attention. There were bruises on her shin. Her bare toes were filthy, the nails broken. Her voice was a terrified whisper; she seemed to be praying in another language, perhaps Russian or Polish.

From behind me I heard the sound of another door opening; footsteps; heavy breathing. Baz Singh brushed past me, heading for the door. He reached out, grabbed the handle, and as the door edged closed I glimpsed a small, thin female figure, dressed in cheap lingerie, move past the narrowing gap. Pale skin and track marks, dirty bottle-blonde hair over dark eyes. Open mouth, face scruffy with tears.

Then she was gone, and Singh was guiding me back towards the stairs.

"There's nothing in there for you, Thomas. Just business."

"Who was that man?" My voice was low, struggling to emerge from my throat. I coughed, and then asked the question again. "Who was he?"

Singh shook his head. "That was Mr Shiloh," he said, his eyes unable to meet my gaze, his face going suddenly loose and bloodless, as if the bones behind had suddenly turned to jelly.

I knew better than to ask any more questions, and allowed him to escort me down the cramped staircase, back along the hallway, and out onto the street. The watery sunlight seemed too bright, stinging my eyes, and the city air smelled clean and fresh as pure oxygen. I felt giddy; my head began to swim and my knees threatened to buckle.

"Thank you again, Thomas," said Baz Singh, and I was moving slowly away, crossing the street, unable to stop myself from walking away from the Blue Viper and the menacing little bald man and the girl – the mysterious girl shut up in that grubby little room above a strip club. There were tears in my eyes, rips and gouges in my heart, and a small, dark kernel of terror clenched tight inside my belly.

I had never seen the strange man before, yet something about him was familiar. Mr Shiloh. The name was familiar, yes, but I was sure that it was from a song or a poem. It took me a while to realise that what I had recognised was the darkness that had been pasted to him like a second skin: it was exactly like that which clung to me, isolating me from my fellow man. This Mr Shiloh's darkness matched my own.

The sky darkening, the world turning, turning, slowing, I found the nearest bar and sat in a corner nursing a large whisky. When I stared into the depths of the drink, my mind caught up in its calming motion, I saw layers of reality, states of being overlapping each other like the torn and discarded pages of an old book. When I looked up, out of the window, I saw the exact same thing outside in the street.

SEVEN

I was drunk when I arrived home later that afternoon. Not falling-down drunk, but enough that I wasn't quite sure about my thoughts and feelings, or confident in my natural bodily movements.

It had been a long time since I'd lost control to that extent and allowed myself to use alcohol as a crutch. And why? – because of a glimpse of one man, and the total apathy of another towards the brutal death of his daughter. I'd seen a lot worse, experienced far grubbier situations, but something about this entire affair had hit me hard, right in the gut.

I drank several glasses of cold water and made a fresh pot of coffee. The real stuff and not that desiccated crap from out of a jar. Sipping my drink, I stared up at the kitchen ceiling, at the floor above me, and imagined their bodies, their slim, delicate bodies swaying in an ethereal breeze.

The image from the television earlier that day was still in my mind, like a stain. Something swinging, and attached to a rope.

Swinging.

I closed my eyes, tried to shut out the image. It did not work: they were still there, those girls, both before and behind my eyes, playing some kind of grim waiting game that I could only ever lose.

Unable to resist the call of my new housemates, I put down my cup, got to my feet, and climbed the stairs. They were all there, out on the landing – even Kareena, with her beautiful silken hair knotted at her throat and her blue tongue and her bulging eyes had finally left the room to join them. Their forms were diaphanous, like images projected against the wall, but also they held a sort of firmness, a sense of being there, in the moment, that a simple image could not duplicate.

As I watched, Kareena slowly raised one hand. Her fingers elongated and the index finger slowly straightened to point at me, singling me out for a task that I could not possibly ignore or turn down. This was not an invitation; it was a command. I stared into her pale eyes, the pupils large and grey, as if something had burst behind them and the blood had drained away. Her lips were full and blue; they pouted at me, not promising a kiss but poised on the verge of a scream.

I turned around and went back downstairs, suddenly sober and completely focused. Turning on the stereo, I took a deep breath and thought about my dinner date with Ellen. At that moment, it seemed like the only normal thing in my life – everything else was wrapped in a black mist, vague, formless and threatening. It was all beginning to form the same endless nightmare.

A concert was being broadcast on the radio – the London Philharmonic playing film scores by Ennio Morricone. The music was wonderful, and seemed to calm me, so I turned up the volume and went into the kitchen for more coffee. The afternoon's alcohol intake was losing its grip and I began to feel less paranoid. I wondered if I'd done the right thing in staying on Baz Singh's payroll, then remembered that I never really had a choice anyway. It wasn't blind sentiment, or even the threat of violence from Singh's heavies, that had forced my hand, but the fact that this was all starting to feel like so much unfinished business. It felt personal somehow, as if I were more directly involved than it first appeared.

It felt as if I were the focus of these dark acts.

I had a few hours before I needed to leave for my dinner date with Ellen, so decided to take a bath. First I booked a taxi from a local firm I often used and sat down to think about what else I might be getting myself into.

I hadn't seen Ellen for ages – far too long. She had moved to California chasing her dream job as a medic on the US space programme fourteen years ago, and other than a few stilted phone calls early on we had not kept in close contact. We'd come face-to-face on two occasions since her move abroad, and one of those times, three years ago, had ended with us having some kind of row brought on by the attraction that never seemed to fade between us. It made me feel guilty and afraid; it made her feel angry that we could never pursue it further, even after my wife had died.

Especially after my wife died.

That last meeting had been when our communication had effectively come to an end.

But before that, years before that...

I'd been a lost soul when I got out of hospital after the accident. I'd spoken to many people – surgeons, psychologists, faith healers – some of whom believed me and others who thought I was suffering from posttraumatic stress disorder. Ellen, a familiar face from my youth, was the only one who actually *listened* to what I had to say instead of giving an opinion as to why I *thought* I was seeing ghosts. Her belief or otherwise was irrelevant. Without realising, she gave me the answer to a question I was too afraid to ask.

And now here she was, back in my life.

As usual, I decided to use the downstairs bathroom, but this time so that I could avoid the swinging girls upstairs. They had been quiet for some time and the last thing I wanted to do was disturb them. I sat on the edge of the toilet seat as I ran the water, my thoughts drifting. I imagined Ellen's face, but every time I did so it was overlain by Rebecca's features. My ex-lover; my wife: the two women who had shaped me.

The hot water formed a skein of mist that rose from the tub, hovering over the taps. I watched the misty mass, imagining that forms were shaping themselves within it. The steam writhed and bulged, as if something inside wanted to be free, and the image unnerved me. I stood, went to the window and opened it, letting in fresh air that smelled like rainfall. The larger part of the steam dispersed, but strands of it hung in the air like ectoplasm. As I watched it, I began to see a bald head forming out of the vapour – Mr Shiloh, the man I'd briefly met at the Blue Viper as he strode from that upstairs room.

I blinked, shook my head, bit down against the inside of my cheek. When I opened my eyes the vision was gone, the air was clear. He was no longer there. He never had been.

I took a long soak, letting the heat and the water soothe my aching limbs. I felt old, outmoded, like a once flashy appliance that had now gone well past its sell-by date. I brought up my hands and moistened my face, a benediction by my own hand because no one else would see fit to bless me. Self-pity flooded in. I felt like giving up, switching off, and the lure of my dead family felt stronger than it had for a long time – almost strong enough to tempt me. I stared at the razor perched on a shelf above the bath for a long time – too long to be serious enough to use it.

After a while I got out of the bath, dried myself off, and traipsed through to my bedroom. The girls hung above me in silence – I could imagine them up there, watching me. The only movement in the house was the slow, unseen rotation of their hanging bodies.

I closed the door and lay down on my bed, feeling more tired than I knew how to deal with. I reached across and turned on the radio, tuning it to a local station that played easy listening music – light jazz, movie soundtracks – and rested my head back on the pillow. The music washed over me, pressing me down into the pillow; my eyes shut beneath its rhythmic weight. Soon I was dozing, and I knew I was dozing, but it felt good all the same.

The door opened and a thin figure entered the room. I was unable to properly lift my eyelids so could see nothing of this figure except a blurred outline, but I sensed that it was female. She stepped lightly, her feet making no sound on the floor, and came around to my side of the bed. She had no aroma; the air around her was still and flat and dead.

I murmured something but could not be sure what it was – meaningless words, a garbled phrase, perhaps even my wife or daughter's name. It could have been anything; it was probably nothing. Nothing at all.

Time seemed to slow down, becoming frozen, and the whole wide world held its breath. Animals outside in the fields and hedgerows stopped in their tracks and cocked their heads to listen; aeroplanes stopped dead in the sky above the house, their contrails forming scribbled anchors to the ground; all the nearby towns and cities wound down, the people in the streets and houses dipping their heads and closing their eyes.

The woman in my room bent over me. Her hair was long and soft; her breath was still, hardly breath at all. Her skin radiated a distant heat, like that of an old fire long extinguished yet still capable of flaring back into life.

I felt her fingers on my bare chest, tracing a line down and across, across and up. It seemed to go on forever, and I knew that she was marking me, branding me as one of her own. When finally I managed to open the stone slabs of my eyelids, she was gone. The door was closed, but a subtle vibration remained in the atmosphere, as if someone had just strummed a chord on an acoustic guitar.

I looked at my chest, the muscles in my neck aching as I peered downward. My entire upper torso felt pinned to the bed but I managed to gain a line of vision along my trunk.

Words of ash were scrawled across my ribcage, a blackened message – or a grim reminder – from somewhere far beyond: *memento mori*.

I struggled off my back and onto my feet, heart racing and muscles pumping like balloons filling with air. My feet got caught in the duvet and I tripped, hitting the floor heavily and rolling. Breathing out of control, I got back up on my feet and leaned against the bedside cabinet. The red numbers on the radio alarm clock were going haywire, spinning through their sequence so fast that they were creating nonsense figures. The figures began to look like words, so I looked away, down at my chest. The blackened scrawl was no longer there.

Overcome by a feeling of immutable dread, I sat on the bed and waited for the atmosphere to rebalance. I breathed slowly, silently counting to one hundred, and eventually felt calm enough to carry on.

I dressed in a black suit and went through to the study, where I sat at the computer and waited for it to boot up. When I was able, I accessed my email account and checked for messages. Nothing but junk. Closing the programme, I once again opened the photos DI Tebbit had sent me and stared at each one in turn.

The names ran through my head:

Sarah Dowdy.

Candice Wallace.

Kareena Singh.

Three pretty little things – pretty little dead things – hung like party favours on my upper floor. The dream now felt like a message. Or an order.

The girls in the photographs looked completely different, yet they were also the same: all victims. There was a cast to the eye, a subtle shadow that could only be seen if you looked close enough and knew exactly what you were searching for.

I studied their faces, the angles of their limbs, the soft curves of their bodies, but nothing stood out against the background of misery and early extinction. There had to be something, a common factor other than their shared role as dead girls in someone's twisted movie-in-the-mind. This was more than some maniac going around killing girls. There was something *other*, something of the beyond about the whole shoddy affair. I just needed to find the link, the connection between three young girls and the realm of spirits. Three young girls and the presence who had invaded my room to leave a message I didn't even want to think about.

I reached out and picked up the phone, dialled the familiar number. It rang seven times before he answered, and his voice sounded harried, stretched to its limits.

"Tebbit," I said without preamble. "It's me. I need to ask you a question."

"What is it, Thomas. I'm worn out, need a drink. Do you have anything for me?"

His usual dismissive manner was absent. The desperation he must have felt was palpable, like the undeniable presence of another being sitting at his side as he spoke.

"These other girls: Dowdy and Wallace. Was there anything peculiar about the bodies, other than the fact that they were found hanged, of course?"

"What do you mean, Thomas? This whole fucking thing is peculiar. I don't know what you want me to say."

A bird hooted outside my window. Slow shades of an early darkness crept through the glass and across the floor. I licked my lips; they were bone dry. "Were there any messages on the bodies… cut or burned into the flesh?"

"Jesus, Thomas, don't you think I'd tell you if there was anything like that? I'm not stupid. I know the kind of thing you'd be looking for and something like that would stand out right away."

The bird hooted again, but this time it didn't sound like a bird at all – more like someone impersonating a bird.

"I'm sorry, Tebbit, I didn't mean to imply that you were in some way unobservant. It's just that you might have been told not to inform anyone of certain particulars. Okay, I'll try another tack here. Was there anything about the bodies that struck you personally – maybe right at the back of your mind – as being weird or unusual? Anything at all – no matter how inconsequential it might seem."

The line hummed, as if distant winds were blowing and I had suddenly been connected to their dim wailing. I listened but it made me want to hang up the phone. The sound was awful, like the ceaseless weeping of a distant crowd of mourners.

"Okay, I mentioned this to my superior officer and he looked at me as if I'd lost my mind, but there was something... something odd..."

"Tell me about it. It might be important."

He took a breath before continuing – I actually heard him suck in the air, hold it, and then let it out again, slowly. Slowly. "Ash. Sarah Dowdy had a small amount of ash in her pockets. Candice Wallace had ash on her teeth, as if she'd tried to swallow it. Nobody else noticed, but Kareena Singh was found next to a small pile of ashes, as if a tiny fire had been lit and then put out."

I thought again of the message I'd seen on my chest.

"Ash," said DI Tebbit, in a hoarse whisper, before ending the call.

I sat with the telephone receiver in my hand, listening once again to that unearthly wailing and wishing that it would stop, wishing that it would leave me in peace. But I knew that it never would.

EIGHT

I finished dressing in a hurry and went outside to wait for the taxi. The unnatural darkness had lifted and it was actually a pleasant evening. The rain had let up, the sun hung low in the sky, spreading the remnants of its warmth, and the sky itself was a pastel painting brought to life. Birds sang their final chorus before dark and as I listened I detected a shrill sense of panic in their warbling tune. In my experience, no matter how beautiful the world might seem at any given moment, there is always darkness waiting to encroach, a dusky invader forever poised to break through and cause havoc. Just like that terrible wailing over the telephone wires, it is always close enough to reach out and touch you.

The taxi pulled up at the bottom of the drive and the driver hit his horn. I nodded, and he raised a hand in response. I hurried down to the car and climbed into the back seat – I never sit in the front; it usually dissuades them from making small talk if you sit behind.

The taxi moved off with a jerk, rejoining the road and climbing the hill away from my old house. I glanced back, out of the rear window, and admired the rugged detached stone property. It had been our dream house when Rebecca and I

86

had first moved in with our infant daughter, but now it held only shimmering nightmares. As usual, I wished that I had the strength to put the place on the market, but as it receded into the distance I admitted that I never would. It was home, and that meant a lot.

Home. I barely even knew what the word meant anymore.

The taxi headed towards the airport, and then down through Yeadon. Pleasant green spaces became small clusters of houses became a series of short high streets boasting pine furniture outlets, fish and chip shops and tatty looking public houses advertising "Fine Food & Ale."

Before long we were travelling down Stanningley Road, past a cluster of Indian restaurants and fast food venues where men stood outside and glared at the passing traffic. The driver was taking a long route to boost his fare, but I didn't care enough to complain. Along a narrow alley, a man pushed a small wheelbarrow; behind him, two dogs fought beside an overflowing rubbish bin. People smoked outside pubs, crowding around the doorways in a way that surely deterred passing trade. Sullen faces peered through the fading light, their eyes containing only suspicion.

By the time we reached the Armley Ridgeway I was ready to get out and walk. Only the depressing sight of a sex shop hoarding kept me inside the car. A feeling of claustrophobia pressed against me, pinning my body to the seat, and the driver kept flicking glances at me in the rearview mirror. I finally jumped out of the vehicle at the roundabout near the Travel Inn, stuffing money into the driver's fist and not waiting for any change as the lights cycled to green and the traffic began to move forward around me. I made the opposite kerb safely, yet I felt dogged by a strange sense of muted terror.

It took a while to cross the adjacent road; traffic was heavy this close to Leeds centre and nobody seemed prepared to let me step out without sounding their horn. At the next green light I lurched off the kerb, slamming into the side of a Mazda and almost falling bodily onto the dusty bonnet of a black Ford Focus.

Once in the centre proper, I began to feel calmer. My mood lifted as the last dying rays of sunlight caressed my cheek, and as I drew closer to the Crowne Plaza Hotel, I almost felt normal again – whatever the hell normal is.

I slipped into the pub opposite the hotel and ordered a single malt, downing it swiftly before the barmaid had even returned with my change. "Another?" she said, grinning. I shook my head and pushed for the door, nerves almost forcing me to change my mind. What was I doing here? Surely this was the wrong thing to do. Ellen and I were history. Whatever we had once shared should not be resurrected. Then I remembered that she wanted to ask me something – a favour of some kind – and I eagerly accepted the justification to keep our dinner date.

I saw her as I entered the rotating glass doors. She was standing in the foyer next to a cheap potted plant, a few steps away from a circular sofa occupied by four or five women in skirts so short I could see the meat of their thighs as they crossed and uncrossed their legs. Ellen waved as I made my way across the open space towards her, the other hand going up to push her hair behind one ear.

She looked good, as if the years had never passed. She had cut her hair short and lost some weight – rather than curvaceous, she now looked tanned and athletic, as if she worked out a lot. She was wearing a simple black dress with a thin, long-sleeved cardigan over the top. It was attractive but not overtly sexy, and I wondered how long she had agonised over which outfit to choose.

The women on the sofa were speaking in what sounded like Russian or Polish – an eastern European language I could not quite place but had heard recently in the little room above Baz Singh's club. One of the women laughed and the sound was so shrill that it hurt my ears. One of her companions slapped her thigh.

"Thomas." Ellen's voice held the slight tinge of an American accent, which was to be expected as she'd spent so long in that country. It made her sound like a different person, someone I didn't really know. The nerves increased, and I lost my footing on the carpeted floor, almost stumbling into her.

"Hello, Ellen. It's nice to see you." I held out a hand, then pulled it back and leaned in for a quick embrace. She kissed my cheek. Her lips felt like silk; her skin smelled of lemon.

"You too, Thomas. You look good – if a little on the skinny side." She smiled: a flash of pure-white dentist-cleaned teeth in her smooth, brown face. I wondered if she used Botox. Her cheeks were taut yet strangely puffy. Then I realised that she had been crying.

"I've lost some weight recently. Stress: the best diet in the world." She linked my arm and dragged me towards the bar, her feet gliding across the floor as if she were dancing.

The bar area was empty, so Ellen grabbed a table while I ordered the drinks. She was drinking white wine and soda, while I stuck with the whisky. I moved back across the room, hanging onto the drinks, and lowered myself into the chair opposite.

"Thanks. I need this," she said, grabbing her glass and swallowing a mouthful of drink. "God, when I said you looked thin I meant it. What have you been up to?"

I considered lying to her, but she knew what I did for a living so any level of dishonesty would only have insulted her. "I had a very bad experience about a year ago, and it left me in a bit of a state. I lost weight, lost focus, and I'm only just getting back on track."

Ellen's hand strayed across the damp tabletop, as if of its own volition. By the time she realised what the hand was doing, it had already grasped my arm. "Really? Was it that bad? Are you okay now? I mean, really? Are you okay?" her eyes widened, and within them I saw a strange light that I had not witnessed for a very long time. The luminescence caused by someone who cares, a person with whom I had a strong connection – a person that was still alive.

I nodded my head. "Yes. Yes, I think so. It was bad for a while, but I think I'm back on track now. I... I haven't been using my ability." I had never been comfortable with that word, but what else could I call it? "I've been moving in what you might call mortal circles for quite some time now, but it's isn't that simple."

"What do you mean?" Her mouth was a hollow circle; her eyes glowed.

"The dead always want me back." I smiled, finished my drink.

"Jesus, Thomas, you always were such a fun date." A smile tugged at the corners of her mouth, uncertain yet wanting to come out into the open. I laughed lightly, giving it permission to come forth, and Ellen took her hand away from my arm and grinned.

Despite my levity, I felt anything but at ease. Although I had intimated that something major had happened, I knew that I would never actually tell Ellen about the events that had shaken me so much that I had tried to block out the dead. In truth, there wasn't that much to tell. It involved an old, supposedly lost piece of film, a late night meeting between government representatives, the scientific community, and a woman who had attended in the name of the church. None of them had survived that night; I was the only one left alive. Nothing tangible had actually occurred, but madness and death had been the result of us viewing that film. Everyone but me had seen something on the screen: the living, the dead, or the exalted; the end of the world and the beginning of something else. All I had witnessed was a blank space, an empty screen, despite being there only because I'd thought I might just catch a glimpse of my wife and daughter in the footage. All that remained was an acute sense of disappointment and the feeling that I had inadvertently opened myself up to something, some darkness at the edge of the world.

"So," I said, pulling my thoughts away from the memory of that night. "How have you been? Things still going well with the job?"

Ellen placed her glass on a paper beer mat and scratched her nose. "Yes, it's great. I've been working with trainee astronauts, of all people. Getting them in shape, testing their bodies for the effects of anti-gravity and other imposed forces. It's interesting work. Despite having very little funding these days, the space programme is still developing new technologies."

"Ah," I said. "It's a long way from a grotty little GP's surgery in Horsforth."

We continued with this kind of small talk, saying too much while not really saying much of anything at all. You know how it is when you meet up with an old lover; the air between you is swimming with things you cannot name and the words you speak, however banal they may at first seem, are always loaded with an additional emotional weight, a resonance that even casual onlookers are able to observe.

Since our initial exchange, I could sense that Ellen was deliberately keeping the conversation away from my ability and the way I made my money. She had never been able to fully comprehend the extent of what I could do, and even though she had been instrumental in my acceptance of my own unique view of the world, I still did not know if she fully believed what I was capable of.

Despite her intimate knowledge, Ellen barely knew anything at all.

"How about you take me to that Italian place you mentioned? I could murder a nice big bowl of pasta." She stood, picking up her handbag from the table.

"I'm sure that's not a term they use in the States. You can take the girl out of Yorkshire..."

"Oh, shut up, you twat," she said, sticking out her tongue.

When we left the hotel the women from the circular sofa were still there, but one of them was leading a fat man in an expensive suit towards the stairs. The man's hand strayed to her buttocks, his fingers splayed across the tight material of her short skirt. I wondered, briefly, if the women knew Baz Singh.

We crossed the road at the lights and I led her down a side street. Bins overflowed with fast food waste, a small black cat hissed at us from a high concrete step before a closed metal door, and something skittered in the shadows of a recessed parking space cordoned off by a stout padlocked chain.

"Lovely Leeds," said Ellen, leaning into me as we stepped onto the main street.

"Nothing like California, eh? With all those gangland drive-by shootings, plastic TV stars and steroid-chomping muscle men in tight little DayGlo shorts."

A group of young men crossed the road and lurched into our path, jostling me as we brushed shoulders with them. They laughed as I stumbled off the kerb, and one of them stared at me as if he wanted to hit me. I smelled booze in the air and broke eye contact. The dead I can deal with, but as far as the living are concerned I have never been what anyone might call a tough guy.

"Assholes," muttered Ellen, tightening her grip on my arm.

The restaurant was called *La Tosca*, and was situated in the basement of an old building that had once been some kind of financial institution but now served as business units for small companies and one-man-band financial advisors. We ducked beneath the awning, glancing up at a sky that threatened rain but didn't quite seem up to the challenge, and entered the darkened space.

The place was only half full, which meant that we got to choose a seat in the window – which, being a basement window gave us only a view of the stubby retaining wall and some fancy cast iron railings. Still, it was a nice place, and the food was never less than excellent. I ordered a nice bottle of red wine and we sipped it as we perused the menu, our attentive waiter standing quietly off to one side.

"What are you having?" Ellen glanced at me over the top of her menu, her blue eyes darkening a shade in the dim, cramped room.

"Are we having starters?"

She nodded, her smile hidden by the cardboard rectangle upon which was painted a bunch of grapes and a wine bottle. "I'm starving. Missed lunch because I had a meeting."

I glanced at her. "Anything important?" Her dark eyes darkened further still, and I wished that I'd kept my mouth shut.

"I'll tell you later. I don't want to spoil the food." She ducked her head behind the menu and I ran my eyes across the lines of Italian recipes, my hunger abating.

I had a bruschetta starter followed by a simple peasant's pasta dish of tagliatelle, vine tomatoes and garlic. Ellen started with a tuna and bean salad and her main course was something with chicken – I can't recall exactly what, but it certainly sounded tasty.

We ate in silence for a while, and when the main courses arrived I observed that Ellen's eyes were moist. She'd clearly been crying before we met – I'd noticed that immediately back in the hotel foyer – but nothing had been said or done since that moment to prompt such an emotional response.

"My super-ghost senses tell me that all is not right in the world of Ellen Lang." I set down my cutlery, leaned across the table and rested my hand on her wrist. She hadn't taken a bite for several minutes; her hand remained immobile at the side of her plate.

"I didn't want to go into this here, while we were eating, but something major has happened and I really don't know who else to turn to."

I squeezed her wrist and took my hand away, giving her some space. "We're old friends, Ellen. God knows, I owe you a lot more than I could ever repay... which means that I'll do anything I can to help you, whatever's going on."

She sighed, lightly, and put down her fork. Then she took a huge swallow of wine, almost emptying the glass. I topped her up and waited.

"Have you seen the news lately, Thomas?" It was the second time she had asked me the same question in less than twenty-four hours.

My mind flashed on the images of the dead girls, the ones whose ghosts were even now hanging in my home. "A bit. Not much, though. I'm working on something that seems to be taking up a lot of my time." I thought it a pretty good answer under the circumstances; it didn't let on too much of anything. Not that there was much to let on anyway.

"I never really told you where I grew up, did I? Just that I was a local girl, Leeds born and bred." Her eyes glimmered.

"No, you never told me. I don't think it ever came up in conversation. You don't know the street where I lived as a boy, either."

She nodded, her mouth a thin line bisecting her face. "Well, I was born on the Bestwick Estate. You look surprised."

"No," I said. "Well, perhaps a little." I smiled, not wanting to give her an excuse to stop what she was trying to say.

"Well, my parents were poor – the whole family was, actually. But dad worked day and night, all kinds of terrible shifts, just to put me through medical school. It was a hell of a financial strain. I still have family there, on that horrible estate. It's much worse now than it ever was when I was a girl, but it was always rough."

I waited, uncertain if she wanted me to comment or was merely pausing for breath.

"You might have seen on the news today that a young girl has gone missing, a nine year-old called Penny Royale. Well,

Penny is my cousin Shawna's kid, and they're all distraught. The whole family. "

I waited for the distant sound of a hammer falling but it didn't come. The news was relatively shocking, but I'd always known that certain members of Ellen's family were not exactly upstanding members of society. One of her brothers had served time for manslaughter when he was nineteen, and an uncle once robbed a post office in Manchester.

"Anything to say?" She blinked slowly, her eyes still moist but her face more relaxed, as if by simply unburdening herself of this narrative she had found some kind of solace.

"I did see that news story, and to be honest it barely registered on my consciousness. I thought it was just another missing child. It's a sad indictment of modern society, the fact that I can even dismiss it in that way, but that's what I did. Have the police been any help?"

"Not much. Oh, they're trying their best, I'm sure, but in a situation like this people's expectations and the limitations of the authorities rarely correlate. I spent this afternoon out there, at Bestwick, trying to console our Shawna. It was an impossible task, and left me worn out. I almost didn't come this evening, but I knew that if I spoke to you, of all people, I'd feel better."

Was she admitting that she was using me as an emotional support, or did her words represent some kind of backhanded compliment? I was so unused to social relationships that I had no clue. All I could do was wing it and hope for the best. "I'll take that as a compliment." I smiled.

"It was meant as one. Pudding?" The non sequitur stunned me for a moment, and then I realised that once again our waiter was hovering, dessert menus clutched in his hand.

"Yes, why not. I think we could both use the light relief."

After I'd paid the bill (despite Ellen's argument that we go Dutch), we went across the road for a drink. There was a little bar that I knew from way back, and it was always dark and quiet – the perfect place for a chat.

"So, give me the details," I said, my fingers wrapped around a cold Guinness glass. Whisky, red wine and now Guinness: my head was going to be pounding tomorrow. But at that point I didn't care, not about anything but Ellen's soft face and her sorrow-filled blue eyes.

"Penny was on her way home from school. It's a short walk, and all the local kids go the same way, so it isn't a problem for a nine year-old to be walking the route alone, certainly not in broad daylight."

Or so everyone thought. Of course, I didn't say this, but the words echoed in my mind, refusing to shut up.

I sipped my drink and glanced into a far corner. Shadows were gathered there, shaped a little like a human form. I knew there was a ghost there, and that it was watching me, but I had other, more important things on my mind. Thankfully this one kept its distance. Some of them are polite like that. Some of them.

Glasses clinked; someone across the room coughed into their fist; the jukebox came on, the volume low, and I heard the opening bars of a Johnny Cash song ease its way into the room.

"Nobody saw anything. They don't know who took her, or where she was when she vanished. By all accounts Penny is an odd little girl – odd, that's the exact word they used. Basically, she's a loner, likes her own company, and loves books. She's very bright…" Ellen's voice trailed off; she was unable to finish.

"Just like you at that age?" I didn't need an answer, but Ellen nodded anyway.

"Okay, it's clear that you want to ask me something. The only thing that's puzzling me is your reticence."

Ellen looked up at me, her blue eyes, her red lips, her pale, pale skin catching and holding the meagre light in the room.

"There's a press conference tomorrow, at the community cen-tre. If you're willing, I'd like you to come along with me, to hold my hand." She smiled, but it was fleeting, and filled with such an immense pain that I could barely even hold her gaze never mind anything else.

"Moral support? Is that all? Surely you need more than that. Come on, Ellen, just ask me." I knew; I had known all along. It always, always comes down to this.

Ellen stared directly at me, her gaze unflinching. "I want… I want you to tell me if she's dead."

NINE

I looked at Ellen across the table, staring into the warm depths of her eyes. The things stirring there, reflected in her pupils, were clearly memories. But they were mine and not hers. Only mine.

I am due to leave hospital in three days. The surgeons have mended whatever was broken and patched me up so that it is difficult to see the joins. But more is broken than my insides, and perhaps something old and previously ignored has even been fixed. I have to think of it this way – in terms of physical properties and parts of me that I cannot name. Otherwise I might go insane.

One of the nurses picked up on what had happened with the dead motorcyclist, and she has been questioning me ever since. After a concerted effort on her part, I finally broke and told her what I saw and what I did with the knowledge. I expected mild concern, even laughter. What I got instead was utter belief. Nurse Haggard believes in what she calls the flipside; her late mother had some kind of latent mediumistic skill and she is herself (so she claims) slightly attuned to the dark. She feels things, senses subtle changes in the atmosphere, but has never actually seen anything that could be described as a ghost.

Before the accident I would have called her a kook. Now I think she might be even closer to the truth than I am.

I have reluctantly agreed to accompany Nurse Haggard to the house of a friend, where I can test my burgeoning ability. This friend of hers – a Mrs Taylor – wants me to contact her dead son.

I lie in bed fully clothed, waiting for my chaperone. I can barely believe what is happening; when did my life turn into such a series of weird events? None of this seems real; it is all so strange and complex.

After midnight she comes to me, this dark nurse of night, and she walks the ward like a spectre. "Are you ready?" she asks, leaning over me and casting her cold gaze across my body.

I nod, terrified to speak in the hospital gloom. I am not ready; of course I am not. Not ready for any of this...

"Are you sure you want to do this? You can back out at any time. No one will think any less of you."

"I'm sure," I say, not sure at all. Not wanting to even think about any of it. The lights above my bed and strung along the ceiling flicker, as if mocking my reply. I stare at them, feeling the strobe effect as it throws my senses into disarray, and they settle at last. In my newfound state, I cannot be sure if it was caused by an electrical fault or some kind of otherworldly presence. Perhaps it is best that I don't know.

Nurse Haggard helps me out of bed. I am still a little stiff, especially since I have been lying down for such a prolonged period of time. The muscles in my arms and legs tend to seize up, the barely mended bones beneath cowering under layers of knotted flesh.

Layers and layers... layers of flesh and of fantasy. Layers of something I am unable to grasp.

She leads me out of the ward and into the corridor. I have spent the last few days in a communal ward, and most of the other patients are either asleep or do not care that I am out of bed. Someone is mumbling in their sleep. A young man with both legs in plaster a few beds down from mine twitches as he dreams of motion, like a dog chasing rabbits in its sleep.

"This way," says Nurse Haggard, allowing me to lean on her sturdy shoulders until my muscles loosen. She is a broad woman, heavy around the waist and with large, firm breasts. I am not attracted to her at all, yet I feel an erection stirring in my trousers. Self-disgust prompts me to push Nurse Haggard away, and she shoots me a look of confusion before hurrying ahead to check that the route is clear.

She is too keen, this woman, and too ready to exploit whatever it is I can do. If I can do anything at all, that is, and the first time wasn't simply a fluke.

We are not accosted as we leave the hospital building and walk to the car park. There are a few loiterers – those waiting for loved ones to be operated upon, nightshift doctors and nurses – who barely even look our way as we pass. We are just two people walking the halls at night: there is nothing unusual in that.

Nothing unusual on the surface, at least.

Nurse Haggard's little canary-yellow Fiat is parked in a staff space near the main gate. I clamber into the back, flopping into the cramped seat, and realise that I am breathing heavily, as if I have run a mile. It is going to take me a long time to fully recover, despite feeling as if I am well on my way to full health.

Nurse Haggard starts the tiny car and backs it out of the space. The trees along the inside of the wall shudder in the headlights and something – an owl, or some other night bird – takes flight from a low branch, ejecting a white spurt of shit onto the dusty bonnet. Nurse Haggard does not even notice the defilation of her vehicle, but I smile nervously, wondering if it is some kind of omen of which I need to take note. The car judders slightly; the engine is cold after being parked there for most of the day, but Nurse Haggard gives it some accelerator and things even out.

Evening-out. That's a concept I've come to hate. The surgeons and physiotherapists all tell me that things will "even out", that my mind will begin to heal as soon as my body is better. None of them seem to believe that I have seen something ephemeral – something ghostly. In the end, I stopped telling them and pretended that it had been a simple hallucination caused by a combination of stress and painkillers.

Sometimes lies are the only truth people are prepared to hear. Sometimes lies are better.

Nurse Haggard takes us along streets I do not recognise, up through Chapeltown and the rougher areas where the Yorkshire Ripper once plied his trade. Before long she stops the car outside a long terrace of Victorian houses, each one set back from the road at the end of a stubby little patch of garden. We sit in silence for a while, listening to the sound of the night. A man walks past on the opposite side of the road, his hands thrust deep into his pockets. His thick dark beard makes me think again of the Ripper, of dead and eviscerated prostitutes with hammer blows to their skulls and staring eyes that have seen the long, pale face of their own demise. Lengthy shadows lean from darkened corners, and then duck back into their hiding places.

The man hurries by, a rucksack hanging loose over one shoulder: a night shift worker on his way to clock in.

"Shall we go in?" Nurse Haggard turns around in her seat to stare at me. I can barely make out her features in the darkness; her eyes are sunken hollows in a head that could be not much more than a grinning skull.

I nod. "Yes," I say, because I know that she will be unable to see me properly in the back of the car, leaning back in the seat that stinks of sex and old cigarette smoke. I don't really want to go inside, but think that it must surely be better than the atmosphere in the car.

I follow Nurse Haggard out of the car, along the street, and through a low metal gate that squeaks when she pushes it open. It isn't a scary squeak, like the ones you hear in films, but something high-pitched and almost comical. I watch her wide back as she walks towards the front door of a large double-fronted house with beautiful but grimy bay windows. Grey nets hang in those windows, and I wonder who lives there with Mrs Taylor, the woman who wants me to find her son.

I am tempted to run, but my body aches. In truth, the fear is submerged beneath a wave of curiosity. Can I really do this? Am I capable of communicating with the dead?

Nurse Haggard knocks once on the door and it is opened almost immediately. A sallow girl with lank shoulder-length hair and wide, moist eyes steps backwards into the doorway to let us in. The hallway beyond is dark, the stairs wide and not very welcoming. Why is it so dark? Is it simply for effect or because someone has neglected to pay the bills? By the look of the girl, with her yellowish skin and too-thin arms sticking out of an old-fashioned house dress, I decide that the latter option is probably closest to the truth.

I follow Nurse Haggard inside and the girl closes the door behind us. I never see her again, but I find myself thinking of her often. I don't even know if Nurse Haggard saw the girl – she certainly did not acknowledge her when the door was opened to allow us inside. Was she a ghost, or a living ghost drifting through the rooms of that house, pining after her dead brother/lover and weeping into the watches of the night?

If this possibility even crosses my mind at the time, then I am unaware of it.

"This way," says Nurse Haggard, in a whisper. The walls are covered in heavily patterned paper, some of it peeling away up near the ceiling. Wooden dado rails trace a line through the maze, showing us where to go.

We enter a reception room at the end and on the left side of the hall. Inside there is a very fat woman sitting at a low coffee table. She has a glass before her, perhaps filled with water or perhaps with vodka – some clear liquid, at least. The fat woman smiles at me and I feel sure of something for the first time since seeing the ghost of the motorcyclist. "Hello, Mr Usher. I've been waiting for you." Her voice is as squeaky as the gate, and I stifle the urge to either giggle or scream.

"Hello, Mrs Taylor. I'm… sorry for your loss." I do not mean to be so glib, but I can think of nothing else to say to the fat woman with the glass of clear liquid. I stare at her thin lips, her loose cheeks, and eyes that have never stopped weeping.

She weeps for the world, I think. But that isn't right. Nobody weeps for anyone but themselves.

"Please sit down next to me, Mr Usher. I think it might be the best place for you, close to the source of grief, as it were." Again that empty smile: there is nothing behind it, just another row of smiles – a mirror-maze of twisted expressions – each one as vacuous as the first.

Nurse Haggard has gone quiet. Her task is done. She sits in a high-backed chair against the wall and takes a paperback book from her pocket. She recites softly from the book, but I cannot hear what she is saying. It must be a prayer or incantation, or a collection of such. Whatever she is saying, it sounds creepy and I know that it is part of what we are about to try to do.

Again the urge to flee almost overcomes me, but I suck it up, swallow it down. Push it away.

I sit down next to Mrs Taylor. She places a chubby hand on my knee and squeezes. I feel sick, yet still, again, there is that sickly sense of arousal. She licks her lips. I close my eyes. When I open them again she is no longer smiling.

"I don't know what I'm doing here, but Nurse Haggard seemed to think that I might be able to help. I'm new to this… I'm not sure what it is I'm capable of, or how to control it, but

I do know that I saw something a few nights ago and I have no doubt that I will see something again. I just don't know where or when that will happen."

Of course I have doubts: about everything.

Mrs Taylor nods her big head. Her greyish hair moves independently from the rest of her, like a small animal attached to her scalp. "I know all about you, Mr Usher. I know what happened. I've been to so many so-called mediums and mystics that I feel as if I've worn myself out on the afterlife. None of them have been able to contact my David, but a few of them have faked it."

"I see." The pain, the loss, the desperation, is written all over her smooth, fat face. I realise now that her smile is not just empty: it is dead. I wish that she would stop saying my name; its overuse is somehow redefining my identity, diminishing it as we speak.

I realise that this woman – this grief-stricken shell – knows more about my situation than I do. She is certain that I will see something, and that certainty bleeds through her skin and seeps into the room, where it latches onto me.

"All I ask is that you give it a try. Just empty your thoughts and try to let my David in. If he's here, he'll come to you – I'm sure of it. If not, I can go back to my grief and stop spending all my money on frauds and bastards." Once again she squeezes my knee; then her hand slips up my thigh, moving towards my crotch. I hold my breath, expecting the worst but her fingers linger at the very top of my thigh and go no further. "If my David doesn't want to speak to me, I can put everything behind me and try to get a life back. Do you understand, Mr Usher?"

"I think so." I can only hope that I did not understand her correctly. The thought of this woman naked suddenly fills my head, and it repulses me.

Nurse Haggard gets up and turns out the lights. The only source of illumination is now provided by what little light bleeds through the net curtains from the street beyond. Shadows curl and shudder; the walls bow inward; the ceiling lowers, trapping us there, in the dark. The room is different now, an alien place. I feel as if I am leaving the familiar world behind.

"I'll do my best for you, Mrs Taylor."

"That's all I ask," she says, lifting her hand from my thigh, but slowly, so that her little finger brushes the crotch of my pants.

I try to rid my mind of all thoughts but those of the woman and her son, who I have never seen. I do not ask for a photograph. I do not need to know what he looks like. My new, rapidly improving instincts tell me that if his spirit is here – or indeed any part of it; a splinter, perhaps – he will make himself known to me. I know then what I hadn't even guessed at before: I am like a magnet for wraiths and phantoms, and as soon as they become aware of my presence they come to me, drawn by whatever it is I carry inside me like a light that never goes out – only dims, remaining visible in the outer darkness.

Blackness moves behind my eyes, an ocean of nothingness. I reach out to him, to this spirit, but nothing responds. I sense other movement somewhere in the house, on the upper floor, but it is not a young man. It is an old woman – ancient, really. A woman with no teeth and a bald head, who was once dragged out of this house and killed in the street by a mob who despised her for the things she had done to their children.

I feel sick with horror; the shabby spirit enjoys my discomfort.

Hastily I leave the ghost of the old woman behind and mentally grope elsewhere in the darkness, looking for someone else. There is no one; even the bald old woman has gone now, either unwilling or unable to communicate with me.

"I can't… not here. Nobody here. I'm sorry." But I am not sorry, I am relieved.

Then, gradually, I begin to sense a blank spot under the house, a place where there is no kind of energy at all. It is like a huge gaping pit, unseen yet clearly there, beneath the foundations, and it swallows whatever energies are close by. Something stirs within the depths of that pit. Not a ghost, but something else. Like a lumbering patch of nothing; a lacuna. Like a blank giant waking from a deep sleep, this gap, this interstice, reaches out towards me, displacing the earth and the air and hungry for my energy.

I feel afraid.

I feel sick.

I feel... I feel... I feel but I don't want to feel. Not this. Not anything.

Then, just as I am about to scream, it halts.

Nothing moves.

Nothing stirs.

Nothing.

"David?"

I open my eyes and see a thin figure standing before me, head bowed, arms hanging boneless at his sides. He is a black shape sliced from the night: a ragged cut-out who has been shoved forward to please us. That's exactly how it feels: as if this presence has been sent to appease us – to appease me, or whatever power I carry. It is a peace offering, a desperate gift to ensure that I leave without stirring up any more trouble.

But trouble is the last thing I want.

"That's not David," says Mrs Taylor, her pitch rising even more than is normal. When she begins to scream I think that she might never stop.

The dark figure blends back into the darkness of the room, and by the time Nurse Haggard has turned the lights back on there is nobody there, just a stain on the carpet where something has stood and burned the evidence of its being into the fibre.

I am a magnet for ghosts. As they become aware of my presence they come to me, drawn by whatever it is I carry inside me.

I don't want trouble... I don't want anything. Not this.

I am a dark magnet: a dark attractor. Pulling forth whatever spirits are near, be they good, bad or merely indifferent to the theatrical posturing of the living.

But magnets are uncontrollable. They attract whatever nature intends. Place a magnet on a table scattered with iron filings and you cannot pick and choose which ones will be attracted. It draws them all towards it, including those damaged or spoiled.

Including the broken ones.

This is the first time I start to consider that what I obviously have, what I possess, may not in fact be a gift, and that it might not necessarily be a tool for good. Like most things in life, its nature is at best ambiguous, and I need to make a decision regarding how to proceed.

I wonder, not for the last time, if I am strong enough to even begin to pursue the limits of my own darkness.

TEN

It was late when we finally left the pub, and I was rather unsteady on my feet. I didn't like the way I was constantly turning to alcohol lately. It seemed like a step backwards, a step I no longer wanted to take. The air was damp but still there was no real sign of rain. There were very few people on the streets; they were all either home by now or perhaps en route to their own or someone else's beds, or had more likely moved on to late bars and nightclubs.

Still the occasional figure staggered across the road ahead of us, or dodged out of an adjacent side street. I heard the sound of glass breaking. Somebody laughed, long and loud, but I had no idea where they might be. There was a slight air of menace, as there usually is in every big city, but beneath it I sensed something more – a strange churning savagery that seemed to be drawing near.

Filings drawn to a magnet.

"This is me, then," said Ellen as we stood in the wash of light that spilled through the hotel doors. Her dark blonde hair was in disarray and the skin around her eyes was still puffy, but she looked beautiful. She clasped my hand, unable or unwilling to let it go.

"So we'll meet outside the community centre tomorrow at eleven?" I tightened my grip on her small, thin hand. Skin and bone: easily broken.

"Thank you, Thomas. You always were such a good friend, and..."

"And what?"

"And more. So much more."

There came a moment then, as we leaned into each other and the streets and the buildings receded, that it would have been such a simple thing to turn back the clock to a time when my family were still alive and I had betrayed them with Ellen. It would have been the easiest thing in the world, but just because something is easy that doesn't make it the right thing to do. I drew back slightly, just an inch or two, but it was enough to break the spell. Traffic noise returned to fill the gap we had created, and the bass-heavy throb of music in some nearby club matched the beat of my heart.

"Goodnight, Thomas," she said, turning away yet still reluctant to relinquish her grip on me. Our hands were the final thing to part, and as I watched her climb the steps and enter the hotel it was all I could do to stop myself from following her inside. The Eastern European women were still there, warming the sofa in the foyer, and one of them stared at Ellen as she passed, heading for the stairs rather than the lift. I noted the hunching of her shoulders, the tension contained within her posture, and for a moment I wished that I had acted upon that momentary weakness of the will.

I slowly made my way along Wellington Street, walking in the hope that I might rid myself of the state of arousal that was fogging my brain. There was a taxi rank outside the train station, in the large bus terminus, and at this hour the queue would be short.

It took several moments for me to realise that I was being followed, and not with great subtlety. I became aware of the sound of footsteps matching my pace, and of the sense of being stalked. Not wanting to turn around and draw attention to the fact that I knew they were there, I crossed the road, glancing both ways for approaching traffic and so that I could catch a sly glimpse of the footpath to my rear.

There were five of them, walking in unison, and each wore a black hooded sweatshirt. The hoods were pulled up to cover their heads and the drawstrings pulled tight to mask their faces. All I could see through the small gap at the front of each hood was a circle of blackness. No features were visible; I could not even make out the shape of a skull beneath the dark material, just soft looking oval mounds.

I increased my pace, stepping as quickly as I dared without giving myself away. My initial instinct was to assume that these kids were muggers, simply wandering the city at night to pick on drunks and lone women making their way home. This gave way, though, to a more sinister suspicion. It was the fact that the hoods gave only on to darkness that made me realise that what was following me might not be entirely human. They may have been human once, perhaps even recently, but now they were something else altogether. Not ghosts or wraiths, but creatures akin to those things: entities bound to darkness. I could feel it in the air that shimmered between us, taste it in the drizzle that strained to fall from grey and bloated clouds, hear it in the troubling song of distant emergency sirens.

Something had sought me out, and this time it was not prepared to take no for an answer.

The five hoodies crossed the road behind me, making not a sound as they followed. This alone was enough to confirm my suspicions: a group of normal kids would be jeering and acting in as threatening a manner as possible. These things were as silent as the spaces between the stars.

I crossed to the other side of the road, pausing for a moment while a black taxi cruised past me in the darkness. The driver was staring dead ahead, but the passenger – a slim girl with buzz-cut hair and smeared eye makeup – turned to watch the kids as they mirrored my movements. The taxi sped up and went through a red light. The girl's face stared at me out of the rear window, nothing more than a pale blur behind the glass.

The street had become unusually quiet and empty. It wasn't right, not in the centre of a big city at this hour. There should have been at least a few pedestrians – night-time drinkers and last-gasp revellers – patrolling the footpaths, but the only other people in the vicinity were the hoodies at my heels.

Just as I had the train station in sight, another group appeared, this time up ahead of me. They stopped a few hundred yards away, effectively blocking my route to the station. They all wore the same apparel: dark jeans and training shoes, dark grey or black hoodies pulled up to obscure their faces.

I cut along a side street, knowing that it would eventually lead me to the station. Footsteps sounded like clapping hands behind me, a round of applause to reward my decision to go off the main drag and enter an even less populated area. I started to run, not caring now that they saw my panic. I didn't want this; it wasn't fair.

My tattoos were writhing on my back and arms like snakes. They were agitated, trying to tell me that these things in pursuit were far worse than ghosts – possibly worse than anything I'd ever encountered. The streetlights flickered around me, threatening to plunge me into complete darkness. Lights in the surrounding buildings went out, small squares of black appearing in the walls of flats and offices which offered no shelter.

Drizzle fogged the air, picking the right moment to turn into proper rain. The pavement seemed to pitch upwards and sideways, trying to throw me off its back like a bucking bronco battling its rider. My throat was tight; my lungs began to ache. My terrible fitness levels were causing me to stumble, and I almost went flat on my face in the road. I prayed for a car to appear – any kind of vehicle, as long as it contained someone I could reach out to, showing them how afraid I was.

The footsteps behind me sounded closer, but I did not look back. I could not look back.

Then, finally, I saw the lights at the back of the train station. The road inclined towards this relative sanctuary, and despite the fact that I was almost gagging from the exertion I ran faster, spurred on because I was almost within touching distance of safety.

Safety. As if there is ever such a thing as safety.

The second group of hoodies – or perhaps yet a third group – appeared at the crest of the hill, stopping at the railings of a large, detached office building. They leaned against the gate posts, staring at me. Some of them had their hands stuffed into the large frontal pockets of their hooded sweatshirts; the others held their fists at their sides, as if readying for a fight. Still I could not make out a single face. Dark openings leered at me, and as I stopped running, trapped on all sides, I suddenly realised that the last thing I wanted to see was whatever the darkness concealed.

The group began to move down the hill towards me, walking in a line; a slow procession of dark urban monks. I glanced over my shoulder, at my original pursuers, and saw that they too had slowed to a measured pace and were advancing in a similar fashion up the steep incline.

I stared in panic at the darkened buildings around me, hoping for a single light. There were none. Nobody was home. Or if they were, they were not open to visitors. From the bottom of the hill a surge of darkness began to rise, coming up behind the marching hoodies. The streetlights went off, one by one, that terrible darkness ascending slowly towards my position halfway up the hill. It was like a vast cloud of blackness, gathering speed now, eager to reach my position, and soon it engulfed the figures which were even now advancing upon me.

I fell to my knees, vomit rising in my throat. My tattoos were burning, as if hot brands were being applied to my skin. I had never felt anything like it before, and the realisation almost broke me. What were these things, and what did they represent? Was the encroaching darkness their master, or did they command it like so many dark lords with a pack of hunting hounds?

When I looked up I was surrounded. The darkness hung back, behind the figures, so that all I could see was them, staring down at me from behind their sweatshirt hoods. The rest of the scene – the road, the side streets, the suddenly distant station – had all vanished, as if I'd been transported to another place entirely. All I could see of their forms before me was the hands that hung out of the sweatshirt sleeves, and they were thin, clawed, and almost skinless. The hands of old men, or newborn babies: creased, papery flesh, bloodless and with the blue bulge of withered veins showing close to the surface. The fingernails were half as long as the fingers they grew from. And they too were white, bleached of all colour, like shards of exposed bone.

At first I thought I saw vaporous breath streaming from the holes at the front of the hoods, but then I realised that they were billowing darkness, like a black mist trailing from a crack in reality. Darkness… or was it ash?

"Please," I said, hating the way my voice cracked, ashamed of the terror held in the word, wrapped up in it. "What do you want with me?" the circle tightened around me; the gaps closed.

The gaps always – always – close.

A flower of ash bloomed from the front of each hood, as if a series of small chimneys were dispensing soot or industrial waste. It fell in small puffs, and lay at my feet, blackening the concrete paving stones and staining like dark patches of blood or oil spilled after a riot.

It felt as if I were being tugged; every muscle in my body fought against some kind of negative energy that was pinning me down and allowing that darkness to enter me. Then, in an instant, I knew that I was stronger than they were. The hooded figures were not touching me, because they couldn't. For some reason they were not yet strong enough – but I also knew that soon they would be and I might not get another chance to escape them.

This realisation brought with it a welcome sense of power.

"No!" I screamed, getting to my feet and moving towards them. Ash drifted in the air, clogging my nose and filling my mouth with the dull, flat taste of an ancient fire.

It took me a few seconds to realise that the figures had reared back, away from me. I knew that it was nothing I had actually done, but my forceful refusal had somehow allowed reality to bleed back in and triggered the street to grow more corporeal around me. The figures parted and I saw two men running in our direction, mouths open as they shouted words I couldn't hear. Shortly the sound rushed back in and I could make out angry yells, obscenities. The men, it seemed, were coming to my aid. They thought that I was being attacked by a gang of youths.

When I turned around I was alone once more on the footpath. The two men hurried to my side, one of them grabbing my shoulder. "You okay, mate? We saw those little bastards push you down and thought you were about to get a kicking."

His friend continued running down the hill for a short distance, clearly puzzled as to where my assailants had gone.

"Thank you. Thank you, yes. I'm fine." My mind raced, looking for a cover story. "I've had a bit to drink this evening, and I think they saw me as easy game. You've saved me from being mugged." It sounded plausible, and the man relaxed as his friend returned, shrugging and anxiously scanning the area for lingerers.

"Are you hurt?" The second man – the one who'd run after the figures – stared into my eyes, looking for signs of… what? Drunkenness? Injury?

"No, I'm fine. You got here just in time." I brushed down my coat and stood against the iron railing, feeling the reality of cold ironwork biting into my back and enjoying its unflinching rightness.

"Shall I call the police?" The first man had a mobile phone in his hand. Its bright little light glowed beneath his stubbly chin, making him, too, seem demonic – not unlike the beings who'd chased and cornered me.

"No harm done," I said, forcing a smile.

"Waste of time, anyway," said the other man, placing a hand against my arm. "They'd never catch the sods. Things like this happen all the time – state of the nation, I reckon."

I nodded. The man did not know the half of it.

My two erstwhile saviours accompanied me to the station, where they saw me into a taxi. I thanked them graciously, and made a fuss of how they'd turned up in the nick of time, but deep down I knew for a fact that if I had not been able to reject that other, darker reality they would not even have seen me as they passed the spot where I cowered, surrounded by things that I could not even begin to identify.

The taxi pulled away from the rank, and I watched the men through the rear window. They stared after me for a while, one of them raising a hand in farewell. Then, satisfied with their night's work, they began to regale the females behind them in the taxi queue with their tale of bravery. I wished them well, and hoped that they at least got a couple of phone numbers out of it.

I dozed in the back of the taxi, my head filled with the remnants of the darkness that had swept up the hill towards the station, hungering for whatever was locked within me – the roots of my ability, perhaps, or simply my basic humanity. Before long I was home, paying the driver and walking slowly along the driveway to my front door. The upstairs lights were on, just as I'd left them, and through the landing window I glimpsed movement that could only be something swinging from the ceiling, its rhythm graceful and eternal.

I locked all the doors and windows, and then I climbed the stairs to bid my constant companions goodnight. They were fading, their forms less defined than earlier that day, and I wondered if they spent the hours waxing and waning, coming in and out of existence as the tidal pull of another place tugged at their shabby presence.

Before returning downstairs, where the bed sheets were cool and clean and creaseless, I went to the landing window and looked out upon the street. A group of figures stood at the corner a few hundred yards from the end of my drive, their faces covered by hoods. Despite there being no way that I could pick out their features, I felt them staring at me as I studied them. I watched for an hour, wishing that they would leave, and when finally they did I stood there for an hour more, praying that they would not return.

The ghosts on the landing didn't scare me, but these hooded figures terrified me to the core.

Then, at last, I let sleep drag me downstairs to my mattress, and rested more soundly than I had for many years. It proved to be the last good night of sleep I would ever have, but right then there was no way I could know that, so my thoughts remained untroubled as the house settled around me and all the ghosts of my life watched over me, only some of them wishing me harm and the others simply judging me from a distance.

ELEVEN

I woke at some point long before daylight. That brief and wonderful period of deep sleep was shattered. On instinct, I got out of bed and went to the patio doors. The curtains were already open, even though I remembered closing them before climbing into bed.

The landscape outside was the one from my dream: a long expanse of burned ground, with no sign of trees or flora, just smoke rising like a sullen ground mist. A hill was located a couple of miles away, and at its apex a single tree was ablaze. The fire was pale, and looked as if it had been going for quite some time. It didn't look like it would expire any time soon.

High up in the branches of the burning tree, coiling inside a cocoon of flames, was a figure that must once have been human but now resembled a length of blackened meat slung onto a ferocious barbeque and left to char. The form turned in the fire, rotating like a child's wind-up toy, and slowly, jerkily, it raised its arms from its sides to adopt an attitude of crucifixion.

When I woke again I was still standing there, at the glass doors, but the curtains were closed. I reached out a hand and grasped the edge of one curtain, afraid to pull it open yet terrified that if I did not I would never see the real world again.

Then I looked down, past my sweating shoulders and the protective talisman's inked there and across my chest. Upon my stomach, left there to remind me more than terrify me, was that same ashen message I'd seen once already:

memento mori

I knew what it meant. Remember that you shall die.

It was a sentiment I'd actually heard more than once before, but right then I did not want to think about it. I knew I'd have to face the not-quite-suppressed memory at a later date, but it could wait until I felt up to the task. In the meantime I returned to bed and thought about sleep instead; because thinking about it was now all that I could manage.

TWELVE

The following day I arrived late and sat for a moment in my car outside the Bestwick Community Centre. I'd left giving myself plenty of time to get there, taking into consideration the fact that I liked to drive slowly, obeying every sign and speed limit, yet I hit some road works on the motorway that held me up by twenty minutes. I realised that I should have called a taxi in the first place, but by then it was too late to make any difference. I was on Baz Singh's payroll and could always charge him for transport even when it wasn't really to do with his case – I should have no qualms whatsoever regarding scalping him for a few quid if it meant that I could leave the car at home, but the thought of being in control of my own movements had just about outweighed my distaste for auto vehicles, so I'd decided to open the garage and give the ageing motor some air.

The Bestwick Estate was located in the dip of a slight valley, with a more affluent area perched above it, the denizens of which looked down in judgement upon the fallen. It was a typical Northern council estate, with badly maintained properties, unkempt gardens, and a proliferation of satellite dishes nesting in the eaves of the cramped houses and boxy blocks of flats.

Most of the gardens contained the latest housing estate must-have items: a yapping dog, a huge trampoline and a tatty St George's cross flag dangling limply from a dirty pole. These places all look the same, and in my experience the people who live in them are generally all from the same stock: ill-educated, angry, under-nourished, and sadly lacking in the wherewithal to even try to escape the clutches of their poor standard of living. It was ex-prime minister Margaret Thatcher's dream become reality: the underbelly of a society in a world where, according to the famous Iron Lady, society itself was nothing but a myth.

Tiredness was stretching my patience and my usual empathy had been replaced by a surly species of general contempt. It wasn't healthy – I knew that – but what else could I do but be a slave to my emotions, just like everyone else?

I exhaled deeply and climbed out of the car. I was keen to get out of that grubby tin box and my eyes constantly scanned the street ahead, as if I were expecting trouble. Always expecting trouble.

I watched a battered Vauxhall Nova as it sped along the road and around a corner, past a row of shops with timbers across the doors and windows and a bare plot of land where someone had set fire to an old sofa. The furniture still smouldered, as if it had done so for a long time and would probably continue forever. Some fires never go out, and the smoke from such conflagrations will gather and mass and wait for an opportunity to choke anyone who might stray too close.

"Got a light, mister?"

I turned to face a small boy, aged possibly seven or eight. He was standing in the gutter holding a cigarette to his lips. His hair was shaved very short, almost down to the bone, and his face was gaunt. Haunted eyes stared at me from a narrow skull, and I wondered why he wasn't at school.

"Sorry. I don't smoke."

The boy shrugged but didn't leave. Instead he lingered, sucking on the unlit cigarette and staring at me. "Who are you? You a copper?"

I smiled and glanced down at my suit. This kid probably only ever saw men in suits when his mother was in court or if the council or bailiffs came knocking at his door. "No, I'm not a policeman. I'm here to see someone."

"You come to see that thing about the missing girl, Penny?" He kept staring at me, his large forehead smooth and grimy, his bald chin jutting.

"Do you know Penny Royale?" I bent down to his level, my knees protesting loudly at the movement.

"Yeah. Went to my school, didn't she. Weird lass. Always reading them books and sticking her hand up in lessons an' that." He turned to stare along the road, and I saw a long, messy scar, like burned tissue, down one side of his neck. Something caught my attention – movement from the other side of the road – and I looked towards the smouldering sofa. Another boy stood next to it, his hair smoking. His clothes were burnt rags.

My heart sank; here was another one come to taunt me.

"Your brother was killed in the same fire where you got that scar." It was not a question; I knew it as certainly as I knew my own name. The presence of the smoking figure was impossible to ignore, and his story came to me unbidden. Just like always.

The boy glared at me, but his eyes were wet. "Fuck off."

"He's over there now. He's waving at you, and calling your name." I studied the smoking boy, trying to make out what he was saying, but the distance was too great for me to fully understand what message he was trying to convey – if there were any message at all. Often there isn't. Sometimes they just appear and hang around for a while before moving on.

"How do you know about our Jordan? He's been dead for years." The boy's cheeks were white; his too-large eyes had consumed most of his face.

"Jordan loves you, and he's watching over you. He wants you to try your best, I think, and not to make the same mistakes that he did." I was making it up as I went along, but I sensed that there was something of the truth in what I said.

The boy on the patch of waste ground stopped waving, nodded his head. He held up a hand, the fingers splayed apart, and then he stepped back into the smoke that was still churning from the old sofa and became part of it, drifting into pieces and finally slipping from view.

The boy at my side was backing away. He was halfway across the road before I turned my attention back to him, and had already made his decision. "Paedo! Fuckin' weirdo!" he screamed, weeping openly now and hating me all the more for it. He ran, and I felt my heart sink. There went another one I was unable to help. Yet one more nameless victim in the long line that stood behind me, lost in time and darkness.

I walked around to the back of the community centre, where the staff car park was already filled with police vehicles and a few local journalists stood outside the fire door smoking and chatting about the missing girl. A few of them recognised me; one of them, a young woman whose name I could not recall, nodded at me, a tentative smile playing across her thin lips. I nodded back, but didn't break my stride.

I could see Ellen through one of the ground floor windows. She was sitting in a small room, with one arm around the shoulders of a short, overweight woman with badly bleached shoulder-length hair. Ellen looked up just as I approached the window. Her face was drawn; she looked tired. She gave me a worn-out smile and beckoned me over with a small nod of the head.

Just as I approached the back door of the building, the journalists and other people hovering in the car park answered some unheard signal to head inside. I was caught up in the crowd as they all tried to squeeze through the same access point at the same time. Beyond the bodies who'd somehow barged their way in front of me, I saw Ellen waiting alone in the doorway of the same side room from which she'd summoned me.

"Glad you could make it," she said, looking pale and tired and as if she did not want to be there, not really.

"Sorry I was a bit late. I had a rough morning. Where's your cousin?" I glanced into the room and saw that it was now empty.

"She's in there." Ellen motioned towards the main hall, inside which everyone else seemed to be congregating. "The fun and games are about to begin." The look on her face was one of cynicism mixed with dread. Her eyes were flat, like old pennies, and I wanted to reach out and hold her but the old guilt resurfaced to stay my hand.

"Shall we?" She moved forward, stepping in front of me, so I had only a partial view of the room we were heading towards. I caught sight of a bunch of red plastic chairs set up in rows before a raised platform or stage, and on that stage were a series of Formica tables pushed together to form a long, low desk. Behind this makeshift desk were four people: Ellen's cousin, Shawna, looking drawn and ghost-like, a man who could only be her husband judging by the way he was tightly holding her hand and staring straight ahead at the gathered onlookers, and two uniformed police officers.

One of the officers was my old sparring partner Detective Inspector Donald Tebbit. The other was a man whose face I vaguely recognised, and I took him to be Tebbit's superior officer. He was large – easily the most imposing figure at the desk – and grey-haired with watery eyes and a nose that looked like it had been broken countless times in the past. He stared dead ahead, his gaze unflinching, and I understood immediately that this was not a man to be messed with.

Chair legs scraped across the wooden floor and muted coughs and snorts sounded as the stragglers – me included –

made themselves comfortable. Ellen had snagged a couple of seats near the front, next to some other friends and family members I'd never seen before but recognised by the nature of their sadness – slumped shoulders, empty faces, features blurred by loss. It was a look I knew intimately. I had worn it myself now for years, with no regard for fashion.

"Ladies and gentlemen." It was the large man seated next to Tebbit. His voice sounded exactly as I'd expected: a low, sombre tone, the words chosen carefully. This was a man who left nothing to chance.

The crowd settled, went silent; they were captivated by his voice.

"Ladies and gentlemen, I'd first like to thank you all for attending this official statement – both members of the press, a lot of whom I recognise, and other interested parties. My name, for those of you who don't yet know me, is Detective Chief Superintendent Norman Scanlon. I am heading up this case, with the day-to-day running of things being taken care of by my colleague Detective Inspector Donald Tebbit, seated at my side."

Tebbit seemed to beam; the compliment of being called a colleague rather than an assistant was not wasted on him, and I silently congratulated Scanlon on his use of basic psychology.

"I'll say nothing more today, and hand you over instead to DI Tebbit, who is more than capable of fielding all questions and filling you in on what we know – and, more crucially, what we don't yet know."

What we don't *yet* know.

Again, the subtle use of psychology, making everyone aware that during the course of the investigation they would get to know whatever they needed to help find the missing girl and nothing more. *Bravo*, I thought. *You know exactly what you're doing.*

Tebbit coughed into his closed fist, swallowed, and seemed to grow a little in his chair. "Thank you, sir. Okay, then. As DCS

Scanlon has already said, thank you all for coming today. Let me begin by telling you what we already know."

Feet shuffled; the crowd leaned forward as one; someone coughed loudly.

"Penny Royale went missing on her way home from school two days ago, October twenty-first, at approximately three-fifty in the afternoon. We at the West Yorkshire Constabulary have committed every available resource to finding her, but we are also appealing to the general public to help us in any way they can. At the end of this press conference, I shall read out our emergency hotline numbers, which will be manned twenty-four hours a day. This has been a very tough time for the family, and rather than sit and detail every nuance of the case, Penny's mother and father would like to say something directly to you all."

Muted whispering. The shuffling of feet. This was why they were all here, to watch the monkeys perform. I could sense the press leaning forward in their plastic chairs, straining to get closer to the shattered parents. A few camera flashes went off, and the TV crews lined along both sides of the hall shifted their lenses towards the Royales, who sat in the glare of lights like frightened animals.

"I'd like to ask you all to remain silent during the announcement, and keep your questions until later. There'll be plenty of time to answer everyone."

Murmured voices. Again, the restless shuffling of feet.

Mrs Royale leaned forward across the table, her hands clutching a sheet of foolscap paper that had been folded and unfolded countless times judging by its shabby appearance.

"I…" Her voice was breaking before she'd even begun, and her husband reached out to take the paper. Mrs Royale snatched it away from him, as if his attempt to take over had been an insult. Then she closed her eyes for a couple of seconds, opened them and continued, reading directly from the sheet of paper now clutched so tightly in her hands that I was afraid it might tear.

"I would like to speak directly to whoever has our Penny." Her accent was thick, making her sound dull and uneducated in the way that pure regional accents often do. "Whoever you are, wherever you've got her, I just want to tell you that our Penny is a good girl. She sticks in at school, has a lot of friends, and wants to work with animals when she grows up."

A pause, during which it seemed like nobody dared breathe.

"Our Penny won't give you any trouble. Just tell her what to do and she'll help you. Penny doesn't want to be hurt, and I'm sure that you don't want to hurt Penny."

The constant repetition of the girl's name was surely the work of some police advisor: the woman had probably been told to make sure that any potential kidnapper identified with Penny, seeing her as a real human being rather than a thing to be coveted and kept.

"Our Penny belongs at home, with us. We love her very, very much, and would like her to come home. We promise that we'll try and understand why you've taken Penny, and we'll make sure the police give you all the help you need to sort out your problems. Our Penny can help you, too. She's a good girl. A very good girl. Please just let her go – even if you open the door now and let her out. She'll know her way back to us… she's a good… a good… good girl…"

Mrs Royale had done well right up until the end, when her voice seemed to fade away into a series of quiet sobs. Her husband held her hand, but it was limp in his grip. The woman looked deflated, as if all the air had been let out of her in one go, and she slumped so low into her seat that it seemed for a moment she might fall to the floor in a heap.

Then something happened that took me completely by surprise. From the far side of the raised platform, where he must have been standing quietly and watching events unfurl, a man walked over and approached Mrs Royale. He was short, solidly built, and bald-headed, wearing a simple dark suit with a white T-shirt underneath. It was the man I'd brushed up against at Baz Singh's place, the Blue Viper. The man Singh had called Mr Shiloh.

He crossed the stage and knelt down at Mrs Royale's side, one hand slipping into hers and the other arm going around her shoulder. She leaned into him, and he whispered something into her ear. She smiled, briefly, and then buried her head in his neck. Mr Royale looked on, helpless yet not objecting at all, as if this were all perfectly natural. Mr Shiloh kept whispering into the side of Mrs Royale's face, his skin shining like plastic under the bright lights. Again I was struck by his lack of energy, the strange neutrality that radiated from him, as if he were a blank sheet of matter waiting to absorb the energy of others and reflect it back at them. The image I had was of the neck of a bottle floating upon an endless sea, the remainder of the receptacle resting beneath the water, but with the bottom smashed off, so that the entire ocean had *become* the container. And it would never, ever be full enough to cease swallowing whatever it came into contact with.

How, I asked myself, could a man of such unassuming stature seem to contain the whole world?

The room erupted into chaos; members of the press all tried to ask different questions at the same time, creating a sound not unlike the mad chattering of a group of chimpanzees. Cameras flashed like indoor lightning and the television crews trained their lenses on the centre of everyone's attention: the poor, weeping parents and their stolid companion.

Tebbit tried to field the ensuing questions as best he could, but I'd already heard the official version of events. My job here was to look from a different angle, to bring my own unique perspective to the tragedy. My job was to see that which no one else could.

And what I saw most was Mr Shiloh.

"Who is that?" I leaned in close to Ellen, aware that I sounded slightly panicked.

"Who do you mean?"

I turned to face her, camera flashes haloing her features, and stared into her lovely blue eyes. "That man, the bald one. I've seen him before. Who is he?"

Ellen looked at the stage, and then turned back to me. "That's Mr Shiloh. He's a friend of the family." She didn't look too convinced by her own description. "Apparently he's been around for years."

I felt cold inside that warm, cramped room, and when I looked back towards him, the man they called Mr Shiloh caught my gaze. Held it. Held it. And did not let it go, even when I frowned at him to make my displeasure clear. It looked like he was trying not to smile – or struggling not to laugh – but I couldn't be certain. I could be certain of nothing, not any more.

Something within this dark little man of infinite capacity recognised me; and something inside me knew him too. The horror of the moment was greater than I could even begin to comprehend, and I felt lost in its baleful shadow.

THIRTEEN

Loss is another country, a strange and welcoming dominion into which all of mankind must one day fall. Some of us walk there regularly, knowing its pathways by heart, and others merely visit briefly, keen to leave before the terrain becomes one with which they are too familiar.

The landscape of my grief was a place I knew well. I had spent far too many years traversing its dense interior, mapping its ever-changing borders, and then I had finally reached a point where I was happy to call it home.

After the meeting broke up, I found myself standing outside with Ellen looking up at the dark scudding clouds and wishing for rain. I'd made a hasty getaway to ensure that there were no awkward moments with DI Tebbit. I wasn't sure how official my involvement with his murder case might be, and the presence of his superior officer made me nervous.

Besides, I wasn't yet sure if I wanted him to know that I'd been dragged into all this stuff about the missing girl.

"Would you drive?" I dangled the car keys from my middle finger, giving a little cock of the head as Ellen rolled her eyes.

"You still don't like to, eh? Even after all these years?"

There had been a time, immediately after the accident, when I'd refused to even get into a car. That feeling passed, as feelings do, and bit by bit I talked myself around and finally forced myself behind the wheel.

"If you wouldn't mind." I smiled.

Ellen took the keys and opened the driver's door, and then she climbed in and popped open the passenger door as I walked around the front of the vehicle. I remembered something my father had said, decades ago and long before his early death: if a woman opens the car door for you, she's a keeper. I don't know what data he based this theory on, but right then it seemed like sound advice.

"Are you sure you don't mind coming back to their place?" Ellen started the car, pulled out from the kerb and headed off down the hill. "It's still not too late to say no." Despite her words, her face said quite the opposite.

I sat in silence, hoping that she read my unwillingness to talk as an affirmative. I could easily have asked her to drive me home, or back to her hotel, but events had conspired to ensure that I became involved with the disappearance of Penny Royale. If I'd felt like a screw was turning before, I was certain now that some kind of knot was tightening around me. The fact of Mr Shiloh's presence linked everything in some way, and I felt that I needed to hang around and find out what that connection meant. In other words, I was by now too far into this to back out.

Ellen swung the car around a corner and we passed a row of shops that looked like they were stuck in the late 1970s. The streets were filthy, with litter gathering in the gutters and plastic bags gusting on the breeze. The front doors of many of the houses we passed were barred by metal gates fixed to the external brickwork – drug-doors, as we used to call them in my younger days. The gates could be locked from the inside, giving a dealer ample time to either flush their stash down the lavatory or escape out the back way if the police came calling.

Before long we arrived at a small cul-de-sac with a street sign covered in spray paint. As far as I could tell, the street name was Tilly Road, but some wag had adapted the letters so it read Titty Rod. At least the local vandals had a sense of humour, however primitive their jokes might be.

The street was filled with cars; they lined the verge on both sides, some of them double-parked. A few of the neighbours were standing out in their front gardens, gossiping over the fences, and others merely peeked out of their windows, unwilling to let themselves be seen in full view. A TV camera crew had set up on the corner, but they were otherwise occupied drinking coffee from Styrofoam cups and chatting idly as we approached.

"All I'm asking you to do is meet the family. Let them tell you a little about Penny, and see if you pick up on anything." Ellen had turned off the engine and she sat staring through the windscreen, her eyes large and moist. "I don't know how this works, but maybe you'll see or hear something?"

"I'll do what I can, Ellen, but you must know that I have no control over what it is I do. I could pick up everything, or I could pick up nothing. There's no way of telling which way this will go."

She turned to face me at last, a gentle smile warming her features. She slipped a hand onto my thigh and blinked. "I know, Thomas, but it's enough that you're willing to try. If you can pick up nothing that might mean that she's alive, yes?"

I nodded. "But it also might mean that I simply pick up nothing."

We left the car and headed towards the Royale house, with me bringing up the rear. A few men stood outside on the untidy lawn, smoking stubby cigarettes and staring aggressively at anyone who passed by the gate. They stared at me, too, even though I was with one of the family. Ellen strode by them, all business, and pushed through the unlocked front door. I followed, feeling wired and paranoid and wishing that this would all just go away. Somewhere overhead, thunder rumbled. I glanced up, but could detect no sign of rain.

At the end of a long hallway was an open door. Low voices drifted from inside the room, and Ellen went in without knocking. The woman from the press conference was sitting in an overstuffed armchair in the far corner, dabbing at her face with a paper tissue. An older woman with the same badly bleached hair was kneeling at her side, clucking like an old hen.

"Shawna," said Ellen, going straight to the chair. "I've brought him."

Shawna Royale looked up at our approach, and the light that flooded her face made me queasy. What I saw there, behind her waxen features, was a combination of unalloyed hope and something darker, something that did not quite fit in with the rest of her bloated washed-out appearance. But the tears she'd shed at the press conference were still visible, and my heart went out to her for her loss.

"Mr Usher," she gasped, standing unsteadily.

I went to her and took her outstretched hand, almost pulling back because of the desperation I sensed. I felt no presence in the room but that of the living. If Penny Royale was dead, then her shade had not yet found its way back here to this tawdry little room on a dead-end street populated by the lost and the forgotten.

"Please, don't stand. Sit yourself down, Mrs Royale."

"Call me Shawna," she said, doing as I'd asked. She sank too far into the seat cushion, and her black skirt rode up to reveal a bare patch of pale, blotchy thigh.

The older woman drifted away across the room, as if she were a phantom. I had to look twice to make sure that was not the case, but she was certainly alive and well, if a little absent.

"My neighbour," said Shawna. "She's been good to us."

I nodded and patted her hand, unsure of what else to do. Someone pushed a kitchen chair behind me, and I eased myself down onto its hard wooden seat.

"I'm not sure what Ellen has told you about me, but I can offer you no promises. The particular ability I possess is rather random, I'm afraid. I have no active part in what happens. Sometimes I see things, and sometimes I am given clues and messages. That's all. I don't really communicate directly with spirits, but I can often understand what it is they need. They don't talk to me directly, just through signs and gestures. I am, basically, what my name suggests: a simple guide."

It felt like the whole room had gone silent and everyone was listening to my spiel. I glanced over my shoulder to make sure, but no one would meet my gaze.

Shawna Royale leaned slowly forward. "I know about what you do. But right now, any help that we can get is better than nothing. We just want our Penny back, and whatever information we can get our hands on might just be the one thing that leads us to her." As if confirming what she'd just said, her hand gripped mine. The bones in her knuckles cracked, and I tried my best not to wince in pain.

"I'm not sure what it is exactly you'd like me to do, but for what it's worth I offer you my services. Ellen is an old friend, and I owe her more favours than I could ever repay."

Shawna smiled, showing her yellow teeth and swollen gums. Up close, her hair was greasy, and I wondered when the last time was that she'd bathed. As if in response, I caught a sour whiff of body odour. Turning away, I scanned the room, looking for something to divert my attention. There were photographs of Penny Royale everywhere, on the walls, on shelves, even resting on the dusty tiled area around the base of the fireplace.

"Help me find out if my daughter is still alive. It's all I ask." When I turned back around Shawna's face was far too close to my own, and I almost reeled back in shock. "I want my baby back." Beyond the hope, beneath the despair, was another emotion I could not quite name. I have a knack with understanding the dead, but often the obscure demands of the living are simply beyond my ken. Whatever is was – this other, hidden emotion – it was lost on me. For now.

"I'll do my best, Mrs Royale – Shawna. I promise."

She would not let me go; her hand gripped my forearm as if someone had bolted it there. "Do you feel her now? Is she here? In this room?"

Now everyone was looking at me. As I stood, turning to inspect the crowded lounge, I noted that every eye in the place was upon me. "No," I said, as clearly as I could. "No, your daughter is not here... but that doesn't mean that she isn't elsewhere, waiting to be seen." I felt like I'd let her down, dashed her slim hopes.

"I hope you're wrong, Mr Usher. I hope you don't feel her anywhere, not ever."

I nodded, smiled, and let Ellen lead me out of the room, along the hall, and out past the smoking doormen. She drove the car again; I was not up to any kind of additional stress.

"I think that went... well? Is that even the right word?" She shot me a glance, looking nervy and on the verge of tears.

"As well as can be expected, I suppose, under the circumstances. I just hope that your cousin isn't expecting too much. Whatever the hell it is I can do, I'm not the master of it. And whenever I do seem to think I have any control over it, there's always a disaster of some kind."

We didn't speak for a while, and I stared out of the window as Ellen drove back towards the city centre. I knew that we were heading for her hotel, but I didn't quite know how to react to the situation. Things were moving too fast; the world was spinning like an out-of-control carousel, and the ornamental horses were coming apart, sending wooden heads and hooves flying off in all directions like deadly debris.

That was exactly how it felt: like I was dodging mental shrapnel.

"Did you feel anything in there, or were you telling her the truth?" Ellen still stared ahead, through the windscreen. The car in front stopped suddenly, the driver slamming on his brakes as a cyclist veered into his path. Ellen reacted calmly, as if expecting the sudden halt. I closed my eyes on old, worn out memories.

"I felt nothing, Ellen. I can only see them when they want to be seen, but I can feel them when they're near. There were no ghosts in that room – in fact, it was remarkably free of activity for a house of that age. Usually, in every home I enter I can sense layers of the dead, going back through time to before the building was even constructed. It's actually rather strange when I don't feel that, but it does occasionally happen."

Ellen drove down the ramp into the hotel car park, not even asking me if I was interested in accompanying her inside. "I need a drink," she said, pulling into an empty space. "So do you." She turned off the engine, handed me the keys, and stared at me like it was a challenge.

"Yes, you're right. A drink would be... well, crucial, if I'm honest."

She smiled, the moment broken and the tension dissipating. "I'm sorry, Thomas, I'm just a bit stressed. All this is just too much. I mean, seeing you as well as Penny going missing. Everything at once... it's just too damn much."

I opened the door. "Come on. The first round's on me."

We entered the hotel and made straight for the bar, where a bunch of men in business suits had commandeered most of the tables. We sat at the bar, squashed into high stools like oversized children, and raced each other to the bottom of the glass. The whisky tasted like fire; it should have been cleansing but it simply stirred up old memories, ghosts I thought I had put to rest.

"Another?" Ellen was already signalling the barman.

"Fine. Make it a double." I decided to leave the car there, at the hotel, and whatever happened later would happen without my resistance, even if it meant me getting yet another taxi home on Baz Singh's tab. I didn't want to think about it too hard, not yet. Thinking could come later, after I'd loosened the cogs of my brain with alcohol.

We went upstairs sooner than I expected, Ellen in the lead and armed with a bottle of decent single malt and two glasses. The afternoon was darkening; the sky looked black through the tinted lobby windows. Rain began to spatter the glass, but gently, as if it were attempting to lull us into the right mood; a drizzly serenade for reluctant lovers.

The lift seemed to be moving much too slowly, and as it climbed I felt us drawing together, as if by some form of magnetic attraction. Ellen's leg brushed against my thigh; her gaze caught mine, unable to let it go. We stared at each other, her holding the bottle and me grabbing onto the glasses. Time seemed to bend. Seconds overlapped, folding into one another. The decades fell away like shed skin.

We did not kiss. We should have, but we didn't. I couldn't quite break through the barriers the years of hurt had built around me like a callous.

Once inside Ellen's room, however, those barriers began to fall, breaking apart and tumbling like the walls of a biblical city breached by a single supernatural note blown through a blessed horn. We sat on the bed and sipped our drinks, all talk forgotten. The forces around us were larger than we dared think, and I almost expected the walls to crack and the floor to shudder, sending us sprawling into each other's arms.

But that did not happen. It took natural forces, human desires, to bring us within touching distance.

"I don't think I can do this," I said, gritting my teeth.

Ellen's hand went to my face. Her fingers traced the line of my jaw, fingertips rasping on the stubble. She said nothing;

she did everything. Her other hand went to my chest, stroking me there, massaging me through the thin material of my shirt. I reached out and cupped her heavy breast, hurtling backwards in time. She gasped; I twitched in shock; we both began to breathe in synch.

The old guilt flooded in, filling me up, and for a moment I felt that I might drown. If Ellen and I had not made love that single time years before, when I'd betrayed my family, I would not have felt this way. It would have been easy to fall into bed with a woman – this woman – who I had always loved yet never been able to admit it.

I strained against my inability to embrace the moment, feeling simultaneously trapped and set free. Ellen kissed my neck. Her lips were like fire and ice; her breath burned my frozen skin and froze the flames of my ardour.

I had spent all the dark years since their death searching for my family's ghosts, and not once had I found them in any substantial way. All I ever had were times like these – moments of guilt and loss and bereavement. I had seen too many ghosts to count, yet I had never encountered the only ones I had ever wanted to find. I could not summon them, nor could I create them from the dust of my memories. They were lost to me, wandering in some void that I had not even come near. If all the layers of reality were to be peeled away, leaving only the final reality, the one that lies beneath, would I find them even then?

When I kissed her, Ellen put her arms around me, running her fingers across the nape of my neck. "I'm sorry," I said: to my dead wife, my dead child, my cold, dead heart. "I'm sorry."

Later I sat on the end of the bed and stared at the dark screen of the television. Ellen sat behind me, miles from sleep, studying me. "Those names tattooed on your back. What do they mean?"

I closed my eyes and listened to the sound of my heart beat-ing. "They're the names of all the people I have failed. I add each name to the list in the hope that it might be the last. Sometimes it seems like I'll run out of skin before I run out of people to fail."

I felt the mattress shift and heard the bedclothes rustle as she leaned forward; then I felt the heat of her hand on my back, laid out flat between my shoulder blades. "So many names..."

I nodded. Tears filled my eyes.

So many names.

"Are you sorry we did that?" her voice was quiet, like the night, like the voices held always within the dark.

"I can't be sorry, but I do feel that I've failed them again."

"Your family," she said; a statement not a question. "One day you're going to have to let them go."

"I can't," I said, staring at the dead screen and thinking that just for a moment I saw something moving in there, a flicker, a reflection of a memory. "I can never let go, not until I've seen them and I know that they've forgiven me."

"What's to forgive?" The hand drew away from my skin; Ellen sat back against the pillows, understandably aggrieved. "What's left to forgive after all this time? It's been over twenty years since we did what we did – and they've been gone al-most as long. Fifteen years, Thomas. Fifteen years of grief. How long until you forgive yourself?"

"What's left to forgive? Far too much to speak of." I stood and went to the window, glancing out into the darkened street below.

Fifteen years of grief...

Standing in a bus lay-by across from the hotel was a short, broad figure with a bald head. He was staring at the window, as if he had been doing so all night, waiting for me to look out. He nodded once, and I knew him. I knew him but I could not say who he was or what he might be. Like a song from the depthless regions of space, he was a thing that should not be, an echo of a scream made by someone who had never existed.

When I turned back to face the bed, Ellen was already asleep. Or perhaps she was only pretending.

FOURTEEN

I left early the next morning, before breakfast. Ellen watched from the bed in silence, allowing me the space to make a fool of myself. I washed and dressed and kissed her cheek, then headed for the door. I paused with my fingers around the door handle, knowing that I should say something but unable to speak in case the wrong words came out.

"Just call me later, when you've had time to think." Her voice was not filled with anger, nor where her words unpleasant. She was simply voicing an undeniable truth.

I opened the door and left her there, possibly thinking worse of me than she ever had before. During the drive home I thought about Ellen, trying not to allow Rebecca and Ally into my head. It was difficult, but I managed – my usual penchant for self-flagellation was put on hold for now. Instead I thought about other things from the past: the things that came after.

My memories are all in present tense; I can relive them no other way because they are always happening, even now. Running on an endless loop like a faulty film strip. They will probably never stop.

Fifteen years of grief…

• • • •

When finally I leave the hospital (to the great relief of Nurse Haggard, who has now run out of ways to sensibly avoid me), I am unable to go back home. There are too many memories residing in the empty rooms, and the walls and floors and ceilings are strewn with reminders of what I have lost. My family sit in the musty darkness, waiting for me, but I know that I will be unable to see them.

And do I really want to see them? It is a question I cannot even begin to answer.

I check into a cheap city centre hotel and try to come up with a plan, a way of helping people deal with their grief whilst helping myself come to terms with my own pain and the things it has made me able to do.

One of the other guests has just lost her father, and I offer her a shoulder to cry on. It doesn't end well. When I tell her that I am trying to contact her late father, she thinks I am mad and runs from me in tears. I begin to think the same: that I am mad. Is that what's happened? Have I stepped off some mental ledge?

I leave that hotel and try another. This time I am more careful, but the end result is the same: however hard I try, I cannot get in touch with the spirits I choose. It takes me weeks to realise that it is they who must come to me, and all I can do is wait.

Wait to see if I am sane, or if the whole thing is a product of my unresolved guilt and overpowering grief.

I drink a lot and watch bad daytime television. The counsellors the hospital recommended have no idea what I am experiencing, and I go through them like a series of cheap suits that don't quite fit, feeling slightly sorry for them as I fail to keep appointments or follow up phone calls. I do talk to the surgeon who patched me together after the accident, and he helps without realising that he is doing so. It is because of him that I do not open my veins in a warm bath, and I'll always be grateful for this at least.

I begin to feel hemmed in, as if the city itself is preventing me from reaching out. I need a new environment, if only to find some space to breathe. Thoughts of suicide now put behind me, I am at last able to picture a future that doesn't involve the grave. But only if what I feel is true; only if the ghosts are real.

I find the number of a caravan park in a local newspaper. When I ring the number I'm told that the only caravan available immediately and on a long-term lease is one of the older models, with basic amenities. I don't mind; the sub-standard living quarters will be part of my punishment, a self-imposed isolation from my fellow man. All I need to go with it is a medieval hair shirt.

I am checked into my new accommodation by a small yet morbidly obese man in a stained shirt and torn jeans. He doesn't say much as he hands over the keys and briefs me on the rules of the site – no parties, no loud noises after 10pm, no breakages. I smile and nod in all the right places, and I am glad that he shows no interest at all in the reasons behind my being here. Anonymity seems to be something I can get used to.

After the caretaker has departed I walk to the site shop and stock up on supplies: eggs, bread, milk and lots of alcohol – as much as I can carry back to the caravan in three trips. I plan to lose myself in booze, to ride the waves of whisky and wine until it is time for me to come up for air, or perhaps drown in the process.

The message I received in hospital prompted me to make a firm decision. I told myself that I would deal with my loss by trying to help others who have suffered similar bereavements, but it didn't quite work out that way. I imagined myself as some kind of supernatural crusader – a champion of the grieving. But instead I found out that I was even more lost than those whom I sought to help, and the realisation of my impotence almost broke me in half.

I went looking for ghosts and found only glimpses of something I could not understand. The spirits I wanted to grasp remained out of reach, eluding my attentions, and I found only scraps and strays. The fragmentary messages these fluttering shades offered meant nothing to me, and after a short time I realised that whatever was happening to me – this strange thing I was perhaps capable of – was entirely beyond my control.

So I made my way here, to this squalid camp site, where I could be alone with my demons and try to silence them with an ocean of drink...

I spend six weeks locked up inside the caravan, drinking heavily and staring at the walls; eating little enough to stay alive but not enough to give me much energy. I had originally planned to lose myself in thoughts of my dead loved ones, but I'm unable to focus and my mind feels plucked at from all sides, as if small hands are raking through my subconscious, looking for gaps.

At the end of this six week period I receive a visitor and everything changes.

It's close to midnight and I'm still awake, drinking as usual. The whisky is running low but I don't want to communicate with anyone to restock my supplies. It's a tricky dilemma, the solution of which is taking up much of my diminishing mental faculties.

There is a knock on the caravan door. At first I think that I must be hearing things, but when the knock is repeated I realise that there is indeed someone out there, trying to get my attention. I wonder if it's a ghost – the very thing I've been waiting for. I've had plenty of glimpses in the past few weeks, but nothing solid or tangible: fleeting wraiths gliding through the trees, a woman standing knee-deep in the river at the west end of the caravan site, a small child staring into the shower cubicle with a strange grin on his face...

I knew they were ghosts because nobody else could see them, but I also doubted my own ability to recognise what was real and what was not.

Because I was stupid enough to ask if he could see the child in the shower, the caretaker now thinks that I am some kind of lunatic. He doubled my rent, but that doesn't concern me. The insurance money is enough to keep me going for some time yet, even after I've paid off the mortgage on the house my dead wife and daughter loved.

I realise that I have been lost in my thoughts for several minutes, and go to the flimsy caravan door. I can sense someone still standing on the other side. This is not the result of any kind of special power; it's always so simple to pick up the presence of another where before you were completely alone.

"Who is it?"

There is no immediate answer, but I hear the sound of feet shifting on the metal steps outside the door. Whoever it is cannot decide whether to stay or flee.

"There's nobody home." I turn away from the door, giving them the easiest option.

"Thomas? It's Ellen. I'm sorry to disturb you this late, but I've only just managed to find out where you were staying."

I turn back to the door and approach it slowly. Then I open it and see her standing there, the black sky creating a dramatic backdrop behind her, and I feel like crying. "What do you want?"

"Can I come in? I've gone through a lot of shit to find you. The least you can do is to offer me a drink." She is wearing dark jeans and a brown leather jacket. Her breath spills from her lips in thin white plumes: more ghosts, but these ones lacking either form or substance.

I turn away, not inviting her inside but not telling her to go away either. I leave the decision to her. She follows me into the caravan, closing the door firmly behind her. "Nice place," she says. "I'm sure you and the cockroaches are very cosy."

I try not to smile but it's impossible, yet the expression feels all wrong. I shouldn't be smiling when my family are dead; I should be screaming into the void and raging at the cosmos, attempting to tear down the walls of heaven.

Something like that.

Ellen sits down on the cushions opposite me. Only a scarred foldaway dining table separates us, but we might as well be on different planets. She stares into my eyes and I'm unable to hold her gaze, so I pour whisky into two glasses and slide one across to her. Without flinching, she picks up the glass and finishes the drink in one.

"You've become a cliché, Thomas. Do you know that? A walking, talking cliché from a bad film. This isn't you – this drinking and moping. You were always more proactive than that." She holds my gaze, staring me down, challenging me to disagree.

"I know." She is perhaps the only living person to whom I cannot lie – including myself. "I tried, I really tried. After what happened in the hospital I thought I had a way out of the black hole I'd found myself in, but it didn't work out that way. All that's happened is that I have more questions than answers."

She drops her gaze, and then brings her eyes back up to face me. This time they are softer, and filled with an understanding that she could not possibly fake. "We've already had this discussion, Thomas. What happened at the hospital, with that girl, was weird, but you can't hang your hopes on it. I admit that I can't explain it, but have you considered that it might have been a fluke? I'm not saying it didn't happen the way you and the witnesses say it did, but it may have just been a one-off, a psychological glitch."

An owl hoots outside the window; wings beat frantically against the darkness. "I have thought about that, Ellen, but I've seen things since – things that can't be explained away. I don't know what's happening to me, or what caused it, but the fact remains that for some reason I can see fucking ghosts."

My own sudden certainty takes me by surprise. "I see them, but I can't touch them or speak to them. Most of the time they ignore me, but some of them seem to be looking for me – or at least for someone like me." I'm breathless, my lungs aching and my mind tied in knots. "I think the dead need someone to guide them."

There it was: the truth. I had stumbled upon it without even realising.

Ellen presses on, undaunted by my ranting: "I came here to give you some information. I wouldn't do this if I didn't think it might help, so listen up and remember what I'm about to say." The caravan rocks slightly on its base, as if a large animal has brushed against it en route to the adjacent woods. "I've found out the name of the man who caused the accident."

Darkness spins and whirls before my eyes, burrowing deep inside my vision. Ellen's voice becomes faint, as if I am hearing it from a great distance; then it increases in volume, and becomes almost too loud to hear.

"What did you say?"

"The man who caused the accident is living in council accommodation in Luton. As you know, he received a suspended sentence for dangerous driving and lost his licence. He has no memory of the accident, and he's on all kinds of medication. I know it's not exactly compensation for your loss, but his life is ruined, too. It seems that he blacked out before the accident, and when he returned to himself it was all over and he was in the back of an ambulance." Her face is pale but her lips are dark. I can see them moving yet am unable to associate the words I am hearing with her mouth, her face. It is like a voice in my head, telling me things I don't want to hear.

"Why? Why are you telling me this?"

Ellen stands and comes round to my side of the table, squeezing in beside me on the bench that doubles as a rude bed. "Because I think you need to go and see him, to confront him with your pain. What happened was a tragedy, but it was also an accident, and it has ruined both of your lives. You're trying to drink yourself to death while grasping at ghosts, and he's already slashed his wrists and taken an overdose of sleeping pills. Maybe together, if you meet and open up to each other, you can save each other."

Is she crazy? How the hell am I meant to face the man who destroyed my life? Accident or not, the events of that night tore open the seams of my reality and twisted the rest out of shape, removing from my existence the only two people who meant anything to me and slamming visions into my head that I cannot even begin to deal with.

"I don't think that's a good idea. I can't promise how I might react if I ever saw him."

Ellen reaches out to me, both physically and emotionally. I wish I could thank her for her efforts, but it all seems so silly, such a waste of positive energy. "That's why I'm coming with you."

FIFTEEN

Someone was waiting in my front garden when I pulled into the drive early that morning. It was a young female police constable and she was just turning away from my door as I entered the drive, as if she'd been ringing the bell for some time and had finally given up. She smiled when she saw me; her face was round and pretty and there was a deep sense of sadness hanging from her like tattered threads from an old coat. She had recently lost someone, but I didn't know who it might be – perhaps her father or mother; maybe even a sibling. The faded ghost stood behind her, too far back to identify. By the time I'd climbed out of the car and was moving towards her, it was gone.

I used to find it annoying when they did that, but these days I simply accept it. They slip between the folds, glimpsed for a moment, and then they are gone, leaving nothing more than a psychic ripple on the fabric of this version of reality.

"Mr. Usher? Thomas Usher?" The constable's voice was pleasant, with a singsong lilt I enjoyed.

"Yes. Are you looking for me?"

"I'm Police Constable Sarah Doherty. DI Tebbit sent me. He's been trying to reach you and was worried that you might be in some kind of trouble. Is everything okay?"

I smiled, nodded. She was a nice girl and I was sorry for her loss, whoever it was she had lost. "I'm fine. Been off the radar for a few hours, that's all."

PC Doherty was standing with her weight on one foot, one hip thrust out to the side. "There's been a development in a case I believe you've been helping us with. DI Tebbit would like to see you as soon as you're able to come to the station."

"You mean now?" I looked down at myself; I hadn't changed these clothes for two days. "I really could do with a long bath and a short drink. It's been a very trying twenty-four hours."

"I'm sorry, sir." She looked it, too; as if she really did regret having to come for me. "But DI Tebbit said to tell you that it involves you personally, and I'm not to leave without you."

"Am I under arrest?"

"No, no, not at all. I'm sorry if I gave you that idea. Please, don't misunderstand me." She raised her hands in a defensive gesture, clearly uncomfortable. "I can wait for you if you like. I'll sit in my car while you do what you have to do, but please don't think that you are under any kind of official pressure. DI Tebbit said that you'd be very interested in what's happened, and he told me to stress the fact that it's in your best interests to see him as soon as you can."

I felt sorry for the girl for having been used as a messenger, and decided to go with her to the station. If Tebbit was this desperate to see me – desperate enough to waste valuable police resources on summoning me – then it must be important. Tebbit may be many things, but he was not a man to waste people's time. "Give me a minute, Constable Doherty, and I'll be right with you. I just need to go inside and change. Then we can go and see your boss."

I was inside for just over half an hour, enough time to grab a quick coffee, change into a clean suit (dark suits were like a uni-form to me; I simply changed into a clean one every couple of days, which meant that I didn't have to think too much about trivialities like clothes) and pull myself together after last night's monumental occurrence. I wasn't quite ready to examine how I felt about Ellen and me making love, and the sex had been oddly unsatisfactory rather than the glorious culmination of years of yearning that I (and surely she) had expected.

Back outside, I climbed into the back of the police car and stared at the back of PC Doherty's lovely neck as she drove. The chestnut hair that hung out of her ponytail was fine and full of static electricity; her neck was pale and smooth and the thin black edge of a tattoo poked out of her shirt collar. Briefly, I wondered what her story was – because everyone has a story, no matter who they are.

The two-way radio barked at us and Doherty reached out to turn down the volume. "Sorry about that," she said, glancing at me in the rearview mirror.

"No problem." I felt uneasy. Virtually my whole adult life had been lived at speed, events moving past like shooting stars, and now, just when I was trying to slow things down, the world was spinning faster than ever. None of it made any sense; I felt lost inside someone else's bad dream.

I stared again at the back of the constable's neck, at the sliver of tattoo she thought she was hiding. Then I thought about my own tattoos, the protective ink that adorned my body and the names I carried with me.

"Who did you lose?"

Her shoulders tensed and the car swerved almost imperceptibly towards the centre of the road before she righted it. "I'm sorry, sir? What was that?"

"Someone you love has died recently. I can see it on you, like a stain. So who was it? Who did you lose? I'll understand if you don't want to talk about it, but it's in my nature to pry about these things." I was doing this to divert my thoughts from Ellen, and felt guilty for using the girl in this way.

There was a long pause, during which I decided that I had probably offended her to the point that she wanted to shoot me. Then the tension went out of her shoulders and she looked at me again in the mirror. "So it's true, then? What they say about you back at the station?"

"And what's that, Police Constable Doherty? Just what do they say about me?" Suddenly I was very interested in what she had to say.

"That you talk to the dead." The car tyres thrummed on the road surface. Sunlight glinted off the windows.

"No. I can't talk to the dead, but they communicate with me all the time. The problem is that I can't always understand what it is they're trying to tell me."

"I lost my father a week ago, but you were wrong about one thing." The tension had returned; her shoulders were hunched as she turned the wheel and guided the car through a gap in a line of stationary traffic.

"What was that?"

"He wasn't somebody I loved. In fact, I hated him. I'm glad he's dead, and if you even try to tell me that his ghost wants to apologise for all the things he's done, I'll fucking kill you."

I said nothing more – what was there left to say? I should not have interfered, but over the years I've learned that if I don't then the dead often interfere with me, and the results can be dreadful. So I ask awkward questions and I hurt people with my unthinking demands, but sometimes the outcome is worth the hassle and bad deeds can be laid to rest.

"We're here." She parked the car and got out to open the door for me.

"I'm sorry," I said as I stood from the back seat. "I learned a long time ago to ask first and apologise later."

She nodded and walked away without another word.

I entered the main building and went straight to Tebbit's office. He was on the telephone when I walked in and motioned for me to sit down. I waited for him to finish his call – it was something to do with a case other than the two I'd somehow become involved with. When he put down the phone he smiled at me, but there was little genuine mirth in his face. He looked ill, ashen, as if the tumour inside him was having a good day, eating away at him and taking its fill. I wondered if he would ever feel bad enough to see a doctor, and then remembered how stubborn he was when it came to matters of his health. The promise I'd made his dead wife was still relevant. She wanted him to pass quietly in his sleep, with a minimum of fuss, and not have to worry about anything but his work in the meantime. What I didn't know was if she knew for a fact what would happen, or if she was orchestrating his peaceful demise from elsewhere, a spiritual surgeon assisting her patient's death from another ward in a different hospital.

"You wanted to see me?"

"Thanks for coming. Before I start, though, I have something for you." He reached into a drawer and pulled out a small cardboard box, which he pushed towards me across the cluttered desktop.

"What the hell is this?" I stared at the box as if it were an alien artefact.

"It's a mobile phone. Pay-as-you-go. All you need to do is keep it topped up – the cost of the phone is being covered by us: essential expenses. When I couldn't get in touch with you, I thought something had happened. I thought you might be dead, or something. I don't want that to happen again, not when you're helping us out like this. Call it peace of mind."

"Whose? Certainly not mine, with that thing in my pocket. I'm sorry, but I quite like not being able to have you track me down at all times of the day and night." I reached out and touched the box with my fingertips, as if it might bite.

"Come on, Usher. Take it. As a personal favour to me."

I sighed and picked up the box, took out the phone and glared at it. I looked at Tebbit, at the bones beneath his flesh, the tumour inside his skull, and I nodded. "Okay. A favour to you. Just don't abuse this. I'm a man who values his privacy."

Tebbit rested his hands on the desk and steepled his fingers, pressing the pale tips against his shadowed chin. "The reason I called you here is because Byron Spinks has asked to see you."

Kareena Singh's boyfriend: the man who everyone but me had down for her murder. Two questions came immediately to mind: how the hell did he know who I was; and why did he want to see me? It made little sense, but then again not much of this whole situation did. By now I was just letting it all come at me, fending the blows as best I could and waiting for the next one to fall. I felt like an old boxer returning to the ring for one last fight, but who is unfit to throw gloves with his much younger opponent. All I could do was stand my ground and hope that my technique would get me through to the final bell.

"Well, that one took me by surprise. Did he say why he wanted to see me?"

Tebbit shook his head. "I'm afraid not. He asked for you late last night, apparently after waking up from a bad dream. He was screaming and wailing so much that he woke up his whole cell block, and when they finally calmed him down he begged them to bring you, said he had something he needed to tell you." A clock ticked too loud from its nail on the wall. Sunlight glimmered through the windows. Footsteps ran by outside the office door. "I'm as puzzled as you are, but Spinks was wound up enough that the prison governor got in touch with my DCS on the spot. It's the most the prisoner's said since we arrested him."

"Ah, yes," I said. "An impressive man, your boss. I saw him at the press conference yesterday."

Tebbit sighed; a long, drawn-out sound. "That's another thing I wanted to see you about. What the hell were you doing there,

Usher? I haven't seen you in a year, and then all of a sudden I can't wipe my arse without you handing me the paper."

I'd expected this and had an answer ready. "I was there in a purely personal capacity. A family member, Ellen Lang, asked me to accompany her to the Community Centre. She needed some moral support."

Tebbit looked at me as if I were covered in something unpleasant. "Come on, mate. I don't believe that for a minute. I know that you and Lang are old friends, but I also know that you were there at the direct request of Mrs Royale. I've already warned her to keep you out of this, but for some reason she doesn't want to listen."

The clock had stopped ticking. I glanced at it and for a moment thought that the hands were moving far too quickly around the face; then, abruptly, it started ticking again and everything was normal. "Okay, I'll admit that I was there in a professional role. Ellen asked me as a personal favour. She wants me to see if I can pick up on anything – if the girl, well, I'm sure you get the drift, Tebbit." Even now the antipathy between us could not be held back; despite the mutual respect we had for each other, we shared a vague and complex dislike. It had always puzzled me. Surely friendships weren't meant to be so complicated.

"Just be careful. Please. This is sensitive."

I nodded and placed the mobile phone in my lap. "I do have a favour to ask you. There was a man at the press conference, he ran onto the stage when Mrs Royale broke down. He calls himself Mr Shiloh. What do you know about him?"

"Why do you ask?" Tebbit leaned forward in his chair, his hands parting and opening, the palms pressed flat against the desktop.

"He interests me. I think I might have seen him somewhere before, but can't quite place him." There was no way that I was willing to tell Tebbit exactly where I'd seen Mr Shiloh before, and that he was a possible link between Kareena Singh's death and the disappearance of Penny Royale. I'm still not quite sure why I kept it from him, but the information seemed private in some way, personal only to me. It was an insane notion, yet it felt right.

"We've already checked him out and he comes up clean. He's an immigrant, born in Russia and brought here by his uncle when he was six years old. His parents were killed during some political rally, and the boy was shipped over here for protection. He has no criminal record, so his past is sketchy at best, but we're reasonably certain that he has nothing to do with the girl's abduction, if that's what you're getting at."

"So you're now officially calling it abduction?"

Tebbit's face seemed to flatten. He realised that he'd said too much and let slip information that was supposed to be kept in-house. "You didn't hear this from me, but we now have a witness who says that he saw two men in hoods following the girl home."

At first I thought the clock had stopped ticking again, but it was still going. I could barely speak, but hid my horror well. "Hoods? What, you mean like monks?"

"Don't be silly, Usher. The witness described two youths in dark hoodies following the girl for part of her route and then vanishing minutes before we think she was taken."

"Oh. I see. That puts a new spin on things, then, doesn't it?"

"Indeed." He sat back in his chair, preoccupied – which was the only reason, I think, that he failed to notice my mildly stunned reaction to the mention of hoodies.

"Right then: Spinks. How are you fixed for a prison visit this afternoon? I can come and pick you up myself and we'll get there for around three o'clock."

"That's fine. I'll be ready when you arrive."

"Just one thing." He leaned forward again, serious. "Don't mention any of this to Baz Singh. I know that you're still on his payroll, and that's your business, but what we've discussed here is mine and I do not want some cheap wannabe gangster party to this level of information, even if it does concern his daughter's death. That man is trouble, and I don't want to give him an excuse to get involved more than he already is. Imagine the PR nightmare we'd have on our hands if we had to arrest the grieving father of a murdered girl."

I stood up, sliding the mobile phone into my coat pocket, where it didn't quite fit. "I'll say nothing. This is between you and me."

"Thank you – and I'll see you later. Make sure you stick some extra credit on that bloody phone."

I left the office and walked down the stairs, too afraid to climb into the small metal box of a lift. The world was closing in on me again, and I felt threatened from all corners. The only person I could possibly trust was the woman I'd upset this morning, and I was afraid to make contact with her again until both our emotions were under control. I wished that I could drop the act and go to her, but then I realised that it was not an act at all. I could barely grasp how I felt about Ellen, but one thing was certain: there was love between us, and that counted for a lot, even in a world as dark as this one was rapidly turning.

PART TWO
THE ONLY WAY UP IS DOWN

"Remember you shall die."
Anon

SIXTEEN

It has been said that ghosts exist only because we believe in them, but I'd argue that the flipside of this rather glib theory is equally as true: we only exist because ghosts believe in us.

Before the accident I had not so much as encountered the notion of consensual – or consensus, if you want to be pedantic about it – reality. In those days I was content to plod along like everyone else, believing in the world I saw around me and represented on television, and not even realising that all it took for that version of reality to shatter was for enough people to believe in an alternative.

The world was so simple then: black and white, with easily defined edges. Now it isn't so straightforward, and nothing I see or feel can be trusted. It's all open to interpretation, and sometimes interpretation is all I have to go on.

Our reality – the one we choose to believe in – is merely a layer, and beneath it and on top of it are other layers, each one equally as real. These different realities exist simultaneously, barely interfering with the other layers, but often, where these separate realities touch or fold or crease, seepage can occur. They can even tear or break, and that's where the real problems start.

I'm sorry to destroy everyone's nice rosy view of things, but ghosts are not the forlorn souls of the departed. They are just beings that have transformed and moved on to another layer, and when we catch sight of them what's actually happening is that reality is warping, twisting, folding, creasing – or even tearing apart at the seams.

That's when they come through – the lost ones, the ones who have wandered off the beaten track and somehow crossed over into another layer of reality, our layer. They cling to their old forms, trying to convince themselves that they belong here, but most of them just want to go home. Some of them, however, go looking for trouble and tend to fight against any attempt made to intervene.

Part of my job is to repair the damage, and to help the ghosts on their journey to wherever it is they need to be. The most absurd thing about it is that I don't even know where I'm supposed to be going or how I might get there.

"You're quiet." Tebbit wanted to talk but my thoughts were focused elsewhere.

"Sorry, I'm preparing myself. Trying to clear my mind and attune my senses. I'm sure you wouldn't want me to miss anything."

Tebbit made a noise in his throat that I took as some kind of affirmation. He clearly wasn't sure if I was being serious or not, and to tell the truth nor was I.

We were in an unmarked police car on our way to see Byron Spinks. Tebbit had picked me up, as promised, and I only made him wait fifteen minutes before coming out to meet him – purely for the hell of it, you understand.

The car joined the Armley Ridgeway and we left it at the exit leading to the prison. Tebbit had sorted out the arrangements in advance, so we were expected. The guard on the gate waved us through without so much as a smile as soon as Tebbit announced himself and flashed the requisite ID and paperwork.

I pulled out the mobile phone Tebbit had given me and started to fiddle with it, opening and closing the screen, pressing buttons, holding it to my ear. "It's a wonderful thing, this little device. I know I should hate it, but it's just too damned clever to dislike."

Tebbit chuckled as he negotiated the narrow approach road. "Glad to hear that, Usher. At least I won't have to worry about you going silent on me again."

"I'm touched by your concern," I said, flicking the phone. "I managed to retrieve my own number, charge the thing and top it up with some credit early this afternoon. Did you know there's even a camera on here? I only found out because I accidentally took a snapshot of my left nostril."

Armley Prison loomed large in the windscreen, an intimidating grey stone structure with something of the gothic about its sullen presence. Tebbit stared at the building; there was a look of intense loathing on his face that was softened by what I thought might be admiration. He'd sent so many criminals here, and possibly failed to send so many more, that his feelings regarding the place were clearly mixed.

Tebbit parked the car and we got out, both of us staring up at the jail. The old grey stones were stained by time, holding within them the regretful tears, guilty screams and possibly repentant prayers of all who had been sentenced to spend time there at Her Majesty's Convenience. The place was more haunted than just about anywhere else I had stood: ghosts skulked between the bricks, lay nestled under the rafters, and stared down from the turreted roof as we passed beneath them.

But I wasn't here to see any of them. I was here on other business. The business of the living.

"You look scared." Tebbit stopped and watched me, his eyes narrowing.

"I am. Always. There are so many spirits here… and so much pain and heartbreak. It's a hideous feeling to be standing here, in the shadow of such desperation." I looked at the ground and tried to compose myself, blanking them out. My tattoos were going wild, as if trying to peel away from my skin and go slithering out of the prison grounds. I recited a quick verse I remembered from *The Tibetan Book of the Dead* and then raised my head to stare down the building. The building stared back, not budging an inch, and I realised the folly of my bravado. The best I could hope for here was to get out unscathed.

The check-in process was interminable. Even though Tebbit was a Detective Inspector on a pre-arranged visit, we still had to go through the pantomime of an intensive search-and-question routine. I have my rites and rituals; the system has its own, and their gods, too, must be appeased.

Corners were being cut and people were looking the other way just to get me here, to interview the man alone, but still we had to endure the rigmarole, the pretence that this was all official and above board. Everyone knew that it wasn't; they were all aware of who I was and what I did. The worst kept secret in town, that's me.

Much later I found myself outside a small room with a narrow steel door. On the other side of that door sat Byron Spinks, a man accused of a particularly nasty murder – a man who had asked for me specifically, and who refused to speak to anyone else.

"He's been more or less uncommunicative since he got here. Won't tell anybody anything, and sits facing the wall in his cell chanting some kind of prayer. I didn't even know he was religious until we locked him up." Tebbit walked towards another door, this one made from sturdy timber and with a reinforced glass window framed in the upper portion. "I'll be in here. There's a two-way mirror, and I'll be able to see and hear everything. He said he won't talk unless you're alone. You'll be fine, though. He's cuffed to the table."

I nodded, not sure what to say. Tebbit walked through the door and closed it loudly behind him.

"This way, sir," said the enormous prison guard who stood behind me. His eyes were as hard as stone and he looked like he could bench press Mike Tyson. "I'll be right outside the door so can be in there in a second if you start to feel uncomfortable. I wouldn't worry, though. He's been meek as a lamb since his arrival, apart from that nightmare he had. The only thing he's asked for is to see you." The guard unlocked the steel door and stepped to one side.

I glanced at the guard, smiled, swallowed, and lunged into the room before I could change my mind. It was a very small room and the lighting was poor. One wall was taken up by a huge mirror – I assumed this was the two-way viewing system, and Tebbit and others were even now sitting behind it, studying my every move, absorbing each nuance of every little thing they saw.

The room was like a film set. The walls were painted the standard prison-grey; the ceiling was a slightly lighter shade, and stained with nicotine from a million historical cigarettes. Byron Spinks was sitting behind the desk, silver handcuffs around his big wrists and a chain leading from them to the underside of the table, where it was no doubt fixed to metal rings which were in turn bolted to the heavy piece of furniture. The table legs were bolted to the floor. The chair legs, too: eight bolts, two for each leg.

"Hello, Byron." The door slammed shut.

Byron Spinks blinked at me, his dark-stubbled head looking grimy and swollen. He was wearing a simple grey T-shirt and dark blue jeans – modern prison-issue fatigues. He smiled. "Mr. Usher?"

"Yes, Byron. I'm Thomas Usher. I believe that you asked to see me?"

His smile was genuine. Probably the most unnerving thing about the expression was the fact that it was real, not faked for the occasion. "I'm so glad to see you."

"May I sit?" I indicated the chair opposite.

"Please." He nodded briskly; an eager child keen to have an authority figure join him in his games.

The chair was hard, uncomfortable. My buttocks began to ache after only a few seconds pressed against the moulded plastic surface. "What can I do for you, Byron? I must admit that I was puzzled to hear you'd asked me to come. After all, we don't know each other, do we?"

Other than the sound of our voices, the room was silent. There was no air-conditioning system, not even a fan; and no radiators were fixed to the walls. It would be hot in here in the middle of summer and freezing cold during the winter months. Presently, it was chilly enough for me to leave my coat on but not unbearable.

"I know you," said Spinks. "At least, I know of you."

My throat was dry; it felt like it might close up at any second. "And how is that, Byron? Where have you heard about me?"

The smile did not waver. He clenched his big hands on the desk and I was glad that he was chained. His forearms flexed, the muscles bulging, and I almost expected his biceps to pop. "They told me."

"They? And who are they?"

"Them."

This was getting me nowhere. "Who, Byron? Who exactly do you mean?"

"Them out there and Them in here." He raised a hand to gesture beyond the walls, and then pointed at his own head, indicating that he also meant the voices inside his skull – the ones that perhaps had told him to kill? But no; I didn't believe that. There was more going on here than a simple crime of passion. Intimidating as he was, I doubted that Spinks had killed his girl.

I decided to change the course of the conversation in the hope that it might help me get some sense out of the man.

There was a tattoo on his left bicep, vaguely tribal in design: thick black Olde English lettering in the shape of an M and a T. "That's nice work. I have a few of those things myself."

He glanced at his arm, at the ink, and a look of shame crossed his face. "That's an old one, from years ago. I don't like that any more. I should get it removed. I don't like to talk about it."

I remembered the phone Tebbit had given me. "Do you mind if I take a photograph of your ink, Byron? I like to document tattoos – let's call it a hobby. I like to think of myself as something of a connoisseur of skin art." I had no idea why I was doing this, but there was something about the tattoo that seemed important, and its wearer was not talking. His ink called to my ink like another animal of the same basic species.

"Go ahead," he said. "Knock yourself out."

I took out the phone, fumbled for a while as I tried to locate the correct function, and then took a snap of Spinks's arm. "Thank you." I put away the phone, hoping that I'd managed to save the photograph in its memory.

"I have a message for you," said Spinks. The smile had now faded. His hand dropped back to the table.

"From whom?"

"From Them."

No surprises there, then.

"When did you receive this message, Byron? In here? In the jail? Was it from another prisoner?"

He shook his head; the skull looked so very heavy, heavier even than his conscience. "Last night. I had a dream. One of Them came to me and told me to deliver a message. A personal message. I wasn't allowed to pass it on through anyone else, just to tell you to your face." He shifted in his seat, suddenly on edge. "They said that if I delivered the message They would let me go. That I could be free. I want to be free, Mr Usher. I so want to be free. It's been years since I could call myself a free man, and it's what I've been waiting for." Tears filled his eyes, spilling over onto his sharp cheeks. He didn't wipe them away; just let them fall, an anointment, of sorts, or perhaps a form of self-cleansing.

"So give me the message, Byron." I did not want to hear what he had to say. Everything in me was screaming to get up and leave; my tattoos burned like acid; the voices in my own head were yelling so loudly that all I could hear was a dirge.

Byron Spinks leaned forward, as if he was about to whisper. His eyes were wide, fearful, and yet brimming with hope. "Memento mori," he said, his voice sounding different, the timbre slightly off, the way he formed the words all wrong somehow, as if he were trying to impersonate himself and not doing a very good job of it.

I tried to push the chair backwards, forgetting that it was attached to the floor, and succeeded only in pitching bodily over the side and onto the floor. I scrabbled there on all fours, like a crab, losing all sense of my limbs as they struggled to push me upright. The words echoed inside my head, unlocking doors that should never be opened, moving along passageways that had not seen the light of day in a long time.

Byron Spinks was silent. The smile had returned, but this time it made him look retarded, as if his brain had been fried by an electrical charge. He pursed his lips, as if blowing a kiss, and slowly closed his eyes. There was ash on each eyelid. Black-daubed fingerprints made by a nightmare hand.

I got to my feet and headed for the door, shaken and paranoid and wishing that I had never come here, to this awful place.

"Wait." It was Spinks. He sounded normal again – whatever that word even means. "There's more to tell."

I turned around to face him and waited for the rest. All I wanted to do was leave, but I was deep inside this now – locked inside a crazy whirlwind of events. "Go on." My voice was strained, breathless. I was shaking with adrenalin.

"I didn't kill Kareena."

"I know you didn't, Byron. But who did."

"Them."

I bowed my head, sick of it all. Sick, sick, sick.

"We were out there shooting a homemade porn video. She liked to get it on film, you know. It made her hot."

I kept staring at the floor, waiting for him to tell me something I didn't know or had not already guessed.

Sick.

"I filmed them all at one time or another – all those dead girls."

I lifted my head and looked at him. His face was solemn, almost serene, in the dim light.

"Candice, Sarah and Kareena. I filmed all three. Met them other two at the Blue Viper, and sweet-talked them into going on camera…only Kareena didn't need no convincing. She was already into the scene." His jaw was tight; the muscles there twitched like buried insects.

"What do you mean? How was she already into it? Do you mean pornography? She was into pornography before you even met her?"

Spinks closed his eyes. The ash was no longer there. I could almost believe that I'd imagined it. "She was the one got me into it, wasn't she? I met her first, and she helped me get to grips with the other two. They all knew each other, see. Worked in the club, and then on the films. Films Baz Singh sells through a mail order company and a website that's not even registered to him."

Sick.

"How long had she been dealing in pornography?"

He paused, blinked, and then continued as calmly as if we were discussing the weather: "Since she was twelve. Her dad got her into it."

Sick.

I didn't know how to respond. The words drilled into my temples, going deep into my mind, churning up so much hatred and disgust that I felt nauseous. "Her father? You mean Baz Singh?"

"Aye. Baz Singh. Only he isn't her real dad. She told me once. She was adopted when she was a baby, and they raised her for what she always called a special purpose. As far as I could see, that purpose was shagging. She was such a great fuck… did it like her life depended on it. Liked it any way you could think of. She said her dad showed her all the best moves." The ghost of a smile wafted across his features as he no doubt recalled some wild night in bed with Kareena Singh.

"I have to go now, Byron. But thank you."

"She was a great shag. A bit sick, though, sometimes. But a great shag."

"I know, Byron. I know she was."

Sick.

He kept repeating the words as I banged on the door and waited for the guard to let me out. True to his promise, he was prompt and a few seconds later I was standing out in the hallway, bent double and retching as I tried to rid myself of the image of Baz Singh, my current employer, inducting his own pre-teenage daughter into the dubious pleasures of low-rent pornography.

SEVENTEEN

There are times in life that no matter how fast we run events conspire to change our chosen means of escape. It's like trying to flee whilst wearing roller skates: no matter how quickly you move your legs, or in which direction you turn, the lower half of your body, from the waist down, will follow its own route, steered by those silly little wheels you suddenly realise aren't really that much fun after all.

My own life had been littered with such moments, and this was just one of them.

We were heading back towards Millgarth police station in Tebbit's unmarked car. There was an uneasy silence between us that I could not quite understand, but I put it down to the strange experience I'd just had – and Tebbit had witnessed – with Byron Spinks. The meeting was playing on my mind, causing me to doubt certain things I'd been led to believe. If Baz Singh was the absolute scumbag Spinks had implied he was, then I'd been fooled. Again. People were always fooling me, taking advantage of my lack of connection with them. I understood the denizens of elsewhere all too clearly, but the complex psychological imperatives of my fellow man remained a mystery. I was getting better though, improving my game. I just needed a little more practice.

"That tattoo on his arm. Do you know much about it, what it means?"

Tebbit didn't respond immediately to my question; he kept staring at the road, his face slack and lacking any kind of expression I could name. Then, gradually, he came out of himself, asserting his presence in the moment. "It's a gang thing: a sort of brand. The MT is a street gang, they run around the Bestwick Estate causing us all kinds of trouble, and have done for years."

"I see. I'd guessed as much. What's Spinks's involvement?" The traffic was light, the shops and offices in the area not yet ready to give up their workers. I watched people through their car windows. They all looked so bemused, as if life itself was puzzling them.

"He used to be a member, back when he was in his teens. We arrested him for a burglary and after that he changed his ways and left the gang. Baz Singh gave him a job in one of his restaurants: after-hours security. He built himself up from there and eventually became head doorman at the Blue Viper." Tebbit's voice was strained; he sounded tired and irritable.

"Do you think the gang have anything to do with Penny Royale's abduction? Perhaps the two cases are connected."

Tebbit shook his head, still staring at the road. His eyes were flat and lifeless. "No, they're not into kidnapping, it's out of their league. Your average youth gang doesn't possess the intellect to pull off something like this – they go strictly for the obvious stuff: drugs and robberies and the odd rape." The cynicism was audible in his words, shaping them into something sad and bitter and twisted.

"I'm sorry I couldn't be of more help. I realise that you were probably hoping for a confession." Somebody leant on their car horn and left their hand there; the sound was reminiscent of a child's wailing lament.

"Not your fault, Usher. Don't mind me, I'm just tired. Tired of it all. Dead girls, missing children: the whole fucking thing.

It's endless, like a tide of bad things that we can never hold back, just wade about in the shallows trying to clean up the mess..."

"I know." The car horn stopped abruptly. "I'm sorry. Do you think Penny Royale is dead?"

He paused then, as if he could not quite think of an answer. "I don't know. Do you?"

"I haven't seen or felt her, but that could mean anything. Maybe she's dead and doesn't want to come to me, or perhaps she's still alive and chained to a bed somewhere on that horrible estate." I wished I had not said that. The image it created and held in my mind was almost too much to bear.

We reached the station in silence, and when we left the car Tebbit raised a hand and headed towards the scowling facade of the ugly main building while I walked the other way, along Dyer Street and towards the centre of town. The area around Eastgate was busy so I had to dodge the crowds that were smeared across the footpath as I headed towards the Headrow. I had the weird feeling that everyone was looking at me but averting their gaze whenever I caught their eye. Couples walked slowly, hand-in-hand, ahead of me, solitary pedestrians crossed the street to stand in front of me and block my path and traffic slowed as it drew level with my position.

I began to feel hungry. I could not remember the last time I'd eaten, and my stomach felt light and empty – my head, too. There were countless cafés and restaurants in the area; I just had to pick one and head in that direction. It was too early in the day for a curry, and the last time I'd had a Chinese I had not enjoyed it. Italian sounded good – a pizza, maybe, or a light pasta dish – so I searched my memory banks for a decent place located not too far away from where I was standing.

There was a small Italian café along one of the streets that bisected the Headrow. I had eaten there many times, and despite the place changing owners more times than I changed my suit, the food was never less than excellent. I hurried along the main drag, looking for the correct street, and soon recognised it because of the tiny news stand on the corner that sold hardcore pornography alongside the daily newspapers. I wondered if Kareena Singh might have appeared in one of those skin mags, or if she only ever starred in her father's films...

Cutting along a narrow side street, I crossed the road and passed a second hand bookshop with a "Closing Down Sale" sign in the window, a computer repair centre with whitewashed windows and a boarded up building that I seemed to remember had been a printing firm the last time I'd come this way. The recession was slowly tearing the city apart, piece by piece. But it seemed to me that another kind of recession – one of the human spirit – was developing behind the scenes, and its collateral damage would be even worse.

The café was a few hundred yards up the slight rise, and if you didn't know it was there you could easily miss it. There was no sign above the door, the windows were dark and hung with heavy net curtains, and the front door was nondescript enough to suggest that the building was a residential property rather than a quaint little eatery.

I opened the door and walked in – glad that it was not locked. The counter was at the back of the dining room, and a short slim man wearing too much hair gel was busy with a coffee machine that made noises like a cat choking on a fur ball. He had his back turned towards me, and the sound of the machine was so loud that I decided to wait until he noticed me. Several tables were littered around the room, all set for lunch with plain white tablecloths and simple table settings.

In one corner sat a young couple sharing a pizza. The girl had blue streaks in her shoulder-length dark hair and a ring through her nostril, while the boy wore a smart business suit. This odd couple were feeding each other from a huge central plate, their eyes locked onto one another's face. The only other customer was an older man in a long raincoat who sat near the toilets drinking white wine. There was no food at his table, but two empty carafes sat before him, and the third was already halfway dead.

"Help you?" The man behind the counter was now looking at me, a crooked smile on his thin dark-skinned face. I had not even been aware of the coffee machine going silent.

"Table for one, please."

"Sit anywhere, sir. We're quiet today. Can I get you a drink?" He came out from behind the counter, stepping off the box that he obviously kept there, and I was surprised to realise that he was little over five feet tall, even in his Cuban heels. "Here all right?" he pointed to a table, dragging his arm through the air in what he clearly thought was a dramatic gesture.

"That's fine," I said, and took a seat.

"Drink?"

"I'll have a large glass of house red, please."

The man produced a menu from I don't know where and slipped it onto the table in front of me, then he skipped back behind the counter, hopped back onto his box, and began to pour my drink. He was humming a little tune under his breath as he worked, and I could not help but smile. He brought my wine and took out a little pad and pencil, raising his eyebrows as I tried to decide what I was hungry for.

I ordered a seafood pizza and sat back to wait for the food to be prepared. The man disappeared out the back, where the kitchen was located, and I heard him talking to someone who I assumed must be the chef. They laughed together, a comfortable sound that I found relaxing after the stress of the last few days, and the man did not reappear right away.

I sipped some wine. It was marvellous: plummy and spicy and soporific, as good red wines should be.

I thought about what Byron Spinks had said as I waited. His message had been chilling and once again opened doors in my psyche that I was not quite ready to step through – not again.

I closed my eyes and wondered who "They" might be, and if they were as dangerous as they sounded. Spinks obviously thought so; he'd been terrified when I left the little interview room. Terrified and somehow distant, as if his mind was elsewhere and his body could not quite catch it up.

"I wouldn't worry about him."

The voice came from out of nowhere, and at first I thought that it was inside my head. But when I opened my eyes he was sitting there, opposite me, his hands laid out flat and unmoving on the table and his dark eyes staring right at me. Mr Shiloh; the one man I had not expected to bump into today.

"Pardon me?" I tried to remain calm, pretending that this kind of thing was perfectly natural and not really very shocking at all. The air shimmered around him, as if reality was trying to come apart. He had stepped through a fold, a kink between different states of being, but not in the same way as a ghost. Ghosts get lost, they lose their way; Mr Shiloh was here for a specific purpose and could seemingly move through these metaphysical gaps at will.

"I said not to worry about Spinks. We'll take care of him." His smile was hideous, more like a leer. His plastic face shone greasily under the fluorescent lights and his hands did not move from the table. He was wearing the same dark suit – or another, identical one – as last time I'd seen him, but this time the T-shirt under the jacket was grey. Like the prison walls; like the sky when it threatens rain.

"What are you doing here?" I kept my voice low, calm. The couple in the corner began to giggle, but when I turned around they were silent, stony, and glaring at me. The old man in the corner shifted in his seat, but when I flicked my gaze across at him he was motionless.

"Fascinated, aren't you?" Mr Shiloh's voice held no trace of an accent. The words were dry and clipped, as if he was reciting them from a sheet of paper. He looked bored, vaguely disinterested, and the only reason I knew he was talking to me was because those dark unblinking eyes never left my face.

And that was another thing: the blinking, or lack of it. I'd been with him for a little under five minutes and he was yet to blink. What kind of person doesn't blink every few seconds? It's impossible not to blink; nature demands that we continually moisten our eyes in this way.

But Mr Shiloh did not blink. I doubted very much that he even breathed.

"Fascinated by what?" Still I managed to maintain the illusion of calm.

"By me; by Them." I knew he didn't mean the other customers in the café – although I was indeed interested to know if they were with him or if I was simply imagining that they were acting strangely. No, he meant the same Them that Byron Spinks had been so afraid of.

The man who'd taken my order still hadn't come back into the front of the café. I wondered if he was in on this, too, or if Mr Shiloh could somehow control people's actions, make them move a little bit slower than usual, or force them to carry on a conversation that they might otherwise have ended five minutes before. There was power in this man; I could sense it. I just didn't know what kind of power it was, or what its source might be.

I stared at Mr Shiloh, taking him in properly for the first time. The other two occasions I had seen him, I'd been taken unawares and not had the opportunity to study him, to examine the features that now sat before me, immobile and unknowable as those carved upon an Easter Island statue.

The first thing I noticed was that he had no eyebrows. The fact had not registered before; I'd just known there was something peculiar about his face, beyond the plastic complexion. Nor did he have any trace of stubble. His skin was too smooth, hairless. Staring at him, I failed to detect even the slightest hint of the normal pores that mark the human face. He did indeed look false – like an oversized doll. His hands, on the table, large as they were, also looked all wrong, rubbery; like the hands of an old Action Man doll I used to play with as a child. I imagined that if I were to reach out and grab one of his fingers, bending it back as far as it would go – way beyond snapping point – the finger would simply flick back into place when I let it go. He looked… undamagable. That's the only word I can think of to describe it, and it probably isn't even a proper word.

Consensual reality, but on an individual scale: the ability to make things so by the relatively simple act of belief. If Mr Shiloh believed that he could bend his body back into shape, then who was I to argue?

"Who are you?" At last my voice began to betray unease. I had to force the words out, as if they were large lumps stuck in my throat.

He smiled. He smiled and it was vile, perverted, like the grin of a father before he penetrates his own daughter: a dead, decayed expression that was almost enough to make me vomit. I coughed into my fist, trying to quell the nausea flooding my system.

I looked at my wine glass and saw that it was now filled with blood – there were even small chunks of tissue floating near the surface, and what looked like part of a human ear, possibly the lobe.

It was like a mockery of the Catholic mass: *drink my blood, eat of my flesh…*

"Who are you?" I whispered it this time, as if the answer – when it finally came – would be too fearful to hear; as if the question itself was a form of blasphemy.

"Oh, I'm just a fellow pilgrim travelling the road to enlightenment." There was a note of humour in his voice that was, in many ways, even worse than the plague-ridden smile.

"Mr Shiloh… that isn't your real name. Who are you? What are you?"

"You can just call me the Pilgrim," he said, smiling again.

I didn't know what to say.

"You got my message, I take it. A rather dramatic way of getting it across to you, I know, but so much fun. Such acts relieve the boredom of being down here among the meat, and I'm all for relieving the boredom."

Still I could muster no response.

"Its okay, Thomas, you don't have to speak – not this time. We will have time aplenty to talk, and next time we meet I'm sure you'll have a lot more to say. Perhaps then I'll have more to show you. Just be aware that we have been watching you, and we have been waiting. We've nudged you occasionally across the years, just to make you travel in the right direction, but know ye that enlightenment is close at hand." He let out a soft chuckle, barely there at all. He was having so much fun. "Sooner or later we'll open our hand and show you what we are holding there, glowing like enchanted gold in the palm. Until then, I bid you bon appetite, and hope that you enjoy the rest of the show."

Something strange happened as he stood out of his chair and at first I couldn't quite grasp what it was. As he raised himself up to his full height, looming upwards rather than standing in any kind of natural way, his hands remained flat on the table-top, his arms stretching as he pushed himself up and away from the table. Those hands were still there as he headed for the door; I could not take my eyes off them. Then, finally, just as the door to the café opened, the hands lifted from the smooth table cloth and he looked the same as he had before.

Instantly and blissfully unaware, as if he had only been gone for a few moments, the man from behind the counter arrived with my meal. The pizza was large and flat, with a nicely browned crust, but the stuff on top – the melted cheese, bright red tomato sauce, mussels and prawns and squid – looked like something dredged up dead and decaying from the ocean floor.

...drink my blood, eat of my flesh...

I paid my bill and left, surging out into a day that now felt tainted. There was no sign of the Pilgrim – the being that I now suspected might be my self-appointed nemesis. Things seemed to have returned to what we like to call normality, and the streets were filled with people who, whatever they did to delay the moment, would die some day soon.

Every face I saw hid the shape of a skull, and every skull was a shell encasing nothing but empty air.

EIGHTEEN

There is an old Biblical proverb that states "in the kingdom of the blind the one-eyed man is king". I've never agreed with that way of thinking. To me, the experience of being the only one able to see that which everyone else around you cannot, even if you are only capable of half-glimpses, is terrifying.

It's my life; it's how it feels to be me.

In the kingdom of the blind the one-eyed man is always on the verge of losing his mind, because the things he sees and the company he keeps are almost unbearable…

The early evening rush hour was starting in earnest, so I stayed away from the main drag, wondering why I hadn't simply gone home after the prison visit. Deep down, I knew the answer to that question: Ellen was in the city, and for some reason I wanted to stick close to her location. There was no real threat to speak of – no one had attacked her, or even mentioned her name – but still I felt that I should remain close at hand in case any trouble started.

There was also another reason, and it had taken me longer than it should have to even consider it as an option. It had been a long time since I last called in to see Elmer Lord, and a visit was long overdue.

If anyone could give me more information on Spinks's tattoo, it was Elmer. The man was an expert tattooist, a part-time mystic and practitioner of holistic and other alternative remedies. He had even been known to climb into the ring for the occasional boxing bout. Elmer held a degree in psychology that he had never told anyone about but me, and I was certain that he possessed other qualifications he had mentioned to nobody. A true renaissance man, Elmer had been inking me for as long as I could remember – he had designed and drawn all of my tattoos, and knew the intimate story behind each one.

Elmer had also given me my very first tattoos, the ones that I could now hardly bear to look at. I had gone to him in shame and told him what I had done, then described what I wanted to mark the occasion, and rather than judge me he simply got out his needles and his ink and he began to tattoo me. During that first session, he revealed to me the power that can be summoned by and held within certain designs placed upon the human body – and when I asked him to design something to protect me, he nodded, then got out his pad and began to sketch.

Elmer's new studio – Lord of Ink – was located down near the Playhouse, so I about-faced and began to make my way down to the bottom of the hill, moving in a direction roughly parallel to the busy Headrow. The back streets were much quieter, and the people I saw there were in less of a hurry to get wherever it was they were going. Indeed, some of them were clearly going nowhere at all, just milling about in search of something, but even they probably couldn't tell you what that thing was. Killing time; winding away the hours until something happened to change their lives.

The Playhouse was a construction site, the building webbed with scaffold and with men performing spidery movements across the heights. I stood and watched them for a while, a strange wistful feeling enveloping me. Someone on the roof – a dumpy man in a yellow hardhat – paused in his work to wave at me, and I nodded before moving on and crossing the road at a set of traffic lights. I passed a Japanese restaurant where I'd once been hired to investigate a haunting and a joke shop with wizened green faces strung like a row of grim spectators in the dusty front window.

Lord of Ink was a few yards along a dead-end street. The shop's simple black-and-red-lettered awning shivered in the breeze. I paused in front of the place, examining the colourful tattoo flashes and photographs of Elmer's work that were on show in the neat window display, then I reached out and rang the bell. Elmer didn't run an open house: he worked by appointment only, and was so in-demand that even then you had to come armed with a personal recommendation from a previous customer. He did not do scrolls with the word "mum" at their centre, football badges or cartoon British Bulldogs with spiked collars. The work he chose to create was considered an art form, and he charged accordingly. Elmer had inked rock stars and gangsters, celebrities and lowlifes. Often he turned away potential customers purely because he felt that they had not yet earned their ink.

The intercom crackled. "Yeah?"

"Elmer, it's me, Thomas Usher. Do you have time for a chat?"

There was a long pause before the speaker crackled again, the voice breaking up but still discernable. "Usher? Good God, amigo, I thought you were dead. Come on in – I'm finishing up with a customer, but you can wait a few minutes, yes?"

The buzzer sounded and the inner locking system made a sound like gunshots. I pushed open the door and entered a short narrow hallway, the walls hung with yet more framed photographs which constituted examples of Elmer's more esoteric work. The stuff in the window was for show to the general public: as good as it was, it was bread-and-butter work of a kind he no longer did. This stuff – the real skin art – was spectacular. There were photographs of elaborate back-pieces that were actually prayers made flesh, lifelike portraits meant to act as living tributes to those who had passed over, and countless protective diagrams adorning arms, legs, and even shaved heads (the wearer would then grow his or her hair back to cover the charm, so that its presence was kept secret). A lot of these were based on Southeast Asian and Oriental originals, but Elmer had worked his own particular brand of magic to personalise each one so that it fit the wearer's needs and circumstances.

I reached the end of the hallway and climbed the wooden staircase. A single bulb lit the way, and it was festooned in dusty cobwebs. At the top of the stairs was a door, which I knew would be unlocked. I turned the handle and walked into the infamous Elmer Lord's parlour of pain.

"Usher. Good to see you, my man. Grab a chair and I'll be with you in about ten minutes. Just need to do the finishing touches on this outline." Elmer was straddling a man who sat facing backwards in an old leather chair, his bare back covered in intricate black lines.

"Thanks, Elmer. Sorry to burst in on you like this."

The tattooist did not look up from his work. "Anyone but you, amigo, and I'd send 'em away. You're welcome here any time."

I sat in silence while Elmer finished up, not wanting to distract him. I knew how important the inking procedure was – how it could be a form of spiritualism in and of itself, especially in Elmer's place. Glancing around, I admired the work on the walls. Again, there were countless framed photos and flashes, each one depicting a unique and unusual piece of ink.

The tattoo studio itself was spotless. Despite the bland frontage and the shabby hallway beyond, Elmer kept his workspace in pristine condition. Various spells and purification rites were carried out on a monthly basis, and an elderly Thai woman took care of the accumulation of more earthly dirt once every couple of days.

"Won't be long now. Almost there."

The dark-skinned man in the chair was thin but wiry; he had the body of a lightweight boxer or martial artist. His silken hair was long, worn in a ponytail, and his arms were branded with what looked to me like some form of tribal scarification. He had his eyes closed and his lips moved as he quietly recited something – a prayer or the name of a loved one. He didn't even know that I was there; such was the depth of his meditative state.

Elmer was outlining a huge and intricate mandala on the man's broad back: a complex concentric diagram with a heavily stylised shark at its centre. He glanced up and caught me looking at the piece.

"It's his spiritual self, the form of his unconscious. Inside, under the skin, this man is pure shark…" Then, leaning back and raising the tattoo gun away from his customer, Elmer slapped the man on the base of the spine. "All done, amigo. You can come back in three weeks and I'll begin the colouring."

The man stood and turned before a full-length mirror. When he smiled, I caught sight of gold teeth in his mouth. "Thanks, Elmer. That's good. I'll see you next time."

Elmer gave the thumbs up and watched in silence as the man put on his shirt, a look of sadness blurring his face as his work was covered up. "See you, amigo. And remember to recite that verse – every night until you come back."

The man nodded, gave a strange half bow, and then left without saying anything more.

"There goes the next world kickboxing champion, Usher. Remember his face. He's going to be a big star – trophies, movies, the whole damn lot. I guarantee it." He smiled, quickly and slyly, and then hopped to his feet to embrace me. Slapping me on the back, he shook his head and laughed. "God, it's good to see you, amigo. I really did think something had happened to you."

I smiled, turning away and sitting back down. "I had a rough time, saw some stuff I didn't want to. Some people died. I thought I could stop doing what I do, but recently that's been proved wrong."

Elmer sat opposite me on a large beanbag. "You can never turn away from who or what you are, amigo. That thing you do – the power you have – it defines you. You are what you do and you do what you must."

Elmer was a small man, with long, thin limbs and a squat, slightly rounded torso – I often thought that he resembled a little spider, and had told him so on many occasions. He always found that funny, and one day surprised me by showing me a new tattoo of a black widow on his elbow. Last time we'd met, Elmer's hair had been short and dyed a shade of blonde that was almost white. Today he had a shaven head, which showed off the tattoos at the rear of his skull and a nasty scar that he always joked was the result of a teenage experiment in trepanning. At least I had always hoped that it was a joke. With Elmer, it was often impossible to tell.

We talked for a time about mutual acquaintances and shared experiences, as old friends do, and Elmer cracked open a nice bottle of Laphroaig whisky from his store at the back of the studio. The whisky was a welcome treat, and as the warmth bled down my throat and into my stomach, settling me after my strange meeting in the Italian café, I finally began to relax.

"I must tell you the reason I'm here, Elmer."

He reached over and poured me another two fingers of whisky. "There's always a reason with you, amigo. Never a social call." He grinned, and I knew that there was not a hint of harshness in his words. Elmer Lord and I were both men for whom social visits do not come easily; there is never a time when we are able to ignore what bubbles beneath the surface of things, darkening our time in this life.

"I have to show you something." I reached into my pocket and pulled out the mobile phone, then fumbled to retrieve the photograph I'd taken in Armley Prison. Finally it appeared on the tiny screen, and I handed the phone to Elmer, who rose into a shallow squat to accept it. "Have you ever seen this tattoo before – or one like it?"

Elmer stared at the phone. His expression didn't change but I sensed a mood-shift in the air, as if something large and dark had just passed through the room, casting us in its shadow. His eyes narrowed slightly, then, giving away the trepidation that he was trying so hard to hide.

"Well?" I sipped my drink, attempting to remain relaxed. It was not easy.

"Where did you take this, amigo?" He closed the phone's lid and passed the contraption back to me, and then slumped back into his beanbag.

"You probably know about the Indian girl who was found hanged a few days ago?"

He nodded once.

"Her boyfriend has been accused of murdering her, and this is his tattoo. I went to see him on remand – he asked for me. Told me that he was innocent and hinted that something unnatural was behind it all, that someone else was pulling the strings." I left it at that: Elmer didn't need to know any more.

"This," he said, "is a design I know well, amigo. It's the mark of a gang called The MT. They've hung around the Bestwick Estate for years, putting their fingers in every illegal pie they can find."

"I gathered that from the police, but I thought you might know something more… something that perhaps they don't." Flattery never worked on Elmer, so I didn't go any further along that particular road; I just gently reminded him that I was aware of his vast network of contacts.

"Okay, amigo, I'll tell you what I know." He stood and stretched his rangy limbs, pouring another drink. He glanced at my glass, saw that it was still half full, and put back down the bottle. "The MT is ostensibly a youth gang, muscle for hire, but they also have dibs on a lot of the organised crime in the area. Prostitution. Loansharking. Drugs. Robbery. You name it; they're involved in it somewhere along the line. The thing is, they began life as something entirely different." He walked to the window and tilted the blinds, looking out onto the street below. None of this sounded anything like the hoody-wearing entities that had chased me through the streets of Leeds.

"What does that mean, Elmer? Please, anything you have could be useful. There's a young girl gone missing–"

"Penny Royale," he said. "I heard about it." He turned back to face the room, his eyes filled with a sorrow I'd rarely seen associated with his features. Then I remembered that Elmer's sister had gone missing when they were both very young, and she had never been heard from again. It was part of the jigsaw of his pain; another piece in the puzzle that made up his intriguing personality.

"Yes. And I think that this gang – this MT – are involved in both of these crimes. I can't be certain, but what is certain anymore? I just feel that they are the crux, the locus, of a lot of bad things."

Elmer nodded. He sat back down on the beanbag, seemingly more relaxed. "Back in the 1920s there was a man called Mathew Torrent. He was a local cloth merchant, ran a couple of boutiques in Leeds and Bradford. A rich and powerful man in the local community, by all accounts – what few accounts there are, anyway, because his name seems to have been erased from all public records and official documentation."

I stared at Elmer, wondering where this was going.

"It seems that Torrent was also something of an occultist. His nickname was the Beastly One, and from what I've heard, amigo, he made Aleister Crowley look like a fat children's entertainer." He raised his head and looked at the ceiling, at the fan which circled there almost silently, above the battered leather tattoo chair. "We're talking much more than a few upper class idiots reciting satanic verses and killing chickens, by the way. The Beastly One operated a few notches up from that: ancient rites, demon-raising, blood orgies and even human sacrifice, from what I've heard."

The fan whispered, as if increasing in volume: double beats. I could have sworn that it was saying a name. My name: *Usher-Usher-Usher-Usher…*

"How do you know all this? I've never even heard the name before, and let's face it I mix in a lot of the same circles as you." I wasn't sure if I really wanted to hear any more; and I wanted to hear it all.

"I've tattooed all kinds of people in my time, amigo. You know that. And I never reveal my sources." Again the brief ghost of a smile. And again. Then it vanished.

The fan kept on whispering:

Usher-Usher-Usher-Usher…

"Go on," I said.

"According to local legend – which is, after all, quite possibly all this is – Matthew Torrent set up the MT as a sort of pressgang for potential victims to be sacrificed during his meetings. He handpicked some of the foulest characters he could find, put them through some kind of sophisticated training-come-brainwashing rituals, not unlike the secret al-Qaeda terrorist training camps we have now in this country, and branded them all with his initials. MT: Mathew Torrent." His face went pale, as if he were remembering information that he didn't want to pass on. "They were a nasty bunch, these guys. Very nasty, amigo. They soon latched on to the other meaning of the letters – the fact that it also represented the word 'empty', and began to make sure that's what they were. Empty. Walking voids, bereft of human compassion and driven only by an urge to commit atrocities, each one worse than the last. They would creep about wearing hoods to cover their faces, and in time they even refuted their own identities, becoming a single nameless entity."

I stood and crossed the room to the window where Elmer had been standing only moments earlier. I reached out to the blinds but didn't open them. This sounded more like a description of the thuggish hoodies I had encountered: nameless, faceless, their features masked by darkness. "And this current incarnation is an offshoot of that vile bunch? Is that it?"

I heard the beanbag rustle as he adjusted his position. "This modern lot are nothing compared to the old-school members – they're just problem kids looking for something to hold on to, and the myths and folklore that's grown up around the gang ensures that they are always operating at full strength – there's basically a frigging waiting list to get in. These days it's more like muggings and drug drops than satanic orgies, amigo, but they're still a dangerous crowd."

The room was growing dim; the sun must be going down outside. I had not even realised how late it was. "What happened to Torrent? How come he's been expunged from the records?"

Elmer was now standing behind me. I could smell his whisky breath. "There are a few stories, but the one that crops up most often is that he had a sister, a child his mother had given birth to before she died under suspicious circumstances back in mother Russia, where they originally came from – they were part of some kind of exiled political group who came to England for asylum. After he managed to escape, Torrent sent for this infant sister. He got her out, and he raised her as his own child.

Nobody knows the name of this girl, the sister, but I've heard corroborating stories from two independent sources that she was killed and Torrent left the area. Because of his bad rep, he was kind of erased from local history. His actions were considered an embarrassment by even the criminal classes, so everyone played ball and he wasn't even spoken of in the worst kinds of pubs and ale houses."

I turned. Elmer was right in front of me. "Killed? How?"

"Another Russian immigrant with mental problems thought she was entering his dreams, and he abducted her. He took her out to a hill somewhere, lashed her with ropes into the branches of a tree, and set fire to it. He burned what he thought of as the witch – Baba Yaga, he said, was her real name, and he swore that she was evil, an ancient Slavic bad spirit in human form."

I almost fell down; my legs began to ache, my ankle bones crumbling to dust.

Burned. In a tree. Burned, probably to ash.

Burned.

"Usher, are you okay, amigo? It's an upsetting story, yes, but I'm sure you've heard worse." He grabbed my shoulders and gently pushed me across the room, to the tattoo chair. I rubbed my cheeks, my chin, scratched at my throat. "What is it?" Elmer's face had darkened; I was touched by this show of genuine concern.

"Something you said… it just hit a spot, you know. Pushed a button." I tried to smile but it didn't work. I probably looked like I was grimacing.

Russia. Witch. Tree. Ash. It was alike some twisted children's rhyme, the words spinning through my head on a repeating loop: *Russia-witch-tree-ash. Russia-witch-tree-ash. Russia-witch-tree-ash.*

Elmer walked around the chair and stood before me, his tattoos glowing in the dim light and his small eyes looking tired but not quite empty. Not quite MT.

"There's one more thing," I said, arching my back and shuffling in the chair. "Have you ever heard of a man called Shiloh? He calls himself Mr Shiloh."

Elmer shook his head. I knew he was telling the truth; that he had never heard the name before. I could see it in his face, in his eyes, and in the way he had answered without pause. Here was something that even Elmer Lord possessed no knowledge of; a person whose identity the best scavenger of information I knew could not even help me with. I felt cold. The fact that Elmer didn't know who Mr Shiloh was seemed somehow more unnerving than the story of Mathew Torrent and his terrible gang of abductors.

"Who is he, amigo?" said Elmer. "Who is this Mr Shiloh?"

I thought of the mandala Elmer had been creating when I arrived. The shark at its centre, with a grin not unlike the one I had faced over a small café table not long ago.

I got to my feet, only a little unsteadily, and placed a hand on my friend's arm. "I truly don't know, but I have a feeling that he wants me to find out... and he's enjoying the mystery."

NINETEEN

Elmer saw me to the door and down the stairs into the grubby little hallway. We didn't speak until we had reached the main door to the street, and even then all we managed was a couple of goodbyes and a see-you-later. Elmer watched me as I walked down the street, heading back towards the bottom of Eastgate. I didn't turn around to acknowledge his gaze.

The sky had darkened a few shades and clouds had moved in to provide a lid to the world. Traffic was slow-moving. I passed the aftermath of an accident involving a moped and a white van. Two men sat on the kerb, one of them with his head in his hands and the other walking in slow circles, sucking on a cigarette.

I reached the Crowne Plaza Hotel, where Ellen was staying, and stood staring at the building's hideously modern façade. There were a million reasons why I shouldn't go in there and only one why I should – yet that single pro outweighed all the cons as easily as one evil deed measured against ten good ones in the fabled scales of justice.

And when the memories came, I was unable to stop them.

Ellen drives the rented van because I am still unable to get behind the wheel of any vehicle without either weeping uncontrollably or throwing up: a strictly Pavlovian response which embarrasses me more than anything else about this whole situation.

I have not driven since the accident, and have no plans to start again any time soon. I watch the side of her face as she negotiates the insane road system, heading somewhere called Marsh Farm on the outskirts of Luton. We already know that it is an unpleasant area with a bad reputation, known for a high percentage of street crime and problem families, but we have made the decision to travel there. *I* have made the decision after a long conversation with Ellen in my rented caravan where she told me that if I didn't do this she would walk out of my life forever.

I don't know why I was unable to let her leave, but the important thing is that I wanted her to stay. She is my friend; she means everything to me. I do not want her to view me as a lost cause, even if that's exactly how I feel.

It is night. The streetlights are primary smears against an urban backdrop of inner-city ruin. We enter a grubby suburb, and soon the only buildings around us are high-rise residential dwellings: the slums of the future, and some that have already become the present-tense definition of that term.

The streets are barren, like a set from a film, apart from a few tired-looking teenagers outside a row of boarded-up shops. They watch us as we pass, their eyes dead, and I feel a sudden surge of adrenaline enter my system. Fight-or-flight: the instinct for self-preservation. It's like being on an animal reserve, or a safari park in deepest Africa, where even though the beasts are enclosed within a compound they are still close enough to the wild state to be considered dangerous.

"We're almost there," says Ellen, keeping her eyes on the road. She looks scared, her face a pale blob in the darkness, and when a cluster of fireworks go off somewhere to our right, on a dark stretch of waste ground behind some houses, she jerks in shock, as if the sound were a series of gunshots.

"It's okay, Ellen. We're safe."

She turns to me and smiles, light from one of the streetlamps stitching the side of her face with shards of white. Her blue eyes are large and, I think, rather beautiful; she looks like a woman I might have fallen in love with had the timing been right when we first fell into bed together.

She looks like someone I might have loved a long time ago.

Ellen parks the car in a space outside a ten-storey block of flats. All the windows on the lower levels are either smashed or boarded up with timber sheeting. We sit there for a few moments, not speaking, just waiting. The night lets out a breath; in the distance, a dog barks incessantly; the chesty sound of a small, ragged engine approaches and then slowly fades away.

"Are you ready?" She places a hand on my thigh.

It is a simple question, but one that I fear I cannot answer. "You tell me." I turn to her, cocking my head to one side in a gesture of bemusement.

"It's enough that you're here, that you're willing to try this. It could be the thing that saves your life."

I rest my hand over hers, squeezing it tightly. "It might also be the thing that finally destroys me."

We leave the car and cross the car park, walking over shattered glass, crushed plastic bottles, discarded condoms and flattened cardboard boxes. A young girl is perched on a concrete bollard at the end of the long, thin pathway that leads to the building's main entrance. She is openly smoking a joint, and she stares at us as we pass within touching distance. "You police?" she asks, glaring at me.

I shake my head but do not speak. Ellen grabs my hand and holds on tight. The girl tells us to fuck off and then laughs manically, swinging her legs and slapping the bollard with the soles of her feet.

The foyer smells of old urine and dirty sheets. The elevator is broken so we have to use the stairs. Four flights, past all

kinds of rubbish: an old fridge on the first half landing, its door
open to reveal black mould shaped like a human face, a child's
doll with its legs removed and its eyes gouged out, what at first
looks like a dead cat but proves to be a mutilated teddy bear,
several dirty syringes. The lights in the stairwell are working,
but only just: ascending the stairs is like climbing through the
different levels of a strobe effect, and I imagine for a moment
that we are entering some kind of weird themed nightclub, a
post-modern study in urban squalor.

"Flat Number 411," says Ellen, breaking the uneasy silence.
There are no sounds from behind the apartment doors, as if
their inhabitants are poised on the other side, listening to us,
trying to guess who is coming – friend or foe – from the rhythm
of our footsteps on the concrete floor. I cannot rid myself of the
image of many people crouching behind those doors, ears
pressed to the wooden panels, listening to us as we pass.

Crouching and listening. Licking their lips.

Soon we are standing outside the door to Flat Number 411.
I look at the metal numbers fastened to the wooden door, the
way they have slid sideways because one of the screws has
fallen out. I imagine what kind of man is behind that door – is
he a monster, or simply an empty shell who is suffering because of what he has done. I am not sure which option I prefer,
but I know that a monster will be easier to hate.

"Ready?" Ellen leans against me, her shoulder brushing the
top of my arm.

I nod. My mind is numb; my heart is racing; my blood is
thin and fast in my veins.

She reaches out to knock on the door, but I grab her hand
to stay the action. "No. I'll do it. It should be me."

I take a long, deep breath, look down and close my eyes.
And then I look back up, at the door, at the crooked numbers
that should mean so much but actually mean so little. I knock
on the door, three times, briskly: a charm. Then we wait.

We wait.

I wait.

It takes ages for someone to answer the door, but eventually it opens, moving slowly on silent hinges to reveal a ribbon of darkness beyond. I stare at that band of black, and bit by bit a face takes shape, shimmering forward like an image from a nightmare. The man is very pale, with gaunt features. He has short hair – the kind that looks like it is falling out because it is so thin and unmanageable. His eyes are coloured such a light blue that they look almost grey, and he has thin, wispy stubble on his chin.

Not a monster, then. Not a monster, but a man; or a monster dressed as a man.

Ellen takes the initiative: "Mr. South? Mr Ryan South?"

The man nods that long death's head, becoming all too human, and suddenly vulnerable. He shuffles backwards, his skinny body retreating a few hesitant steps inside the apartment as he opens the door wide. "Please," he says – mutters, really. "Please, come inside."

I feel that if I take one step forward I might tumble into an abyss, but Ellen – dear, dear Ellen – is there to catch me, to steady my body and my nerves. She holds my hand, refusing to let go even when I try to pull away from her. "No," she says, only once. But it is enough to tether me to the moment, and to reshape the reality that was threatening to skitter away from me and transform this meeting into something else entirely – something from a bad dream that never, ever goes away.

Ellen leads me along the hallway, past the grim walls with their outdated coverings and dusty framed pictures, the old-fashioned radiators that the council have not yet replaced, and the stained and peeling skirting boards. The carpet beneath my feet is filthy; little puffs of dust shoot up with every footfall. Cobwebs gather in the corners; dirt streaks the walls and paintwork.

"This way. In the kitchen. It's the only room I keep tidy these days. I'm afraid I can't manage much more." Ryan South moves slowly, like a man in his eighties. I know for a fact that he is twenty-nine, but even his appearance gives the impression that he is an old, withered man whose time left on earth is limited.

We move to the door at the end of the hallway, and on into the kitchen. The room, as promised, is cleaner and brighter. A table has been set for tea, but it looks as if a child has carried out the task. Small cups and saucers like those used by old women in sheltered housing; tiny cakes with fancy sugared icing; a chipped plate stacked with cheap biscuits.

Cheap. It is all so fucking cheap.

In that moment I feel such an exquisite sense of sadness, and an unwanted surge of empathy towards this man. He regrets so much of what he has done, what he has caused, and knows of no way to make things better. So he struggles on, with his chipped plate and his cheap biscuits, and he clings to the hope that someone else might make the situation better for him.

And that someone, no doubt about it, is supposed to be me.

We sit like schoolchildren playing house as South pours the tea. It is dark, stewed, but Ellen thanks him anyway. I remain silent, not yet trusting myself to speak. This wreck, this man-child, is the tawdry reality of what I had built up to be a ferocious demon in my mind. All this time, recovering in hospital, and afterwards, as I climbed nightly inside a bottle, I pretended that he was a huge beast of a man, a snaggle-tooth dinosaur who licked the blood of my family from his lips and laughed as he did so.

But here he sits, this Ryan South, this destroyer of worlds, and the only word that comes to me is: pathetic.

"I… I'm glad you could come." He is speaking to me but looks at Ellen, as if he can't quite bring himself to see my eyes in case the faces of my dead family are reflected there.

Pathetic.

Ellen turns to glance at me, sipping her tea.

"I thought it might help. If I saw you… confronted you." The words hurt like razors being drawn from my throat. One by one, they slice the flesh.

"And am I what you expected? Am I a monster?" It is as if he is reading my mind.

I look at Ellen, then back at South. Ellen is still looking at me, so she doesn't see it, but for a split second I am convinced that when I turn back towards him, Ryan South is sticking out his tongue. I blink, utterly taken by surprise. "No," I say. "No, I don't see a monster before me. I see a ruined man." His tongue was triangular, pointed. I am sure of it. But no, how could that be? It's impossible.

South finishes his tea and pours another. He is weeping now; his cheeks are wet and his eyes are shining. "I haven't been able to leave this flat since it happened. I'm trapped here – imprisoned by my own remorse."

Is it just me, or do his words sound rehearsed, like he's reading aloud from a pre-prepared speech? I cannot quite pinpoint what it is about his voice, but there is a certain inflection, or lack of it, that reminds me of a newsreader or perhaps an actor not quite ready for the main roles but experienced enough to carry off character parts.

"Shall I leave you two alone? To talk?" Ellen begins to stand.

"No." The word comes out louder than I expected, and Ellen is shocked into immobility. She hovers with her backside a few inches above the hard wooden seat, unsure whether to complete the act of rising or to let herself fall back into the chair.

Again, when I look over at South he has an odd expression on his face. It looks like he is gurning: his mouth hangs open, the pointed tip of tongue lolling from between his thin lips, and I swear that he is giggling silently.

Not so pathetic after all.

"Please, Ellen, stay. Stay with us. Look at him."

She looks at me; at South. He is normal again, that sad, flat face churning out waves of despair. What is going on here? Am I experiencing some kind of breakdown? Perhaps the idea of finally meeting the man responsible for the deaths of my wife and child has led to some kind of mental burn out – a blown fuse in the damaged circuitry of my brain.

"I'd just like to say that I'm sorry. So deeply, deeply sorry." His eyes bulge and sparkle, as if he is holding in laughter.

Ellen sees nothing. She nods at me, urging me to respond. As far as she is concerned, there is some righteous healing taking place, and she will not rest until I open myself to its power.

What a heap of shit; what a travesty.

The ceiling light flickers and Ryan South seems to move bonelessly in his chair, his arms slithering across the table. His face is so pale now that it is white – albino. His lips are jet black and his teeth are pieces of coal stuck into his swollen gums. The flickering stops, and once again the man seems exactly as he was when first we entered his apartment: a carefully drawn portrait of sorrow and regret.

Pathetic once more.

I glance around the kitchen, past Ellen's caring face, and watch as something rises from the sink. I can see the sides of the metallic bowl, the mixer tap, and a dark, bulbous shape as it lifts itself from the drain, inching towards the surface. When I blink the vision is gone; there is nothing there but a slightly scratched sink with a bent tap.

"Ellen?"

She smiles at me, her eyes filled with concern. "What is it, Thomas? Do you have something you need to say?"

I look at Ryan South, at his narrow face and his wispy hair; his mouth is twisted into what I can only think of as a snarl. "What happened out there, that night? Out on the road?"

Ellen faces him, and he once again adopts the attitude of a remorseful killer. "I… I still don't know. I'd been to a party, but I

wasn't drunk or stoned – not that night. I passed the breathalyser
test when the police arrived. It was all so... weird. One minute
I was driving along the road at a steady pace, listening to some
music, and the next I was hurtling the wrong way through some
roadworks. I have no idea how I got turned around... I blacked
out... like I wasn't even me anymore." He begins to sob, his hands
making fists on the table. His nails are very long, like those of a
guitar-player. There are dark hairs across the back of his hands,
a thick hatched pattern that worries me but I do not know why.

"That's okay, Ryan. You can cry. It might help." Ellen
reaches across the table and grasps his hairy white hand. I
almost push her away, but I know that would be madness.

But, then again, this whole situation is mad.

"I'm sorry... you should be the one crying. Not me." His
eyes flick upwards, and through the tears I see something stir:
a huge darkness peering from behind his skull. Now I know;
at last I am certain. Everything I have seen is real.

"We should go," I say, at last. I stand and kick away the chair.
It upturns and clatters on the floor, making a sound that seems
deafening in the enclosed space. "We should go now, Ellen." I
lurch out of the kitchen and down the gloomy hallway, knocking pictures off the walls and banging into a radiator that hisses
at me as I veer away, raising my arm in a protective stance. The
pictures lie face up on the floor. Now that the dust has been
disturbed, I can see that they are all images of death. Mono-
chrome photographs of people lying in state, arms crossed, eyes
stitched shut, like Victorian death poses. Anatomical sketches
of a baby holding open a wound in its sternum. A naked man
on a mortuary slab, one of his legs peeled away to the bone.

Ellen follows me, apologising to Ryan South, telling him
that it will be better next time. When I look back at the pictures on the floor I see landscapes and still-life studies: fields
and meadows and fruit in bowls – an accumulation of Pound
Shop tat which serves as a façade of normality.

But for a moment I saw through the lie, and stared into the depths of another place, an alternative reality. And in that moment I knew... I knew.

Back in the car, driving away from the high-rise, I glance over my shoulder for one final look at the festering nest of nightmare. On the fourth floor, from an upstairs window that I know – just know – belongs to Ryan South, I see a china-doll face so thin that it is painful to look at staring at me from the darkness, an expression of utter delight twisting its features into a demonic mask.

The face pulls back, swallowed by blackness, but its image lingers on my retina like a photographic double exposure.

Finally I am sure. At last I know that I am not losing my mind. The things I see, the ghosts that hover at the edges of my vision – real. All real. Every bit of it.

Once we are off the estate and onto safer ground, Ellen pulls over at the kerb. She parks opposite a fast food place and I watch the young customers queuing for their pizzas and kebabs and burgers. Tears pour down my face, my neck. Ellen reaches for me, pulls me into her embrace. "There, there," she murmurs into my ear. "There, there, Thomas. I'm proud of you. That can't have been easy." She smells of fresh sweat. The side of her neck is damp and smooth. "Can't have been easy..." Her hands are shaking.

No, it was not easy. Not easy at all. But next time I will come prepared, and it will be the easiest thing in the world to face my demon. Because now I know who he is, or at least what he looks like – and I will recognise him anywhere, even if he hides in plain sight, just as he has done tonight.

Darkness surrounds us, pressing against the car, but I am finally at ease with the night and whatever it contains. Now, I realise, there are much worse things than simple darkness.

TWENTY

Staring up at the Crowne Plaza Hotel, I retreated from the memories. It was not time – not yet. Soon, yes, but not now. Dusk had turned to evening, had become night, and the hotel windows were ablaze with illumination. I tried to guess which one was Ellen's room, and if she was in there, but couldn't even recall on which side of the building it was located.

Then, in one of those strange quirks of circumstance that you think happen only in books and films but actually happen all the time in real life, my mobile phone rang. I looked at the number on the screen but did not recognise it.

I pressed the button to answer the call and raised the phone to my ear. "Hello?"

"Thomas. It's me." Of course it was her; it couldn't have been anyone else.

"Hello, Ellen. I've been meaning to call you."

"Me, too," she said, and there was a crisp lightness to her voice that made me glad I was there, only yards away from where I hoped she was sitting or standing or lying on the bed with the hotel phone in her hand, rubbing one bare foot along the opposite shin. Perhaps she was even looking out of the window – which I suddenly remembered was indeed situated at the front of the building. Hadn't I stared out of it only last night to watch Mr Shiloh watching us?

"Where are you?" I looked across the road, judging how many minutes it would take me to get over there, how many steps it was from one kerb to the other.

"At my hotel."

"Me, too."

She laughed and I was in the middle of the road, moving across at a jog, and then landing safely on the other side. "I'll meet you in the bar in five minutes," I said.

Entering the hotel, I glanced at the sofas in the foyer to see if the same Eastern European women where there from before, but the sofas were empty. Few people were present on the ground floor, but as I looked up I saw a handful of residents moving between floors, crossing landings and ascending the wide, carpeted staircase.

I made my way to the bar and ordered a pint of bitter. The area was empty apart from a suited man with an open laptop resting on his table and a middle-aged couple who were chatting quietly in one corner. I took my pint to the table farthest from the other customers and sat on a stool to pretend to watch the muted sports programme on the wall-mounted television screen above the fruit machine.

Ellen came in when I had swallowed only half of my drink. She looked trim and relaxed in dark blue jeans and a pale blue open-necked shirt that went well with her flashing blue eyes. Her hair was pushed back from her face, and she was wearing very little makeup. Either she didn't want to make too much of an effort for me or she was confident enough that she looked good without the slap on her face. The latter seemed a pretty safe bet, as she had never gone in for elaborate beauty routines. She was what my old man would have called a natural heartbreaker.

"Hi," she said, slipping onto the stool opposite. Her neck was flushed. Her eyes jittered around the room, unable to settle on my face.

"Drink?"

She nodded. "That would be good. Get me a half of whatever you're having."

I returned to the bar and ordered another pint of my own to go with Ellen's smaller glass, and then brought both drinks back to the table.

"Cheers," said Ellen, raising her glass and taking a swallow. "That's nice."

"Listen. I just want to say something before this gets even more awkward between us than it is now. I mean, I suppose I want to apologise." I gripped my glass but didn't pick it up.

"Apologise for what?" Her eyes flashed, but I couldn't quite read the emotion bristling behind them.

"For not treating you with the respect you deserve. For failing you as a lover. For... for last night." I paused, trying to judge the reception.

"It's okay, Thomas. I do understand how you feel, you know. Remember, I was there from the start of this thing. I know how guilty you still feel about Rebecca and Allyson – guilt about what happened between you and me all those years ago, and guilt about the accident. I'm sorry, too. I shouldn't have pushed you." She licked her lips, betraying her nerves.

I sighed, finished my first pint and took a sip of the second. "Yes, I do feel guilty about us – about the past. If Rebecca and Ally were still alive, I probably wouldn't feel it so intensely, but it all got mixed up with the accident. My feelings for you have always been... complicated. My family's deaths simply made them even more so. I... Jesus, I just don't know how to do this, what to feel, what to say. It's all such a mess, inside here." I pressed a hand to my heart, trying so desperately to make her understand things that even I couldn't get a grip of.

"Let's just enjoy our drinks and see what happens. We've been dancing around this thing for so many years that it's bound to feel weird now that we've stepped over the line. I don't want you to hurt any more than you always do." She sipped her bitter. Her lips were beautiful.

"Is that how I come across? Like a hurting man, someone in constant pain?"

She leaned across the table, her eyes now piercing right through me. "Yes, Thomas, that's exactly how you come across. It's what you are. I don't think I've ever seen anyone who carries so much pain around with them, and as far as I can tell you have no one to share it with. You're God's lonely man, a person whose troubles run so deep that they've become like blood, like oxygen. Take away your pain, your guilt, and there's nothing left to drive you. And I don't want to be responsible for that."

The couple in the corner stood up and left. The man with the laptop tapped at his keys, lost in whatever paperwork was so important that he worked on it in a hotel bar instead of enjoying an evening meal or meeting up with friends or colleagues.

I blew air out between my lips and ran a hand through my short, dry hair.

"For a long time the thought of seeing Rebecca and Ally again – the hope of glimpsing their ghosts – kept me going. It was the reason I didn't take a long dive off a high bridge or go to bed with a gun in my hand. Then, gradually, the grief and the remorse turned into something else. I've learned so much since this stuff started happening to me, and the most important thing I have discovered is that death is not the end. It's not the beginning, either. It's just... another thing, the next thing, an experience we all go through.

"It's difficult moving on when I know that my family are still there, that they still exist, and all I need to do is open the right door..." I took a long swallow of my beer to hide the tears that

I could feel trying to spring forth. It was the first time I had spoken of this with anyone, and rather than feeling like a burden being lifted it felt like a lid being opened, the contents of an old, secret box exposed to the air, where it might suddenly turn to rot.

Ellen sat back on her stool, crossing her legs. "Wow, Thomas, that was… intense."

I smiled, despite the stew of emotions behind my words. "I know. I've never told anyone that. You should feel honoured."

"I do understand, you know. Not all of it, of course, because all the strange stuff that surrounds you scares the hell out of me, but the rest of it – the deep wounds and the emotional torment – I can get my head around."

I ordered more drinks and we relaxed. We even chatted about her time in America. How she had first been drafted in to work with trainees on the US space programme because of her expertise in the physiological studies of weightlessness and other esoteric interests she had developed when studying medicine, and been surprised by how quickly her career had taken off. She was happy, she said, and there had been a few men, but nobody important, nobody special.

It seemed to me that there was a profound emptiness in her life, and that she filled it with work. But her journey over to England because of the disappearance of Penny Royale, her cousin's child, whom she barely even knew, spoke volumes about the things she secretly craved.

We all have our secrets, and often it takes but a single phone call to lay them bare.

"Have you eaten?" she asked me, eventually. I told her that I hadn't even thought about dinner, and she insisted that she treat me to something there at the hotel. We adjourned to the dining room, and continued to skirt around the issue that stood between us like the decaying corpse of an elephant in the room – the fact that, although it had not yet been mentioned, I was staying the night.

After dinner we had some brandy and held hands across the table. The intimacy felt right this time; it no longer felt dirty, a grubby little affair to be ashamed of. It felt real and wonderful and like something I had been searching for without even re-alising. I even entertained the thought that I might return to America with Ellen, set up and start again, putting the ghosts – my own and those belonging to others – behind me for good.

Such is the folly of romance.

It was late when finally we retired upstairs. I took the lead this time, just as a man should, and I held her hand tightly as we walked along the landing to her door. She glanced at me before slipping the key-card into the lock, and we shared a smile when the green light above the handle failed to illumi-nate. Ellen wiggled the card a few times, and eventually the light came on, the locking mechanism clicking loudly to allow us access.

The room was dark, the curtains were drawn. We lay down on the bed and just held each other for a while, allowing the moment to take its own shape and develop its own momen-tum. When we kissed it was with a hunger that was almost frightening: her tongue pushed between my lips; I bit down on its end, causing her to draw breath and moan.

This time the sex was better – not perfect, but better. We found a rhythm and stuck with it, moving with a lack of ur-gency but an excess of passion. I came first, but she was not too far behind. In time, I knew, we would find the perfect mid-dle ground and we might be good together – at least as good as we were outside the bedroom, and when we both stopped trying so hard to pretend that we were no good to anyone, even ourselves.

Ellen fell asleep in my arms. I watched her in the darkness, picking out the side of her face and her sharp cheekbones. Lift-ing the bedclothes, I stared at the curve of her back, the way it sloped down to her firm, large buttocks, and then admired her trim thighs. She shifted on the pillows, her face coming round towards mine, and she opened her eyes. I knew she was still asleep, that this was simply a nocturnal twitch, but it felt good to have her watching me.

I kissed her cheek, the side of her mouth, and ran my hand along her waist. I think I probably dozed off for a while, comfortable with the position we had adopted, and when I opened my eyes again I knew that it was late, approaching the early hours. There is a certain fragile quality to the darkness at that time of the night, a caught breath that hangs in the air, waiting for something to happen.

I knew without looking that someone was standing at the end of the bed; the only information I did not have in my possession was the identity of this third person in the room. I rolled slowly onto my back and peered into the darkness, my eyes adjusting to the black space. The furnishings came into focus first – the bedside cabinet, the chair by the window, the tall wardrobe standing farther along the same wall – and then the shape of the figure sketched itself into the gloom. It was a man – I was sure of that – and he was standing a foot or so away from the end of the bed with his arms held straight down by his sides.

"Who is it?" I whispered, afraid but curious. The figure shuffled, taking a tiny step either backwards or forward, towards the bed. Then, at last, I recognised the contours of a face I had only ever seen a few times in my life, and each of those was a recent sighting.

The figure at the end of the bed, watching us in silence, was Byron Spinks, the man accused of killing Kareena Singh (and no doubt, in time, the other two hanged girls).

"Hello, Byron. What can I do for you?" I held the panic inside, wondering how on earth he had managed to escape from the jail, and why Tebbit had not called to warn me that the man was on the run. Then, as I came fully awake, I began to realise my mistake. This was not really Byron Spinks before me. It was his ghost. Byron Spinks was dead, and like so many others in his position, he had come to see me.

I climbed out of bed and walked towards Spinks, acting much stronger and more confident than I actually felt. He turned and moved towards the bathroom. The door opened before him, swinging outward before he had even reached it, and the light came on. The illumination was meagre, barely real light at all: more like a torpid flame flickering from a place I did not want to see. I noticed that Spinks was naked, and that he had blood on his back.

I stood and stared, knowing that I would follow. I always did, in the hope that I could help. It was what I did, what I was supposed to do.

Spinks entered the bathroom and seemed to vanish from sight, as if the small, rather cramped room had suddenly become infinite. I followed him inside, certain that I had little choice in the matter. Whichever way I tried to turn, I knew that the bathroom door would be waiting for me, and it would not close until I used it.

The room was immense. The usual bathroom fittings of bath, shower rail, sink and toilet had been erased, and the only familiar item to remain was a mirror of tarnished glass. My bare feet skimmed across something soft, like a powder – or perhaps ash. The weird sketchy light flickered as I approached the mirror, and once I was standing an arm's length from it, the murky glass began to clear. Byron Spinks stood inside the mirror. He was a reflection of nothing, a copy of the man who would never physically stand anywhere again, certainly not in the same form he had occupied since birth.

"Why have you come to me, Byron? What is it you want me to see?"

This close, and now that the darkness had lifted, I could clearly see his wounds. There was a slash across his chest, dried blood smeared above and below it. His throat had been gouged, but the wide rent was dry. One of his eyes was gone, and in its place there was a ragged black hole.

"What is it?" I kept my nerve; I always do, somehow.

Over his shoulder an image began to form out of the greyness. A vast open area, like a field, but burned, razed, leaving only the charred stumps of trees and bushes and blackened grass. Far in the distance, shimmering gently, was a hill, and upon that hill was a burning tree. The shape writhing in the flames had once been human, but now it was merely an approximation of the human form. And before it was human it had been something else. The geometry of that former self was struggling to be born again in the blistered mass that danced at the heart of the pale fire.

Fear threatened to overwhelm me, but I sucked it up, chewed and swallowed. This was my job; it was what I did. I had to see it through.

Spinks held out his arm in an expansive gesture, as if he were offering me this sight as a gift. To the left of the hill something staggered into view. At first I could not tell what it was, but despite the spastic movement it didn't seem like an animal.

Then, gradually, the thing hove into frame.

It had four hideously long scrawny legs, like those belonging to a giant chicken, and perched atop those ugly clawed limbs was a crude hut with no doors or windows. There was, however, a single stunted chimney sticking up from the pitched roof, and from it poured a ribbon of black smoke that coiled and entwined with that of the fiery tree.

I recalled my visit to Elmer Lord, and that he had mentioned the Slavic spirit of Baba Yaga. I knew that the spirit was said to have lived in a similar chicken-legged house with no doors or windows, and that she entered by the chimney. But I also knew that these old myths and folktales were simply created by mankind to codify the things that we cannot understand: comforting visual touchstones meant to hide the multitude of possible truths, yet which lie in wait like spiky borders to the pathways of a terrible maze.

Every witch and warlock and monster is just a mask for something worse. Behind all the stories, under all the great archetypes, hide the things which we all fail to see or believe in – the tumultuous landscapes our consensus renders unreal. But everywhere there is a great and languid darkness, and beneath that there is yet another darkness, and on and on with no real end. Layers of reality, levels of existence, and the only thing standing between what we know and what we cannot know is our unquestioning belief in the world we choose to see around us.

The absurd little hut tottered on its oversized chicken legs, the whole surreal construct unstable and ready to fall. It stumbled forward onto one knee, then the other, and the heavy upper part crashed to the ground, shattering into separate pieces – pieces that became smoke and drifted over towards the flaming tree, which remained as solid as ever, an image that even I could not disbelieve. Even when all the other false images were stripped away and destroyed, this one remained in view, burning forever.

Forever burning. Blazing. An eternal and unquenchable fire.

"Who is she?" The question didn't really matter. She could be anything those who believed in her wanted her to be.

Byron Spinks slowly shook his head, lowered his arm, and coughed up a single black plume of ash. A matching one trailed from his shattered eye socket. Then the mirror went dark and I was standing in an ordinary hotel bathroom, my bare feet cold on the tiled floor, looking at nothing but my own naked reflection in the mirror above the sink.

There was ash on my face and in my hair; smudges of ash lay across my shoulders like a terrible shawl.

Two words were scrawled backwards in ash across the tarnished glass of the mirror.

I didn't need to look at them to know what they said.

TWENTY-ONE

When I woke up, Ellen wasn't in bed next to me and the television was on. The set was tuned to a local news programme, and inevitably they were screening footage of the Royale's press conference and Shawna's tearful breakdown before the cameras. The camera cut away before Mr Shiloh made his well-timed entrance, but as I leaned forward across the mattress and peered at the screen I just about caught a glimpse of what looked like the sleeve of his black suit moving in from stage right.

The bathroom door opened before I had the chance to find the remote control and change the channel. Ellen stood there with her head wrapped in a towel, smiling at me. "Morning," she said, moving towards the foot of the bed. She glanced sideways, drawn by the television, and caught sight of a straight-faced newsreader sitting before an enlarged background shot of her cousin taken directly from the press conference footage. "Oh," she said, letting the towel unwind from her damp hair. "Oh."

"I was going to turn that off. Thought it might upset you." I sat up in bed, rubbing the back of my head and wondering if I'd bumped it against the headboard during the night. I'd had a pain there ever since Byron Spinks had shown me those weird visions in the mirror.

"No, it isn't that. Not really. It's just…" She dropped her gaze and pulled the other towel – the one encasing her wonderful firm body – tighter.

"What?"

She moved to the side of the bed and looked down at me. "I was going to tell you this last night, but with everything that happened… you know, between us… well, it sort of slipped my mind in all the excitement." She bit her lower lip and shrugged her bare shoulders. It was a strangely childish and unguarded gesture, and made her look even more beautiful.

I smiled. "Go on." Shifting across the mattress, I made room for her, and she sat down, pushing her legs together. I reached out and stroked her arm. The skin was still wet, and warm to the touch.

"Shawna didn't believe you when you told her that Penny was still alive."

"Probably… I said she was *probably* still alive."

She cleared her throat. "I know. Probably. But she didn't believe you, anyway. She got a phone call from a man – a medium – who claims that he has a message from Penny, and he wants to pass it on. It's almost as if she wants the child to be dead – as if she can cope better with the thought of her death rather than someone holding her against her will."

I closed my eyes and tried not to yell. If there is one thing I hate in this world, it's fake mediums: tawdry pier-end show-men making a few quid off the back of the deceased and exploiting the pain of the loved ones they leave behind. "Who is it? What's this man's name?"

"I remember his name because it's so cheesy, obviously a stage name. He calls himself Trevor Dove. Do you know him?" She shuffled closer to me on the bed, caressing my leg with her wet hand. I stared at the back of her hand, at the tiny water droplets – seeing whole universes expand and explode within them – and wondered where all this would end.

I didn't know Trevor Dove (and that most certainly was not his real name; he had changed it to reflect the supposed spirituality of his act) personally, but I had heard of him from other sources. He had a television show on one of the minor satellite channels and toured with a travelling medium set-up, moving up and down the country performing for money. His act was as cheesy as it came, and his appearance matched the tacky showbiz elements of his routine. He usually wore pale blue suits and his hair was bleached blonde to make him look younger. He worked out at a gym, sported a tangerine-orange solarium tan, and – if one Sunday newspaper was to be believed – he slept with many of the grieving young wives and mothers that he counselled in his hotel room after the shows. And also with some of the distraught fathers and brothers.

"When is your cousin seeing this man? Or is he coming to her home?"

Ellen cast me a sideways glance, her lower lip rising slowly to cover the upper. "I'm afraid she's going to him. She's been invited along to one of his stage shows, today in fact."

I wanted the bed to swallow me up. "Where and at what time?"

"Three o'clock, at some second-string place behind the Alhambra theatre in Bradford. It's a matinee." She leaned back against the headboard; it creaked like old bones. "There'll be an audience of pensioners and desperate housewives, all there to see him speak to the dead while they hope that he doesn't pick on them."

"Great," I said, mostly to myself. "This is just great."

While Ellen continued to get ready in the bathroom, I picked up the phone and dialled the number for Millgarth police station. After being bounced around a few different departments I finally got through to Tebbit, who was in a mellower mood than when I'd last seen him, immediately after the prison visit.

"How are you, Thomas?"

"Not good. I have something I need to ask you."

"That's strange," said Tebbit, "because there's something I need to tell you."

I waited, and when it became clear that he was waiting for me to ask my question first, I ploughed on. "It's about Byron Spinks. I think I already know the answer, but... is he by any chance dead?"

I sensed Tebbit draw back from the phone – there was a sudden flat sound, as if air had rushed into the space between the side of his head and the earpiece. "Jesus, Usher, that's what I wanted to tell you. He died last night. There was some kind of commotion, a fight with another inmate, and he was stabbed to death in his cell."

Things were getting weird again – as if things were ever anything but weird in my life. "What happened? Tell me what you know."

Tebbit sighed; I could hear his distaste at the accrued years of crime and terror as it flowed between his lips like bile. "It happened about an hour before lock-up. As you know, Spinks has been spending most of his time alone in his cell, but after your visit he seemed to come out of his shell a bit. He still didn't talk to anyone, just walked around the block, like he was biding time for something. Then, when he returned to his cell, someone followed him. There was no prior trouble between these two men. They barely even knew each other as far as anyone can tell. But the other man was armed with a weapon made from a sharpened spoon and he followed Spinks in there and started slashing."

I recalled the vision from last night: the cuts and gouges, the blood... and the ash he had coughed up before leaving me.

"A couple of witnesses who arrived after the attack began told us that Spinks didn't seem to be putting up much of a fight. They say he just sat there, on the floor, and let the other man cut him.

One of the men said that Spinks was smiling. Another said that he was praying, but in no language he could understand."

I clenched my teeth and tried to stop the dizzy feeling that was building inside my head. "Anything else, Tebbit? Is there anything you're leaving out?"

"There were some words, Usher. A weird phrase scrawled on the cell wall."

I knew what was coming; it was clear as day, obvious as the sunrise. "Was it a message, Tebbit?"

The room felt vast, like an empty amphitheatre. I hoped that Ellen would stay in the bathroom just a little while longer, so she would not see the panicked state I was in. My hands were shaking. There was sweat on my face.

"Yes," said Tebbit. "I think so. Remember those words he said to you, just before you left?"

"Memento mori," I whispered, hearing once again a rush of air inside the earpiece and sensing that someone else, someone other than Tebbit, was listening.

"The strange thing is," said Tebbit. "The really strange thing…"

"Was it written in blood?" Again, I already knew the answer but was hoping for something else, something different.

"No. It was written in ash."

"Thank you, Tebbit. You've given me the answer I was dreading."

"What does it mean, Usher. What does it all mean?"

Written in ash.

"Memento mori? It's Latin. It means 'remember you shall die'. The world of the arts is littered with examples of this throughout the ages. Medieval Europe was obsessed with the notion. It's a reminder… a reminder of our mortality." I knew what he was asking – that he meant everything, and not just that damned message, but for some reason it was all that I could focus on, so I chose to bore him with sterile facts.

"Don't bullshit me, Usher. What's going on here? My arse is on the line – I have those fucking hangings and now Penny Royale to deal with. It's too much, and now *you* seem to be what's linking the two cases." I could hear the rage in his voice, but he was doing a good job of holding it back, strapping it down so that it could not escape and do any damage.

I closed my eyes. The wind-sound was now inside my head.

"The two cases are linked. You're correct in that assumption at least. But it isn't me that ties them together. The common denominator here is the MT. That gang, those seemingly invisible thugs. Baz Singh has something to do with it, too, but I'm not yet sure what or how deep his involvement might be. Spinks was the string, I think, that held it all together, and now someone's gone and cut that string, leaving a whole lot of loose ends." Of course I knew more than I was letting on, but my own understanding of this knowledge was limited. I couldn't very well tell him about Mr Shiloh, or the clumsy illusion of the Russian witch spirit that had been torn down and revealed to be just another false front, another sham.

Everything about this was intangible, tough to pin down, and I couldn't risk sending Tebbit and his officers off track in their investigations. Let them do the official stuff, the legwork, and I would take care of the rest.

I always had to take care of the rest.

"What is it you're not telling me, Usher. You promised me full disclosure." His voice was hard as slate, sharp as the blade that had killed Byron Spinks.

"I don't know. I honestly don't know. There's so much more going on here, and we've only glimpsed the very tip of it. I think it all goes back a long way, but perhaps even farther back than even I can imagine. There are forces at work here that I don't understand. Another reality is converging with our own, and believe me when I tell you it's bad news for everybody."

That seemed to shock him. He went quiet for a moment, and then I heard the sound of his breathing. "My head hurts, Thomas. I've been getting these headaches…" I thought of the tumour I knew was growing inside his skull, and of the promise I had once made his poor dead wife not to mention it. Right now, that promise was more difficult than ever to keep. "My head hurts so I'm going to go now. Just let me know when you have something… tangible. Something I can move on without my boss sending me to the fucking loony bin."

With that, Detective Inspector Donald Tebbit hung up the phone and I was left listening to the crackling of dead air on the line. Deep within that pulsing white noise, for the briefest of moments, I could have sworn that I heard someone giggle.

When Ellen once again emerged from the bathroom I told her that I was going home for a change for clothes and that I would meet her in Bradford later that day, so that we could both attend Trevor Dove's ridiculous public sham of a mass séance, or whatever it was he had planned.

"Why don't I pick you up and we can go together?" she said, towelling her hair. She had put on her underwear, and the banal sight of her drying herself off made me feel slightly uncomfortable: I could not shake the conviction that we had once again become too familiar and just like last time, the timing was all off. My previous good feelings about this were fading fast. Now it all seemed like just another bad move in a game that had been lost from the very start.

But my involvement with Ellen was not a game – it was serious, and I knew that I was messing with her life. With both our lives. I didn't want this to go wrong; I needed it to work out this time.

It had to work. Because right now it was all I had.

"Do you know how to get there – to my house?" I knew she'd never been there before, even in the old days, or in the older days before that.

"No, but if you write down the address on that cute little hotel notepaper I'm sure I can find it. I'm a woman of the world, you know. I've even been in a space rocket." She grinned, despite the darkness that even now was closing in on us both.

I jotted down my address and directions how to get there, then we kissed – rather awkwardly, I thought – and I left.

Another taxi: yet another chitty to claim back from Baz Singh. I knew that I would have to contact Singh again, and soon, but other things kept diverting my attention. I wondered if he'd heard yet about Byron Spinks's murder, and if, like me, he suspected darker motives than a simple prison-ground difference of opinion.

Once I was home I went straight into my room and took off my clothes. I felt grimy, as if I'd been wearing the same outfit for weeks, and the house seemed like a mausoleum. Cold, dark, filled with nothing but death.

After a shower and brush-up, I put on one of my usual dark suits and trudged upstairs. The three girls were still there, but only just. They were fading for real now, their outlines barely even visible against the patterned wallpaper, like old stains.

They swung slowly to and fro, as if caught in a strong breeze, and they no longer had the strength to acknowledge me. They had become just another reminder, a gentle prod to push me in the right direction – part of the vast *memento mori* my life had somehow become. Spinks was there with them, and even he wasn't much more than a heavy blurring in the air. He sat in the corner, with his back against the wall, gazing calmly up at Kareena. His position reminded me of when I'd found him in the warehouse, staring up at her body and keening like an animal.

"Don't worry," I said, quietly. "I'm still on your side. I'll find out who did this so you can move on."

I turned around and left them there, four wan phantoms jittering in and out of focus like pictures from a faulty television signal. Their increasing lack of solidity felt like a warning .

that time was running out, and I needed to help them before that happened.

I had made a promise a long time ago that I would always do what I could to help the spirits that came to me. Sometimes my help is the exact opposite of what they need and their names join the ever-expanding list tattooed upon my back. Three – now four – more names would take up a lot of skin. I feared that I might run out of space.

But now it was time for some research, before I once again entered the tide of insanity. Knowledge is power, and at the minute I felt completely unarmed.

Downstairs, I booted up my laptop and logged on to the search engine I always used. The first name I typed in was Mr Shiloh, but the majority of the search results that came up seemed to relate to the Biblical location of the same name. It was an ancient city in the Ephraim hill-country, and considered by scholars as the capital of Israel – indeed the centre of Israelite worship. The Hebrew bible mentioned it as an assembly place for the people of Israel, where there was once even a sanctuary containing the Ark of the Covenant.

Blah, blah, blah. So far so Indiana Jones. It was all very interesting, but there was nothing to link the mythical place to Leeds street gangs, a Russian witch, an abducted child and three hanged girls.

The next search result was a transvestite nightclub in Essex called Lady Shiloh's. That didn't sound too promising either.

The name of Mathew Torrent brought up even more obscure links: a baker in Leicester, the obituary of an American writer of pulp science fiction novels, a Swedish printing company specialising in religious pamphlets. To my stressed mind, even these seemed linked in some way to what was happening all around me. Part of the darkness I could feel creeping towards us all.

I killed that window and opened another, heading straight for a few websites of my own. Over the years I had seen hundreds of specialist sites appear online dedicated to the subject of the paranormal. Most of them were superficial and aimed at the credulous, with faked photographs of "ghosts" and orbs and spooky little kids in white dresses. The ones I wanted were far more esoteric.

I know little about computers other than how to hit the keys with my fingers, but I do accept that the internet is a rubbish dump for information – just not always the right information. Looking for absolute truth online is like looking for a diamond in a council tip. It just isn't going to happen. But if you are careful, and use common sense, it is possible to glean a few salient facts from the endless pages of puerile nonsense at your fingertips. And if you wade through enough garbage dumps you will eventually find a hidden gem, probably one that somebody else has thrown away, thinking it useless.

None of the usual sites provided anything regarding Mr Shiloh or the mysterious Torrent, so I logged on to the last resort, a little place on the web where the real weirdoes hang out. I didn't like going there often as it tended to attract extreme personalities, usually with their own strange and sometimes borderline psychotic agendas.

The site had started life as a sort of repository for Fortean stories and anecdotes, but over the past five years it had transformed into something a little bit scarier. People with avatars like Deadmum, Bileduct and Lady Oesophagus gathered there to trade insults and information. Some of what they said was even interesting. A small amount of it often proved valuable.

The site search function failed to bring up anything pertinent regarding the names of Shiloh and Mathew Torrent (although, apparently, the transvestite club in Essex has a ghost called Matt), so I headed for the site's discussion forum. Keeping a low profile, I logged in under an anonymous account and scoured the discussion threads.

After an hour of wading through disturbing tales of suburban poltergeists, a demon in a toilet bowl, and a harrowing account of a Catholic rite of exorcism carried out in 1971 on a pregnant woman on a camp site somewhere near the Lake District, I found a single abandoned post from another anonymous user with no responses attached. The message was dated over a year ago, and according to the site's records only seven people had ever logged on to view it.

In the body of the post I discovered that someone had uploaded an old, slightly degraded black-and-white photograph – obviously scanned from a historical newspaper article – and asked the question: *Who is the man in the photograph? There seems to be the ghost of a little girl sitting on his shoulder.*

These odd websites are littered with such stuff: old photos apparently containing images of the departed. Again, most of them are either faked or simply flawed.

I couldn't see the supposed ghost, but what I did see shook me a whole lot more than any photographic phantom. The man was standing outside a shop with a large awning proclaiming "Torrent Fabrics". He was wearing an old-fashioned suit with a bow tie, and with what looked to be a white handkerchief tucked into his breast pocket. A trilby hat was perched upon his head, so I couldn't tell if he had any hair beneath it, but there was little doubt that the face and sturdy physique belonged to Mr Shiloh.

My new friend; my nemesis; my horror – they call him Mr Shiloh.

So Torrent and Shiloh were one and the same. I was slightly ashamed that I hadn't seen this one coming, and in retrospect it seemed obvious. Shiloh/Torrent had created the street gang known as the MT. An ex-member of the MT was linked to the three hanged girls. Hooded youths had been seen following Penny Royale home on the day she disappeared. Mr Shiloh knew the Royale family. Baz Singh knew Mr Shiloh. Baz Singh's daughter was one of the hanged girls... blah, blah, blah. Fill in the blanks.

Round and round we go: wheels within wheels, stories wrapped up in stories.

I switched off the laptop and poured myself a drink, stared at the rather beautiful and expensive amber liquid as it sat in the glass, and then drank it down like it was medicine – which, of course, it was.

TWENTY-TWO

Ellen arrived at two o'clock that afternoon. I glanced out of the window and saw a little red Smart Car coming up the drive. I guessed that she must have rented it, and then I thought how absurd she looked driving such a tiny, stylised vehicle: like a kid in a clown's car.

She parked and got out of the car, looking up at the house. She had never actually seen the place before, and I wondered how it might strike her to finally be here. The house was in a nice semi-rural area, surrounded by fields, with plenty of space separating it from the closest neighbouring properties. Rebecca and I had gone into some serious debt to afford it, but she and Ally only got to enjoy the benefit for a short time before the accident.

Ally had loved the house: the open spaces, the old, scarred brickwork, the large rooms and high timbered ceilings. Whenever I walked the rooms of the big old house, I knew that I'd give anything to hear even the smallest echo of my daughter's laughter following me. Alas, that had never happened, not even once. The rooms remained silent; the house was truly empty, even when I was home – *especially* when I was home.

Empty, even with ghosts of hanged women swinging on the upper floor.

I went to the front door and opened it before Ellen reached the worn stone step. She smiled at me, the weak sunlight catching in her hair and lightening it a shade, her eyes flashing, her cheeks holding rose petals. "Hi." She was subdued, as I had expected. I think she felt slightly uncomfortable standing outside the place where my family had once dwelled, if only for a brief span of time.

They may not have lived there for long, but the house stood in their shadows.

"Come on in. I'll be ready in a moment." I stepped back from the door and beckoned her inside. She followed me, leaving the door open – perhaps subconsciously, as an escape route if the emotions held tight within the place became too much for her to bear.

I decided to cut short her discomfort and grabbed my jacket off the hook by the door. "I won't bother giving you the grand tour. There's nothing much to see here, these days." I couldn't prevent the note of self-pity that tinged my voice.

Ellen simply nodded, silent now that she was inside. I could tell that she just wanted to leave.

We went back out to the car and she pressed the key fob to release the locks. "Nice motor," I said. "Looks like a real monster."

Ellen smiled, shook her head. "Please, don't start. It's ridiculous, isn't it? But it was all they had left at the rental place."

Ellen slipped into the driver's seat and I squeezed in beside her, making a show of huffing and puffing. "Oh, shut up," she said, still smiling.

The little car moved surprisingly fast along the narrow country roads. I felt myself become tense and gripped the seatbelt. "Slow down a little, eh? I know this is a toy car, but it's still a death machine."

Ellen began to say something, and then thought better of it. She must have suddenly remembered the reason why I was so nervous travelling at any kind of speed. Whenever I drive my own car I go well under the speed limit, no matter who is sitting up my arse and in what kind of vehicle. I know from bitter experience how speed can kill.

Traffic wasn't too bad so we arrived in Bradford a little before 3pm. Ellen parked in a space so tight that I couldn't even see it until the car had slipped neatly between two other vehicles. "Magic," she said, winking at me. "These little babies are designed for urban stealth parking."

We got out of the car and walked down to the Alhambra theatre, and then cut up behind it until we were standing before a small, rundown building with its sign hanging askew on a rusty bracket. "Here we are. King's Theatre." Ellen stepped towards the door but held back, as if she really didn't want to be there. "This is going to be horrible," she said.

I reached out and grabbed her hand. Squeezed it. "It's okay. Let's just try to stay calm and observe. If things get out of hand, I'll step in, but try to keep it as low-key as possible."

She nodded. I smiled, but behind the smile lay only a sheet of ice.

It was ten minutes before three and I knew that everyone would be sitting down and waiting for the show to begin. I walked through the glass double doors, up a short flight of carpeted steps, and towards the ticket booth. A young girl with bright green hair sat behind the counter reading a paperback book. As I got closer I saw that the book was a Stephen King novel, and she was reading so intently that she failed to register my approach.

"Excuse me."

The girl looked up, a slightly aggrieved expression on her face. Clearly she didn't want to be disturbed from her reading. "Yes? Help you?"

"We're here to see the Trevor Dove medium show, but I'm afraid we didn't book in advance. Are there any tickets still available at this late a date?" I smiled, trying my best to seem dull and inoffensive. It seemed to work a treat.

The girl looked down at a computer terminal, tapped a few buttons, and nodded. "Yep. Still a few left. How many do you need?"

"Two, please," said Ellen, now at my side and pulling out her purse.

The girl printed out the tickets, one eye still on her novel.

"I'll pay," I said, reaching into my jacket pocket.

"Don't be silly, Thomas. You're doing me the favour here, and I'm not about to let you pay for the privilege." She scowled and opened her purse, talking out a credit card.

I held up my hands and stepped back. "Fair enough. I'm not going to argue with you today."

Ellen smiled; that was one small victory under her belt. She always was an independent lady.

We headed for the double doors at the bottom of the stairs, which led to what a sign rather ambitiously described as the Main Stage. From the look of the place I doubted there were any other stages in the building, so it had assumed the title by default.

Ellen pushed her arm though the crook in my elbow and held me. It felt good, pure, and I hung on to the sensation for as long as I could, with a vague notion that I might need the memory at some unspecified time in the future to arm me against the dark. Life is full of such small moments of unacknowledged intimacy, and what I have learned is that they are valuable weaponry against despair.

The room we entered was like an old music hall, with drapes laid against the walls, red velvet chairs aligned in neat rows and a nice long stage at the front. The audience was impressive; there was barely an empty seat in the house. Dove's television show was something of a cult item, and despite not pulling in huge viewing figures for the cable channel who broadcast it, revenue from tie-in shows like this one must have been enough to keep the man in business.

Just as we grabbed a couple of seats near the back of the hall – the only two empty ones within range, next to a group of giggling students – the house lights went down, a tinny electronic version of Mussorgsky's *Night on Bare Mountain* started playing, and the curtain went up jerkily. It could not have been better timed if we had been following a script. Perhaps we were; maybe, at some points in all of our lives, we are following scripted directions without ever knowing that we are doing so.

The crowd began to applaud as a tall, lean man in a powder blue suit emerged and strutted onto the stage. Trevor Dove cut an impressive figure mainly because of his height – other than that, the silly suit, bleached hair and fake tan made him look shallow and pompous, and more than a little vainglorious. He strode to the front of the stage and took a modest half bow. On his head was strapped one of those portable microphones the pop singer Madonna made popular in her live shows back in the Nineties; the whole affair already had the air of a carefully choreographed musical act.

The soundtrack faded and the star of the show began his spiel.

"My name is Trevor Dove, and I welcome you, friends, to my evening of spiritual adventure."

More applause. The students on our row were still giggling. I looked around and noted that there was a mixed crowd in place to view the entertainment: old ladies hoping for messages from loved ones, middle-aged women on a girls' day out who would probably go on for a curry afterwards, students like the ones next to Ellen and me, and a smattering of hardcore ghost-groupies after their latest fix of this sanitised version of the paranormal.

It took me a while to locate Shawna Royale, where she had been placed in a good seat close to the stage. Her husband wasn't with her (an unbeliever?) but it isn't an overstatement to say that I was stunned to see who was accompanying her. Baz Singh sat at her side, looking rather uncomfortable in a pinstripe suit and heavy overcoat. I stared at him, thinking for a moment that I was seeing things – I had no idea why he might be there, or who had invited him.

"Do you know that man sitting next to Shawna?" I nodded in their general direction and Ellen squinted to see in the dim light.

"I recognise him, yes, but I don't know his name. God, this is rubbish, isn't it?"

"Ellen. This is important. What is that man doing with your cousin?"

Ellen turned to look at me, her face suddenly serious. "Sorry, Thomas. I don't know his name, but he's a local businessman who's organised a fund to help look for Penny. He gathered together a few more prominent local figures and they all chipped in with some cash to kickstart the thing. It's probably some kind of tax write-off."

My mouth had gone dry; I licked my lips but there was no spit on my tongue to do any good.

Trevor Dove continued with his introduction, pacing the stage like a rather light-footed caged tiger in pastel colours. His voice, with its modified Yorkshire accent, sounded camp and affected: it was staged entirely for the local crowd.

"Now, friends, I must warn you not to expect too much from me. The spirits – our friends on the other side – do not always come forward in the way we would like. Sometimes the wrong ones step forward into the light, and other times, even when we connect with someone we know, the messages they bring are confused and uncertain. They speak to me in code. A smell. A colour. A vision of some kind. They are never direct, and always go round the houses, as my old mam used to say, to get to the point. So I must ask all you friends to be patient, to be calm and polite in the hope that we get something of value coming through from the other friends – the ones we've all come to meet."

The music had finished now, and the applause was more of a ripple this time rather than the clamorous noise from before.

The audience were settling; Dove had them eating out of his hand. The man was a pro.

"First I do have someone here, a friend who has passed over, who seems to be telling me about some washing, or a washing line. Does that mean anything to anybody here?"

Several hands shot up. I shook my head and fought the urge to leave.

"This is pathetic," said Ellen. Her former light humour had disappeared and in its place there was a quiet, simmering anger. She clearly didn't enjoy the thought of this showman conning her cousin and feeding off the family's pain.

"No… no, it isn't washing, not really. It's a peg. That's it, isn't it, friend?" Dove glanced to the side of the stage, as if he were speaking with someone who stood there. "Come on, friend, can you be more specific?" A peg… peg… Peg! That's it, it's a name, isn't it, friend?" He turned back to face the hall, his eyes wide and filled with a sort of fervour that I could not be sure was entirely faked. "Is there a Peg or a Peggy in the room? Have you lost someone?"

Most of the hands that had been raised dropped; only one remained in the air.

"Stand up, please, won't you, friend?" Dove had now adopted the warm persona of a caring family member. "Don't be frightened."

An old woman slowly stood, clutching her handbag to her chest. She was wearing her hat indoors, as if she was afraid to put it down in case someone stole it. Her smile was weak, uncertain, and even standing she hunched her shoulders as if she were still sitting down.

"Are you Peg, friend? Is that your name, dear?" Dove kneeled down at the front of the stage, opening his arms in a broad, showy gesture of inclusion.

The old woman coughed lightly. "No… no, it isn't me. My sister, she was called Peggy. We lost her, oh, six weeks back now. To the cancer."

Applause rippled gently around the room; someone gasped; the students giggled into their hands.

"Well, friend, Peggy is here. She doesn't seem to have much to say – her presence is weak – but I think she just wants you to know that she's always watching over you. Is that all right, friend? Does it make sense to you?"

The woman was weeping openly. She nodded her head and dabbed at her eyes with a paper tissue she had produced from the sleeve of her dress. "Thank you, Trevor. You're a very kind young man." Adoration poured from her eyes along with the tears, and I began to feel nauseous. The old man sitting next to her reached up and touched her arm; she sat, smiling and dabbing with the tissue. The applause intensified, and when Dove raised his hand it slowly died down.

"Thank you, friend. You enjoy the rest of the show, and I'll leave your Peggy's love with you." He stood and walked back to his mark, his strides long and confident.

It went on like this for some time: Dove making vague allusions to people who may or may not be dead and hoping that one would stick; performing like a high wire artist, constantly and minutely readjusting his position to prevent a fall. He was very good, of his kind, and possibly did possess some minor mediumistic intuition, but the rest of it was pure bluff and bullshit. He hid his secrets well, too. Behind the glitter and the sham he was virtually unreadable.

Then, almost an hour into the show, he called for Shawna Royale.

"I can see… I can see a coin. A penny. It's Penny, and she has a message for her mother. Now, I've been contacted by this one before, and she knows that her mummy is afraid. Could Penny's mum please stand up and make herself known to us? That's right, friend, you come forward. I have a message from someone who says that she's your little girl."

Shawna Royale stood and took a hesitant step forward, towards the base of the stage. She held her hands out at her sides, as if balancing on a ledge, and licked her lips. Her yellow hair was pulled back into a severe ponytail that showed its dark roots, her face was red and blotchy from all the crying she'd done, but she had managed to make an effort and put on a nice dress. My heart went out to her in that moment, and to all the other mothers and fathers and sisters and brothers and grandparents who are taken in by low men like Trevor Dove. All those weeping people reaching out in the darkness and grasping for something – a life-line, a name, a face, a vague message couched in general terms that could, really, be from anyone and to anyone. But they believe it every time; they need to; they have to. It's all they have.

Then, as Dove turned a certain way and one of the stage lights caught his pale blue suit, I saw it: his own feeble ghost. It was very fragile, like a silver spider web spun in the shape of a tiny figure, but it was there, sitting on his shoulders and clinging on to the sides of his head. He turned again and it was gone; he turned again and it returned.

I stared at the image, peering inside it to reach its secrets. It looked like a small boy, possibly a sibling judging by the proximity – the ghosts of friends keep a respectable distance but family usually cling like limpets. It was small and monkey-like; very young and showing obvious signs of distress.

"She says she loves you, Shawna. Friend. She says she loves you very much, and that she misses you." His face was awful, a puerile mask of empathy that I wanted to smash. Shawna Royale was shaking; great silent sobs wracked her entire body.

"She says that someone took her and killed her. A man... a big man with dark features... he was wearing strong aftershave and he hurt her... hurt her all over." His eyes were closed; his face went pale beneath the orange tan. Oh, he was good. He knew how to earn his money, this paranormal whore.

The ghost on his shoulders dropped off and stood beside him, becoming slightly clearer. It was definitely a small boy, and there was blood on the front of his pants, dripping down his legs. Suddenly I knew everything I needed to know about Trevor Dove, and the nausea I'd felt earlier transformed into pure rage.

"Stop this!" I stood and glared at the stage, aware that I must look like a madman but unwilling to let this carry on for much longer. "Stop this offensive rubbish! Penny Royale is not dead."

Trevor Dove shuffled round to face me, his eyes filled with tears. "What is it, friend? Are you hurt? Are you in pain? Did you come here hoping that someone might pass on a message from the other side? Have patience, friend. We all get a turn."

I am not proud of what I did, but I had no choice in the matter. It had to be done; the ghost needed someone to usher him from his brother's side. And that, after all, is my job in this life.

"There's a small boy standing next to you. He has blood on his crotch and running down his legs. His name is..." There was a large M on the boy's shirt, so I took an intuitive guess, my voice turning cold and sharp. "His name is Michael. He was your brother, but now he's dead. You raped him, probably on a regular basis, and he cut himself down there to make you stop." I remembered reading somewhere, perhaps in some magazine in a dentist's waiting room, that the psychic's younger brother had taken his own life when Dove was thirteen. He claimed, in that interview, that the suicide was pivotal in his choice to use his gift to "offer aid to all the grieving friends, wherever they are."

Dove looked like he was dancing. He was shuffling on the spot, unable to respond in any meaningful way, other than through this unconscious motion. His feet did a little soft-shoe shimmy across the stage; his face went pale beneath the tangerine tan.

"Michael has been with you since it happened, and he just wants to go. He has somewhere else he needs to be, but the lies you tell to these poor people are keeping him trapped here. You have to stop this. It's hurting people. The brother whose life you helped to end insists upon it."

Shawna Royale crumpled to the floor, sobbing. Trevor Dove began to scream, and leaped from the stage to run in my direction. The students had finally stopped giggling.

I didn't even feel the punch when it landed. I was too busy watching the boy on the stage. I wished him well as he turned and walked away into darkness, at last starting out on the road to another version of reality, where he might finally find some kind of peace and his wounds would at last begin to heal.

TWENTY-THREE

We were all in the foyer.

Baz Singh was standing beside the chair, shaking his head in what I could only assume was a demonstration of utter confusion. Ellen was holding a handkerchief to my cheek and inspecting the damage with narrowed eyes. "Doesn't look too bad," she said. "I don't think you need stitches."

Dove's roadies had eventually dragged the raging medium off me, but not before he had cut my face with one of his ostentatious gold rings. I almost felt put out that he had not called me "friend" even once during the fracas – the closest he had come to it was to yell the word "fucker" over and over again.

I leaned back in the chair, pressing the base of my skull into the wall against which it was positioned. I was beginning to think that I might have acted in haste. All things considered, I could have handled the situation better. My jaw ached; my pride was bruised. The blood still felt hot on my face.

"What the hell was all that about, Usher?" Baz Singh was riled; his eyes were popping out of his sweaty face and he was grinding his teeth. "I mean, what are you even doing here?" A couple of his employees hung around in the background, chatting quietly. Big men with big muscles: the brothers or cousins of those I'd met at the Blue Viper during my last visit to the club.

"Friend of the family," I said. "And I could ask you the same question."

"Bastard!" The voice came from the other end of the foyer, near the doors. I looked up to see Trevor Dove being shepherded out of the building by his cronies. There was still a crowd out there, and I knew that he could easily have sneaked out the back way – but it seemed that he was trying to save some face, to show the fans that he was not harmed by my accusations. But I knew otherwise. The very fact that his brother's ghost had now moved on was proof enough that things had changed, and I hoped that Dove would be answering a lot of questions from interested parties over the next few weeks. So would I, of course, but hopefully Tebbit could keep attention away from me at least until I was finished with everything else. He had done it before, and there was a good chance he would be doing it again.

I knew how to become invisible when it was required. Like a shy ghost.

It occurred to me that I was beginning to rely on Tebbit's influence a lot. Much more than I liked.

"I am here," said Baz Singh, drawing my attention, "in the capacity as head of the 'Pennies for Penny' fund. We have been raising money in the local community to help the Royales in the search for their daughter, and if Trevor Dove could prove that the poor little girl was dead, he was due a reward." He stalked in little circles, shining the floor with the leather soles of his expensive shoes.

"Well you wasted your time. That man is a fraud. I've saved your fund some money." I opened my mouth, working my jaw. For an effete showman, Trevor Dove packed a mean right hook.

Baz Singh stalked away from me, crossing the foyer to stand with his men. They talked in whispers, glancing occasionally in my direction. I wondered what Singh was telling them, and when one of them laughed I decided that I was better off not knowing after all.

"Shall we go?" Ellen was standing now, the paper tissue still clutched in her hand. There were spots of blood on it, but nothing that looked too horrendous.

"Yes. Good idea. Where's your cousin?" I stood, peering around the emptying foyer. Shawna Royale was loitering by the door, perched on the threshold, and she was locked in an animated conversation with someone I couldn't quite make out because of the angle of the open door. I took a step to the side… and saw Mr Shiloh with his hand on her arm, his hairless plastic face shining pale in the harsh light from the ceiling-mounted fittings.

I started to go over there, in the mood for a confrontation, but Mr Shiloh looked up, locked eyes with me, smiled, and stepped out into the street. By the time I was standing next to Shawna Royale, the Pilgrim was gone. I couldn't see him on the street, nor could I make him out in the back of any of the cars pulling away from the kerb or moving slowly along the road.

But I knew he was there; he was still there, hiding in the shadows, and watching me. Always watching me.

"Will you take me home?" Shawna's voice was small, weak and bruised. She had gone through a rough experience this afternoon, and it was the least I could do to accompany her home.

"Yes. Of course. Ellen has a car. We're parked round the corner." I took her arm and guided her outside. I glanced once over my shoulder to make sure that Ellen was following. We reached the car and climbed inside, the three of us packed like maudlin circus clowns into the silly little vehicle – me in the back and the two women in front. On another day it might have been funny; right now, it was simply uncomfortable and even slightly degrading.

We passed Baz Singh on the kerb outside the Alhambra, and it seemed for a moment that he exchanged an unreadable glance with Shawna Royale. But by the time I had registered what was happening, the moment had passed me by.

I studied the side of Shawna Royale's face as we moved smoothly through the late afternoon traffic. Rain clouds were gathering, massing their forces for an onslaught, and pedestrians hurried through the early gloom. Her cheeks were streaked with red lines, brought about by the constant tears, and her skin was greasy and mottled. She wore the appearance of someone suffering greatly, but not for the first time I had a sense that there was something else going on beneath the surface. There was something about the way she acted – or perhaps the way she looked – that didn't ring entirely true. Sly glances exchanged with Baz Singh aside, I felt unsure regarding her true motives for being there, and I felt guilty for thinking that way.

"How do you know Baz Singh?" There was silence in the car for a moment, and then Ellen cleared her throat, as if trying to break the tension.

"I've known him for years," said Shawna. "Back when he used to manage his dad's restaurant, we'd go in there for curries and chat with him after closing. Nice man."

Baz Singh could be described as many things – among them a borderline gangster, an unrepentant pornographer, a possible abuser of his own dead daughter – but nice was not a word I'd put near the top of the list.

We soon left Bradford and headed towards Leeds, joining the ring road as the clouds darkened and the inside of the car became humid. Silent sheet lightning flashed for a moment directly above the Bestwick Estate, and I fought against an almost overwhelming feeling of impending doom, knowing that I was merely responding to the worsening weather.

The estate was quiet; the changing conditions seemed to have kept everyone sensible indoors. Curtains were closed at most of the windows, and as usual the occasional group of teenagers huddled inside shadowy shop entrances and the doorways of boarded up ground floor flats. Ellen parked the car outside Shawna's place and we got out without waiting for an invitation. Shawna led the way along the cracked concrete path and Ellen and I followed in silence.

Inside, Shawna put on the kettle. "Terry's at the club, drowning his sorrows in brown ale." It was the first time I'd heard her mention her husband's name. "It works for him, anyway." Bitterness tainted her words and I imagined the gulf that must have widened between the couple since their daughter's disappearance. If they had been struggling to get along before, then surely by now they must be almost completely estranged.

Ellen and I sat at opposite ends of a long, sagging sofa. We looked at each other, and then away, inspecting the ornaments and bric-a-brac that littered the room. Photographs of Penny stood on every shelf, hung on every wall, and I stared at the face of that poor child, hoping that I was right about her being still alive. Whether or not she was safe was another matter entirely, and one I was not yet ready to consider at any great length.

Shawna brought through a tray containing cups, a plate stacked with biscuits, and a tea pot. Ellen poured and we drank our lukewarm tea, not one of us quite willing to be the first to speak.

"I'm sorry if I embarrassed you," I said, at last, to the room in general. "But that man was after money, and nothing else. He was lying to you. Believe me when I tell you that your daughter is not dead. Penny's alive... somewhere. I just don't understand why so many people want to believe she's dead." I stopped there, before I said too much; before I said too little.

A flash of what looked like anger coloured Shawna's face and I wondered what I had said to upset her. Then, abruptly, her mood changed and she put down her cup on the table by her chair. "No, I'm sorry. I'm taking this out on you. I was so desperate for some news – for any kind of news – that I was even willing to hear that my daughter had been murdered. Can you even begin to understand that? What it feels to know nothing, to be so much in the fucking dark that you'll clutch at any promise of news?" Her eyes were lowered; she was staring at her feet.

She needed something from me – perhaps a lifeline, perhaps an indication that someone understood what she was going through – so I gave it, as best I could. "I know what it is to lose someone, and how your emotions can get tied in strange knots. Believe me, I know."

She raised her eyes and they were clear: no tears, no grief, not a hint of turmoil. Clear as a deep blue ocean at midnight.

"We should go. Will you be okay, honey?" Ellen stood and walked across the room. Her legs tensed in her tight jeans and when she knelt at her cousin's side I felt a shameful thorn of lust pierce my side. There were things she and I needed to speak of; a mess that needed tidying. I only hoped that I had the right tools to do the job.

We left Shawna there in the darkening living room, cradling her cup and staring at the wall. Whatever was going on inside that woman's head, we had no business trying to get a glimpse of it. In my experience some emotions are just too private and painful for others to even begin to fathom, yet people still insist upon lining up to take photographs.

We left the squat building and walked towards the car, the mood between us difficult to read. It had always been this way: we made things complicated simply by being in each other's company.

I smelled smoke in the air. The clouds grumbled far above us. The lightning from before had not returned. Not yet.

When the car came into sight, Ellen stopped and grabbed my arm. "Thomas."

I looked over at the small vehicle and saw that a group of youths in dark hoodies were standing grouped around the bonnet. One of them had lifted the bonnet, and was reaching inside to interfere with the engine.

"Hey!" I yelled, jogging forward and wishing that I was more of a fighter; that my skills lay in my fists rather than my broken mind.

"Thomas – don't!"

When the group turned as one, heads swivelling in my direction like mechanical toys, I wished that I had taken Ellen's advice long before it was offered.

The black hoods showed only darkness; no features could be seen. These were the same figures that had chased me to the train station when I'd left Ellen's hotel – the same dark entities who had been the harbingers of a greater darkness, and this time they seemed bigger, wider, and brimming with more power.

This time they were up for the fight.

I stopped running and stood watching them, waiting for the first move. The figures stood and stared, blackness billowing within their black cotton hoods. Long, thin, pale hands slid from the cuffs of their arms. Sharp white nails glittered in the early sodium-tinted darkness. Then, one by one and all across the estate, the lights went out: house lights, streetlights, garden lights, wall-mounted security lights. Each was extinguished as if by a colossal hand passing over a series of tiny flames.

Darkness flooded in, moving through the streets like floodwater. It surged towards us, sluicing through the narrow alleys and ginnels, washing over roofs and splashing against walls.

The hooded figures raised their heads and arms, offering those blackened hoods to the even blacker sky, and then they began to wail. The noise was like sheep being slaughtered, or the screaming of cattle as they are herded over the edge of a cliff. I pressed my hands against my ears and turned around, looking for Ellen. She had already started to run, and she looked back at me as she flew towards the corner of a nearby high-rise.

"Keep going!" I ran after her, following her across a car park and towards a fence that had been partially broken down at some point, probably by vandals. "Go! Go!"

I was close behind her as she ducked through the gap in the fence, her jacket sleeve catching on a loose timber and ripping along the seam. She didn't stop; she kept on running, terrified of what was now in pursuit: the original members of the MT. Mathew Torrent's old playmates come back to hunt us down like dogs in the street. Or perhaps, as history might suggest, to pressgang us into God knew what kind of arcane rite or ritual.

I gained on Ellen as she moved across a patchy area of grass, the haphazard remains of an old bonfire standing clumped at its centre. The charred timbers of old furniture, door frames, and what looked like the shell of a television, were still piled there like an offering to some obscure modern deity. We were almost abreast of the dead pyre when another group of dark figures stepped out from within the unstable tower of blackened detritus to block our path.

They stood there, stiff and motionless, blocking our way.

We halted, breathless and panting. The air clouded in front of our faces; faint ghosts giving up the chase. I stepped close to Ellen, and then in front of her, trying to protect her from these things. One of them hissed like a big cat; another giggled like a naughty child. Wisps of ash fell from the dark holes of their hoods, floating on the air like satanic tickertape. They passed their hands in strange patterns before their dark hoods, disturbing the air and conjuring something from the gathering darkness.

The long white nails on their long white fingers carved long black strips from the night.

"Thomas… what's going on? What do they want?"

Before I had time to answer I was hit from behind: a sharp, hard blow to the back of the head. I went down onto one knee and tried to rise, but one of the figures ahead of us stepped forward and kicked me in the face. As I fell I saw the same figure approach Ellen. It pulled back a hand and half-slapped, half-punched her between the eyes. I heard the sound of her nose breaking, and felt it as if I had experienced the blow myself.

I couldn't work out why they were doing this. Surely they could kill us with a blow, rather than beat us up like common street thugs on a violent spree. These were now powerful entities, and they didn't follow the rules that we so fiercely believed in – so why were they not simply ripping us to pieces?

It made little sense, but unfortunately my head was hurting too much to think about it. A smoky darkness filled my mind, clouding my senses, and I barely knew where I was.

Gaining my feet, I hurled myself at the nearest figure. It was an instinctive act – pure blind aggression. My hands sunk into the soft material of the hooded shirt, sinking deep into the spongy matter beneath the clothing. I struggled with the figure, trying to grapple it off balance, but its strength was far greater than mine and it simply flipped me and threw me to the ground.

More proof that these things could kill us with ease, if that's what they chose. Or if that was what they had been sent to do...

Maybe they had only been sent to warn us, or to weaken us to the point that we backed off. But why were our lives – or was it just my life – so important to the Pilgrim?

Again I was up, raging now, refusing to allow these creatures to hurt Ellen. Two of them bore down upon me, the darkness at their core billowing forth and ash falling down like black snow, covering my face in a greasy layer that smelled of cooking pork, or burnt human flesh.

They pressed me down into the ground, silent and unstoppable, and in my panic I managed to reach up and grab the side of one of the hoods. The sooty material slipped sideways, and then back, uncovering the soft-looking head beneath. At first I was confused, not understanding exactly what I was seeing, and then it registered that I was looking at the *back* of a head. Dark, greasy hair, all knotted and crawling with lice, the back of a skull where there should have been a face.

A human head, but worn backwards. A head worn the wrong way round, like some hideous Halloween mask.

I screamed, batting at the head and attempting to push myself backwards across the slippery grass. Sooty ash fell from the dirty scalp, dark dandruff drifting down towards me. The head flopped on its neck, moving like a stuffed toy: loose, almost boneless.

Then, in turn, the rest of the figures calmly removed their hoods, pushing them back to reveal the dirty, tattered backs of heads.

Ellen was barely conscious; thank God she didn't see what followed.

The heads slowly turned in unison, pivoting on thin necks and rotating through one-hundred and eighty degrees to show me what was on the other side. They stared at me through eyes that I knew far too well: my own eyes, wide and blinking as if emerging from a dark cave.

My own eyes.

Mine.

My eyes looking right at me.

Each of these awful figures bore the exact likeness of my own terrified face, reflected back at me like in some carnival sideshow of mirrors. I saw the pared-down image of my own fear multiplied – and surely there is no more horrible sight in this world than that of your own face filled with indescribable terror?

My eyes looking right at me.

I slumped, defeated. The ground held me like a desperate lover, unwilling to let me go.

Mine.

The figures replaced their hoods, reached down and grabbed Ellen, carrying her past the skeletal bonfire – lifting her above their heads (*my* heads!) like a trophy.

They formed a grim procession, holding her aloft, and what came to mind was a heavily choreographed dance of death. I tried to crawl across the grass but bile rose in my throat and my limbs began to shake. I vomited and rolled over onto my back. I stared at the barely visible moon and the pallid stars, trying to perceive what hid in the spaces between the constellations.

The darkness around me seemed to writhe, folding in on itself like a snake swallowing its own tail. A snake with my face: my own private Ouroboros...

Then I saw nothing – nothing but a thin rain of black ash.

TWENTY-FOUR

Awake? Unconscious? It was impossible to tell, but time bled backwards for a little while, showing me the past in a new way, and from a different angle. This past, these historical events, became as real to me as the present.

At that moment in time, I doubted that I would ever see Ellen Lang again.

Ellen is late. We meet in a small café in the centre of Leeds, where she often goes for lunch with colleagues from the surgery where she works. I sit nursing a cappuccino and watching the other customers, my leg shaking in a nervous palsy under the table.

An old couple sit by the door, holding hands across the table. The man is wearing an eye patch and the woman keeps glancing at it nervously, as if whatever it is meant to hide might emerge at any second. A group of four women talk about politics at a corner table. One of them cannot keep her hands still; she says more with the movements of her fingers in the air than she does with her words. A mother sits with her small son at a table next to the toilet. The boy is slowly eating a huge ice cream sundae, and the mother gazes absently at the top of his head. She looks on the verge of tears, and I wonder what has pushed her to this juncture.

A short, slim waitress dodges tables and clears dirty dishes. Her chestnut brown hair is coming free from the elastic band she has used to keep it back from her face; sweat shines on her forehead. Her eyes are so dark that they are almost black.

The air around the waitress stirs, like a heat mirage. Ghosts follow her, not quite visible but present at her every move.

I turn away, look down at my coffee. I did not ask for this ability. Is it a gift or a curse? Probably both. Wherever I look, whoever I am with, spirits writhe constantly in the background. Some of them step forth, wanting to be seen, but others remain on the sidelines, ignoring me. I can feel their hunger and sense their sadness. They are lost; every one of them is looking for a road to follow yet many of them choose to delay their journey even when that road is found.

Most of them are looking for something... often they are looking for me.

The strip lights buzz and flicker. The sky outside is dark with slashes of light carved into its mass where sunlight struggles to penetrate the clouds. It would be a nice day if only those clouds would clear.

The waitress pauses by an empty table and reaches out a hand to support her slight weight as she stumbles a little. I am just about to rise and go to her aid when she moves on, heading towards the counter where she puts down the plates she is carrying. She wipes the sweat from her brow with her apron, picks up the plates, and takes them through to the kitchen. The door swings behind her, smooth and silent on its hinges.

Ellen and I had met at a student house party in Headingley years before. I was missing Rebecca because she'd stayed at home with a bad cold and Ellen was accompanied by a languages student with a bad lisp. She ditched the languages guy that night, after realising that he was basically socially inept.

Nothing happened between Ellen and me. Not that night. There was an attraction between us from the very start – that very first time we saw each other it was like someone had turned on all the lights in the room. Unfortunately the timing was wrong.

The timing is always wrong.

Even on the night we slept together, our timing was off. Rebecca was pregnant with Ally by this time and I was struggling to cope with it all. I had left Uni and was getting by working long shifts in a factory doing shitty work just to pay the bills. Ellen was still at Medical School, studying towards a future in which I knew I would feature less and less.

I was weak; she was weak.

It happened only once, and I spent every moment afterwards regretting what we had done. My regret was an insult to Ellen: she didn't deserve to be treated like that.

Weak. I was always so very weak.

"Sorry I'm late."

I turn in my seat to see her standing there; looking for all the world like that ambitious young girl I'd first met at the party so many years ago. Her long hair frames a face that is pretty but never beautiful – not unless you get to know the person underneath. Then, and only then, does a woman like Ellen shine and by that time you are totally smitten without ever having realised it.

"It's okay. I was enjoying the time alone. Just… thinking."

"About the accident?" She slides into the seat opposite, brushing crumbs from the table.

"A little," I say, not wanting to tell her the truth: that I have been thinking about her.

It has been three months since we went to visit Ryan South in his little flat in Luton. We have not been back, but Ellen keeps pushing for it. Things have changed. I am beginning to come to terms with what happened (but never to accept it) and tentative plans are forming. For the first time since Rebecca and Ally's deaths, I allow myself to think that I might just have a future, but am unsure what form that future might take.

I have Ellen to thank for this. She has given me a push right when I needed it.

"How are you feeling? I haven't seen you for a couple of weeks. Sorry about that – been busy." She smiles, but it is a small, fragile thing that disappears just as quickly as it surfaces. She looks pale, drawn, as if she has not been sleeping well.

"I'm... well, I think I'm fine. I don't feel like killing myself anymore, which is a bonus. I've also moved back into the house."

"I need a coffee. How about you?" She turns around in her seat to signal the waitress, who has by now come back through from the kitchen. The air around her is still moving, but not nearly as much as before.

"I'm okay," I say, swirling the dregs in my cup. It is my second cappuccino and I think it best not to order a third. I struggle to sleep at the best of times, and more caffeine would be asking for trouble.

We don't say anything else until Ellen's drink arrives, and then she takes a long draw from the cup before looking me in the eye. "I have some news."

"Yes," I say. "You mentioned that when we spoke. What is it?" There is a heavy weight in my chest, trying to drag me down. I am expecting something bad but am not sure how bad it might be. Has Ellen somehow guessed the thoughts that have been coalescing inside my head since she took me to Ryan South's place? But no; that is impossible. I don't even have a firm plan, just a series of unconnected thoughts that, when placed together, add up to form something stupid – stupid but undeniably appealing.

"I've been offered a job in America. Florida. They called me a week ago and I've been dreading telling you since then."

Somebody drops a glass on the floor and the waitress moves swiftly across the room to clear up the mess. It is the old man with the eye patch, and he seems more upset than he should be at such a clumsy act.

"I see." I do not see. I don't see anything at all.

"I applied over a year ago. A friend got me through the door and I had a telephone interview, then they flew me out there. I hadn't heard anything, so just assumed that either the vacancy had been filled elsewhere or cancelled altogether. Then, a few days ago, I got a phone call…" She stops there, looking away. Her eyes are wet.

"I don't know what you want me to say."

She turns back to me, her head whipping around to glare right at me. "It's not what I want you to say… it's what I need you to say. And the very fact that you can't fucking say it speaks volumes." She looks down, at the table. Her hands are tearing apart a paper napkin; pieces of white paper lie on the table top like tiny drifts of snow.

"I…" But there is nothing there. I cannot find the right words – any words.

"It's never going to happen, is it?" Her voice is close to breaking; I can hear the regret lodged like crumbs of food between her teeth. "The timing is always wrong. It always was wrong, even that night we finally got our act together and fucked."

Her use of such a coarse term shocks me; I have never seen what we did as fucking. As far as I am concerned, we made love, and that's why I always feel such guilt. A meaningless sex act is easy to forget, but true lovemaking scars you deeper than bodily wounds, and for so much longer.

"I can't tell you what you need to hear, Ellen. There's too much going on. My family are dead, and I feel somehow as if I'm to blame. I see ghosts everywhere, but never the ones I want to see – never the ghosts of my wife and child." I am crying now, but silently. I clench my hands into fists.

"You are crippled by guilt, Thomas. Crippled. Guilt about the time we slept together, guilt about their deaths, guilt that you think you should be able to see their ghosts but can't. Have you ever thought that all this might actually be in your head? That maybe the only phantoms stalking you are those created by your unresolved guilt?"

I lower my head. This is the first time Ellen has ever verbalised any kind of doubt regarding what is happening to me. I have always known that she does not fully believe it, that she is simply keeping an open mind, but to hear those words feels like a physical blow.

My own doubts were blown away when she took me to see Ryan South.

The waitress passes our table. The hem of her apron brushes against my forearm and when I look up she is smiling at someone across the room – the man behind the counter, who is calling her over. The air shivers around her, a riot of subtle movement. I can hear nothing but a wind rushing in to fill up the gaps. The waitress moves slowly, each muscle prominent on her legs, her shoulders. She is a machine, a beautiful meat machine designed only for forward motion, never looking back at what she has left behind, heading always towards extinction.

I am suddenly aware that I am being allowed a glimpse behind the scenes here, but I understand nothing of what I am seeing. The scene looks fragile, like it might come apart at any minute, and I fear for what might happen if, like the glass dropped by the old man, it breaks and shatters into pieces.

Then all sound returns and I hear the clatter of cutlery, hushed chatter, chair legs scraping across the tiled floor, and Ellen's voice.

I hear Ellen's voice and she is saying goodbye.

"I'm sorry. This is for the best. We can't go on like this, turning in silly circles. Me waiting for you to wake up and you punishing yourself for the things you think you've done. It has to end."

Her face is hard yet brittle, like porcelain.

"I know. You *should* go. Whatever there is between us, it will always be there, but neither of us can allow ourselves to be tied down by it. You have to make your own choices and I have to make mine. I do thank you, though, for pushing me. If it wasn't for you I'd still be sitting in that caravan, trying to drink myself to death."

She reaches out across the table and holds my hand. Her fingers are cold when they should be warm. "Just promise me you'll go to see that man again – Ryan South. I really do believe that your salvation lies in contacting him again. You changed after that first time. Things got… well, a little bit brighter. Push it harder, further. Force the issue."

I nod, stiff and unfeeling. "Don't worry, Ellen, you have my promise. I will see him again." If only she knew the truth – but even I don't know that.

She stands briskly, without saying anything more, and when she leans across the table to kiss me I feel like holding on to her so that she cannot go anywhere. But I do no such thing. Instead I keep my arms limp at my sides and let her kiss the side of my mouth.

I close my eyes.

When I open them again she is gone.

My friend, my last best chance at redemption: gone, gone, gone…

At that moment in time, I doubt that I will ever see Ellen Lang again.

I say her name, like a tiny prayer.

I speak it again:

"Ellen."

TWENTY-FIVE

Ellen.

When I opened my eyes I didn't know where I was, or why my vision was so occluded. I strained to see beyond the clammy darkness that hung in tatters before my eyes, but it was impossible. Raising a hand to my face, I rubbed at my eyes and managed to pull away the ashen caul that I found there, clinging to my face like a secondary skin. I spat, wiped my mouth, and rubbed more vigorously to clear the stuff from out of my eyes.

There was no sign of the hooded youths. Wherever they'd taken Ellen, it seemed that they were long gone by now. It could have been hours ago or it could have been only minutes since she had been snatched. I had no way of knowing which.

I tried to sit but felt too dizzy to move. The next time I tried, it was easier and my head had just about begun to clear. I blinked but the sky remained dark. I was lying upon a soft mat of black ash and my clothes were covered in drying vomit. I touched my face again – tentatively, now that I was fully awake – and felt the raised areas around my chin and cheeks, the blood that had dried on my skin. There was little pain now because of the adrenaline rush I'd experienced during the fight, but I knew that I would be aching by morning.

If morning ever came.

"Welcome," said a familiar voice, and when I looked up I saw the Pilgrim standing before me, naked and glistening like plastic under the sickly light of the moon. Mr Shiloh, Matthew Torrent... whatever he called himself. He stared down at me with an amused look on his face, his pale lips locked together in a grim sneer.

His chest was smooth and unmarked, and like his head it was completely lacking in hair. Again I thought his skin looked rubbery and malleable, as if no matter how hard I hit him he would feel no pain – he would just absorb the blow as he waited for the next one.

If I threw something at him, the missile would bounce off him like throwing a tennis ball at a wall. If I blew him up with explosives, the separate pieces would simply come together again and reconfigure. If I cut off his arms, legs and head and buried them, he'd carry on moving like a decapitated earthworm.

As my gaze travelled across his alien form, I saw that he had no nipples. Nor did he possess a navel – which meant, of course, that he could never have been born as other mammals are born: he had never been delivered by a human pregnancy. I'd already suspected that he was not human, and here was the proof.

A mad thought entered my head: had the Pilgrim been hatched from an egg, or grown in a dish in some cosmic laboratory?

His thick legs were also totally without hair, and where there should have been genitals was only a smooth expanse of leathery hide. Not a blemish marked the shadowed spot, and somehow this sight was the most horrific of all. He was not like other men; he was not a man at all. Was he even a beast, or simply some kind of conceptual entity that had crawled into our reality through a loophole in the human psyche? Was he just a bitter little homunculus looking for kicks to relieve his dreadful ennui?

None of it made any sense. Like the ever-changing rules of dream logic, it seemed that the Pilgrim remade himself as he went along, constantly tweaking and tinkering with the rules of his own being.

"Once again I apologise for our methods, but some rituals are necessary when one is preparing the way. I'm sure you, of all people, understand that – the unique power of the rite, the techniques involved in conjuring certain altered states and atmospheres." He smiled, and once again I was reminded of a shark. His eyes were black and tiny; they seemed to both swallow the light and negate it. His face would have looked more at home cruising through the ocean depths, searching for prey.

And he was playing with me like a shark tormenting a wounded seal.

"Where's Ellen?" My breath was thick in my throat. I felt that I could hardly stand, so stayed there on the ground to wait for my strength to return. Right then, it felt like this would never happen – that I would be grounded forever.

"Ah, the lovely Miss Lang. Quite an interesting relationship you have there. It's been like watching a soap opera all these years." The smile stayed in place, even while he spoke. "Ill-fated lovers. Most entertaining, I must say."

"What do you mean, all these years? I don't understand." I gripped the earth with my fingers and tried to push myself up, but it didn't work. I fell back, rooted there.

"You'll learn, in time. Or perhaps you won't. It means little to me, or to those I serve and who, in turn, serve me." He turned and walked slowly over to the old bonfire, stopping in its stark night-shadow. He had no cleft in his backside, and no buttocks: just an unbroken area of pale rounded flesh.

He did not eat. He did not shit. He did not live as we live, but existed inside a rarefied bubble of his own devising.

"I've given you enough clues to start piecing this whole thing together, Mr Usher. I'm afraid that I'm becoming rather bored with the game now, and am forced to escalate events – to rush onward towards the exciting climax." His body swerved, as if he were dancing. His limbs moved as if they were boneless, bending and flexing in the air. He even clapped his hands, but silently.

I had no idea what he was talking about. I had never seen this man – this thing – before that day at the Blue Viper, when he'd walked out of an upstairs room and left a woman in tears. How could he claim to know me so well?

"Please… where is she?" There was ash in my throat, but it would not budge. I couldn't even summon enough energy to cough, or to vomit.

"They have her. The Empty Ones. The MT. Oh, how very clever, don't you think? I do like a good, dramatic name for the bad guys." He spun on his heels, the entire bottom half of his body turning first and then the upper torso corkscrewing around afterwards, creasing the flesh at his waist. His eyes were now black as tar, and their intensity made me feel even weaker than before. There was a great and limitless emptiness at his core, but I could also see that he was the servant – or perhaps the priest – of some other, greater force that so far I had barely even glimpsed.

A priest: a dark priest preparing the way, clearing a path.

"Look at it," he said, raising one arm and casting it back, beyond the point that any human shoulder joint could endure. There was no crunching sound of bone breaking; his arm simply bent backwards and stayed locked in place.

Behind the Pilgrim, towering in the dark distance, I could make out a shape. It was that damned house on fowl's legs, but this time it was different. It was now constructed of concrete, and as it tottered on the spot I saw that it also possessed doors and windows, all of them boarded with heavy security shutters. It was a derelict witch's house: the blasted place at the end of every modern-day fairytale, but one that no author had ever been brave enough to write of.

The blasted heart of the estate: the core of all this urban despair.

And behind even this, another sight: a hill, a tree, with pale flames clutching at the sky, and something twisting within the grasp of those flames, as if dancing in triumph. I could see clearly now that the blazing shape had once been a child, a small girl – perhaps even Mathew Torrent's infant sister. But before that, it had been something else, another form entirely. The young girl had merely been a potential vessel – perhaps the first – meant to carry this thing into the world: an unwitting carrier for a dark parasite whose appetite for horror was infinite.

There are things beyond this world and beneath it, energies that have no formal shape and which experience unnameable hungers, and often they catch sight of us, and we pique their interest. There is no hate, no antagonism: theirs is not a human scrutiny. They simply notice us and drift towards us. But if they are to enter, a door of some kind needs to be opened, a way prepared, and a good way of doing this is by the application of ritual – the content of these rites and incantations matters not, because they are only a means to an end. They are metaphor, a way of creating a mood. A level of belief is all that is required.

Belief is the key to it all.

There is no good or evil. No God. No Satan. Everything is real and it is also unreal: all is simply a matter of consensual belief. We fabricate our myths and our legends – our own pathetic little metaphors – simply to hide the face of that which we cannot comprehend. And sometimes, sometimes, that face is the same as our own.

But occasionally a door is opened, a rift occurs, a layer of reality is breached, deliberately. A way is opened to allow these forces inside.

Then, and only then, is it possible for some *thing* to pass through.

"Is this really what it's all about? Your sister was meant to be a host for something you wanted to bring through? Then, after she was killed, you had to start all over again?"

He laughed, but it was not a human sound at all. It was more like the whining of a small machine, an engine gearing up for mayhem. "That's only part of it. The other part – the main part – is creased up on the ground before me, writhing like an ant."

"What have I got to do with any of this? I know nothing about these things. You brought me into this, when you announced yourself at Baz Singh's nightclub." Again I struggled to stand, and this time I got as far as a low crouch, with my hands placed flat on the ground to support me.

If I could keep him talking, appeal to his colossal sense of hubris, there was a chance that I could gather enough strength to fight back.

"Oh, that silly little man. He thought that sodomising his own daughter was the height of perversion, and that if he gave her to us as a form of sacrifice he could even bargain his way into some kind of forbidden knowledge. Such a petty little atrocity: one that even amused me – for a little while. We used the girl, of course. She was one of those who prepared the way, providing a little death to tease the palette. Oh, such pretty, pretty little dead things, hanging there, all in a row – all in a row on your upstairs landing."

The Pilgrim stalked towards me, his hands increasing in size as they opened like hideous flowers.

"But alas, alas – it all becomes so dull in the end. All of it. I have walked between the lines of realities for so many centuries, and nothing ever interests me for long. I have served many and lorded over millions more. I am the Pilgrim, and this, dear friend, is just another step along the way, yet another stopping point on my great pilgrimage through the realities."

The derelict tower at his back swayed, the concrete creaking, rubble falling from somewhere within its bulky mass. Then, slowly, the Pilgrim set off towards the other side of the patch of waste ground, where he ducked through a rent in the opposite fence to the one where Ellen and I had entered. He didn't stoop to go under the post – he simply folded, passing through the gap in an instant.

He had grown bored of me, like a child torturing an insect, and now he was done.

His face peered back through the jagged gap; his voice hovered in the darkness: "I was there all along. Watching and waiting. I was there when it happened – when your family died. And I was there when you did it."

I closed my eyes, wishing that I could block my ears just as easily.

"I was there. I was inside him."

I didn't want to think, not about this. Not now.

"I helped you do it. I did it for you."

Not yet.

The tree beyond the chicken-footed tower blazed momentarily brighter, its cold fire chilling the sky like ice, and then, like a lamp being dimmed, it went out, taking the image of the Pilgrim's awful, white-staring face with it...

That was when I heard the screaming.

Unable to decide which way to turn, I simply dragged myself to my feet and tottered over to the nearest possible point of support – a small, half-demolished wall. I leaned against the bricks to catch my breath, and once again someone screamed. It sounded like a woman, and it was coming from behind me, back in the opposite direction to that in which Ellen and I had run.

I stared at the other fence, noticing that the tower and the tree were gone, and then I turned around to follow the sound of the screams.

Ellen.

Limping, yet aware that I was not badly injured, I crossed the car park and headed back towards Shawna Royale's flat. There was a small crowed gathered outside, spilling across the path, and I could hear music. It was almost as if a party had been broken up, and no one had thought to turn off the stereo when they all rushed outside to see why someone was yelling.

I brushed past teenagers who smelled of cannabis, a middle-aged woman in her nightdress, and two young men holding hands with the same girl. Reeling along the footpath, I saw it before I even registered what it was, and when the realisation hit me I was too shocked to do anything other than keep on going, keep limping towards the thing that swayed in the still night air.

Ellen.

They had not even cut her down. Nobody had thought to lend her some dignity, some final vestige of humanity, as she hung there, bruised and limp and dead. So very dead.

Ellen.

Her body was suspended from a short length of rope that had been attached by a bolt to the lintel across the double doorway to the block of flats. Her feet made tiny circles in the air a few scant inches above the ground. Her neck had been unnaturally lengthened, as if whoever had done this had then dangled from her legs, pulling her down with their body weight in order to snap her spine.

Ellen.

Blood on her face. Eyes wedged open, with one bulging out to rest like a peeled boiled egg upon her sunken blue cheek. Lips blue-black. Skin slack and bloodless. She smelled of shit and urine. I would never hear her voice again; never feel her touch; smell her breath. Kiss her body – her twisted, broken body.

Ellen.

I fell.

Ellen.

I fell down.

Ellen.

I fell down on my knees.

Ellen.

I fell down on my knees and began to scream her name.

TWENTY-SIX

Millgarth police station. Again. But this time I was not in one of the main offices, or even a quiet side room. No, the room I was in was located deep within a part of the station I had never seen before but always suspected existed. Most official buildings have their secret places; the hidey-holes where hushed conversations and clandestine meetings are held. Millgarth police station was no different in this respect: it too had its underbelly, and I had been swallowed by it.

Swallowed alive… but only barely.

After I collapsed before Ellen's strung corpse, someone had finally decided to make a 999 call and summon the emergency services. I'm still not sure who arrived at the scene first, police or ambulance, but one of them put in a call to Millgarth and tipped off Tebbit – the right thing to do, of course, considering he was in charge of the case.

When he arrived Tebbit dragged me to my feet and bundled me into the back of a patrol car. Then he had driven us here, to the station, and we had descended underground, to the basement level, inside an old lift with clanking cage-like doors.

"I'm lost here, Usher. Really lost. This whole thing has gone completely out of control." He was pacing the floor, clenching and unclenching his fists, and his face was dark and troubled. He kept pausing to rub or scratch the side of his head, but it never lasted for longer than a few seconds.

Scratch-scratch.

"What the hell is going on?"

Scratch-scratch.

I looked up from the desk, from the names brutally etched into its wooden surface. I could barely see anything beyond the veil of grief, and although I realised that I probably owed Tebbit some kind of explanation, I felt unable to form the right words.

The room was tiny, with a single bare bulb hanging from the dirty ceiling. The walls were unpainted plaster and the floor was stained concrete.

"My DCS wants me to put you in the frame for everything. He thinks you're guilty as all hell." He stopped pacing and turned to face me. He looked on the verge of tears.

So Detective Chief Superintendent Norman Scanlon thought I had killed Ellen and abducted Penny Royale. How neat and tidy – and wrong. So very, very wrong.

"Come on, man. Talk to me. Tell me something here, so I can do something positive instead of making you into a fucking straw man." His eyes widened, filled with something I didn't recognise. Could it have been compassion?

Scratch-scratch.

"I didn't do it. Not any of it." My mouth was parched; there was ash in my throat and I couldn't seem to get rid of it.

"I fucking know that, Usher. Jesus, if I thought for a minute that you were even remotely involved in any of this, I'd kick your arse right into a cell. I brought you down here to hide you, not to interrogate you. I need a reason to put you back out there on the streets, so you can help me find whoever is doing this shit." I had never heard him so angry, yet also so calm and cold and razor sharp. Tebbit knew exactly what he was doing.

"I'm sorry. I know… I should have known." I pressed my hands into my cheeks, then against the side of my skull. "That man I mentioned to you – the Russian immigrant, Mr Shiloh. Have you found out anything more?" I was operating purely on my energy reserves now, and pushing all thoughts out of my head. If I stopped to think, I would go under and drown in my own grief.

Tebbit shook his head. He looked very tired. "That's a blind alley, I'm afraid. I contacted Interpol and a bunch of other international agencies, but none of them had anything on the man. That was unusual in itself, so I dug deeper… and got nowhere. He has all the necessary credentials, of course, but he's clean. Too clean. I could find nothing but the most basic official paperwork. That's all. Nothing else."

I scored the top of the wooden desk with my fingernails, trying to cause myself pain, to bring me back from the edge. "He's not real. He's something I've never seen before. Not a ghost or a lost spirit… something… demonic."

"I thought you didn't believe in devils and demons."

Scratch-scratch.

Old Scratch? But, no; there was no such thing as the Devil. Not in the way Tebbit meant.

I looked up at him again, trying to see beyond the surface of things and into the endless void beneath. "Maybe I was wrong."

"Who else? Who else is involved?"

I pushed back from the desk, feeling suddenly confined. "Baz Singh is into this up to the collar of his Gucci shirt, but I don't really know how. He's put together some kind of fund to help the Royales, and I've seen him with Mr Shiloh. It's all very vague. I have nothing solid, nothing that you could use to arrest anyone. All I have is feelings and hunches. Things I've seen and felt, but no real evidence. Dead girls and pilgrims. Sighs and whispers. Blood and ash."

"I need more than that, Usher." He stalked over to the desk and lowered himself so that he was looking directly into my eyes. "Your spiritual mumbo-jumbo isn't going to work with this one."

I licked my lips, feeling tense and nervous. "Oh, I think that's the only thing that *is* going to work. Mumbo-jumbo, as you call it. It's the only weapon I have." I stood and walked to the wall, smashed my fist into the concrete just to feel the pain. Plaster cracked. The lone light flickered, casting thick shadows into the corners, and I felt poised at the edge of crossing over, hovering between states of reality as if my loss was acting as a bridge.

"*Mumbo-jumbo,*" I whispered.

The shadows crept towards me, reaching out like old friends. I was certain that they were smiling, smiling… smiling at me.

Everything had changed. I was no longer trying to fight the visions that assailed me – no, by now I was opening myself up to them. Let them come, and I'd take them all on. So what if I was a magnet for the darkness at the edge of the world, the gulf that could possibly consume our reality? If that was what it took, then so be it. Let the whole damn thing come pouring towards me, along with whatever shitstorm it contained.

I was through running; there was nowhere left to run. All I had, all I was, all I had ever been, was my mumbo-jumbo.

"I'm sorry, Usher. Genuinely sorry… Ellen Lang seemed like a nice woman, and I know you were close. But you can't blame yourself for what happened – it wasn't your fault."

I turned away from the wall, smiling. I felt insane, utterly insane. "Shut the fuck up, Tebbit. You know nothing about me, nothing about her. You don't even like me. But that's okay, because we have this weird relationship and we help each other out, don't we? And this time is going to be the last. This time I plan to bring down the walls of reality and avenge their deaths – all of them. My wife, my child, my lover. Guilt be damned: this is about vengeance." It felt so good to get that out of my system, even if I wasn't sure that I entirely believed it. The power was in the saying; the magic lay in the words and the emotion they contained. Even violence could be a form of incantation.

"Are… are you okay, Usher?" DI Tebbit looked terrified. Not scared, or even afraid, but terrified. I wished that I had a mirror, so that I could look into it and see whatever he had just witnessed. Had I transformed into a monster, with bolts of black energy fizzing from the ends of my hair? Had I become death? It certainly felt as if I held death in my hands, and it was a good feeling – one that I could get used to without any problem at all.

"Let me out of here."

The emotions behind my words churned and boiled; they were pushing against the surface, getting ready to explode. I knew that I could use this power – tap into it and utilise it to cross over and navigate the fold in reality where I would find Mr Shiloh, the hooded figures, the house on its hideous chicken legs, and hopefully Penny Royale.

Tebbit paused, and then nodded, stepping towards the door. "Just help me stop this thing… whatever the fuck it is." He unlocked the door and glanced along the corridor. Then he pulled his head back into the room. "Come on. Before anyone notices you're here."

Scratch-scratch.

My first port of call was Lord of Ink. I suspected that Elmer Lord knew just a little bit more than he had told me, and if anyone could give me a pointer to follow, it would be him. I realised grimly that my tattooist was the only person in the world who I could trust. Nothing, I thought, could be more pathetic than that.

This time I went round the back way, ducking along a narrow alley and climbing over the wall to his property. I found myself in a small, rectangular yard, with weeds growing up through cracks in the concrete surface. There were empty crates and barrels stacked against one wall, and a small herb garden contained within a jerry-built greenhouse was situated near what looked like an old water feature gone dry.

Action was good for me; it helped me to not think about anything beyond the moment.

The ground floor windows had been painted with white-wash, preventing anyone seeing inside. I had no idea what Elmer might keep there, under the stairs, but I assumed from the heavy wooden hatch set low in the rear wall that the place had at least a small cellar or basement.

The other door, the one I thought must lead into that down-stairs hallway from the opposite end to where I'd entered last time, was firmly closed. I banged upon it, shouting Elmer's name. It took him a long time to answer, but eventually I saw his face appear at one of the upstairs windows. He waved and disappeared. After a short while the back door opened.

"You okay?" His face was etched with concern. I knew only fragments of Elmer's life story, but we had been more than casual friends for a long time. "Why didn't you use the front door?"

"I'm feeling paranoid." I shot him a tiny smile. "I need to speak with you. I need your help."

He stepped aside. "Come in. I'll help you however I can – you know that, amigo."

I didn't speak again until we were sitting in Elmer's studio, another bottle of whisky sitting on a table between us. This time he sat in the tattoo chair and I was resting on a high stool. I was on to my second glass. "Elmer, I don't want to offend you, but I know you were holding something back before. I need you to be honest with me. Someone has died–"

"I know," he said, taking me by surprise. Registering my expression, he continued: "I still have contacts on that damned estate. I told you I grew up there, didn't I? A lot of my early years were wasted in that place…"

I remained silent.

"Okay, amigo. Here it is." He got up from out of the chair and walked around it, so that he was facing me. Then, taking me by surprise yet again, he quickly took off his shirt. His copious tattoos ranged from the primitive to the most sophisticated examples of skin art I had ever seen. There were brutal prison tats, beautiful oriental images, and so many colourful tribal designs that it was almost like looking at a human kaleidoscope.

"Wonderful… but what specifically am I meant to be looking at?" Anger brimmed behind my face; it felt like my skin was crawling across my skull.

Elmer's face sagged; a great sadness was suddenly exposed there, behind the mask, for just long enough for me to see how deeply it penetrated. "Here," he said, pointing at the upper part of his left shoulder.

"The demon?" It was an elaborate oriental demon of a kind I had seen before, probably hanging on his wall.

Elmer nodded. "Look closer. Look under the colouring and between the lines. Between the lines."

For a moment that sounded like the most profound advice I had ever been given, and I understood fully why he had repeated it. I stared at the tattoo, straining to see beyond the ink.

"Can you see now? The demon is a cover-up job. I had it done by a friend, a long time ago. It's covering something I'm ashamed of."

I still couldn't tell what he meant: the tattoo looked fine to me, even if one of its edges was slightly ragged, forming a strange bulge in the side of the demon's head.

"Look, amigo. Look and see. There it is… like I said: between the lines." His finger traced the outline within the outline: the lines that formed the letters.

"There's an M…"

I could barely believe what he was showing me. What he was telling me.

"And there's a T."

"What does this mean, Elmer? Tell me it isn't what I think?" I backed away, feeling as if all of a sudden I didn't know Elmer Lord even half as much as I'd thought I had only seconds before.

"No, amigo. I used to run with them when I was a boy. There's a lot you don't know about me, and most of it you never will. Things I've seen and done that I'm ashamed of. This is one of them – that's why I had the tat covered up. But scars run deep. You can only ever cover them, and not remove them completely."

I took a single step forward, if only to let him know that I believed him. My hands were shaking; I couldn't trust them to stay at my sides.

"They have bases all over that area, amigo. The whole place is like a rat's nest, littered with tunnels and bolt holes. But there's one place – it's the last place I heard that they'd been sacrificing animals and practicing rituals. At the back of the estate there's a bunch of derelict buildings. Condemned bungalows, garages that are falling apart, and a high rise that's barely even standing anymore. Look for them there."

I recalled the terrible visions of the last few days – the not-so-grand illusion of the house on chicken legs that had then surreally become a concrete version of the same. Now I knew where to look, but what I didn't know was how to get there. In this world I would find little or nothing of use; I had to push myself over and into that fold or crease in reality to get close to what I needed. Only there could I even begin to commune with these things: the dead, the undead, and the things that lie between.

Between the lines.

There was one more place I needed to visit before I could make preparations to go looking for the missing child, and it was somewhere I had grown to despise. I took a taxi to Bradford, and told the smirking driver to drop me off at the Blue Viper. It was afternoon already and the sky was growing dull. The rain had held off, but its threat was never far away. But even if the weather stayed dry, it felt like it was raining on me.

I had a few loose ends to tie up to before I went any farther towards the dark. There was a good chance I might not make it back here, to this sunny but often overcast little enclave, this world, this Earth. This beautiful reality. If everything I had learned over the years was even remotely true, then where I was going there were no guarantees, no escape routes or safety nets.

Unusually, there were no heavies hanging around outside the club. The main doors were locked but the side door looked unsecured; its security barrier was pulled back and sticking out from the frame. It looked as if someone had either gone in or come out pretty fast, neglecting to lock up as they went.

The Pilgrim's words came back to me: *Oh, that silly little man.*

I looked again at the unsecured door, and everything became achingly clear.

Breathing slowly, I reached out and turned the door handle, hoping that it would not budge. The handle turned and the door opened. I stepped inside, closed the door carefully behind me, and began to climb the stairs. It was dark in there – darker than it should have been. It was as if night had fallen, but only inside Baz Singh's club. I could hear a distant moaning, muted by the walls and the doors, but not unlike the sound of people having sex. I continued up the stairs and took a left, heading directly for Singh's office.

The office door was open wide, and through it I could see his desk. The desk lamp was flickering madly, as if insects were trapped inside the bulb and fluttering against the glass. As I approached it popped loudly, the bulb turning to dust. I kept on going, refusing to be spooked – this was just another game, or perhaps part of the biggest game of all. I felt the Pilgrim's hand at work here, and the thought carried with it a strange feeling of contentment. Know your demon; face your demon; put a name to your mortal enemy.

I know now that my own enemy has many names and wears faces without number: because he is legion.

I stepped into the office. Lying on the desk was the gun Baz Singh had offered me what felt like years ago but had been only a few days before. There was no smoking barrel, like there always are in the movies or in the lyrics of those crackly Delta blues songs. It just sat there, on its side, on an oversized ink blotter. The blinds were drawn; there were black streaks on the dusty material, as if someone had dragged their scruffy fingers down the entire length of the blinds.

I turned and left the office, heading for the little room where I had first encountered Mr Shiloh, the Pilgrim, menacing a prostitute. I passed the top of the stairs, glanced down them, but saw nothing moving. Nothing but shadows, Nothing but dust. Or perhaps ashes.

This door was closed, but there was a smear of red on the wood beside the handle. I knew it was a sign, a signal, and that I was meant to go in there. Part of me screamed to run away, but the rest of me – the stone-cold-hard-as-grief rest of me – stood my ground. I pushed open the door and watched it swing inward, disturbing the already flickering shadows within. The walls were bare, but there were more smears of blood, some at waist level and others, puzzlingly, up near the ceiling.

There was a flat, dull, coppery odour inside the room: a slaughterhouse stink that forced its way up my nose and down my throat, almost making me gag. The television in the corner was playing with the sound turned down. I turned to face it, looking at the screen, and saw footage of Baz Singh sodomising his daughter, poor dead Kareena, his hands gripping her hips and his body thrusting hard up against her. I tried to avert my gaze but couldn't seem to work the muscles in my neck.

I watched for a few moments more, noting the look of un-alloyed enjoyment on her face and the expression of pure horror that twisted his features into an ugly mask.

It was wrong, all turned around: the rapist looked like a victim. Kareena, it seemed, had gone willingly into this particular dark-ness, and was forcing her step-father to acquiesce, to enact his own part in the sordid ritual that the Pilgrim had surely set in motion. Once again, the truth was the opposite of my suspicions.

Finally I dragged my eyes from the screen and gazed along the floor. There was a trail of blood. Just blood. Nothing more. It led along the floor and stopped at the bed, where it began again, but patchy, more like separate stains now than a con-stant track.

There was something under the blankets. Some *things* under the blankets. They were humped in places, as if a number of items had been placed on the bed and carefully covered up. Fresh red stains bloomed even as I watched.

I looked back at the screen. Then back at the bed. How many of them were under there, taken apart and left on the mattress for me to find? Was it just Singh and his doormen, or perhaps even the rest of the Singh family – whom I had not yet met, and now never would? If those shapes rustled or squelched I did not hear, and if they writhed and twitched I did not see; for I was focused upon something else, something deep within my own being – a sudden and curious sense of righteousness.

I looked again at the television. I studied the intense look of horror in Baz Singh's eyes: the one true sign that told me he had known for a long time that he was lost and that there was nothing he could do about it. But, I promised myself, if there were any names to add to the list on my back, I would not ask Elmer Lord to make Singh one of them. Only those who truly deserved to be saved were remembered on my flesh; those de-serving souls whom I had failed and continued to fail. The ones who never had a choice.

I glanced one final time at the writhing mounds on the bed, the twisted bloodstained covers, and then I turned and walked out of the room. A wet sound followed me, but I put it out of mind, pretending that I couldn't even hear it. Walking slowly but with a new sense of certainty, I carried on past the stairs, where blackness seemed to reach up and out for me, and returned to Baz Singh's office, where I picked up the gun.

Obscure spells and ancient rites are all well and good when you are dealing with the ethereal, but flesh and blood demons require less subtle methods of disposal.

I had owned a gun once before, but never used it. Oh, I had practiced shooting it, and to a reasonable level of competence, but when the time came, and I was in a position to put all that practice to use, I was unable to pull the trigger.

But this time I would not hesitate. This time I would meet fire with fire, and finally lay ashes to ashes.

TWENTY-SEVEN

It was time.

Time.

Finally.

Time to remember.

I had put it off long enough, and the pressure had become too much to bear. I had hidden the memory even from myself, pushing it beneath the guilt and the grief and the all-consuming desire to try and make up for all of my past mistakes. But this one was perhaps the biggest mistake of them all.

Finally it was time to remember.

This time I am alone on the drive to Luton. I have a lot of time to think about Ellen, and what might have happened between us if I had perhaps allowed things to develop. But I could not let that happen; my ghosts are too heavy to put down and leave behind.

My ghosts are heavy, and I must carry them now forever.

The multicoloured streetlights blur past my windscreen, becoming an ice-cream inferno. People stand in nightclub doorways, scowling at the night. Young women in short skirts and high heels run out into the road, as if flirting with the sparse traffic. Everywhere there are eyes, staring and studying. I feel dissected by their gaze.

Soon I am in the Marsh Farm area. The grey houses beneath a grey sky; the grey lives held within the shadow of short, grey futures. It all looks familiar – like the rundown places from my own territory – and I feel as if I am just a short distance away from where I began.

The streets here are clear of the crowds I saw in the outlying areas. There are no late pubs or nightclubs, just dreary tract housing and looming high-rises. Lights are still on in many of the windows. A lot of the residents in these parts do not work, so they stay up till all hours, drinking or fucking or pursuing less conventional pastimes.

The familiar ten-storey block appears ahead of me and I step on the brake out of some sense of unvoiced fear. The car slows. I turn into the same car park as before, when Ellen brought me here, and sit behind the wheel with the engine running.

I open the dash box and take out the gun.

It is old, scratched, and has tape wrapped around the handle to mend the plastic casing. The gun is a small calibre automatic pistol, with six cartridges in the clip. I know that it is un-marked, with no serial number, because the man I brought it from made sure that it could never be traced. I helped him out with a small problem: his porn shop was being haunted by the ghost of an old prostitute who died in the 1800s, stoned to death by a drunken mob. I helped the spirit find her way back on track, and instead of accepting money I asked if he was in a position to supply me with a weapon. He did not ask what it was for. Nor did I offer the information.

The gun is heavy. Cold. I have practiced many times, out in the countryside, shooting at targets attached to trees. I am not a bad shot, but shooting paper targets is a lot different to killing a man.

I turn off the engine and sit for a while longer, watching the window. Ryan South is in there, sitting with the lights dimmed. Perhaps he is drinking the night away, trying – as I once did – to soak his demons in cheap wine and whisky.

I get out of the car and lock the door, pausing with my hand locked around the handle. If I let go, that is it: the decision made. If I twist and open the door again, I can go home and forget about all of this nonsense.

I wait for seconds but it feels like weeks.

Then I lift my hand away from the car, slip the gun into my jacket pocket, and stalk towards Ryan South's building.

This time there is no one sitting on the concrete bollards, but I remember the young girl who sat there last time, asking if I was the police. I wonder if she is still around, or if in the intervening time she has come to some sort of messy end. The ground is just as scattered with litter as the last time: empty beer cans, crushed fast food boxes, other less identifiable debris...

The foyer still smells like a pub toilet. I climb the stairs, faster this time as I now know the way. I stop at the fourth floor, staring at the door to Flat Number 411.

The door is open; just a crack, but open nonetheless. As if he is expecting me.

Perhaps he is.

I step forward, the world receding to this single point, and gently kick the door wide. The smell that wafts out of the flat is awful; a rotten combination of raw meat and sulphur invades my olfactory system, making me gag.

I step inside without thinking, knowing that if I do stop to consider my actions I will turn around and walk back to the car. This is it: the moment. There is no turning back from here on in.

The place looks nothing like it did last time. I am convinced that the hallway is even longer and narrower than before, and the wallpaper has been messily peeled back, as if by sharp claws. Hanging on the walls are framed pictures torn from anatomical textbooks – images of wounds pulled and pinned apart to show the intricate workings of the human body. I stare at pencil sketches of layers of fat, arteries, and the bone beneath. The human form skinned like an apple, peeled like a banana, chopped in half like a grapefruit.

On the floor there are scattered photographs: naked children, men and women with blood on their clothes, extreme surgical procedures – lobotomies, vivisections, trepanning, and one particularly nasty close-up shot of what looks like an autopsy.

I carry on along the hallway, peeking into the living room. The room has been stripped bare. There is no furniture; there are no coverings on the walls, floor or ceiling, and even the floorboards have been lifted to expose the dark crawlspace beneath. The smell of sulphur is strong here; someone has dug down into the skeleton of the building and revealed something foul.

I move into the kitchen further along the hall. It looks like a butcher shop. The huge, split carcasses of cows and sheep and pigs hang from steel hooks stuck into the walls. A pig's head rests in the sink, covered in flies – the sound of their buzzing begins as soon as I see the head; before that I had not heard a thing. Bones and hooves and fur are stuck to the walls, draped across the dining chairs, and the centrepiece of the small dining table is a slaughtered lamb, its belly opened and books and ornaments shoved into the bloody cavity. Its tiny uterus has been removed and placed alongside it on a dented tin platter.

Then, abruptly, I hear the creaking of floorboards; the patter of feet across the ceiling directly above me. But the feet sound too small, tiny in fact, and for the first time I begin to taste fear. I draw the gun and back out of the kitchen, then turn and head towards the other rooms, moving deeper into the flat along the hallway, which seems to be elongating as I travel along its length.

My hand is steady but my insides are shaking. I must be strong. I have to see this through.

My journey through the flat is silent. No timbers groan and I manage not to stand on any of the filthy plates and crunched up food wrappers strewn across my path. The movement in the flat above has ceased; the building is now as quiet as the grave – and that is exactly what I think of as I continue forward: the ambience of an open grave.

Bugs and centipedes scurry across the wall to my left, plopping onto the carpet at my feet. I focus ahead, at the darkness that awaits me. The further I go (and by now the interior space seems limitless, as if I should have reached the end long before now) the darker the sights I am presented with.

A cuckoo clock hangs on the wall, and as I pass it I realise that it is made of tiny bones (the bones of children?). The clock chimes – a mechanical sound rather than any kind of ringing tone – and two doors open, one at each side of the clock face. From these tiny doors appear two skeletons, but with normal skin-and-hair heads resting above white bone. The figures meet at the end of their bone rails, turn stiffly and kiss, then trundle back the way they came, the doors shutting behind them.

One door now bears a photograph of Rebecca's face; the other has a small portrait of Ally. I dare not even wonder where these photos of my family came from: I have seen neither image before.

Skulls hang from spikes, and above me, from the ceiling, dangle a row of dried human skins. They rustle like paper as I pass beneath them, shifting in a wind I cannot feel. More pictures on the walls show me upright coffins containing the wide-eyed dead; beneath them are names and Latin inscriptions, faded by time and grime.

At last I reach what must be the end of the hallway. There are clothes and shoes everywhere, and the doors have been ripped from the frames at the entrance to the rooms located at this end of the flat. Stuffing from pillows and mattresses covers everything in a strange domestic snow, shifting uneasily as I wade through the soft yellowish mass.

Ahead of me, what looks like a huge, bedraggled lion crosses the hallway, leaving one room to enter the room opposite. It does not see me; it simply walks across my path, its movements slow and easy.

I take a deep breath and carry on, unwilling to react to these images.

The rooms are empty (even the lion has vanished), but the one at the end – the final room – betrays a presence. Sickly light spills across the threshold but does not shift beyond the doorless frame. Shadows skitter on the patch of carpet outside the door, as if silent dancers are prancing within, hurling their bodies through the air and contorting into unusual shapes as they practice some strange choreography. But still there is no sound: the flat is silent as a moonscape, and seems to lack gravity and atmosphere in the same way as that haunted husk.

"I'm here," I say, thinking that I have indeed been expected.

A low, wet gurgling sound floats from the doorway. It sounds like someone laughing underwater, or choking on their own vomit as they try to scream. The sound continues for a minute that seems like an hour, and then gradually fades away.

"I'm here to see you, Ryan. I've come back for another visit." I raise the gun, my finger easing onto the trigger and my stance widening almost imperceptibly as I ready my body for action.

It is by now a familiar stance, yet still it feels vaguely absurd.

I reach the door and stop, afraid to go much further. I do not know what I might see – and that unknown element is worse than anything else in this damned place. Because that's what it is: utterly damned.

"So I must come in, then? You're not going to come to me?"

Nothing. Not even the movement of air inside the still, dense building. Everything is still. Everything is frozen.

I step forward and turn around to examine the room. Looking through the doorway, I am almost relieved by what I see. It is bad – very bad – but my imagination has already conjured much worse. The small, pink bodies of babies have been nailed to the far wall, above the bed: crucified like so many mini-Messiahs. The babies have been painted; their skin is a canvas for signs and sigils and elaborate occult designs.

Painted infants, all bloody and torn.

I know that what I am seeing is not real, not in this world anyway, but the knowledge does not make it any easier to take. I am being given a glimpse into another reality – a place where these mutilated corpses are mere baubles, simple ornaments, and where whoever now controls this environment feels most at home.

"Very clever. Now where are you?"

The bed is covered with offal. I cannot tell if the viscera are human or animal in origin, but the butchered cattle downstairs give me something to hold onto...

Then, as if on cue, the babies begin to stir. Hanging from their tiny pierced hands, they writhe against the wall, toothless mouths open in silent misery, eyelids flickering open to reveal empty, red-rimmed sockets. Each of the babies now has a huge incision in its belly, pinned open with surgical clamps. The sight is an echo of the anatomical photographs I passed earlier, a grim repetition of obscenities. The small bodies writhe against the wall, the lips of their dry, completely bloodless wounds puckering and opening up to show me the pulsing grey treasures held within.

I turn away, half disgusted and half impressed by the lengths to which whatever is in this house will go to try and shock me.

"Very clever," I say, facing the empty doorway and the hallway beyond. "Now let's see something real." I do not sound afraid, but inside I am terrified.

Before I leave the room entirely I look back over my shoulder: bare walls, unmade bed, torn carpet, window with a leather jacket strung across it in lieu of curtains. The tawdry reality I was not meant to see.

Ryan South is waiting for me outside, at the mouth of yet another open door, performing a contortion which in school gym classes we used to call "the crab". He is bent over almost backwards, with his palms flat on the floor, but his head is craned around underneath his back – so far that it does not seem possible for the human body to stretch this way.

"Usher." His voice is low, quiet, almost pleasant to hear.

His head turns through one-hundred and eighty degrees, so he faces me right-side-up.

"Who are you?"

The crab-man shuffles forward and flips upright into a sort of bastardised kung-fu stance: legs apart, torso rigid, arms held across the body and hands pointed like spears. He is wearing a pair of soiled pyjamas. His feet are bare; the toes are long and crooked, the nails yellow and sharp as claws. They scrabble on the floor, sounding like rats scurrying under the boards.

"Who are you?" I say again, staring him down and keeping the gun trained on him, judging his movements.

"I am many. We are one. How's the wife and kid, Usher? Whoops – I forgot. They're in here. With us." Slowly, gracefully, he performs a perfect ballet pirouette, stretching up on those ugly toes. The heaped mattress filling shifts on the floor, rising in small heaves and humps around his feet.

I know enough to realise that Ryan South is not alone inside this body; there are others in there with him, possibly even keeping him prisoner in his own frail cage of bones. "I want to speak with Ryan South. He and I have unfinished business." I straighten my arm and point the gun at his face.

He smiles. A long, thin purple tongue flicks out between his thin blue lips, licking his chin and leaving a trail of yellow sputum. Behind me, in the other room, the babies begin to cry. From the distant kitchen comes the sound of feet and hoofs clattering on the walls and tabletop, of mutilated bodies thrashing and falling heavily to the floor.

"Just cut the fucking act and show me who you are. Or let me talk to Ryan South. It won't take long. I just need him for a minute or two." My finger aches to pull the trigger, but I am not sure if I want to shoot the twisted man before me or use the gun on myself.

Then he sinks to the floor, hands coming up to cover his face. He is weeping: long, heavy, drawn-out sobs. "Please," he wails. "Help me." He moves his hands away from his face and I look into the eyes of the man who killed my family. But then, almost immediately, I realise that he did not do it alone. Whatever was inside him a matter of seconds ago was also there that night: they used him as a puppet, controlling him.

He smiles again, and then shakes his head.

I sink to my knees on the worn carpet. The babies continue to cry, slamming their little crucified bodies into the wall: a choir of wailing stillbirths.

"Is this what you want?" He stands, rising slowly from the white mattress stuffing, like some ancient sea god from the surf. "Do you want to kill him? Is vengeance what you seek, pilgrim?"

I look at the gun, then back at the man who stands before me with his arms outstretched. It is a short distance between the two, one that I feel I could travel if only I knew how to push myself.

"Do it, Usher. Do it, now. Take another step on your journey. The power you have has always been inside you, but it took a little push to release it from out of the depths. Now it calls to you, as it calls to us... and to others without names or faces. Can you feel them spinning towards you across the gulf, reaching for you in search of a way in?" He drops his hands to his sides. "Go all the way. Break on through."

"What do you want from me?" I raise my head and the tears stream down my cheeks. None of this makes sense – even the fact that I am here, with a gun in my hand and a family-sized hole in my heart.

"Shoot him. End his life. Take another step towards the dark." He steps forward, approaching me. His movements are smooth, unhindered.

I point the gun at him and try to pull the trigger, but something inside me snaps and my finger refuses to squeeze. I see it in my mind's eye: finger twitching, bullet firing, head exploding, blood misting before his shattered face. But none of it happens.

None of it happens as I would have wished.

Wished.

Make a wish:

I wish you were here.

Rebecca. Ally. My loves. I wish you were here.

"Let us make this easy for you." He reaches into the folds of his pyjama top and pulls out a thin-bladed kitchen knife. "Just watch." He takes the knife and slashes his own face, drawing a long, deep gash across first one cheek and then the other.

Skin tears like paper, blood flows like tears. He then uses the other hand to grab his lips, pulls them away from his mouth, grasping them between finger and thumb, and neatly slices them off. He throws the meat into a corner, laughing through blood. Bloody laughing.

Then he starts work on the arms. The shoulders. The chest. The belly. The throat.

"Memento mori," he says; they say. Gurgling on blood as if it were nothing but mouthwash. It is the first time I have heard that phrase, but somehow I know deep inside me that I will hear it again... I will hear it again, but I do not know where or when. Maybe when I do, things will become clear, and I will discover the nature of the being that stands before me, performing an act that I cannot.

And I watch. I watch and I gain a perverse pleasure from seeing the man I have grown to hate mutilate his own body in such a way. It is only when I tell myself that he is not doing this to himself – that others are doing it for him – that I finally snap and do what I came here to do.

Too late, much too late, I point the gun and pull the trigger. The gun does not go off. I pull the trigger again and again.

Again.

"Memento mori."

Then I stand back and watch in silence as Ryan South cuts himself out of this world and into another, where something dark waits patiently for him, washing itself in blood. His blood. My family's blood. All our blood.

TWENTY-EIGHT

After watching Ryan South die – or, if I'm to be honest about what happened, after I participated in his death by not stepping in to help – everything took on a clarity that terrified me. Suddenly the world became opaque and I could see the machinery that hums beneath; each layer of reality was etched clearly on the glass, and all I had to do was reach out and touch them.

That was when I began to read books on religion and spirituality, and to study obscure occult texts written by anyone from great religious leaders and half-mad prophets to drunken poets. It didn't take me long to realise that in this context the Dalai Lama had much in common with Walt Disney: both were fabricating their own version of reality, and one was just as relevant as the other.

There is no forbidden knowledge: everything is permissible. We choose which reality we want to see early on in our lives, usually encouraged by parents and loved ones, or enemies and abusers, and we stick to that version for the rest of our days. But sometimes our faith in that choice is swayed, and we begin to see glimpses of something else... something more.

Vincent Van Gogh did not paint in forbidden colours, Bosch's *Garden of Earthly Delights* was not a religious vision, and the strange imagery and eerie mysticism of a painting like *The Fairy Feller's Master Stroke* is just as real as a photograph.

My early studies had incorporated such commonly available volumes as the Bible, the Torah and the Koran, along with several less widely known Muslim and Buddhist texts. And then I devoured every other religious or mystical doctrine I could lay my hands on, however esoteric – texts on occult science and fringe belief systems. From there I had strayed into darker territory, and managed to get hold of books whose very existence was thought to be fiction. These latter volumes confused me even more, providing no real answers, only glimpses of a form of madness that I felt unable to examine any closer.

My studies came to an end one day when I was walking on the beach in Whitby, where I had gone to visit a young girl who was hailed as a natural medium. This girl could speak with the dead, or so it was said, but when I got there all I found was a confused teenager with a lot more imagination than the average thirteen year-old.

Walking along the front, I came to a small fenced area containing a beat-up old merry-go-round and an out of tune calliope. There were various Victorian penny games in what amounted to a tiny arcade, and one of them caught my eye.

I walked towards the booth and looked at the large glass case. Inside it was a clockwork chicken collapsed beside a small toy piano. I fished a coin from my pocket and slid it into the slot. The tiny player-piano started up, and after several failed attempts the bedraggled clockwork chicken jerked to its feet. As the tinny music played, the chicken began to dance. I watched it until my money ran out, and came away with an insight that made me quit the esoteric reading matter and concentrate instead on what was really important – people, and how I might help them.

We are all like that clockwork chicken, dancing to the tune of a toy piano and only ever allowed to stop when the money runs out. But when some unseen hand puts another penny into the slot, we are forced to start all over again, dancing to a hideous tune until our legs break.

We dance and we dance, but we never know whose hand feeds money into the slot. All we can do is keep going until the dance is over.

Back at the house I sat downstairs and stared out of the patio doors into my garden, thinking once again about that stupid chicken in its dusty case – amazed because I hadn't thought about it in years.

It was by now late afternoon and shadows were gathering under the bushes and at the rear fence. A lone butterfly wafted across the lawn, hovered for a while over a certain patch of grass, and then moved on. There were eyes on its wings. The design didn't resemble eyes: there were actually eyes watching me from the insect's beautiful wings. Things were slipping through; or perhaps it was I who was slipping, and inch by inch my grief was pushing me towards the crease in reality where the Pilgrim walked.

I stood and walked to the bookshelves. My hand strayed over the spine of some of the books I had read years ago, looking for an answer when all along I should have been looking for the right question.

I turned away and trudged to the foot of the stairs. Dust motes spun in silence, drifting in the air like unfettered souls. But there was no such thing as the human soul – not in the terms of an isolated entity separate from the body. Mind and body are one; we are what we are and after we die we become something else, moving on to somewhere else. The only question worth asking is, "when"?

Ellen was still there, somewhere. She was dead, but still present in the universe. Just like my family. My acceptance of this was the only thing keeping me going.

Memento mori: Some day you shall die.

The phrase hinted at the only truth that was not open to debate.

The idea of death had not frightened me for so long that it had finally begun to represent some kind of comfort. The one thing that did scare me about my own mortality was the possibility that I might not catch up with my wife and child. Rebecca and Ally had moved on so long ago, and had such a head start on me, that I couldn't be certain they had not left me behind for good.

I started up the stairs, placing one foot in front of the other, just as I always did. The only religion in which I believe is that of forward motion: keep on going, no matter what, and you will always find yourself somewhere, even if it is the place you least desire to be. But perhaps it's the place you need to be.

The three girls were now barely even visible: just smudges in the air. Spinks was merely a dark patch against the wall. Ellen had not joined them; her presence was elsewhere, and I doubted that I would ever see her again.

As far as I could tell, these girls had been used as signifiers; their grisly deaths were nothing more than a method of preparing the way, setting the mood for whatever the Pilgrim was attempting to bring through into our world. I had no idea what that thing might be, but once, a long time ago, he had tried to force it into the body of his sister and failed because of a murderous peasant boy who took it upon himself to kill a witch.

I also knew now that Kareena Singh had gone willingly, and the very fact of her presence in my house meant that, after death, she had come to have second thoughts. Perhaps once she was closer to the thing the Pilgrim was summoning, the darkness at the edge of the world, she had seen its true face and realised the error of her ways. Or perhaps she had simply realised that she had been wrong. I would never know for certain.

The room that Rebecca and I had once shared – the master bedroom – was one into which I ventured rarely, and it had been locked up for many years prior to the events of this endless week. I went in there now, knowing on some level that I had to be close to the family I missed. I needed their help, even if they were so very far away.

I looked around the room, taking it all in. The wardrobe where her clothes still hung, the bed we had slept and made love in, the antique dressing table she had inherited from an old aunt; her hairbrushes on the side, the bottle of her favourite perfume. All of it untouched, left there as some kind of shrine. My eyes stung and my throat went dry. I wanted to walk towards that stuff – her stuff – but my legs had turned to stone.

There was power here, of a kind: the power of those loved and lost, of the ones we cling to even in our darkest hours.

But if this room was one that I hardly ever entered, there was also one into which I had not set foot at all since their deaths.

I turned and walked out onto the landing, feeling the wind-gust of the ghosts out there if not actually seeing their forms, and stepped across to Ally's room. The white door was looking slightly grubby now, and the handle had always been loose. The door was never locked – there was no need; I simply never went inside.

I opened the door and stepped into the past, feeling a cold wind caress me as I crossed the threshold. The posters on the walls were still intact, if a little dusty; none of them had come loose. Ponies and puppies and cartoon characters. The wallpaper was a design Rebecca and I had picked out together: colourful clouds and moons and stars, with cartoon cherubs lounging amid the celestial clutter.

Stuffed toys lay in a group at the top of the bed, clustered up against the headboard. Their glassy eyes stared at me, not judging, just watching, and I felt a tug somewhere deep inside – the tug of a small hand clutching at my heart.

I got down on my knees and closed my eyes. The power was stronger here, as I had known it would be. I could feel them, both of them, and my desire to see them, even one last time, almost overcame me.

I said their names over and over again, feeling something stir. I called upon them to aid me, to protect me as best they could, and I'm sure that there came an answer: soundless, wordless, like a silent breath on my cheek.

I recited lines from ancient prayers once carved in stone, a section of the Torah. Then I spoke the words of a William Blake poem; recited an old Beatles song; a paragraph from John Steinbeck's *Of Mice and Men*, which had always been Rebecca's favourite book. I finished by singing Ally's favourite nursery rhyme: *Baa-Baa Black Sheep*.

It is not the content of the incantation that matters, but the power of the emotion behind it. Magic is an inexact science, and it can often be made up on the spot. This is what most people do not understand: the words, the phrases, mean nothing, but the thing which holds the meaning is what lies *between the lines*. Elmer Lord understood this – it was a similar magic to that inherent in his tattoos. I understood it, too. I always had.

The real magic is interstitial, it lies in-between what we know and do not know. Enchantment lives in the gaps between what we feel and what we say, what we hear and what we miss.

My tattoos became animated, the ink flowing across my body, running in narrow, coloured rivers before returning to recreate the symbols of protection they were always meant to be. I felt my friend Elmer Lord's art within me; I heard the sound of the tattoo gun and felt the tip of the needle pierce my flesh. Then I felt as if I were being filled with positive energy.

I knew that my family were kneeling alongside me and that despite my old betrayal they still loved me, and always would.

I stood and walked to a door in the opposite wall. It was a built-in cupboard, where Ally had always hidden whenever we played hide-and-seek. She kept her favourite possessions in there, the stuff that she wanted no one else to handle. I opened the door and looked inside.

Part of me wanted to see her hiding, crouched in the same spot she always hid. But I knew that wasn't feasible – that it would not be so easy. If ever I did catch up with them, it would cost me more than the simple opening of a door.

It was there. The mirror. I had picked it up in an old second-hand shop for her fifth birthday, when all she had wanted had been a dressing table like her mother's and a full-length mirror. She loved dressing up, and Rebecca allowed her to play with make-up as long as she didn't make a mess.

Ally had loved the mirror; it had been her "bestest present". I wept when she stood before it dressed in some of her mother's old clothes; my little girl turning into a little woman in the glass. The mirror had always remained her favourite thing. Nothing we bought afterwards could ever replace it in her affections.

Scrying is simply another method of creating a formula to access elsewhere. An ancient Arabic treatise, *De aspectibus*, outlines much of the power of mirrors. Its author, a man called Alhazen, studied the subject at length, and his book is considered the ultimate written record of the properties of reflective glass. I had read the volume during my early studies, and it had made such an impression that I had subsequently avoided all mirrors for a year.

Byron Spinks had walked into the mirror in Ellen's hotel room on the night of his death, after he had been killed by another prison inmate who was probably a member of the MT. I had seen him, but I had not followed him. Not then. This time I would. But I would be the one to choose the mode of entrance.

I stared into the mirror, focusing within me. I reached into my body and dug down deep, pushing aside all the things I used as armour – the secret codes of my pain, the razorwire fences of my psyche. Then, finally, I found it: a small dark box with a shiny clasp. I opened the box and tipped out what was inside: the love I kept all for them, for Rebecca and Ally. I let it out into the light for the first time since Ryan South took them from me – since the Pilgrim, as I now knew him, had used Ryan South as a weapon in a Marsh Farm slum to draw me into his orbit.

"I'm ready," I whispered. *"Mumbo-jumbo."*

The room went dark; the mirror turned black.

The glass was fogged, as if heavy, dark clouds churned and boiled beneath it. Some of that fog leaked out, spilling into the room, and slowly I reached out to touch it. The fog was actually ash; it turned my fingers black. I pulled away my hand and raised it to my lips, opened my mouth, and stuck the fingers inside, licking them clean and tasting the ash from a fire that never went out. It tasted of loss. Of memory. Of pain.

Marshalling my terror, I raised my hands, palm out, and pushed… but they came up against the glass, stopping dead. Dead hands. No entry. Puzzled, I stared at the mirror, at the blackness beyond, and glimpsed movement there, the quick flickering motion of an insect scuttling under a rock, or a snake slithering into shadow.

My hands were still pressed against the glass. They were cold. So cold and hard and dead.

Cold hands. Dead hands.

Another set of hands appeared opposite them, the palms locked with my own. These other hands – so white and smooth and like plastic, but ending in smoky darkness at the wrists – flexed and I felt their pressure against my skin and bones. Then, briskly, they clasped me tighter, our fingers locking as if in a child's game.

Their grip was like iron.

I tried to step back in panic, but the hands held me there, and then they began to pull. It was too late for regrets. The time had long passed to change the course of events, but fear and doubt and anger collided in my mind to release me. I re-alised at last that I was not doing this – my own power was not as strong as I'd started to believe.

This was the Pilgrim's doing. He was dragging me into his realm, just as he'd wanted all along. I had no choice now. I had been tricked and cajoled, and now he had what he wanted.

He had me right in the palms of his hands.

I was dragged roughly, violently, into the mirror, afraid of what might be waiting there for me on the other side of the blackened glass, squatting in-between realities and laughing like a jackal.

Here was where the magic lived, where the Pilgrim walked, where the ghosts drifted.

Here was where it all ended, one way or another.

Here was where I finally got to put out the fire.

TWENTY-NINE

When the fog cleared I was standing on a street in the Best-wick Estate, or at least a street on an alternative version of the estate. There was no sign of those terrible disembodied hands, or the thing to which they belonged.

The air smelled of burning: the stench entered my mouth and pushed down my throat, making my insides ache as if they were being squeezed. The buildings around me looked even more rundown than they did on the real estate, if that were at all possible. Windows were mouths lined with jagged glass teeth, doorways were coffin-shaped holes leading into strange black rooms, and weird-looking birds sat along the rooflines, squawking softly.

It was dark here; it was always dark here. Always dark in the Pilgrim's domain.

The sky was burned; the roads and footpaths were burned; it was all burned. Ash drifted like dark confetti, riding air currents that I couldn't feel in this stark, still place. I could sense a great lassitude which threatened to overcome me and drag me down to my knees, but I fought against it with all the strength that I possessed. All I wanted to do was lie down in the road and rest, go to sleep, but I held on tightly to the conviction that if I did so I would be trapped here forever, lost between realities and stored like food in the Pilgrim's larder.

"Mumbo-jumbo," I said again, enjoying the way the words tasted as they filled my mouth. The phrase brought to mind an image of Tebbit, and the plain kind of reality he stood for.

I walked forward, heading in the direction of the waste ground where Ellen and I had been set upon by those terrible members of the MT. As I walked I sensed movement in some of the buildings. Shapes hovered at shattered windows; disjointed shadows writhed in those coffin doorways. It felt like I was being watched, or scrutinised like a specimen in a lab.

Far ahead of me I caught sight of a long procession of figures moving along the burned horizon. They were very tall and painfully thin – like skeletons with tissues of pale flesh pulled taught across their bones. Each of the figures was vaguely humanoid in aspect, yet above the neck they all had birds' heads. Large beaks snapped at the sky and tiny black eyes stared unblinkingly ahead. I could make out nothing more of their features, but even this glimpse was enough to inspire the hope that they didn't turn their attention upon me.

I knew that the Pilgrim was in control here. It was clear that he was able to shape the reality of this place between realities. Everything I might see would be a reflection of his darkling dreams.

I kept on moving, trying to focus on the road ahead. From behind me there came the sound of doors slamming open and shut, like hungry mouths, and when I turned to look the coffin-shaped entryways were darker, deeper than before, and within the wooden frames I could see fine outlines etched into that darkness, like engravings. The outlines moved, struggling to be born from those upright coffins filled with night, and I forced myself to look away before my concentration was lost.

I passed the odd sight of a huge cracked egg at the side of the road. It was at least large enough to hold a human being.

More hairline cracks appeared in the surface of the dirty white shell as I passed by. A black and yellow claw-like appendage struggled from one of them, tearing at the shell and breaking away chunks that fell to the ground to shatter into yet smaller pieces, which then skittered across the charred paving stones.

Before moving on, I glimpsed a pulsing caul-like sheet through one of the cracks in the egg, with what might have been eyes staring through the folds in its pulpy mass. Something called out, but not in any language that I could understand.

Then they appeared.

They.

The MT.

They skulked out from their hiding places behind the grubby, tumbledown buildings and followed me from each side of the road, stalking me like predators following wounded prey. They didn't attack, simply flanked me and matched my strides as I walked.

They were the drones, the workers, the part-time hangmen, but I was here to meet with whoever or whatever was in charge.

Animals walked with them – odd, mishmash creatures made up from differing origins: an alligator with the legs of human children, spiders the size of puppy dogs, with white faces containing a single gelid eye, bats that walked on their wings, dragging behind them silver-razored tails.

The figures paid these familiars little attention, but they turned their sightless gaze upon me. Ash dropped from their black hoods and dissipated in the heavy air. Their hands grasped emptily at their sides, straining, as if they were being reined in by a greater force. I knew that they were acting as chaperones, forcing me along a certain route, but it was the route I wanted to take anyway.

There had never been any other way to take. This was the culmination of a choice made long ago.

I spotted the ruined fence and made for the broken barrier, increasing my speed. I was almost running by the time I reached it, and I crawled through the smashed panel on my hands and knees. On the other side I came upon the old bonfire, which I now realised could only ever have been a funeral pyre. Among the twisted timbers and molten plastic, scorched human flesh had been moulded and fused together to form a nightmarish amalgamation of figures who all screamed silently for release.

I peered at the mess of blasted tissue, picking out a hand, a leg, a pair of breasts, a face... and two eyes flicked open in an incinerated face, peering at me from a mask of ancient agony. The sound of blackened matter ripping apart filled my ears as the figure opened its mouth. I leaned in, urging it to speak, but all that emerged from its lips was a thin, black plume of ash...

I lurched away, heading for the far side of the waste ground, where the other broken-down fence would provide a way out. I ducked beneath the leaning timber frame and rolled onto the rubble at the other side. I was breathing heavily, but not from exertion – the altitude here was like that encountered halfway up a mountain, and it held the air like fluid in my lungs.

The place I had come to see loomed above me, tottering on its tawdry chicken legs. This time the legs were real – massive, scaly and knobbly as old tree branches, they shuffled in the debris that littered the ground, grasping for purchase. Perched atop those terrible limbs was a scorched concrete building with no doors or windows but a single smoking chimney jutting from the pointed roof. The juxtaposition of oversized fowl's legs supporting this grimy modern structure was horrific in a way that eclipsed everything else.

It was beyond the surreal; way beyond terror.

I moved around the building, expecting it to turn and track my route. But it remained in place, shifting its weight equally between the four feet, yellowed talons clutching at the earth.

The structure looked like it might topple over at any second, but it also looked as if it had stood there for centuries, perhaps occasionally moving a few feet from the exact spot where it now stood, but always returning to nest in its own weird footprints.

As I reached the back of the awkward building, I saw that a truncated set of concrete steps hung down from the rear wall. They dangled there in the air, unsupported; the lower steps had crumbled away and rusty steel reinforcement rods stuck out like old, reddened bones. But if I leapt up and reached out, I could grab onto the last tread and pull myself up.

I crept closer to the back wall, bent my knees, and jumped. Missing the stairs by inches with my grasping fingers, I tried again, and this time I managed to get hold of one of those crusty steel rods. I hauled myself up, feeling the strain in every muscle. The chicken legs scuttled; the building moved gently from side to side, adjusting to counteract my weight. Then, at last, I was up there, my chest resting on the steps, and I gratefully dragged my entire body onto the crumbling ledge.

Breathing heavily, I crawled up the half stairway and pressed my body against the small door at their summit. There was no handle, but I knew that I could open it. All I had to do was knock on the door.

After all, I was expected.

I made a fist and brought it down onto the heavy steel door. I knocked once, but the sound was multiplied tenfold, as if I were hammering repeatedly on the door to gain entry. Slowly, soundlessly, the door eased open. I glanced over my shoulder, to see the hooded members of the MT standing below me, looking up at me as I clung to the open door. I took out the gun and pointed it at them, not picking out any single figure but just aiming indiscriminately into the bunch.

They rocked on their heels, swaying gently. And then I was shocked to see them step away backwards, their arms and legs bending the wrong way at the knee and elbow joints. They moved slowly and deliberately, a procession in reverse, and I watched as they blended into the darkness that had now crept in to frame the demolition site like a Saturn-ring of soot.

I pushed through the doorway, swallowing down my fear, and entered a long, dark corridor. I was not surprised to hear the door snicker shut behind me, but what did make me uneasy was the sickly illumination that bled into the space, blooming against the walls and floor. There were no openings along the lengthy corridor, but a sort of sullen swamp light emanated from the stone walls (stone, not concrete; for this was more like the entrance to a cave).

I was terrified, but I bit down on the fear. I had to do this, had to keep moving into the heart of someone else's darkness, if I was to stand any chance of saving the child.

"I'm here, Pilgrim. I'm coming." My voice sounded flat, dead, but he knew that I was here so there was no point in trying to disguise my approach. I took the gun from my pocket and held it tightly in my right hand, suspecting that it would be a poor defence against the being I had come here to confront, yet still taking comfort from its cold, hard weight in my fist.

"I'm here."

I walked forward, moving reluctantly along the featureless corridor. The floor, walls and ceiling were identical and before long I had lost all sense of direction as well as spatial awareness: I could have been walking on the ceiling for all it mattered, and the sensation provoked within me a kind of light nausea. My head began to ache and bile rose into the back of my throat, but I swallowed it down, telling myself that I needed to remain calm and in control.

Always in control, even here, where all control was an illusion.

I was the only hope Penny Royale had left, and that should be motivation enough to keep me on track. I had allowed my own child to die, so the least that I could do was save this one, whatever it cost me. But it was not redemption that I sought, more a sense that I could do something to push back the encroaching tide of darkness that I felt groping towards me.

The structure was much bigger inside that it was out, but the idea of the Pilgrim being able to manipulate space in such a way didn't alarm me. I knew that he was capable of so much more, particularly here, in his own environment. He was a product of the things that slip through the gaps, the wasted ideas and abandoned dreams of the living. His ability to mould those things into this strange between-place was no great surprise considering everything else that I had learned.

He was not a man, he was not a beast. He was something in-between.

I knew that the Pilgrim had been there with me when I confronted Ryan South, the man driving the car that had killed my family. I wondered about other times after that when he may have come to me, and if he had in fact been stalking me since childhood, walking along at my side like a dirty little angel. He had intimated as much during our frightening conversations, but to trust him would be to trust a serpent. I had to make up my own mind and assess whatever came at me. My own sense of reality was vital now; it might be the only weapon I had against such a being as this self-styled Pilgrim.

I had to believe in myself.

The corridor suddenly opened out into a large circular chamber with a high vaulted cathedral-style ceiling. I stared upward, straining my neck, but was unable to see the pinnacle of the ceiling above me. It seemed to stretch on for miles, and my vision ran out at a layer of dusty darkness in which strange winged shapes glided, swooping and darting like bats. There were ledges dotted here and there in the stone walls, and as I watched an occasional figure would step out and approach the edge of one of these balconies, as if peering down at me. None of the figures was human. Some of them could barely be called figures at all: just dim outlines and shifting clumps of darkness.

I realised that I was inside some kind of viewing gallery, not unlike the ones Victorian surgeons had used to demonstrate complicated operations before the eyes of fascinated students and members of the paying public. Had the Pilgrim called these others here to see me? Was this all part of whatever elaborate game he still seemed to be playing?

I lowered my gaze, not wanting to watch the watchers for much longer. Before me, an aperture had opened up in the previously solid stone wall. I moved towards it, still gripping the gun, but before I could enter the Pilgrim himself stepped forward, in all his plastic glory.

"Greetings," he said. His voice was almost welcoming. "I've been waiting here for you. I've been waiting a very long time." Again there was the intimation of so much more than his words could convey. As always, he was playing with me, teasing me with snippets of the truth that became lies by association.

"What is this place?" I stood firm before him, betraying no fear yet feeling plenty.

"This," he said, looking around, "is my home. Or one of them." He smiled and it was like the expression a shark makes before it bites off your leg.

I felt my rage building, but bit down on it.

"Where's the child? Where's Penny Royale?" My hand tightened on the gun.

"This way," he said, giving in far too easily for my liking. I had expected at least a continuation of his riddle-like monologue, but instead he simply turned and walked away, expecting me to follow. His naked body seemed to ripple in the darkness, as if the skin were attempting to leap from his torso.

I glanced around, and then up, before following the Pilgrim through the opening. His stride was long and graceful, like that of a trained dancer. He was brimming with confidence, and knew that I was almost powerless here, in this place. His place.

He stopped before a set of steel doors. I waited. Finally he turned, his face glistening slug-like in the foetid darkness. "I hope you are prepared for what you are about to see." He seemed to grow and swell, taking up far too much room in the increasingly claustrophobic space.

"And what's that?" I stared him down, sensing his pleasure at this whole situation. "What's this all about, Pilgrim? Is it all just part of some endless game that you play? Are you just having fun?" I sounded unafraid but I was terrified.

He sneered, and then laughed. The sound was awful, like the gurgling drains of hell. "Oh, yes. I am indeed having so much fun. But there is a serious side to all this. The stage was set by those pretty dead things, all hanging like party favours and charging the atmosphere like leaking batteries, and now at last we have a vessel fit to contain the multitudes that will follow. Penny is such a lucky little girl. She will know pleasures that others cannot even bear to imagine."

"If you're so powerful, why can't you just open the door all by yourself and let it in – the darkness?" I was beginning to sense the limits of his power, and I doubted that he liked the fact I was constantly shifting my position within our dynamic.

"Even places like this have certain… rules. There is no such thing as true chaos; you above all people should be able to understand that. Chaos is just another name for order."

Something was nagging at me; an idea that had brushed up against me several times now, but was only just coalescing into something that I could put into words. "You're lying, aren't you? You're not some adventurer who cruises the realties for fun. You're trapped here, only able to flit into existence occasionally, when you are allowed… or if you are called. If you were even half as powerful as you claim, none of this would be necessary. None of it."

Something flickered across his face; an expression that could not be described in human terms but might just be a hint of weakness. It was like the tip of a serpent's tail flicking in darkness: sharp, fast, barely even there at all.

"I once had the thought that you might be some kind of priest, and that's not too far from the truth, is it? You are bound here, and your only possible way out is by arranging for something else to pass through, so that you can latch onto its back and ride it. You're like an insect, scuttling around behind the skirting boards of reality, stuck there feeding on crumbs and scraps, waiting to be let out."

The mask slipped, just for a second, and as his hairless face drooped I saw behind it a vast and infinite emptiness: a void that hungered for substance, but was cursed never to attain that which it coveted so intensely.

"This way," he said, and opened the steel doors.

I entered a large room that looked not unlike an average lounge in a normal home. Cheap furniture was arranged around the room, and pictures hung on the walls. There was a gas fire, a faux surround with a mantelpiece, and windows that looked out onto nothing, just an empty expanse devoid of feature and character. The room looked familiar, and it took me a while to realise that I had been inside here before. It was the Royale's living room.

They were all there, inside the room: Shawna and her husband Terry Royale, Baz Singh, in his expensive suit and shoes, Mr Shiloh, his mask now firmly back in place and his Pilgrim identity cast aside like a costume. They were standing in a circle, and at their centre was a cheap Formica dining table. On the table was a girl, lying on her back. A girl called Penny Royale.

She had been stripped down to her underwear, and the bruises on her body stood out livid against the light surface upon which she lay prostate, one arm dangling limply over the edge and the other clasped across her flat little chest as if in some final desperate act of self-protection. Her eyes were wide open, staring beyond us all, and her nose and teeth were broken. Blood had dribbled between her lips and onto her chin. Her left cheek was swollen, the bones beneath shattered, and there were finger marks on the pale skin of her throat.

Her mother stood over her. Her mother stood over her with something shining in her hand. Her mother looked at me as if I was the one committing some kind of atrocity. With something shining. In her hand.

Her mother.

Her mother looked at me and snarled.

Shining in her hand.

As my gaze travelled along Penny's poor little abused body, I saw that her stomach had been hacked open and the skin of her ribcage was peeled back like the flesh of an orange. Blood was beginning to congeal against her pale skin, and her innards hung out of the wound like clumps of red rope.

It was then that I finally looked at the knives: small, sharp blades in all of their hands, which they had been using to skin her.

Her mother, holding a knife.

Her father, holding a knife.

The benefactor of her finders-fund, holding a knife.

All shining in their hands.

Baz Singh had blood on his suit. Shawna Royale had blood matted in her badly-dyed hair. Terry Royale was crying, but the blood on his face destroyed any vestige of sympathy before the notion had even entered my head.

Blood; her blood. Penny's blood. They were all lathered in it.

Blood. Blood. Blood.

"I see you found my little gift," said Singh, nodding at the gun. His face was loose and hung as lifeless as an empty sack. His voice sounded like stones rattling in a box. I stared into his eyes, but the man I had dealt with was no longer in there. Instead there was a gap in the shape of a person – a gap clothed in skin. "I left it there for you. Thought… you… might be able to use it."

I realised then that Baz Singh was begging me for death. He wanted me to kill him, but at that moment the concept of mercy was the furthest thing from my mind.

Mercy was for those who deserved it.

I looked back at the corpse – the partially flensed corpse of poor, poor Penny Royale. She lay there like a slab of meat, a plaything for animals, and my heart groped towards her across that dreadful killing room. I could smell the flat, coppery odour of her blood, even see fine red particles still misting like a light red rain in the air. Seconds earlier, this grubby little coven of would-be witches had been hard at work, looking for the doorway that had been created inside her, and ignoring the precious young life as it bled from her body...

Something caught my eye then; a small fluttering, like the jittery movement of a bird's wings. There was something stirring in the ruin of Penny's belly: a small burned shape that could have been a foetus but was too ugly and mutated to be anything even resembling human. It rolled in the thickening blood and slowly pulled itself partway out of the hole in Penny's abdomen, its mouth opening and a terrible squalling noise issuing forth.

It was burned and blackened, but it was being born – born into this place, a way station from where it might then enter our world, our reality, and possibly stop us believing in the structure of what we saw around us.

"Say hello to our baby," whispered the Pilgrim.

I raised my hand and pointed the gun at the table, at the dead girl, at the thing being sired from her ruin. The creature's small white eyes were upon me; its singed tongue emerged from between cracked lips and flickered back and forth, back and forth.

"No," I said. "No." My mind was racing; images spun before my eyes. Reality falling apart, spinning away from the centre in a whirlwind of unbecoming... Then I pulled the trigger and the squealing thing exploded into a rain of ash.

The Pilgrim stepped back from the others, gliding as if on castors. He hissed at me, his eyes bulging from that smooth, bald head. "Kill them all. They did this – they skinned the girl."

Still, after everything that had happened here, he was playing his little games.

I trained the gun on the Royales and then on Baz Singh's empty features, wondering what could have possibly led them here, to this. Even then, lost in my rage, I knew that the Pilgrim was toying with me, using me for some complex plan, and I fought against carrying out the task he was goading me into.

"Do it," he said, harshly. "Do what you failed to do last time – what you couldn't do to Ryan South. Take a step towards the dark; unleash the true potential of what's inside you, and join me on my pilgrimage. We can work wonders. We can take it all. Release the true nature of the power inside you. Let it out to breach realities, and we can rule over it all…"

I shot him. *I shot him*. I shot him in the head. In the throat. In the chest.

Bits and pieces of him flew off, spinning through the air like yanked doll parts, and I knew that I was not doing him any harm, but I kept on pulling the trigger until the bullets ran out. Then I pulled the trigger again, again, again…

Thick white appendages, like pale, hairless insect-legs, erupted from beneath the sham of his body. They groped in the air, with monstrous pincers snapping, and as I stared at them those hideous limbs began to sprout flowers. Tiny red and yellow and purple blossoms grew at speed from the bleached flesh, their petals opening to reveal tiny mouths ringed with diamond teeth.

The Pilgrim was a thing of masks: beneath each face there hid a new one, and at the bottom of them all was nothing but an endless pit of despair.

Baz Singh chose that moment to strive for redemption. He lunged at the Pilgrim's protean form, grabbing at the flailing limbs that swayed and lashed at the air. One of them cut his face, cleaving it down to the bone, and another latched onto his throat, the blossoms burrowing into the flesh and supping his blood.

Singh grappled with the monster, wrapping his own arms around the now frantic limbs, but he was no match for the Pilgrim. He was cast aside, flopping like a bloodied doll, and came to rest against the table upon which Penny Royale now stirred...

I stared at her poor little body, trying to convince myself that the sight was not genuine, that it was just another of the Pilgrim's games. But it was real. And it was awful. Penny's lifeless body had already hitched along the tabletop, and was now dropping down onto the floor, her back arching as if boneless and her face turned up to the ceiling. The blasted thing in her belly had partially reformed, and was moving her like a sack of old clothes, dragging her off the makeshift altar and towards the gaping onlookers.

I didn't know what to do. Of all the things I had seen, all the ghosts and entities I had ever encountered, this was the worst. It was the worst because, despite being dead, it was still human – still a little girl – and she needed her mummy.

Shawna Royale began to back away, her hands flapping in front of her breasts. She tried to scream, but no sound came; she tried to cry but there were not tears enough to wash away this horror. Instead she sank to her knees, lifted her hands, clasped them together and began to pray. Right at the end, she rediscovered her humanity, but it wasn't enough. It was pathetic.

Penny's stilted corpse jerked its way towards her mother, half walking, half crawling, mostly just flopping like a filleted carcass. It fell upon her, tearing with limp hands and biting with shattered teeth. Shawna just knelt there, her mind gone.

Then the Pilgrim once again stepped forward, those spidery albino limbs having retreated back inside his shell. His cracked face shone; his eyes rolled back in his head like onyx marbles. Through his broken skull I glimpsed pulsing translucent matter, like shredded wet plastic bags slowly filling with air...

His shell reforming from the darkness around him, the Pilgrim shook his head and smiled. "Not ready yet, Usher. Not yet. But some day you will be, and when that day comes I'll be walking alongside you, just as I have been for all these years, giving you a nudge, pushing you in the right direction. You may ignore the dead, but the dead will never ignore you. That slice of darkness inside you, it calls out to them, draws them in. It burns like a flame in the night."

And then he was gone. For now. But his final parting words remained, hanging in the air like ash:

"Memento mori."

I had failed to notice it before, but a strange glow had entered the room. I looked over towards the fireplace, where something was forming, knitting together from the darkness. It was a tree: small, stunted, charred, yet glowing from within. Pale flames licked around the edges of a hole in the trunk, then ignited and traced a route along the withered branches to engulf the whole thing.

The remains of the stillborn creature – the Pilgrim's Mistress partially reformed – slouched across the floor, called back to its prison. It moved slowly, pulling its blackened form along on spindly limbs, even using what few teeth had grown in its tiny, malformed mouth to gain purchase on the carpet. I kept watching as the monstrosity inched towards the burning tree, and stepped back as a tongue of white flame snatched it up and drew it into the silent conflagration.

I walked over to the table, where the others now stood, and dropped the gun at their feet. Shawna Royale was silent beneath the weight of her dead daughter; Terry, her useless husband, was staring at the floor. Baz Singh looked shocked, as if he had been caught in the middle of an explosion.

I picked up the girl and stepped away from the group, resisting the urge to tear them to pieces with my bare hands. I grabbed the table cloth and wrapped it around Penny's bloodied remains, attempting to treat her with the respect she had never been given in life.

I barely noticed as a battered and bloodied Baz Singh struggled wearily to his knees, then bent down and picked up the gun. He took some fresh bullets from the inside pocket of his jacket and slowly loaded the pistol. I could have stopped him, but I no longer cared what happened to these beasts. I had watched a man die before, and knew that I could live with what was about to happen.

Terry Royale had not moved since I entered the room. Nor did he move now, even as Baz Singh pointed the gun at his face. He seemed to welcome the sight of his own extinction.

"Leave," said Singh, nodding. "I'll take care of this." Blood poured from the ruin of his throat and his face was lacerated. He was a dead man anyway; at least this way he could exercise some control over the nature of his exit.

I looked again at the fiery tree. The pale flames had enveloped the charred entity, and rolled it gently in a huge hand of fire. The thing rotated, supported by the living flame, writhing in exquisite agony. It was still small, but it had grown – evolved by flames. As I watched, a single spark drifted from the tree, floated through the still air, and landed on the curtains. They caught fire immediately, going up as if they had been doused in petrol.

I turned and hobbled away from the fire.

The sound of gunshots followed me out of the door, blowing me back towards my own version of reality.

I stepped down from the ruined frontage of the dilapidated concrete tower, being careful not to do any more damage to the girl's body, the heat of the flames at my back and the memory of this night burned into my mind forever. Then I carried Penny home, through the night and the capering shadows, past the old bonfire and the broken down fence.

I carried her home and I put her to bed, and when I looked

out of her bedroom window I could see, on the horizon, what looked like a burning tree on a distant hill. The shape that writhed in those endless flames no longer seemed triumphant; now it seemed agonised, as if the pain it endured was indeed eternal, and was starting all over again.

I turned away and tucked in Penny Royale, aware that even the dead need some form of comfort, even if it is from a stranger.

Then I went downstairs and put in a call to DI Tennant, asking him to come immediately to the residence of Shawna Royale. I used the mobile phone he had given me, and decided that it was a good gift after all. In the end it had come in handy. Again, Tebbit would have a lot of work to do if he wanted to keep my name out of this, but I trusted him to do what was right, what was just.

I stared at the framed school photographs of Penny Royale as I waited for Tebbit to arrive, hoping that the girl might now be allowed to rest in peace. Her death had been needless, part of a failed ritual which was destined never to succeed, and the main culprit in her demise saw it all as part of a fucking game – a game whose meaning I could not even grasp.

Penny's parents would not be found, and her murder would enter the mythology of the Bestwick Estate, where it would be discussed over drinks in the local pubs and on windy street corners by women who wore bathrobes and slippers at midday.

The Pilgrim's motives were less easily resolved. I knew that I had not seen the last of him, but the next time I would be prepared. Now that he had shown his hand, I could take steps to beat it. At least that was what I hoped.

Poor Penny Royale had been doomed from the start – probably sold to the highest bidder before she was even conceived. In return for the empty promise of powers that I couldn't even begin to imagine, the Royales had created a daughter only to act as a vessel for something darker than even they had failed to estimate.

Baz Singh had his own agenda, of course, but I suspected that his daughter, Kareena, had drawn him into the circle rather than him being the instigator, as I had first thought. Whatever good remained in Baz Singh had stepped forward at the end, and he had ceased the operation in the only way he could think of.

The blood on his hands was not on mine; I had other regrets to carry.

I knew that Penny Royale's name would be added to the list on my back, and that Elmer Lord would ink it free of charge, just as he had inked them all. The first name on the list had been that of Ryan South, followed by Rebecca and Allyson Usher.

I did not think the list would ever come to an end, but I could always hope – and believe – that some day it might.

And now, at last, I have visited their graves. The grief I carry always inside me would be too much to bear if I continued to stay away. Once I chose to remember them in my own way, in my own time, but now I must face them where they lie in the ground like seeds awaiting springtime.

Not a day goes by when they are not in my thoughts. They haunt my every movement, but still I have not seen them: they have not come to me in the way that others have, asking that I bear witness to the memory of their passing or simply requesting that I guide them towards the next part of their journey... but some day, somehow, I still hope that they will find their way back to my side.

I read their names carved so carefully in stone and tears fall freely, but these tears are good: they are cleansing, and help show me that I am still alive. There is so much loss in my life, but I have seen what comes afterwards, beyond the loss, and it is just as confusing as the life that unfolds around me. For the first time the knowledge that some day I shall die does not hold me back from the brink: instead it brings a kind of hope and urges me onward. My family are there, up ahead of me, and after this life will begin the real search to find them. I believe that I am up to the task.

I glance up from the graves and see a small girl walking along the footpath, near the line of trees that cuts the main road off from view to create the illusion of privacy in this place. The girl is not my daughter, but she could be; she looks a lot like her. Her name is Penny and it is a name that I can never forget: it is inked onto my back with the rest of them – all the lost souls I could not help, the ones who are no longer around to hear my apologies.

I watch the girl for a while longer, until her outline blurs and blends into the trees: her arms become branches her hair is now leaves. I tell myself that she waves to me as her image fades, but I cannot be sure. She has been absorbed into nature, and I wish her well on her journey. I am sorry that I was not able to help her towards whatever goal she must now reach alone, but at least I tried and she will not be forgotten.

Part of my job upon this earth is remembrance, and I will not shirk the responsibilities that come with it, no matter how hard and painful they might be.

I send my thoughts to the dead ones, the ones I have loved and continue to love, and then I turn and walk away, across the brown grass and the gravel path, continuing on my pilgrimage in the hope that one day I will find a question on which to pin all the answers I have unearthed and the ones that wait to be discovered.

ACKNOWLEDGMENTS

Thanks so much to Steve Jones and Sarah Pinborough for giving me a kick up the arse when I really needed it; to Stephen Volk for some vital comments on an early draft; to Ramsey Campbell, Stephen Volk (again), Christopher Fowler and Tim Lebbon for being kind enough to read the manuscript and give me a blurb; to Mark West for reading when it mattered; to Marco and Lee at Angry Robot for having faith in me; to Jon Oliver for giving me that first important shot at the mass market; to Gary Fry and John Probert for invaluable support and friendship; to Simon Strantzas for brotherhood; to Simon Bestwick for the encouragement; to Andy Cox and Pete Tennant for their invaluable support over the last few years; to Chris Teague for first publishing me; to Mark Morris for being a good pal and offering sound advice; and to Charlie and Emily – my amazing little family – for being the greatest thing that ever happened to me.

If I've forgotten anyone, please accept my sincere apologies. It's been a crazy few years…

ABOUT THE AUTHOR

Gary McMahon's short fiction has appeared in numerous acclaimed magazines and anthologies in the UK and US and has been reprinted in yearly "Best of" collections.

He is the multiple-award-nominated author of the novellas *Rough Cut* and *All Your Gods Are Dead*, the collections *Dirty Prayers* and *How to Make Monsters* and *Pieces of Midnight*, and the novels *Rain Dogs* and *Hungry Hearts*.

He has been nominated for seven different British Fantasy Awards as both author and editor.

www.garymcmahon.com

A THOMAS USHER STORY
THE LATE SHOW

I knew exactly why I'd been summoned to Soho, of course, but still I had no idea what I was doing there. When Professor Theo Dryer had asked me to attend, as a personal favour to him, I felt obliged to accept his invitation. Dryer was an old friend of mine, the head of the Anthropology and Social Studies Department at Leeds University, and the acknowledged leader in his narrow field. There was also the fact that I owed the old bugger a favour or two.

As I stood outside the weather-beaten wooden door on a busy side street not far from Soho Square, where many film production companies and the British Board of Film Classification all have their offices, I considered, just for a moment, walking away. I wasn't sure what I was going to see there, in that room beneath three floors of grubby apartments where "European Models" plied their trade, but something – and I *refuse* to call it my fucking "Sixth Sense" – told me it would lead only to trouble of the gravest kind.

"Are we going in, then?"

Dryer placed a hand on my arm, as if attempting to reassure me. I smiled but he didn't buy it; Dryer knew me well enough to realise that I was nervous. The truth was it went beyond that: if I'm going to be honest, I have to admit that I was afraid.

317

"Yes. I suppose we should. We're expected." I stepped aside, glancing up at the old stone building, and then both ways along the street, which was crosshatched with late afternoon shadow. His own reticence was due to some kind of residual concern at the thought of being seen entering a premises used as a whore house rather than any genuine fear of being followed. I motioned to Dryer, allowing him inside first. After all, he was the important one, the man with links to the government. I was simply his somewhat reluctant guest.

The stairway was long, steep and narrow, with no banister or handrail, and we were forced to place our hands against the flaking plaster wall to aid our passage downward. A single yellow bulb lit the otherwise gloomy space, but it wasn't doing a particularly good job. I couldn't see my feet; they were shrouded in darkness, as if lost in a low-lying fog.

The scarred door at the foot of the timber stairs was closed, and it had no handle. It was painted a putrid lime green colour but the once glossy finish had faded long ago, and now the surface looked decrepit and rough as an old man's cheek.

We stood before the door, neither of us saying anything. The bulb fizzed and hissed above our heads and I was gripped by the sudden fear that it might fail.

"Well, this is it," said Dryer, adjusting his woollen coat. His face was pale and his eyes refused to settle on one thing for longer than a second or two. In all the years I'd known him, I'd never seen him in such a state.

"This is what?" I turned to him, opening my arms in an expansive gesture. "I know the official explanation, but why are we really here?"

"You know as much as I do, Thomas. All they told me was that it was a matter of high importance and that it had something to do with national security. I'm surprised they let you tag along to be honest, but your name seems to open doors even you are unaware of."

I nodded, pretending I knew what he was talking about. "So we're here to see a presentation, a special lecture of some sort. But why here, in this grubby little place?"

Dryer shuffled his feet. There was gravel on the floor and it made a grating sound as he moved. "All they said was that they needed my professional opinion, and when I mentioned you they seemed delighted. They said that your line of work was connected to what they had to show me."

I was none the wiser, so said nothing more.

"Shall we?" said Dryer, licking his lips.

"By all means."

He reached out and rapped his knuckles on the door, to the left of where the handle should be. Within moments it was opened by a large man with a shaven head and a looping black tribal tattoo on the side of his neck. The man's eyes were small, like those of a pig. He looked hard as nails.

"My name is Professor Theodore Dryer, and this is Thomas Usher."

The big man nodded once, and then stepped deftly to the side. "They're waiting for you," he said in a voice that sounded like distant thunder. "Just go down the stairs and wait."

The door closed behind us and we were swallowed by a murky red light that emanated from hidden fittings at the tops of the walls, right up near the ceiling. The air was damp, musty. There was a smell that I could not identify and my insides were gripped with nausea so strong that I felt I might start to dry-heave.

"Are you okay?" said Dryer, sensing my discomfort.

"I'll be fine in a minute. Can't you feel it? The atmosphere."

"It's very cold, and the air *is* rather stale, but that's about it." Dryer slowed his pace, waiting until I drew level. "Is there something... well, you know. Something otherworldly here?"

I laughed; a short, sharp sound in the cramped corridor. I expected it to echo but instead it was absorbed by the clammy bare-brick walls. "Stop being so melodramatic, Dryer. I just feel a bit sick, that's all."

Dryer grinned, and for a moment he looked like a schoolboy who has been caught out in a prank. Then we descended a second staircase, this one metal and obviously recently installed. It was cleaner than the rest of the interior, and its surface was smooth and painted blue.

There was a tiny waiting area at the bottom of this second set of stairs, with four rickety wooden dining chairs arranged against the wall opposite yet another door that was missing its handle. Dryer sat down, resting his head against the wall, but I chose to stand, as yet unsure of what exactly I was getting myself into.

My stomach was still grumbling. It felt like the beginnings of an ulcer, but I'd had the all-clear after my annual medical check-up only three weeks earlier. There was something strange here, something I'd not encountered before: a weird formless energy that was not exactly a bone fide presence, but held some sort of malevolent intelligence all the same.

We did not have long to wait until the door was opened. A short, wide woman in a black smock and white dog collar stood in the doorway, a nervous smile on her face. "Professor Dryer?"

I shook my head and tilted it at my seated companion. "That's him. My name is Usher."

The woman glanced quickly away, and I was certain I saw an expression of mild disdain cross her face at the sound of my name. "Professor. My name is Cleo Quaid, and I'm the one who suggested you come here this evening."

"Ah," said Dryer, standing and extending a hand. "Reverend Dr. Quaid. It's so nice to meet you at last. You've already met my friend Thomas Usher…"

"Yes," said Quaid, shaking his hand with her fingertips. "I am well aware of the reputation of Mr. Usher, and I can't say I approve of his presence here. Sadly, my opinion was not considered important enough to matter."

Frustration vented, she walked back inside the room and left us to follow. I glanced at Dryer; he shrugged, and gave a twisted little smirk. Then he went inside, with me bringing up the rear.

Quaid was standing at one end of the small room, pouring herself a large measure of whisky from a selection of spirits on a small silver tray which rested on a filing cabinet. She was pouting, obviously put out by my presence, but I tried to ignore her surly form as Dryer and I drifted to the centre of the room. Two other men were standing there, talking in low tones, and a third man, this one much younger than the others, stood at a low table fiddling with a small laptop computer.

"Gentlemen! Glad you could make it." Neville Brand, a low-level back bench MP surged forward, a smile on his face and a drink in his hand. Unless I was mistaken, his companion was Lance Benedict, the head of a major digital communications cartel who ran several pay-as-you-view television channels and owned a string of tacky newsstand magazines. My heart sank when I saw him. I'd been warned by Dryer that the smug bastard would be there, of course, but the sight of him affected me more than I'd expected. More than I would have liked.

Not exactly what I'd call good company: doctors, holy fools and media moguls. At that moment, in that squalid little room, I wished that I'd walked away when I had the chance. I still hold to that wish now, with all of my heart.

"I'm particularly glad to make your acquaintance, Mr. Usher. Or can I call you Thomas?" The smile on Benedict's face was enough to make me want to hit him. But I didn't. I remained calm and in control. I had a feeling I'd need exactly these qualities later on in the proceedings.

"Mr. Usher will do just fine, Lance."

The smile faltered; he wasn't quite yet sure what to make of me.

"Don't worry; I don't bear a grudge. I realise you're simply trying to sell magazines, like any other money-grubbing piece of dirt." I held his gaze as I spoke, unwilling to back down until he knew I meant business.

"Please… Mr Usher. Surely that's all in the past?"

"You called me a fraud, Lance. A faker. You even went on some stupid daytime TV show to speak out against people who – now, what were your exact words? Oh, yes: 'feed on the grief of the damaged and the grief-stricken.' Nice turn of phrase. Very poetic."

Benedict took a deep swallow from his glass. His cheeks had flushed red and he was beginning to sweat. "Listen, I apologised for that later. We printed a retraction in *Look Now!*"

"A tiny three-line article stuck at the back of the magazine, under the classified ads. Very noble of you, I'm sure." I had him on the ropes now, and because of a misplaced sense of pity, I decided to move in for the kill much sooner that I'd planned. "That boy, the one I was trying to help rid of his ghosts? Billy Taylor. Fourteen years old, bullied at school, comfort-eating to ease the nightmare his life had become. He hung himself from a tree in a nearby park two days after your television appearance. Did you know that?"

The room was silent. Everyone present was listening, waiting to see what would happen next. I walked away, sparing everyone the embarrassment. Reverend Quaid had now moved away from the drinks cabinet, so I poured myself a stiff measure of rum and stood against the wall, signalling the fact that I'd called a cease-fire.

"If we can all take our seats," said Brand, his political mask slipping back into place. "Then I'm sure we'd all like to find out why we're here."

Everyone moved towards the folding chairs that had been placed at the centre of the room, facing a small screen which was suspended from the ceiling. The young man by the laptop walked across to the light switch and doused the lights. The screen shone white before us, and again I was overcome by a sense of nausea.

Brand stood and made his way to the screen, one of those retractable pointers favoured by university lecturers in his hand. He nodded at the man operating the laptop and a PowerPoint display began to run through its paces.

"This is a scan of the floor plans of a place called Daleside House, an old psychiatric building in the north east, near the Scottish borders." He pointed with his stick and watched us, taking note of our puzzled expressions.

I glanced away from the fuzzy architectural blueprints and studied my fellow audience. Quaid was well into her second drink. Brand was glowering at the screen. Dryer had a bemused look on his kindly face.

"Nothing much to write home about, you might think. And you'd be right... but for one thing. This place, the Daleside, has long been rumoured to be haunted. The area has been the site of strange lights in the sky, mutilated cattle on local farms, and other random occurrences for decades."

Photographs flipped across the screen, grainy images of cylindrical objects in the sky, figures at windows, and a particularly bemusing shot of a tall, skinny man holding what looked like a large squid wearing a sheepskin coat.

I suddenly realised why I was there as part of the group, and once more I felt sick to the stomach. I sensed nothing ghostly; there were no presences immediately apparent inside the room. But there *was* something here, of that I had no doubt.

"A group of property developers recently demolished the building to use the site to build a new residential estate. There were a few problems – horrible smells that wouldn't clear, workmen claiming to have seen things in the empty rooms. The usual stuff. But then they uncovered the bones."

The Reverend Dr Quaid let out a small squeaking cry, but no one else said a word.

"The bones of hundreds of people were dug up in the basement. These bones were... well, they were *deformed*. It seems that an old Victorian doctor in charge of the asylum had been conducting experiments on his patients. Work had to be stopped; the project was delayed. Then, once everything was removed and accounted for, the builders were allowed back in. Within a week they discovered a shaft that ran down the structure, inside the walls. They could find no apparent bottom to this shaft, but on a shelf under the basement they found a battered, somewhat scorched film can, containing a single roll of 16mm film stock."

Dryer coughed. Brand paused, milking the moment. He was a typical politician, always making the most of his part.

"What was on the film?" Quaid's voice wavered; she was scared already, even though we still had not been given all the information.

"That, my dear Cleo, is what *you're* all here to find out." He swung the pointer in the air, like a conductor showing off with a flourish. "Only two people have viewed this film. One of them, a site manager for the construction team, went quite mad and had to be locked up for his own protection. The second person was a low-ranking government official, a young woman who worked for the Health and Safety Executive. Much the same happened to her. She is currently in a secure hospital, after trying to bite through her own wrists."

He swallowed before continuing, loosening the top button of his shirt with hands it obviously took a lot of willpower to keep from shaking. "Due to the fact that the film canister was covered with what look like occult markings, we suspect some type of footage showing satanic rites. Maybe even a snuff film."

"Bloody hell, Brand. What is this, some kind of joke? Are you trying to whip up some controversy before the next election? If you want to be in my magazine, there are better ways of achieving it – a nice little homosexual affair, some recreational drug-taking…"

Dryer laughed, but I was more interested in what Brand had been saying. I'd heard of the Daleside, and its supposed hauntings. As far as these things go, and according to my sources, it was a genuine place where energies converged. I'd heard bad things – very, very bad things – about the former asylum, and the recollection of some of these stories brought on another bout of sickness. I belched, smiling an apology to Quaid, who turned around in her seat. My mouth tasted awful; like rotten eggs.

"Please, this is all true. We've asked you here for your expert opinions on the film. All we can gather is what both of these rather unfortunate individuals kept repeating as they were taken away."

"And what was that?" I asked, speaking up at last. My lips were dry and I felt like I wanted to vomit.

"The thing is, both of these poor souls kept saying *exactly* the same thing. Over and over, like a chant. They said they'd seen the face of the devil."

The sound of shattering glass made us all jump. "Sorry," muttered Quaid, bending over to brush away the fragments of the glass she'd dropped on the floor. "I'm very sorry." Her face had turned so pale that I was about to get out of my seat and offer her a drink of water. "I'm okay… just a shock, you know. A shock to someone in my job."

The joke was feeble but it broke the tension. Even I forced a laugh.

"If any of you would rather not take the risk, I'll quite understand. You can leave now and we'll inform you of the outcome later." Brand leaned forward, as if on a pivot. His eyebrows arched up in such a way that we were in no doubt that he wanted us to stay.

"Just show us the damn film, you pompous oaf." Benedict was becoming impatient; his bluster didn't do much to mask the fear.

"If we're all in agreement, then?"

"Yes, get on with it, man!" Benedict got up and stalked towards the makeshift drinks cabinet to refill his glass. His hand shook as he poured, and he seemed to be muttering under his breath.

The Reverend Dr. Quaid nodded once, and then looked away.

"I'm game if you are, Thomas." Dryer looked worried, but not so much that he was willing to miss this, not unless I suggested we leave.

"Yes. Let's watch it." I was surprised how steady my voice sounded.

"Do you... do you feel anything, Thomas? Any, you know – any spirits?" Dryer's eyes were so wide that I thought they might pop out of his head.

I smiled. "No, old friend. All I feel is slightly ill." I still do not know, even to this very day, why I underplayed my reaction to being inside that room, next to the film can. All I can think of is that I was trying to spare Dryer my discomfort.

While we'd been talking, the young laptop operator had switched on a light and wheeled out a trolley upon which rested a film projector. The film was already loaded into the spools; it was dusty, creased, but still looked to be in reasonable shape.

"You can go now, Travis. There's no need for you to remain." Brand walked to the back of the room and started fiddling with the projector, flicking buttons and rattling the film in the grate.

Travis left the room. The door whispered shut behind him; the light went out, flickering slightly before it died. My tattoos at last began to twitch, signifying something not quite right – not quite *natural* – about what we were about to experience. It wasn't much, simply a brief and passing sensation across my back and upper arms, but it was enough to ensure that I put up my mental barriers and recited a few Romany charms in my head. All the signs were pointing to some kind of vague, possibly transitory supernatural phenomena; there was nothing to tell me I should be overly worried.

It's funny how wrong even I can be.

"Let's start the show," said Brand, still in love with the sound of his own voice, and quite clearly thinking that he was just the cutest thing alive.

The projector made a low humming sound, which was punctuated by the occasional insectile clicking. A beam of dusty light shone out of the front of the machine, and I followed it with my eyes until they rested on the screen.

The screen went dark. No, that isn't quite right. It was more than that; more severe. The screen went *utterly* black.

A chair leg scraped the floor and someone coughed quietly.

The blackness on the screen seemed to pulse, gently at first, but then becoming more insistent. I looked around me, at my fellow viewers, and wondered what they were expecting to gain from this. They were wide-eyed, craning their necks forward, and transfixed by the screen.

My stomach began to tie itself in knots; the nausea returned, but this time with more force. Yet still, I did not have the sense that anything major was about to occur. It was as if there were dim energies hovering at the edges, the vague outlines of the dead looking in at us through a murky window.

"When is this supposed to start?" asked Benedict, his anger and impatience resurfacing. "I'm getting bored."

Then it began.

The darkness on the screen bled to a soft grey, like the visual static you used to see between television stations on old analogue television sets, or that flickering snow that would appear if the transmission was lost. But there was something underneath the swirls of grey and black: shapes, moving, writhing, and shaking what looked like ill-defined appendages. At first I thought we were watching an experimental film, some silly post-modern attempt at cinematic deconstruction put together by an underachieving student who'd smoked too much pot whilst watching third-generation copies of avant-garde animation.

I could just about make out a vision of a barren wasteland, populated by hulking humanoid figures. It seemed to me that they were either copulating or merging. I could not be sure which.

Then I could see nothing, just the visual static. Every time I thought I could conjure an image from the chaos on the screen, it moved, shifted, and I was forced to start all over again. The effect was disorientating, like being on a roller-coaster. Constantly kept on the verge of revelation, it was a strain on each of the senses.

I managed to wrench my eyes away from the screen and examine the rest of the people in the room. Dryer was leaning back in his chair, his mouth open, hands clawing at his face. Benedict was masturbating, his right hand working furiously at his semi-erect member while his other hand reached out towards the screen. The Reverend Dr Quaid was vomiting quietly into her lap.

I craned my neck around to look at Brand, still manning his spot at the projector. He had his eyes squeezed tightly shut and tears ran down his cheeks, making pale tracks in the sweaty flesh. He was singing a song, a children's nursery rhyme: I think it might have been "Humpty Dumpty". I'm still not sure why, but the sound of his cultured tones droning such an incongruous tune was somehow terrifying.

When I looked back at the screen it was dark again. Black. The blackness moved, like tar, like the effluent of the sewers of hell. Shapes – people – struggled beneath its surface; swimmers in that crude adhesive darkness that were being slowly drowned. Or, more likely, I saw nothing but the patterns the rational mind attempts to create when confronted by visual chaos.

I struggled to my feet, heading for the projector. Despite having seen nothing that could be construed as conventionally evil, or even anything more than distasteful, I wanted more than anything in the world to turn it off. Still my insight failed me; I could sense nothing of what was obviously churning beneath the surface, trying to heave into view. Perhaps it was simply too large, too unthinkable for even my perceptions to contain. I remembered a line from a newspaper article I'd read recently about a soldier in Afghanistan; something about the horrors of war being simply larger than oneself.

For the first time, I knew exactly what that meant. Some feelings are just too huge to contain; certain imaginings are too complex to decode.

I lurched towards the projector and turned it off.

The film spun out of the gate, flapping like a tortured snake. It slapped my hands, drawing blood; it was as if the very film wanted to resume its showing, and it would not go down without a fight.

Brand was standing in a puddle of his own urine; the crotch of his trousers was stained. I turned away when the smell of shit wafted into my nostrils.

Of the others, only Dryer was in any fit state to communicate. "Oh, dear God," he said. "What was that?"

Quaid was by now weeping uncontrollably, her face buried in her hands, around which was wrapped a rosary. Benedict had left the room. The door was still open, letting in dim smears of light from the passage outside. I never saw him again. Shortly afterwards, he sold all his holdings in the communications company, took to sea in his yacht, and blew out his brains with a small calibre handgun.

"What did you see?" I had to know. Even with my highly attuned sight, I had witnessed very little; certainly not enough to understand.

"I… I don't know," said Dryer, standing clumsily and turning his ankle as he stepped away from his chair. "I think… I think I saw… I don't know."

The face of the devil.

Just then a young woman walked by me. One second there was nobody near me, the next this girl was drifting over to the projector. She had long blonde hair pulled back into a loose ponytail and her eyes had been messily jabbed out with something sharp, maybe a stick or a short blunt blade. She took the film out of the projector, this wan little phantom, and carried it to the front of the room, where she stepped upwards with one shapely leg, as if taking flight, and vanished into the small suspended screen. She looked back only once, giving me a final view of those sad, ruined eyes.

I did not know who she was – her identity still eludes me – but I was certain that she was claiming the film to return it to the darkness where it rightfully belongs. I can only pray that it remains there.

I turned and stared at Dryer, staggering slightly under the onslaught of so much sensory input.

"I don't know," he repeated, clearly having not seen the girl.

He was not lying. We'd known each other too long to bullshit, and there was no point in hiding anything, not any more. His hair had turned grey at the temples and the left side of his mouth was twisted, as if he'd suffered a mild stroke.

"My chest hurts," he muttered, before falling to his knees.

My friend Professor Theo Dryer died of a sudden massive coronary en route to the hospital, in the back of the ambulance I called. He was holding my hand when he went. I did not see his spirit leave his body. I can only hope that, wherever he has gone, it is better than whatever he glimpsed on the screen in that dingy little basement room in Soho.

Later that same night, Neville Brand left his Kensington apartment and paid a visit to the Reverend Dr. Cleo Quaid in her Battersea studio flat. He raped her first, and then strangled her to death with a set of her own rosary beads. Then he raped her again. After first smoking a cigar and finishing the bottle of whisky he found on a desk in Quaid's study, he walked to the window, perhaps looked up at the stars, and threw himself down into the small paved garden area below the flat. He landed high up on a set of cast iron railings, impaled through the shoulder, thigh and chest. It took him approximately forty minutes to die, and during that time it was reported that several people walked past his suspended body, ignoring his dying moans and not looking up to see where they came from.

I have been unable to trace the young man whom Brand called Travis, nor have I had much luck in tracking down the security staff who let us into the property. As I have already stated, the identity of the ghostly young woman remains a mystery.

The film was not recovered from the scene. The builders working on Daleside House claim never to have unearthed such an item, and the developers have threatened to take me to court if I pursue the matter.

I badly wanted to learn what the others had seen in the film, but now that was obviously out of the question. Had they all shared the same delusion or had each seen their own private version of Satan's features grinning back at them between frames containing a storm of static?

In the final reckoning, I had seen little – next to nothing. But why had that been the case? Had my unique insight protected me from those killing visions, or had it deserted me once more, this time at a crucial moment when I might have peered behind the workings of the world – this one and so many others – to catch sight of the unutterable? It seems to me now that I will never know the truth.

The thing that keeps me awake at night, drinking into the small hours and scratching my tattoos, is the fact that I was not warned of the presence of something malevolent that evening. My perceptions failed me; I had no idea what was coming.

The unswerving confidence I once had in my abilities has reduced to the point that I no longer trust what I see or feel or experience. This realm of the senses has blurred irrecoverably with those other realms beyond – the ones I so foolishly and conceitedly believed that I was beginning to know and even understand.

In my darker moments, when I feel something spinning so slowly that it could be either the world or a thin, black stylus turning somewhere deep inside my burned-out soul, I think that perhaps it is better this way. For if my recent doubts are proven to be true and I am not in fact here to help or offer guidance, but to *usher in the dark*, that sensation might just be the void opening up inside me.

ANGRY
ROBOT

Teenage serial killers
Zombie detectives
The grim reaper in love
Howling axes **Vampire
hordes** Dead men's clones
The Black Hand
Death by cellphone
Gangster shamen
Steampunk anarchists
Sex-crazed bloodsuckers
Murderous gods
Riots **Quests** Discovery
Death

Prepare
to welcome
your new
Robot overlords.

angryrobotbooks.com